SHE WALKS IN BEAUTY

SIRI MITCHELL

BOOKS BY SIRI MITCHELL

Kissing Adrien

Chateau of Echoes

The Cubicle Next Door

Moon Over Tokyo

A Constant Heart

Love's Pursuit

A Heart Most Worthy

The Messenger

Unrivaled

Love Comes Calling

Like a Flower in Bloom

Flirtation Walk

State of Lies

Everywhere to Hide

writing as IRIS ANTHONY

The Ruins of Lace

The Miracle Thief

ABOUT THE AUTHOR

SIRI MITCHELL is the author of 18 novels, among them the critically acclaimed Inspy Award winner *She Walks in Beauty* and Christy Award finalists *Chateau of Echoes* and *The Cubicle Next Door*. A graduate of the University of Washington with a degree in business, she has worked in many different levels of government. As a military spouse, she lived in places as varied as Tokyo and Paris. She always seems to find her stories in places where women come into conflict with their culture.

New York City, 1891
During the opulence, the splendor, and the excess of the Gilded Age

CHAPTER 1

*G*ET DRESSED, CLARA. In your visiting costume. We are going out." My aunt's words were at once both commanding and precise— as precise as her posture: a series of ninety-degree angles. Seated as she was, upon one of my bedroom chairs, she was perpendicular in the extreme.

There were far more important matters to consider than geometry, however. I bit the inside of my lip to hide the smile that threatened to escape. We were going out! And *we* never went out. *We* never went anywhere. Not since Aunt moved in with us the month before. Several times I had been given permission to visit my friend Lizzie Barnes, but only in the company of Miss Miller, my governess.

Aunt rose to her feet from the chair that made a pair with my own. Their plump, pansy-embroidered seats and lilac fringe corresponded with the rest of the decor in my bedroom. Her fluffy Pomeranians, displaced by her sudden movement, began barking and dancing about her feet. "Was I unclear in my diction, Clara? I meant *now*."

"No."

"What? I should not have to strain my ears to hear you."

Indeed, she shouldn't. Her ears had a habit of standing away from her head like soup ladles, as if they were longing to be freed from her relentlessly old-fashioned coiffure, parted in the middle and drawn back into a bun. "No. You were not unclear."

"Very well then." She clucked at her dogs and left the room, accompanied by a frenzied yipping. The three dogs that scampered after her were the most hateful creatures I had ever known.

At Aunt's departure, Miss Miller emerged from the shadows of a corner to part my velvet curtains and draw down the shades on my windows.

"I don't see why she thinks she can order me around like one of her horrid dogs! I'm not some child—I'm seventeen years old."

Miss Miller smiled and walked toward the now-vacant chair. "She's simply used to people doing as she bids."

"Then she ought to have stayed where she was."

"She's taken an interest in your upbringing, and I think it's very kind. Especially since . . . well . . ."

"Since I have no mother."

"I didn't mean to make you feel--. I didn't mean--I'm sorry."

Miss Miller sat as I stood to allow the maid to help me undress.

I could never be upset with Miss Miller. And in any case, Mama had died so very long ago. "We've been doing just fine on our own, you and I."

"But there's your debut to consider now."

"That's months away." More than a year. And I was looking forward to it about as much as a mouse looks forward to being pounced upon by a cat. "Besides, *you* could be my escort!" I ought to have thought of it before. Long before Father had announced that his sister was moving in.

"Nothing would give me greater pleasure, but that's not my place."

2

"Couldn't you, though? Then we wouldn't have to do any of it at all! We could say we were going to one of those balls but visit the Museum of Art instead. No one would have to know." And even if I did have to attend those dreadful events, I could do it with a companion. Someone besides my friend Lizzie, who was bound to be caught up in all of the excitement. And when it became apparent that no one wanted to dance with me, when no one spoke to me, Miss Miller could take me through mathematic drills and converse with me in Italian. It would be as good as being here, in my own room, safe at home with my books.

Miss Miller laughed. "You sound quite desperate."

I was.

She stopped laughing and looked at me with something close to sympathy in her eyes. "I can't escort you. But if I have my way, then maybe you won't have to debut at all."

Wouldn't have to debut?

Miss Miller rose when the maid went to pick up my hairbrush and came close to speak into my ear. "I've written to Vassar College. I'm quite sure they'll be impressed with your studies."

Vassar College? She thought me ready to attend Vassar? My heart thrilled to hear it!

She squeezed my shoulder and then stepped out into the hall, leaving me with visions of college lectures and distinguished professors swirling through my head.

———

AFTER THE MAID fixed my hair, I hurried down to the front hall only to discover that I was early. I would have to wait for Aunt. I might have brought a novel had I thought of it, but there was no use retrieving one now. I didn't want to risk Aunt hearing my steps and lecturing me about my choice in literature.

Five minutes before the stroke of four, Aunt sailed down the staircase, resplendent in a visiting toilette. I fell into her wake as she passed by and followed her out the door to the street. The Victoria awaited us. Aunt stepped up first; I allowed her a moment to sit and adjust her skirts, then I climbed in and settled myself beside her.

In front of us, the coachman took to his perch above the front wheels.

I lurched as the carriage moved forward and had only just adjusted to the sway of the carriage when it came to a halt. The coachman removed himself from his seat.

But. . . we were at Lizzie's house!

It was two houses down from our own and quite similar, with a dozen steps leading up to the front door. It was just as tall and narrow, with a columned front portico; two windows graced the parlor floor, then three on each of the floors above. But there had always been something about the Barneses' home that made it seem less imposing, more inviting than our own.

The coachman presented a hand to help me from the carriage. I stepped aside and waited for Aunt to descend before following her up the steps to the door. A footman answered her ring and extended a gleaming silver tray to receive her card.

We were soon shown into a parlor that had been done up in warm greens and golds. Last year, if I remembered correctly, it had been furnished in dark woods and draped in plum brocade. I rather liked this new look.

Mrs. Barnes was seated on a sofa, Lizzie sitting beside her. They both rose as we walked into the room.

My friend grinned when she saw me, but then checked herself, hiding her enthusiasm behind a delicate cough.

It seemed strange for our visit to be confined to the parlor, when Lizzie and I normally went straight up to her room. But Aunt and I sat across from Mrs. Barnes and Lizzie on chairs that matched the sofa, which matched the curtains and the carpets and the lampshades. The whole of the room gave off an impression of golden dreams and sparkling sunshine.

"Mrs. Stuart. It is such a pleasure to receive you." Mrs. Barnes spoke with the accent of her native South. Honeyed and mellifluous, I never tired of hearing her speak.

Aunt sighed and placed a hand to her formidable chest. "I regret that I have been feeling so poorly of late."

I felt my brows lift in surprise. Most days, Aunt was so firmly in charge of the management of the household that she made the rest of us feel quite slothful.

"Surely your brother, a physician, is able to aid you."

"I am afraid that what ails me is something for which only heaven can provide the cure."

"Oh. Well." Mrs. Barnes's smile wobbled for just an instant. "Of course we must all look forward to drying our tears on the bosom of Abraham."

Aunt had spent much of her life mourning the loss of her husband, a man whose ghostly presence was best represented by the unrelieved black of deep mourning Aunt had chosen to clothe herself in for as long as I could remember. Her eyes deflected to her lap for a moment. "Affliction is the only thing one should expect from life." She closed her eyes, sighed again. Then opened them. "And speaking of expectations, I expect that you're educating your Lizzie in the social obligations of her debut. Next year."

Mrs. Barnes inclined her head. "As I am sure you are cultivating the finer attributes of your young niece."

Being talked about while present created the odd circumstance of trying to pretend one was absent. I tried not to move, not to breathe. For her part, Lizzie looked as if she were trying to do the same.

In the meantime, Aunt nodded. "Of course. Certainly. There

is so much to be taught and so much to be learned that it's a wonder none of these girls wait until the age of twenty to come out."

"Indeed. They say age begets great wisdom." Mrs. Barnes's tone, however, gave every indication that she did not agree with *them*. "Would you care for some refreshment?"

"No. No, thank you."

"Not even some tea?"

"No. It's not necessary—"

Mrs. Barnes leaned back slightly and looked over her shoulder. At the movement, the butler appeared at her side. "We will take some tea."

The butler bowed and left the room, but he returned quite quickly. There was silence for several moments while the tea was passed around. As I sipped from my teacup, I pondered my coming debut with something akin to horror. I hoped Miss Miller's plan worked. If I went to Vassar next fall, it would preclude any possibility of a debut. But what if she failed? What did I want with dancing and flirting and polite conversation? And how could I ever hope to persuade Father to let me attend university?

I saw Lizzie suppress a smile when I bobbled my cup.

She was the only one who knew just how much I dreaded our coming debut. Just as I was the only one who knew how much she longed for it. Were it not for her devotion and support, were it not for the fact that we would be facing it together, I would as soon perish as present myself to the world at large. I did not have hope enough to believe that I could avoid it forever, not even with dear Miss Miller's words still ringing in my ears, but at least I would not have to worry about it this season. There would be time enough for all of that next fall.

Mrs. Barnes and Aunt talked on and on about our joint debut. About how long it would take to have our gowns made, which dances in particular we ought to know. And just how many girls would be coming out with us. I would rather have been up in Lizzie's room pasting mementos into her scrapbook or listening to her rhapsodize over the latest *Harper's Bazar*. Or better, in my own room with just Byron to keep me company.

Lizzie made faces at me, which I ignored, while I tried to tempt her cat out from under the sofa by wiggling the toe of my walking boot. It had been known to pounce at the winking buttons once or twice before.

A clock struck the half hour with a merry tinkling.

Aunt put her cup and saucer down on the parlor table and turned to me. "Come, Clara."

She meant it literally. I gave her my hand and aided her to her feet.

As she made her way out of the room, accompanied by Lizzie's mother, I felt a plucking at my sleeve.

As I turned back toward the parlor, Lizzie caught my arm with her own and leaned close. "We must meet in the shrub bushes two Thursdays from now. At half past three."

I nodded. We used to meet there all the time when Mama was still living. She would send a tray out to us with thimbles of tea for our dolls.

Aunt had already reached the front step and was clearly waiting for me. I hastened from Lizzie and said my good-byes to Mrs. Barnes. The coachman helped us into the carriage and then climbed into his seat. Aunt folded her hands on her lap, smiling with a twisting of her lips. "That was quite satisfactory. Except, of course, the tea she forced on us. Who serves tea during an at-home?"

I nibbled at the inside of my bottom lip. The conversation had disturbed me. I did not wish to talk of debuts any more than I wished to think of them. I would think of Vassar instead. Of Vassar and its great halls of learning; of all the marvelous books filled with knowledge that awaited me next fall. Surely

Miss Miller could persuade the college of my aptitude for study. Surely, she could persuade Father to let me go.

But then Aunt grabbed one of my hands and clasped it between her own, drawing it up toward her chest. "I have made the decision that you will debut this season instead of next."

CHAPTER 2

HIS SEASON? I pulled my hand from her clutches, though I could not seem to tear my gaze from her face. I'm quite certain my eyes registered all of the horror that I felt. "But I'm not ready! I have *dozens* of things left to learn. And you must know that I'm no good at any of them. And besides—I can't debut without Lizzie!"

"You can and you must."

"But you told her mother, you practically *promised* her mother that I would come out with Lizzie next year. We've already planned it." And I had been counting on it if I wasn't to be allowed to go to Vassar.

Aunt slipped a hand into her reticule. It came out with a square of newspaper caught up between her fingers. She extended the scrap to me. "Read this."

———

The New York Journal—Society
October 1, 1891

It has just been discovered that Franklin De Vries, heir to the De Vries fortune, and his brother, Harold, will be returning early from their Grand Tour. Having embarked upon their journey last year, the pair has scandalized England, terrorized France, and appalled Germany. As well as having bought up half of the treasures of Europe, they have also depleted many of its cellars. At least Italy has been spared their presence. Alas, we fear the Continent will never be the same. Travel well, young Knickerbockers! A sparkling social season awaits your arrival!

Aunt was shaking her head as I looked up from the article. "Knickerbockers—those brothers are descended from some of the city's finest Dutch settlers. And younger sons always do seem to get the elder ones in trouble. I am sure it's for that reason they're to come back. But it was this very thing for which I have been waiting." She bared her teeth in a grin, which made her look very much like one of her dogs.

I returned the paper to her.

The carriage came to a stop in front of our house and Aunt stepped out. "The De Vries heir is returning and that changes everything. You must have him."

"But Mother and Mrs. Barnes were the best of friends! It was her greatest wish that—"

"You be married. And it is your father's greatest wish that you marry into money—De Vries money. We lost everything to the De Vries family once, he and I, and well not be placed in that position again. They owe us the heir, even if they don't yet realize it. We've been counting on you to restore the Carter family's honor. And you shall." She turned her back to me and started up the front steps.

Restore the family's honor? Me? I hadn't even realized we'd lost it. Such a grave obligation was worth even a debut. But there was still one very important detail that Aunt hadn't yet seemed to comprehend. I hurried to follow her, tripping on my skirt. "I cannot debut without Lizzie."

"And I cannot account for your contrariness! Brother and I may have approached high society, but we were never truly granted entry. You, my dear girl, shall have it all."

"But—"

"Anyone with any sense would be overcome with joy at such news."

But that was just it. In the grand scheme of New York City's high society, I truly was nobody. I could not see how any reasonable person would expect me to be able to catch the De Vries heir. And Aunt was speaking as if I had already caught him.

———

MISS MILLER FOUND me in my bedroom as the maid was helping me change gowns. "I have prepared a science experiment for us."

I did not answer, but sat on a chair to have my shoes unbuttoned.

"Science is one of your favorites."

I'm afraid that when I looked up at her, it was with misery in my eyes. "Aunt just told me I'm to debut this coming season."

"Yes. Next year. Which is why science and learning are so important. There is a whole world awaiting your arrival, whether it be at college or the finest ballrooms in the city. You must expand your capacities in every way in order to meet all of its challenges."

"No. *This* year. I'm to debut this year."

"This year? But that's ridiculous! You aren't ready. And you've only just turned seventeen."

"Which is what I told Aunt."

The tiniest of creases appeared between Miss Miller's eyes,

but it quickly disappeared. "She's mistaken. I'll speak to her. Your debut has always been planned for your eighteenth year." She paused and gave me a pointed look. "And we're behind in preparing you. I fear I've put aside instruction on social refinements in favor of intellectual accomplishments."

"Which is why we've gotten on so well!"

Miss Miller smiled. "Yes. But you're going to have to promise to exert extra effort next year when we put aside your books for dancing and conversation classes."

"I will."

She raised a brow.

I sighed. "I promise." Now there would be no getting around it. But I can't say that I was sorry to have been able to put off those miseries for another year. In truth, Miss Miller had been postponing my social education for quite some time. At my own urging. Lizzie had been taking dance classes and voice lessons for several years now. But why should I have put aside my real studies—mathematics, and Italian, and Latin—for dancing lessons and lectures on proper comportment? They couldn't be so difficult as geometry to learn. And I still had plenty of time in which to do it if Miss Miller was indeed correct.

LATER, FOLLOWING THE completion of the experiment, we returned to my room so I could record it. Afterward, Miss Miller excused herself and called the maid to help me dress for dinner. But as I came down the stairs on my way to the dining room, I saw my governess being shown to the door. By Aunt herself.

Although Miss Miller was carrying a valise, and wearing traveling clothes, it didn't seem as if she wanted to leave. "I must protest!"

Aunt took her by the arm and pulled her forward toward the

door. "Protest all you'd like. The matter has been decided."

"I may have delayed Clara's social education a little bit, but —"

"A little bit? You haven't educated her at all!"

Miss Miller wrested her arm away and set her valise on the floor. "You have to understand—she's so very bright. To have thrown away these last few years to focus on dancing and etiquette? It would have been a travesty!"

"A travesty? The travesty is that she faces her debut in less than two months and she isn't even prepared for it!"

"But you must be pleased with the progress she's made. Mount Holyoke would be delighted to have her. And I took the liberty of writing to Vassar College on Clara's behalf just last week."

"Vassar? College? What do you think it is that Clara is destined for, Miss Miller?"

"She could do anything she wants. Great strides are being made in science and medicine and—"

Aunt gestured to the doorman to pick up Miss Miller's valise. "I'm sure that's all very true, but there's only one great stride Clara's father and I expect her to make: the one to the altar."

"But really, Mrs. Stuart!" Miss Miller clutched at the handle of her bag.

The doorman didn't seem to know quite what to do.

With a valiant tug, Miss Miller reclaimed her bag and secured the handles between both of her fists. "The days of young girls being rushed into marriage are over."

"Not in this house!" Aunt pushed Miss Miller out the door and signaled the doorman to shut it. When she turned toward the stairs, she saw me. "Miss Miller has gone."

"Where?"

"Away. For good."

"Why?" Why would she send away my teacher and closest

confidante?

"Her personal views are incompatible with the requirements of your education."

"My education? But we hadn't even begun to work on rhetoric!"

"Yes. Well. All good things must come to an end."

"But—"

"I'll hear no more about it."

"You're a tyrant and a bully! And I wish you'd go back to where you came from!" Tears blurring my vision, I ran up the stairs to my room so I could catch a glimpse of Miss Miller. My forehead pressed to the window, I watched her walk down Fifth Avenue. Her back straight, her pace measured, she never, not even once, looked back. And so I sat in the window, a grown girl of seventeen years, and cried as I had not cried since my mother had died some six years before.

After a while, once my tears stopped, once I discovered I could take a breath without a stuttering in my chest, I decided upon a course of action. I decided I would take the situation up with Father. There was a strategy involved in that sort of thing. Father seemed, of late, to trust his beloved sister with everything having to do with my welfare. She had raised him when their parents had died, so I could not be thought to decry her actions. Neither could I be suspected of being ungrateful for her care. She had, after all, so recently sacrificed her own life of noble widowhood within the bosom of her husband's family to come and live with us. Since then, she had ruled the house in righteous selflessness.

———

I WAS LATE in appearing for dinner. Aunt and Father were already seated when I arrived; I encountered their fierce stares when I entered the room. But I couldn't bring myself to care.

We sat in silence and ate in silence, the butler officiating from his place at Aunt's elbow. First the soup course, then the fish course, which was followed by the meat course.

Father stirred in his seat.

I'd always thought myself the most fortunate girl in the world to have such a handsome father. With his silvery hair and neatly trimmed beard, he looked quite dashing. The very picture of respectability. He was, of course, the city's preeminent physician and the inventor of *Dr. Carter's Patented Tonic*. His medicine had made him a fortune. *Dr. Carter's* was advertised in newspapers and on posters throughout the city.

He looked up from his lamb chop and smiled at me.

Returning the smile, I cast a glance at Aunt, to see if she would speak.

She did not.

I could not speak. Not when I had not first been spoken to. Either Aunt would have to say something about Miss Miller or my opportunity would be lost. So, when I reached to butter my roll, I put out my elbow and knocked over my water goblet.

"Clara!"

I folded my hands into my lap and bowed my head at Aunt's admonishment.

"She can't even eat a meal properly and she's to debut this season?"

Lifting my gaze, I saw Father frown. "Debut? This season? But I thought—"

"I know she's only just turned seventeen, but the De Vries heir is coming back from the Continent. There must be no delay."

"Certainly not. Not if the De Vries heir is available."

"There is much work to be done."

Father's frown deepened, and I saw my chance. "If Miss Miller could be persuaded to stay, then maybe she could educate me."

Father's eyebrows rose in alarm. "Persuaded to stay? Why would she have to be persuaded?"

I cast a glance toward Aunt before returning my gaze to my dinner plate.

"Why?" Father was looking at his sister and there was an edge in his voice. "Miss Miller came highly recommended. And I had to pay a fortune to entice her from the Vanderbilts."

Aunt sniffed. Jet pendulums swung from her earlobes as she emphatically cut into her lamb.

Father placed his knife on his knife rest, then aligned the bottom of his spoon with the bottom of his cheese knife. He speared Aunt with his gaze. "My dear sister, you know I rarely question your methods, but I find I must question this."

It was now that I must make my point. Even if I had not yet been addressed. "Really Father, I know nothing at all about society. I am terribly unprepared for a debut."

Aunt sent the smallest of smiles in my direction. "Exactly. It is exactly as Clara has said. She is terribly unprepared for a debut. Miss Miller has completely failed in her duties."

Father's brows rose to a peak and then gathered together as they sunk. "If you think her not ready the why--"

"She will be. Now is the time, Brother. Just think: the De Vries heir. This is the moment for which we have been waiting."

They turned then, both of them, to look at me. And there seemed to be something more than Father's usual good humor lurking in his smile.

———

I RETURNED TO my room after dinner, defeated. Listless, dispirited, I flopped onto my bed. As my head encountered my pillow, I felt something hard. I rolled onto an elbow and lifted up the corner. There was a book beneath it! Two of them.

I pulled them out into the evening's gloom.

The first was my Byron. Mother's Byron. And the edge of an envelope protruded from its pages.

I sat up, reaching out to turn up the gaslight, then let the book fall open on my knees.

A letter. Addressed to me. In Miss Miller's elegant script.

Pulling the envelope from the poem "She Walks in Beauty," I slit it open, then withdrew from it a single sheet of paper.

My dearest Clara,

Do not be saddened at my going. I have long considered you my most accomplished pupil; there is not much more I could have taught you. I only regret that I did not share Riis's book with you sooner. If ever you should need to contact me, I can be reached in care of my sister, Mrs. John Mifflin in Cortland.

Farewell. I remain forever your friend.

Julia Miller

I picked up the other book. The book by Jacob Riis. *How the Other Half Lives.* I opened to the first page and began to read. An hour later I emerged from its pages long enough to turn up the light once more.

Such things I learned about the conditions in which half the city lived. Such horrors! I read of tenement buildings so devoid of fresh air that people slept on the roofs in the summer . . . and frequently rolled off to their deaths. I read of plumbing so antiquated that water did not reach even to the second stories, let alone to the seventh or eighth. Of rabbits' warrens of tiny rooms where a dozen people were expected to sleep. And of diseases I had thought eradicated that swept those buildings each summer, leaving scores of children dead in their wake. All of these things occurred, *occur*, within the city. My city.

Right here.

And the photographs! The haunted eyes of lost souls, of women and children, peered out between the pages. Beseeching, pleading. Begging.

In my city. My home.

I used to love the idea of Lady Liberty, standing in the harbor, welcoming the visitor to the city. Even the thought of her raised hand still thrilled me to no end.

"Give me your tired, your poor,
Your huddled masses yearning to breathe free,
The wretched refuse of your teeming shore.
Send these, the homeless, tempest-tost to me,
I lift my lamp beside the golden door!"

To what end? For what purpose did she greet the immigrant? To welcome him to a rat-infested, disease-ridden hovel? To offer him no home, no food, no sturdy shelter? Lady Liberty, it seemed, had failed to fulfill her promise.

I fell that night into a fitful sleep, haunted by the images of destitute children and by the certain knowledge that dozens of them were living, were dying, in rude poverty every day. But what could I do? What could anyone do? The problem was so vast. If half the city lived in tenements, then that was over one million people. Surely one person, surely I, could do nothing that would affect any change.

———

MISS MILLER'S LEGACY may have been disturbing and dismal, but life without her seemed dull and devoid of direction. Though Aunt had taken it upon herself to improve my social education, there were, as yet, no lessons being taught. For the first two days following my governess's departure, I was left entirely to my own devices.

The third day was a Sunday. As we walked into Grace Church, there was an almost imperceptible shifting in the pews. A shifting toward us. As we began our walk down the aisle, our footsteps echoed up toward the lattice of vault work that supported the ceiling.

Father squared his shoulders.

Aunt lifted her chin.

I tried to ignore the members already in their pews—and their stares. Tried not to think about anyone but Lizzie, taking comfort in the fact that she would face the same gauntlet, the same scrutiny when her own family followed us in.

But they would not follow too closely.

No, each family at Grace Church wanted the aisle to themselves for at least a few moments. The better to be seen; the better to have gowns catalogued and hats critiqued. Some of the most elaborate costumes of the week were worn on Sundays.

I used to stare at the people in the pews as I walked down the aisle. But that was when I was younger. Before I knew that those same people were staring back at me.

Finally, we reached our pew. I took my seat beside Aunt, who sat beside Father.

"Over there."

I looked around, trying to see who it was that had spoken.

"Over. There."

I could attribute the words to no one.

"For goodness' sake!" The words pierced my ears with a hiss. It was Aunt. She held herself so still that she gave no indication of speech. "If you look beyond us, across the aisle, there is a long pew. Occupied by two people."

I shifted so that I could see it.

"Not. So. Conspicuously." The words were spoken through her teeth.

I straightened my spine and then leaned forward, ever so slightly.

"Do you see it?"

"No."

Aunt leaned backward, ever so slightly. "Now?"

Did I? It was so hard to tell where the pews started and stopped. Especially when they were across the aisle. And there were several pairs of people over there. Granted, most of them were surrounded with other people. But how could I tell if a pair that had space around them were *the* pair or not?

"Did you see them?"

I supposed I had. The pair had to be one of those that I'd seen, didn't it? "Yes."

"That is where the De Vries heir will sit. When he comes back to the city. Next to the woman in blue. His mother."

Oh! *That* woman. I had been looking too far down the aisle. Mrs. De Vries was dressed in a costume of medium blue with beige lace at her throat and around her wrists. Her dark blue hat, set atop a piled mass of blond hair, was trimmed in ivory-colored ribbons and a puff of ivory ostrich feathers.

That was Mrs. De Vries?

What conclusions could be drawn about a woman who wore medium blue and ostrich feathers in her hat? About a woman whose family had somehow impugned my own family's honor? Nothing other than the conclusions that might be drawn of any of the other women attending services. Mrs. DeVries was perfectly respectable. In every way. I couldn't draw any conclusions at all.

It would have been nice to know, just the same, that she was nice. That she wouldn't hold it against me that I had been commanded to pursue her son. Especially when it hadn't been my idea. Had I been able to escape my debut by magic or some other dark art, I might just have done it. But my family was counting on me. My father was counting on me. And I couldn't disappoint him.

CHAPTER 3

*T*HE NEXT MORNING, I was called into Aunt's room. She had taken over one of the spare rooms and had it done up in deep reds and dark browns before she had moved in. I had only been there twice since then, but both times it had felt as if I were walking into an underground grotto—a particularly stuffy one. But at least the heavy curtains had been pried apart that morning to allow some rays of light.

The dog lying next to her rolled from its back and barked, alerting her to my presence. Seeing me, she put down her newspaper and raised a lorgnette to her eyes. "I require an apology."

For my calling her a tyrant and a bully, no doubt.

"I'm waiting, *have been waiting*, these five days now."

"One only apologizes for actions one regrets having taken."

An eyebrow poked up from her behind her eyepiece. "I require an apology and I'll get one."

"Then may I suggest you look elsewhere? You'll not get one from me."

Her nostrils flared as she took in a great, deep breath.

"Miss Miller was more than my teacher. She was my *friend*. She'd been my governess since Mama died."

21

"Yes. And I sent her away because she failed to do her job."

"But you didn't even let me say good-bye!" To my complete and utter horror, I felt a tear bloom and then roll down my cheek.

"Then I apologize for my haste in dismissing her." She tipped her head toward me in such a way that I knew it was my turn to reciprocate.

"Then I apologize for . . . having spoken to you in such a loud voice."

"Your apology is accepted, as I assume mine was. Now then, let me take a look at you."

I wiped at my tears as I stood there, not quite knowing what she wanted from me.

"Turn."

Glad not to be witness to her scrutiny, I turned.

"Slowly."

I turned slowly.

"Yes, yes ... no. No, no, no!"

No?

"I must be able to *see*." Aunt gestured to her maid. "Take off her gown."

My gown? I put a hand up to my bodice, but I was not fast enough. No matter which way I turned to try to hide myself, the maid's hands found me and soon I was standing before Aunt in just my chemise and drawers.

"Are those all yours?" One of her fingers was pointing in a rather specific way toward my chest.

"My . . . ?"

"Your bosoms. Are they all yours?"

I glanced down at them. My cheeks flushed with sudden heat. "Yes. Mostly."

"Mostly? What is that to mean?"

Being mindful of Aunt's predilection for proper diction, I tried to choose my words precisely. "I have some . . . padding."

"Padding!"

"In my corset."

She glanced toward my discarded corset. "You call that a corset? I'd be surprised if it even had a dozen bones in it. And it can't even be tightened." She gestured once more to the maid. "I need to see what I have to work with."

The maid did as she was bid and soon I was left bared.

After having rubbed her dog on its ample belly Aunt took up her lorgnette once more. "I see." She sighed and shook her head. "A pity we cannot wait until next year. I would much rather show you in full bloom, but we must make do with what you have." She tilted her head first this way and then that. "It would not be so bad if you were plumper. We could just tighten your corset and let the excess spill out on top. How small is your waist?"

"I do not—"

The maid came at me with a measure and wrapped it around my waist with chill fingers. "Twenty-two inches, ma'am."

"Twenty-two. It could be better. And how large are your hips?" The maid pushed the tape lower, over my drawers, and took my measure. "Twenty-five, ma'am."

"Twenty-five inches? I can't send you out into society with the shape of a young boy. And you're tall enough to be one, aren't you? I can't think why I didn't notice any of this before! We'll just have to cinch you in and plump you up and hope that it can be accomplished in time. We've only eleven weeks until the season begins." One of the dogs on the floor stood on its hind feet and reached a paw out to scrape at her hand. She took it onto her lap as she continued speaking.

"I'll have the cook make a coddle of eggs for you at breakfast, provide a generous wedge of cheese at lunch, and a creamed soup in addition to dinner. Have no fear, you will be plump as a hen in no time." She gave her dog a pat and then took up her paper.

After a moment I realized I was no longer wanted. I pulled my chemise over my head. Aunt's maid hooked my corset atop it and helped me with my gown.

The paper rattled as Aunt's voice floated out over it. "Clara?"

"Yes."

"I will have a corsetiere come tomorrow at two o'clock to fit you for a proper corset. By the time you debut, I expect you will have an eighteen-inch waist."

"Eighteen inches!"

"Yes. The ideal waist is a hand's span. Unless the De Vries heir is a Philistine, he will not be able to span your twenty-two-inch waist. We must give him what he expects if we hope to secure him without undue trouble." Her eyes appeared over the top of the newspaper. "You may go."

I did. But I'm afraid the doorknob slipped from my hand as I shut the door behind me. It closed with a very satisfactory bang.

———

ONCE RELEASED FROM Aunt's presence, I passed the rest of my time in the ladylike pursuits of gluing images into my scrapbook and working on the perforated cardboard needlework motto I was making for Lizzie for Christmas. The handiwork occupied me until lunch and then from lunch until dinner.

The next day the corsetiere and her assistant came at the appointed hour. I heard them at the door and crept to the stairs to watch as the doorman took their cloaks. Once again, I was bid come to Aunt's room. The assistant took my measurements in much the same way Aunt's maid had the day before. The corsetiere looked on as she spoke to Aunt.

"We have corsets made of ribbon and corsets made of cloth. Satin, silk, and sateen. Cotton. Embellished with lace or ribbons or embroidery, in white or in colors as varied as ivory, pink, blue, or red—"

"Really!" Aunt seemed rather offended at all of the choices.

The corsetiere bowed. "With colored gores or without. Corsets with as little as two hundred bones and models with as many as six hundred."

"To begin, we want one that can be secured only from the back."

The woman coughed. "The latest models lace in the back *and* have clasps at the front." She waved a hand. "Lace once and remove as often as you would like."

"We have much to accomplish and very little time in which to do it. There will be no possibility of cheating if the corsets are secured only from the back."

The woman frowned. "I suppose that one could be made that way."

"I suppose you *will* make one that way if you wish to keep our business!"

The corsetiere smiled, though it was a bit thin about the lips. She turned toward me. "How about this one, miss?" She was holding up a model that frothed lace at the top and sprouted ribbons down the front. If I had to wear one, then that was the one I would choose.

"Yes, I—"

"No." Aunt's voice overrode my own. "We don't need furbelows. We need a simple corset. Which no one will ever see. And if my niece is successful in her debut, if she can whittle her waist in time, then we shall call you to create the corsets for her trousseau."

———

THE CORSETS TOOK a week to be made. They were delivered by the corsetiere herself, who had me try them on to ensure a proper fit.

"And how does it feel?"

"I don't think that I can breathe." Indeed, I hardly had breath enough left in my lungs to squeeze out those few words.

Aunt rose from her chair and came over to peer at the corset. "Your body will adjust soon enough. And when it does, you will have an enviable waist." She nodded at the maid, who approached me with a corset cover.

After helping me into the corset cover, she assisted me back into my gown. It fit somewhat tighter between my shoulders, but rather looser down below.

The rest of the day was my own, and so I put the time to use on the motto I was embroidering for Lizzie. When it was finished, it would proclaim *Friendship Love and Truth* in all the colors of the rainbow. But unexpectedly, my back became sore and my neck fatigued. The corset had placed me in an unnatural position, and I could find no comfortable posture in which to sit. Moreover, whenever I moved, at least one of the corset's six hundred bones poked into my sides. I counted the hours until I would be able to take it off and sleep.

But that night, after the maid had removed the corset cover, she handed me my nightgown.

I handed it back. "You've forgotten to remove the corset."

She curtsied. "You're to wear it, miss."

"I know. And I do. I will. But now it's time for sleep." Aunt had trouble finding maids that performed to her satisfaction. I was beginning to think this one's time, too, was limited.

"You're to wear it while you sleep, miss."

"*While* I sleep? But if I wear it, I will not sleep!"

The maid bowed her head and curtsied again. "'Twas the missus's orders."

If I could have reached the laces, I would have untied them myself. I had tried, in fact, that very afternoon. But they were located at the back of the garment and tucked into the corset where I could not find them.

"Your nightgown, miss?"

I surrendered and bowed to her suggestion.

I tried, I truly tried to sleep.

I relaxed my limbs and back completely letting the tension run out from my shoulders to my fingertips. But still I was held in my cage, my back rigid, my hips constrained. I turned to my side, but it was no better. I could pass a hand between my waist and the mattress without touching either.

I sighed and rolled and stared into the gloom for what seemed like an eternity. And then I got up. Or tried to. Since I couldn't bend in the middle, I had to slide along the mattress, let my feet hang out over the edge, and wait for gravity to do its work.

Once standing, I gathered up all the cushions in the room and then used them to prop up my pillows. Eventually, I found the perfect manner of sleep. By using all of the cushions, I created a kind of seat for myself. And it was in that way that I finally, and with great relief, found sleep. While sitting up in bed.

CHAPTER 4

*T*WO DAYS LATER, Aunt surprised me once again by wanting to go out. "You are to wear a walking costume."

"May I ask where we are going?"

"To the dressmaker's."

We stepped out into Father's Victoria. But this time we went quite a bit farther. Along the way, we passed block after block of sidewalks that had been mounded with garbage, carriages parked atop them. Behind the buildings, lacing the streets together, was the elevated train track. Above the din of carriages and the shouts of people, the train's rumble was constant. At one point, as we passed an intersection, I saw the train itself, shooting sparks and raining soot on those who had the misfortune to be walking beneath it. Like some mythical medieval dragon, it left shadow and darkness in its wake.

Aunt wrapped my knuckles with her parasol. "Don't lean out so. One would think you'd never seen this city."

I hadn't. Not really. Oh, I'd gone with Miss Miller in the other direction, to the zoo and the Museum of Art, but I'd never been this far below Twenty-Fourth Street.

When we reached our destination, we descended from the carriage and entered a shop bedecked in crystal chandeliers and silk tassels. It had been done in peach and gold, all warm and glowing. We were shown to chairs so overstuffed that I was challenged to maintain my balance, teetering first to one side and then to another, correcting my posture by bracing my boots against the floor.

Aunt wasted no time in addressing herself to the dressmaker. "My niece must have everything. She's to debut this season."

"*This* season? I hardly think that we will be able to—"

"I hardly think that you will be able to afford not to supply her wardrobe."

The dressmaker's face went perfectly still for one long moment and then she closed her eyes. Inclined her head. "I see." When she opened her eyes, she addressed herself to me. "Please stand." At the wave of her hand, a half-dozen girls appeared. Two of them unfolded a silk-upholstered screen and closed us off from the rest of the shop. The others helped me from my gown. Then one of them took the measure of my arm, another of my back, a third of my neck, and a fourth started toward my waist.

"She's to achieve an eighteen-inch waist by December." My Aunt's proclamation left no reason for the dressmaker to doubt her word.

The fourth girl dropped her measure with a shrug and looking toward the one recording my measurements. "Eighteen inches at the waist, then."

"As to colors . . . ?" The dressmaker stood away from the girls, letting them do their work.

Aunt swayed atop her chair. "White, of course! For her coming-out dress. And for all the balls that will follow."

The dressmaker bowed. "Of course. But for the other events?"

"Something to complement her skin. And something that will make others take notice."

The first girl whispered to two attendants-in-waiting. They disappeared behind a curtained doorway, reappearing several minutes later laden with a colorful array of bolts of material in shades like buffalo red, rosewood, copper, empire green, and sapphire blue.

Aunt frowned. "I want her to attract a man, not a circus!"

The girls bowed and backed away, soon returning with a new assortment of fabrics. This time, the colors were much softer, ranging from a pale Nile green to the lightest blue, from rose to gray lavender. And they seemed to meet Aunt's particular requirements.

Once the colors had been decided upon, Aunt ordered my entire wardrobe for the season. She also ordered several hoop skirts that would hang from my waist. One of the girls brought out the latest model. It consisted of fifteen hoops of various sizes, from smallest to largest, that were suspended on five tapes from a sixth tape buckled about the waist. I would be able to sit, for the first hoop started just above my knee, but I had no idea how I would manage to walk.

Just as I assumed that we were finished, Aunt stayed the dressmaker with a hand to the woman's arm. "And now I wish to consult with you regarding my own wardrobe."

Her wardrobe? It had remained unchanged since I had known her. Black gowns, black hats, black shawls, and black cloaks. If the silhouettes had been altered from time to time, the general aspect of mourning had never been placed into question.

"Yes, madam?"

"I wish to order"—she closed her eyes as if it pained her to speak—"a gown in purple, and one in gray."

Gray? Purple! My debut had accomplished what a lifetime of widowhood had not: It had persuaded her to emerge from deep mourning. Perhaps she would soon pass into other dark colors as well.

"And some mauve cuffs." She glared at me as she ordered them, as if I might dare to question her. "Someone must accompany you to all your operas and balls and parties."

———

AFTER OUR BUSINESS with the dressmaker was concluded, we continued on to Constable's. I had heard Lizzie speak of this famed, elegant store—a genuine department store—but I had never been there. When we arrived, the coachman parked our carriage right on the street, next to two others. After he had seen us on our way, I saw him turn to speak to the other white-breeched servants waiting beside the store.

Two doormen opened twin doors at our approach, bowing as they did so.

Aunt tugged me inside and walked me straight to Gloves.

A clerk took charge of us as soon as we presented ourselves. "We have some very fine gloves from England."

Aunt was already shaking her head. "I want French. From Grenoble. Firsts only."

The man took a measurement of my hand. "Six and one-half." He reached down and pulled a pair of gloves up from the drawer, passing them to Aunt.

She passed them right back. "If she is a six and one-half, then we'll want a size five."

The man frowned but returned the pair to the drawer and took from it a new one.

Aunt examined them for a long moment and then nodded. "We'll want ten pairs of sixteen button in white. And ten pairs of twelve button. In white. And a dozen pairs of six button as well."

"In white?"

Aunt nodded.

"As you wish."

As the clerk put a shopgirl to work packaging up our purchase, Aunt pulled me around the store. She selected a dozen pairs of silk stockings and a season's worth of muffs and parasols to match the wardrobe she had ordered from the dressmaker.

I returned home worn from the noise of the city and fatigued by all the sights and sounds we had passed on our journey. And then I remembered that it was Thursday—today I would see Lizzie!

As the appointed hour neared for our meeting, I tried to find some reason to wander to the garden. It would not have been difficult in spring or summer, but most of the flowers had fallen to the frosts of October and the birds had already fled for gentler climes. I finally decided to simply slip out. But deciding was one thing and doing it was another matter entirely. As I walked on light feet past Aunt's room, I saw her sitting in a chair reading a newspaper.

One of the dogs stood watch by her door. It seemed to eye me suspiciously as I passed and breathed a low growl.

"Who's there?" There came the sound of a teacup finding its saucer.

If I lingered too long, Aunt might lower her newspaper and then she would discover me. And in truth, no one could answer if no one was there. I hurried on down the front stair, the thick carpet masking the sound of my steps.

Once outside, I headed toward the hedge. It had grown since I had last sought its refuge. There had been no reason for meeting in such places once we had given up our dolls and once Miss Miller could provide an escort to and from my friend's house. But how clever of Lizzie to think such a thought! To remember the way from her gate through the neighbor's garden and into mine.

"Lizzie?"

"Clara!" A hand reached out, clutching at my elbow and pulling me straight into the shrubbery. "I've been sitting here for *days!*"

"I'm sorry but..." I steeled my courage. "I have something that I must tell you."

She clasped her hands together at her breast. "And I have something to tell you!" Her blond curls were positively quivering beneath the brim of her hat.

She did? That was good—it would delay me from telling her about the debut. "You first."

"No, you. You said so first."

I nibbled at my lip. I supposed the best thing to do was simply to say it. "Aunt has decided, in spite of everything I could think of to convince her otherwise, that I'm to debut. This season."

I had expected despair from Lizzie, but she gasped and then began to giggle. "But that's wonderful. I'm to debut as well! That's what I was going to tell you."

"You are? But—"

"We'll be together, then, just as we always planned."

Just as we always planned. For the first time since Aunt had announced my debut, I felt hope. Lizzie would make sure I didn't fail. I began to smile. But then I remembered my other secret. I leaned close, not willing to disclose my shame to any ears but her own. "*And* I'm wearing a corset."

"Me too!"

If I could have laughed in relief, I would have, but I didn't have the breath to do it. "Do you find it—I mean—" I stopped and then tried again. "How do you eat?" The problem wasn't actually with eating. The trouble began afterward, once the food lay in my stomach. It simply stayed there for what seemed like hours after meals. I'd already given up eating green apples.

Lizzie wrinkled her nose. "Eating? With the corset?" She

shook her head. "It's a pity one has to at all. But, here! Let me show you." Lizzie began to unbutton her bodice.

"Lizzie!"

"You have to see it. It's the most gorgeous thing."

With a roll of her shoulder, she cast back her garment, revealing the very same corset that I had coveted. The one with all the lace and the cascades of ribbons. Then she pulled her bodice back up and buttoned it closed beneath her chin.

"Now show me yours."

"You don't want to see it."

"But I do—show me!" She was looking at me as if she might start to unbutton my bodice herself. "Did you pick satin or silk?"

"I didn't pick at all. Aunt picked."

She wrinkled her nose. "So is it sateen?"

"Worse. Plain cotton."

She frowned in such a way that I basked in her sympathy. Then her eyes brightened. "But just think: At the end of the season, once you're engaged, you can pick anything you want for your trousseau!"

Marriage. So soon! "But what if there's no one ..." I knew, of course, who was expected for me, but what about Lizzie? What if she went through the entire season, only to have her hopes of true happiness dashed at its end? "What if there's no one suitable?"

"Suitable? Everyone is suitable. At least everyone at a ball. The thing is to find someone manageable. Someone compatible."

"Compatible." I tried out the word for thought. Surely among the hundreds of people in society, there must be one who would be compatible. At least with Lizzie. And surely the elder De Vries would be compatible with me. "Aunt has told me I must try for only one. She has fastened on the—"

"Don't say it! Let me guess." Lizzie closed her eyes, folded her hands upon her heart, and took a great breath. Then she opened her eyes and gazed at me mischievously. "She has fastened on the De Vries heir."

I felt my mouth drop open. "But how did you know?"

"He's the one Mama has picked for me as well. How perfect!"

"Perfect? But if we both--?"

She linked an arm through mine. "When you tire of him, then you shall give him to me and when I tire of him, I shall give him to you. That way we shall both have the benefit of regular dances with him. And every Thursday, at half past three, we will meet right here and discuss how it's progressing."

"How what's progressing?"

"Why, our courtship, of course!"

"But is that permitted?" Weren't we now adversaries, competing for the same prize? And if that was so, wasn't Lizzie sure to win him? There was no one who didn't like Lizzie.

She laughed. "Oh, Clara, you make it sound as if it's a crime."

"Do you really have to be set on him? Maybe one of us could refuse him." I couldn't, of course, but perhaps she could.

"I can't. I wish I could. But Mama, being from the South, with no real connections . . . she thinks we need them. Him. The De Vrieses. I wouldn't tell this to just anyone, but some people haven't really accepted her here. Still. And she wants more for me. So, I can't refuse him, but. maybe you can."

I was already shaking my head. "I have to have the heir. No one else will do."

How had it happened that both of us had been pointed toward the same person? Our debut had been planned for years, but never had I thought that we would be pursuing the same man. We stared at each other for a long moment. The dismay in Lizzie's eyes seemed to mirror my own.

But then a smile banished the consternation, and she broke the silence. "We shall make a promise between us right now.

Never, but never, will we ever allow a suitor to come between us. Say it."

"Never, but never, will we ever allow a suitor to come between us."

She nodded.

"But what happens if ... I mean, he'll have to choose, Lizzie."

"Then he shall choose. If he chooses you, I will be happy and come to your wedding. And if he chooses me, you will be happy and come to my wedding."

"I don't think it's meant to work that way." Lizzie was always so genial, so cheerful, that she refused to see difficulty in even the most impossible of situations.

"We just made a promise. And now there is nothing to do but keep it."

"But how do we know that he will prefer us at all?"

"Why wouldn't he? We're the best catches in the city. Papa has plenty of money and if anyone is to fall sick, your father can cure him. I'm exceedingly gay and charming, and you're exceedingly smart and pretty. What is there not to like about us?"

What indeed?

"Just think: Our debuts await and with them, true love!" Lizzie ducked through the bushes toward the gate in the wall. "Don't forget. Next Thursday. Half past three!"

CHAPTER 5

I HAD NEVER understood before just how precarious life was. How in one moment, there could be nothing but Byron and science experiments and in the next, they could vanish—replaced by singing lessons and etiquette books as if my life itself depended upon them. Gone were my days of laughing and learning with Miss Miller, my hours-long visits with Lizzie in the splendors of her bedroom. My debut had ceased to be a vague kind of doom floating about my future; it had grown wings and teeth and swooped down to carry me away with its obligations.

"Don't light about here and there like a bird!"

I started at Aunt's voice. I had been wandering about the room, loath to sit and make any more pronounced the confines of my corset, but lacking in anything of substance to do instead.

"Your strength, if you have one, is in your aspect. Your clear skin and the sheen of your dark hair. With the least bit of wakefulness at night, with a bit of languor and lethargy, you look quite pallid and tragic. You must put it to good use by walking slowly, like one in mourning, with measured paces. It will give you a certain note of grace."

I had to acquire grace now too? Along with a perfectly pitched voice and an accomplished playing of an especially difficult Hungarian dance by Brahms? "You ask too much."

"Then you expect too little. I can open the doors of high society to you. My marriage to Mr. Stuart entitled me to that, at least. But I cannot make you walk through them with any kind of success. That is up to you." She frowned at me, criticism lending weight to her scowl. "Go now. And think on that. And have the butler deliver the newspapers. I need to know where everyone has been and who they're seeing and what they're doing."

I did think on my success. I thought about it all night while I tossed and turned and sighed and groaned. By this time next year, I might be married. And if not married, then engaged to be so. There was no doubt about that. Only one uncertainty regarding my future remained: the identity of the groom.

If I was going to marry, and it was certain that I was, why should I not marry the De Vries heir? I had almost convinced myself that I should be the winner of that prize. Though I still didn't understand the circumstances of Aunt and Father's determination that I unite with him, wasn't my family's honor more important than Mrs. Barnes's connections? But Lizzie's words kept echoing through my thoughts.

"Never, but never, will we ever allow a suitor to come between us."

Never, but never? How could we possibly keep that promise unless we both decided to cede Mr. DeVries to the other? And why would Mrs. Barnes or Aunt allow either of us to do that?

———

SUNDAY PROVIDED SOME relief from my training, though I should rue the day that I considered a walk down the aisle of Grace Church preferable to an hour spent with Aunt! As soon as I was settled in the pew, I snuck a peek across the aisle.

It was occupied!

By more than just Mr. and Mrs. De Vries. There was another, younger, woman sitting beside them, wearing a hat edged in white fur and a dark green costume trimmed with the same fur. She looked like a Russian princess who had stepped from the pages of *Harper's Bazar*.

On the other side sat two young men, both dark-haired. The first was dressed in an elegant dove gray frock coat, his hair precisely combed away from his brow. The other had the telltale folds of an Inverness cape showing at his shoulders. His hair was rather unruly, his brows thick. And it was he who caught me looking in their direction.

I quickly pressed myself against the back of the pew. But leaning back just a bit, beyond the furthest reaches of Aunt's hat, I could see them still. Enough to know that the young man had done the same. And that he could see me still.

Leaning forward, I took the hymnal to hand and flipped to the morning's first hymn, determined to give him no more thought. Though I did wonder which one he was: the elder or the younger. To which of them was I to be presented? Which young man was destined to be the restorer of my family's honor? And if the De Vries were such a terrible family to begin with, then why did I have to marry into them? Why was it that I had been deemed the sacrificial lamb?

The New York Journal—Society
October 27, 1891

Dr. Willard Carter and his sister, Mrs. Lewis Stuart, will give a tea on Tuesday, November 10, at their residence, 472 Fifth Avenue, in honor of Dr. Carter's daughter, Miss Clara Carter, who is one of the season's debutantes. Mrs. Stuart and Miss Carter will receive on Tuesdays during the winter.

Aunt had hardly finished reading the notice of our tea to me when a coil of anxiety began to tighten in my stomach. I would be receiving. This winter. I hadn't even thought of that! "Wouldn't another day be better?" Like Wednesday or Thursday or Friday? Some day of the week that wasn't quite so close to its beginning? A day of the week that I would have time to prepare for?

Aunt hardly bothered to look up from the paper before replying. "Tuesdays are best. That allows any interested gentlemen callers to see you directly after a Monday evening event. We shall waste no time that way."

"Callers?" In the plural? "But I thought my only interest was the De Vries heir."

"It is. But why would he be interested in you if no one else is interested? We must cast a wide net, and in doing so reel Mr. De Vries in unawares."

———

AUNT SPOKE TO Father about that very thing at dinner.

"We shall give Clara a tea on Tuesday, November tenth. To celebrate her debut into society."

"November tenth? Could it be a different date? I've an appointment that afternoon."

"It's already been announced in the *Journal*."

Father continued eating.

When he said nothing, Aunt spoke again. "You may announce it to all your patients, those with eligible sons. They might be ignorant of their obligations. Now is the time to remind them."

"Aren't our hopes fixed on the De Vries heir?"

"They're old money and they have to be dealt with gently. Discreetly. They might not take kindly to being reminded of their debt. We will rely on Clara's ability to captivate"—she cast a stern eye in my direction—"and on your means of persuasion only as a last resort."

Father picked up his goblet and took a sip of wine. "Gently and discreetly." He set the goblet back on the table. "I don't remember them being gentle or discreet when they lost all of our money during the Panic. I'll never forget it. All of it gone in a single day. September 18, 1873. It was rather abrupt, Sister, wouldn't you say? And their bank was completely unrepentant."

This was how our family had lost its honor? By losing its money? But hadn't everyone's fortunes disappeared in the Panic? That was what Miss Miller had said. Hadn't Aunt married into the illustrious Stuart family? And hadn't we lived here on Fifth Avenue, among Vanderbilts and Goulds, ever since I could remember?

My questions were tempered by the steel that appeared in Aunt's eyes. "This is our opportunity. And it is better for us if our goal can be accomplished without any undue unpleasantries."

———

ONCE THE TEA had been announced, my social education advanced with rapid speed.

"Because this year's debutante will be next year's hostess, that's why! That's why it's important to learn the difference between asparagus tongs and sardine tongs. Especially if you're to be the bride of a De Vries. Understood?"

I nodded.

"So. What is this one for?" Aunt selected a utensil from the dining room table and held it up before me.

"It's a fork." At least that's what I hoped it was. It was shaped like a spoon, but at the very end, where it ought to have been a solid curve, there were several tines. It was a spoon-like fork.

"Yes. It's a fork. Very good. But what is it for?"

"It's for ..." It couldn't be for salad. And it couldn't be for meat; the tines weren't long enough. It wasn't for fish. Or for bread. It had to be for something that was mostly meant to be eaten with a spoon. A jelly? No. Jellies were meant to be spread with a knife. And it was surely not a soup spoon.

Aunt placed the utensil back on the table. "It's for ice cream."

"Oh."

"And how about this one?"

That one was a very spidery-looking fork. It had three long, thin, very sharp tines. So it wasn't meant for placing anything in the mouth. It had to be for stabbing something. Something like a ... roast? No. It wasn't sturdy enough. Something like a cake? No, it would pull right out. It was made for something small but hard. Something like an apple? But why would anyone want to stab an apple? An orange? "An orange." I said it with much more confidence than I felt.

"Close. It's a lemon fork."

On and on and on she went. A dozen forks. A dozen spoons. A dozen knives.

"And this?"

"It's a ..." It couldn't be what I assumed it to be. It was a shovel. A tiny narrow shovel in miniature. But what else could it be? "It's a shovel."

"Yes, of course it's a shovel. But what is it destined for?"

"Something very . . . deep."

"Yes."

"And rather . . . narrow."

"Yes."

I was beginning to perspire behind the ears. "And ... I really don't know, Aunt."

"Well, you'd better know! And I'll tell you now: It's a marrow shovel."

"A marrow shovel." I had not known there was such a thing.

"Yes. To dig it out of a bone." Exasperation was evident in her tone.

"Is there a reason why I couldn't just use a knife?"

"Would you like me to give you a toothpick as well? In fact, why not pick the whole bone up with your hands? And then wipe them on the table linen once they've become soiled? Any more questions?"

I did indeed have more questions. But what I wanted to know most of all was why I had been told to betray my closest friend. But I didn't ask her. I couldn't. I didn't know how to do it.

CHAPTER 6

$\mathcal{B}$Y THE TIME Thursday afternoon came, I was battling a headache two days old.

And Lizzie exploded in a display of hysterics when she saw me. As soon as she could, she latched on to my arm and dragged me through the hedge. "Did you see him?"

"Who?"

"The heir! At church!"

I nodded.

"Then tell me what he looked like. We arrived too early and by the time I knew he was there, we had already left."

"He was ..." I tried to disengage her gloved hand from my arm. "I'm not sure exactly which one he was."

Lizzie only hung on tighter. "What do you mean?"

"There were two. Two young men in the De Vries pew."

"Then tell me what they both looked like and I'll tell you which one he was."

But how could she possibly know? "The first was darkhaired. . ."

She nodded.

"Actually, they were both dark-haired."

"I adore men with dark hair!"

"And the one was wearing a frock coat."

"What color?"

"Gray. Really, Lizzie, could you stop grasping at me?"

She dropped me from her clutches. "And the other?"

"An Inverness."

She wrinkled her nose. "An Inverness? I've never liked them. I hope that one's not the heir. Although maybe . . . maybe I could just throw it away once I'd married him."

Throw it away? She would just throw someone's clothes away?

"Or you could. So. They both have dark hair."

"Yes. The one combs it back, like this." I swept my hand from my brow over the crown of my head.

"The one in the frock coat or the Inverness?"

"The frock coat."

"And the other?"

I shrugged. "He didn't seem to care much where his hair went or what it was doing."

Her lips crimped into a frown and then suddenly lifted. "The one in the frock coat's the heir."

"But how do you know?"

"I just do." That question settled, Lizzie launched into a recital that took at least ten minutes to perform: who had been seen with whom and what they had been wearing.

I had just opened my mouth to ask her about her training for our debut when she spoke again.

"And did you see that woman in church? The one wearing the Havana brown-colored mantle? Mama said she hadn't seen one in years! I can't imagine that anyone would find it attractive."

"Perhaps she was just trying to stay warm."

"Warm! Why would warmth matter on a Sunday morning? One can get by with a stole at a dance and one can wear a higher collar at a reception, but on Sunday morning? Everyone sees you as you are. For a full hour and a half. Some from the back, and some from the side. No, there is no day so important to fashion as a Sunday!"

Lizzie left me quite as pained as she had found me, her words and general good humor ringing in my ears.

———

THE NEXT DAY with Aunt was given over to the practice of polite conversation. I was almost looking forward to it. There were so many interesting things of which to speak. The state of the poor and the Riis book. Tammany Hall and politics. Since Miss Miller's departure, I had longed to find someone with whom to discuss the issues of the day.

"The first rule is that there must be no mention of any unpleasant topic."

No unpleasant topics? "But then what is there of interest to converse about? And why wouldn't I want to know what Mr. De Vries thinks about--" In my haste I had almost confessed to reading the Riis book. A thing that I had now become quite sure I must not do.

"About?"

But then why shouldn't I confess to reading the Riis book? Any person with any kind of conscience would be aghast at the things that went on in the city. I lifted my chin and answered her question directly. "About the Jacob Riis book, for instance."

"And how do you know about the Riis book?"

"Miss Miller gave me a copy."

Aunt frowned. "Lies. Everything that man says is a lie. He's an immigrant, for goodness' sake!"

"There are photographs in the book. I could show you! All those poor people who live in the tenements on the Lower East Side—"

"He's a liar. As for Mr. De Vries, he'll think what any other normal person thinks about the poor: Some races are simply inferior to our own. The Irish, for instance. And the Italians. If they're poor and they live in tenements, then it's their own fault."

"I don't think anyone would choose to live in a building that's falling down upon them."

"Exactly. So if they do, then there's bound to be something wrong with them, isn't there?"

"Do you really think that's what the heir thinks?" Could he truly be so unfeeling?

"That's what most people with any sense believe. If God wanted the poor to prosper, then they would. If they're not, then they deserve what they get. And of course that's what he'll think. Which is why there's no need to mention it. Why speak of such unpleasantness when there are so many other things of which to speak? There must be no mention of politics or religion or any other objectionable topic. Nothing which will offend any of your listeners. Nothing which will lead to any lengthy sort of conversation. And you must always enunciate."

No politics, religion, or any other objectionable topic. What was left?

"Now you may practice."

"Practice what?"

"Conversing."

"With you?"

Aunt looked down, pointedly, at the dog dozing on her lap.

"The dog can't talk."

"And neither can most of the people you attempt to converse with. It is always to your advantage to know how to carry on a conversation with a person who cannot or will not speak."

"I couldn't just say, for example, 'Good day'? And then leave?"

"You could not."

"It's rather difficult to speak to someone who's sleeping."

Aunt roused the dog and then set it on the tea table. It blinked and opened its mouth for a yawn, exposing a row of sharp tiny teeth and a little pink tongue.

"You may begin."

I directed my attention to the dog and, against all reason, began to speak to it.

"I hope you're feeling well today." Or at least better than yesterday, when it, or one of the other two, had dug up a flower bulb and become violently ill soon thereafter. I wish it had died and saved the rest of us from the stench of its indigestion.

"No. No. You may absolutely not ask any person about their health."

I tried again. "It is so very good to meet you."

The dog tilted its head to one side. In that posture, its skull very nearly disappeared into its fur. It looked like cushion. How I wished that I could tuft it with buttons, embroider it with flowers, and give it away as a gift. I smiled. "I have so often wanted to make your acquaintance."

Aunt frowned, but she did not interrupt.

"Did you enjoy the . . . opera?"

The dog said nothing.

"I found it quite uplifting."

Aunt coughed. "Remember that the first opera of the season will be *Romeo and Juliet*."

"Uplifting in a tragic sort of way."

The dog sighed and reached a foot up to scratch at its ear.

With starts and stops and prompts from Aunt, I talked to that dog for what seemed like an hour.

Aunt glanced at the clock on the mantel. "Ten minutes. Not bad. For a start." She kept me practicing until I could talk for half of an hour without a prompt. "Most likely the opportunity to converse will come during dinner or at some reception or other event where you'll also be able to ask for a glass of punch or otherwise distract your conversation partner." She lifted the creature from the table and set it back on her lap. "Now then, a conversation such as that one will always stand you in good stead, even when the person you are conversing with does not wish to respond. Except, of course, if you are being cut."

"Being cut?"

"Being snubbed. In that case it is expected that you would stop speaking and leave the person immediately to his or her own devices."

"What if I am by myself? How would I leave if I'm not to go anywhere unescorted?"

Aunt's brows seemed in danger of disappearing into her hair. "By yourself? When would you be by yourself?"

"I don't know."

"And neither do I. In any case, the proper way to be cut is not to acknowledge that you have been cut, but simply to pretend that it is your decision—in fact, your greatest desire—to leave that person's presence."

It sounded terribly humiliating. "But what if I don't know that I'm being cut?"

"If you are being cut, you will know it. Someone who knows you will suddenly refuse to acknowledge you. Someone to whom you are waiting to be introduced will turn away just as the introduction is about to be made. There are a hundred ways to cut a person and believe me, all of them will register upon that person. For that, after all, is the intention."

I nodded, hoping that it would never happen to me.

"But you must also learn how to cut."

"How to—?"

"How to snub someone."

"Why would I ever want to snub someone?" The dark confines of her room seemed to have swallowed me. Nothing she was saying made sense.

"Not everyone who has met you need be acknowledged. Especially those you meet at dances."

"At dances? Not even those I dance with?" How could I dance with someone without acknowledging him?

"Especially not those you dance with. Not unless it's advantageous to know them."

"But that doesn't seem—"

"A true gentleman will never expect to be acknowledged if the only place he has met you is a dance."

"Really?"

She nodded. "Truly. And in that case, he will provide you with an opportunity either to acknowledge or to cut him."

"He will?" Why would he do that?

"He will. Must I always repeat myself?"

"No." If I raised my hand to my head, I was sure I would feel my temple throbbing.

"Now then. If you do not wish to acknowledge someone, if you wish to cut them, then you must not give them the opportunity to speak to you." Her jet earrings trembled at her vehemence. "You must either remove yourself from their presence, or you must make it clear that you do not wish to speak to them."

"So ... I should ignore them?"

Those stern lips suddenly smiled. "Very good. That is one way in which it can be done. You might also refuse to meet their eye. You might refuse to offer a hand. You might refuse to speak."

"But then wouldn't they keep on speaking? The way that you just taught me to do?"

"Ah. Perhaps, but only on the condition that they did not know they were being cut, and the first thing about cutting is that it must be done in such a way that the person knows he is being snubbed."

I practiced the delicate art of cutting someone in a dozen

different ways and by then, I could not keep myself from objecting to the course of instruction. "I have had a headache for three days now in succession."

"I expected you might. It comes from trying to assimilate *en masse* those lessons which ought to have been taught, little by little, over the course of several years."

"Might I, perhaps, excuse myself? To lie down and rest before dinner?"

"Lie down and rest? For a headache? Certainly not! The most useful remedy is to spend ten minutes walking backward. And it will improve your posture as well." She nodded toward the hall. "Go on. It will be good for you."

I took myself out of her bedroom and into the hall.

"And not too quickly! Slowly. And precisely!"

CHAPTER 7

*M*Y SOCIAL ETIQUETTE was not the only thing to fall under Aunt's mania for improvement. She ordered a new hallstand and a new card receiver for the front hall. She decided the furniture in the parlor needed a rearrangement. And she forced a flurry of new French recipes onto the cook. One morning when she found me in the parlor, she turned her attentions to my person.

"I have come to decide that your lips are too large. Too wide."

I raised my hand to cover them.

"Yes. That is one thing you can do. You can hide them behind your hand." She cocked her head and pursed her lips. "But then one might think that you were yawning. Perhaps better to use a fan. In my day, we all practiced saying the letter P. It had the advantage of puckering the lips. Of making them appear smaller than they were. Try it."

"P?"

"Yes. See? Again."

"P."

"Yes. And you may add prunes and prisms to it. Peas, prunes, and prisms."

"Peas, prunes, and prisms?"

"Say those words over and over and over. When you wake, as you fade to sleep, and anytime in between that you remember. It will have the effect of reforming your lips, of making them plumper rather than wider. And in the meantime, before that work has been accomplished, you must always enter a room with the word *prisms* leaving your lips. Go ahead. Try it." She was waving her hand toward the door.

I obliged, leaving and then, at once, returning and taking up my seat beside her.

"Prisms!" She fairly exploded with the word.

Oh!—I had forgotten. I turned around and tried it once more.

"Prisms." The sound of the word died as I stepped across the threshold of the door.

"Yes. The first impression you make will then be one of elegance. And of a smaller mouth, of course. Now, come here."

I obeyed, letting *prisms* drop from my thoughts altogether.

"Sit."

I sat.

"We must now—" She leaned forward. Looked as if she were trying to peer around my side. "Do you always do that?"

"Do what?"

"Do you always let your shoulders roll forward in such a lackadaisical manner?"

I pulled them up and rolled them back before she could expand her comments. "No."

"What did that Miss Miller teach you that was of any importance?"

Mathematics, geography, and literature. Italian and Latin."

"It is said that Consuelo Vanderbilt's mother had a steel rod affixed to her daughter's spine."

A steel rod!

"Though I don't make it a rule to agree with those types, it is possible that an extreme measure such as that one might need to be undertaken if you cannot correct your posture on your own."

"No!" I straightened as I said it. Edged forward on my seat and folded my hands into each other.

Aunt stared at me for one long moment. Then she frowned. And sighed. "I *have* noticed that the corset has already helped to improve your carriage. If you can endeavor to maintain proper posture at all times, then ..." She sighed again. "You must understand that I am only trying to help you. If your mother had not died, she would have taught you all of this long ago. And there would be no need for my instruction. But really, you cannot hope to succeed in society without such correction."

One of the dogs barked.

Aunt bent slightly and put a hand to its head. "There will be no need for such undertakings if you can manage to cure this deficiency on your own. Understood?"

I nodded.

———

IT WAS WITH great relief that I snuck away to greet Lizzie the next Thursday afternoon. I slipped past the dogs, not daring to look at them for fear they would discern my purposes. Pulling on a cloak, I stepped out the back door and made my way through the garden.

Lizzie chided me as I entered the hedge. "I've been watching you forever. It seemed as if you would never arrive! What were you doing?"

"I was walking. In a ladylike fashion. Aunt says, 'No girl of good breeding ever goes anywhere directly.'" I sniffed the way Aunt always did. "'She is not in a hurry like some common servant. The most beautiful lines in nature are not straight. They are curved.' "

Lizzie clapped her hands. "Wait—wait. I've got one! Mama says to always hold one's hands close to the skirt when walking."

"Really?" I hadn't heard that before. "Why?"

"So that they don't swing about unbecomingly."

I added it to my burgeoning list of things not to do.

Lizzie stepped away from the bushes and drew her hands around in front of her. "I'm not to stand with my hands behind me either."

"Truly? I hadn't known, and I don't know if I can remember."

Lizzie's face flushed. "I can't. So Mama said always to clasp them within each other."

"I'm not to wink."

"And I'm not to let any young man address me by my first name."

I held up a finger the way Aunt always did when she admonished me. "And never, ever allow a young man to take your arm—"

"Because doing so implies that you are weak." Lizzie finished with a giggle.

Those rules were all well and good, but what were we supposed to actually do with young men? "Have you ever wondered, Lizzie, what it is that we're allowed to do? When we're with a young man?"

Her brow furrowed and her laughter ceased. "Well, be kind. And frank. And gracious. And catch one of them as a husband!"

"What if I forget and do something. Or forget *to* do something?"

"Then I shall come to your rescue. And you're to come to mine."

Dear, sweet Lizzie. It seemed she had an answer for everything. And I had only questions. "I don't want to debut." I never had.

"You've never wanted to debut."

I had to smile that she could read my thoughts so well. "I'm not ready. Not like you are."

"Of course, you're ready."

"I'm not."

She leaned forward then and took up my hands, pressing them between her own. "You were born to debut and so was I. It doesn't matter if you want to or not, if you're ready or not. We have to." We did. We had to do it. And that was the plain, simple, unadulterated truth.

———

THE DAY OF my tea dawned cold and cloudy. Rain threatened most of the morning, but by afternoon the clouds had been blown back by a ruthless wind. In the garden, hapless leaves were being tossed helter-skelter. "Do you think . . . ?"

"What?" Aunt was busy watching the maid attend to me.

There were a hundred thoughts to think, but I did not know which one to settle upon. Would anyone come? Would I bobble my tea? Would my hair stay in place? Would I be able to think of something clever to say to all of the people who attended? If anyone attended at all? "Do you think it will go well?"

"Of course it will go well. It has to go well. Like a ship that has just been launched, either you will drift onto a sandbar and be grounded, or you will sail off into the sea with great aplomb. Be warned: We cannot afford to have you flounder upon some desolate shore! Easter is rather late this year: that gives us an advantage. There are eleven weeks between the official start of the season next month and its end at Lent. We must gain as much ground as we can in these next few weeks. You must succeed; you will succeed. The Carter family honor depends upon you. Besides, this tea is more for the mothers than the men. Impress those women, and they will push their sons in your direction."

There were mothers to worry about as well?

I had been put in my dressing sacque, not yet ready to don my gown for the tea. The maid ran a comb through my hair, gathering my locks at the top of my head.

"Stop!"

Both the maid and I jumped at Aunt's cry.

"I think a lesser height is needed. She is tall enough already."

The maid let go my hair and tried again, the tines of the comb creating what felt like furrows in my scalp.

"No. No, I think something less severe. Part it in the middle for just an inch. We'll curl the fringe and then gather the rest around back in a twist, with some small curls escaping at the nape."

The maid let go my hair once more. This time, the part was less brutal, the gathering of locks less violent. But just when I thought myself saved, she secured my hair with pins she sunk into my scalp. And then she approached me with curling tongs.

Aunt buried her nose in one of her dogs as she gave it a kiss. "You'll thank me when you're the focus of the society column in the newspaper."

I rather doubted it. I sat there as the maid passed the tongs back and forth between a candle's flame and then seized my fringe and applied the tongs to it.

Once done, she turned to help me with my gown. But Aunt directed her to lay it aside and tighten my corset first.

"Please! I can hardly breathe as it is."

"The gown is meant to fit perfectly ... as long as the wearer has an eighteen-inch waist."

Eighteen inches? Already? That was one and a half inches less than I had.

"Tighten the corset."

I felt the maid at my back, loosening the laces. There was a moment of sweet freedom when I could breathe unimpeded, and then she violently wrenched the laces, forcing all of the air from my chest. Once I had grown accustomed to the constriction, she helped me into a corset cover, a hooped skirt, and then my gown. It was a traditional white debutante's gown. It had been made in crepe de chine with satin bows fixed to the shoulders and a satin rose set upon my waist at the back. It had no similarity to my former loose gowns. Those had dropped freely from my waist to my ankles. This gown fit the upper half of my body tightly, exquisitely.

And it nipped in at my waist, only to fan out from the hips in a multitude of pleats.

Aunt took me by the hand and led me to the mirror.

The image staring back at me was astonishing.

I was no longer a girl.

I was no longer seventeen.

I was a debutante, a woman. A woman in search of a husband.

"Now, the gloves." Aunt gestured to the maid. "Here is how it's done. First, you must sprinkle them with powdered alum." She took a jar from her pocket and shook it into the glove. "Give me your hand."

I put it in her own.

She pulled me toward the stool in front of my dressing table. "Sit there and put your elbow on the table."

I looked at her with a frown. My elbow on the table? Surely, she was joking. If I was still a bit unsure of fish knives and lemon forks, I knew this rule by heart: No elbows on the table.

"Now!"

I did as she ordered, fearing still that at any moment I might be scolded. But I was not. She simply began to turn one of the gloves in upon itself until the openings to the fingers were displayed. She fit the glove over each of my fingers in turn. Then she jammed my elbow into the table with the effort it required to pull the glove on over them. But she was not done yet. She had not fit my thumb into it. "Brace yourself."

"Pardon me?"

"Brace yourself! With a hand to the knee."

With those words the struggle began. Eventually, after some moments of tugging and wrenching, the feat was accomplished. Aunt waved the maid toward me so that the gloves could be buttoned. Then she stood back, panting, hand at her chest. "It will go easier the next time."

I hoped so. I'd lost all feeling in my thumb. "I can hardly move my fingers."

"I know it. But see how nicely your hand is cupped? Doesn't it look much smaller?"

It was. It did. But was it worth such discomfort?

———

I DESCENDED THE stairs behind Aunt at a sedate pace.

Upon reaching the first floor, Father thrust a bouquet of white roses into my hands. "For the fairest of them all."

I blushed at his compliment.

"Remember, my dear, that you're a Carter and deserving of the very best of them."

Aunt crooked her arm through my own. "And that would be the DeVries heir."

At the new hallstand's mirror, Aunt paused to make an adjustment to her hair. Her mauve cuffs looked unfamiliar against the black of her gown. But for now, jet earrings still dangled from her ears and her hair was still covered with a lacey widow's cap.

After she was done prodding and poking, we walked into the parlor together.

Pillows in profusion dotted the furniture. Lamps, not content with their own lampshades, had been draped with lace and trailed fringe. A collection of family miniatures and fans decorated the shelves. Rugs upon rugs covered the floor. Mirrors reflected back myriad statues and figurines. And bows adorned the chairs. All but one.

All but our revolutionary relic.

That chair sat amongst the others, devoid of any ornamentation. Proud in its rude form, it proclaimed to any who saw it that the Carter family had some connection to our nation's valiant past.

Elsewhere, vases frothed feathers. The desk was embellished with a scarf, as were the piano and the curio cabinet. Mama's collection of bells had been polished and now gleamed bright as stars.

The brocade curtains had been drawn back to expose the sheer lace curtains behind them. As light filtered through their web, it translated the pattern into a series of bars upon the floor.

In the dining room, the table had been laid in lace and the tea set placed in the middle. In addition to a cup for cream and a bowl for sugar, there were all kinds of cold meats, a tiered silver server filled with tea cakes and another filled with muffins. A pyramid of hothouse strawberries. Sparkling crystal pots filled with jellies and tiny china cups of custards. And among all the implements and dishes had been placed nosegays of cut flowers of the most spectacular varieties.

At four o'clock, the first guest arrived. And after that first one, they came in droves. Lizzie and her mother among them. Aunt sneered when she saw Lizzie and her mother. "No doubt trolling for information for Lizzie's tea."

"Lizzie's having a tea?"

"Of course, she's having a tea. Next Monday. At Sherry's *restaurant.*"

A restaurant! Lizzie must be wild with excitement. There was nothing grander than a restaurant. And to hold a tea at one!

Aunt sniffed. "Sherry's. If it must be done at a restaurant, Delmonico's is the only place to do it; he knows the worth of old money. Besides, there was a time when every decent sort of person received guests into his own house, not at a restaurant like some itinerant vagabond. What is it, I wonder, that they're trying to hide?"

I fluttered my fan surreptitiously at Lizzie.

She returned the greeting.

"Stop that! You've guests to attend to. Prospective suitors. Leave Lizzie and her mother to their own devices. They've only come to see what it is that we have. At least they'll see a tea given in a proper manner. And I've no doubt they'll leave before it's over."

Aunt was right. For before I could free myself from the reception line and look to Lizzie for amusement, they had gone.

The receiving line seemed infinite, filled with people, each one of them waiting to be received by me. There were young men of all shapes and sizes. From the one who immediately slunk into the corner and cast malevolent looks at me to the one who treated my greeting as a perfunctory obligation, to be endured only for the sake of access to the bountiful tea table. But there was no particularly dashing young man among them. Not even a rather disheveled darkhaired one. Among all those many guests, I never saw the man for whom I had been prepared.

I greeted both mothers and their sons. Indeed, half my time was spent in greeting visitors. The other half seemed to have been spent in bidding them good-bye. To each of them I said the same. *Thank you ever so much for coming* and, when they were readying to leave, *Good day.* It was only after the last guest had exited the front door that I thought to ask about the De Vries heir.

"Did he come?" Had I missed him? I don't know how I could have. In spite of my responsibilities and the crowds of people, I had been able to visit both the parlor and the dining room. Twice.

Aunt turned from a lampshade she was adjusting. "Who?"

"Mr. De Vries."

"No."

No? What little pleasure I had taken in my tea evaporated. He hadn't been here? He hadn't seen me? What had all of this been for if not for him? All of my work, all of my social etiquette had been put on display for nothing.

CHAPTER 8

THE NEXT WEEK I'm afraid my spirits were still rather low. If Mr. De Vries would not present himself for an introduction, I did not know how I should have the opportunity to win him. As had become my habit, I turned aside the cheeses and sausages at breakfast. Took up a piece of dry toast instead. It was one of only very few foods that did not linger overlong in my stomach. I took a taste of the cook's coddle, of course. Aunt made me. But I always hid the remainder beneath my napkin as I left the table.

Aunt surprised me by speaking to me through the pages of her newspaper. "I have changed my mind. We will be attending Lizzie's tea." Aunt said it as if changing her mind were a daily occurrence.

"We will? Today?"

She glanced at me over the top of the paper. "We would not want to go tomorrow."

LATER, AFTER LUNCH, the maid met me in my room. She pulled a visiting gown of pale green from my wardrobe and laid it across the bed. Then she found my gloves and a pair of bracelets and placed them all beside it. As she was giving a quick tug to my corset laces, Aunt came in.

She fingered the gown on the bed, then glanced back, over her shoulder, toward the wardrobe. "Perhaps your lavender silk would do better."

"The lavender silk? But isn't it meant for receiving guests? At home?" And because it was meant for receiving rather than visiting, it was more subdued in design. More sober. And less pretty.

"Yes, yes. Leave me think for a moment." Lifting her head, she closed her eyes. I could see them at work beneath her eyelids, rolling back and forth. Up and down. Finally, she leveled her chin and opened them. "You must not seem too old; neither must you seem too young. Lizzie is altogether adorable. If you try to compete on the basis of plump cheeks and golden curls, you will surely lose ground to her. Your skin is rather too consumptive to compare favorably with her ruddiness. The best policy will be to keep you present at the tea but apart from her. And what is wanted in a dress is something with vivid color. We must attract attention away from Lizzie. Yes, the green gown will do."

She sat down in one of my pansy-embroidered chairs, her dogs filling the space around her feet.

After being dressed in a corset cover and combing mantle, I sat in front of a mirror while the maid pulled back my hair and began braiding it into a plait that would be looped at the back of my head.

Aunt stopped her. "A coiffure that is rather more refined is what's needed here. We have already announced your entry into society, Clara. You may wear your hair in a more sophisticated design. Lizzie may not. At least not today. And that is an important distinction to make."

She and the maid discussed different options, finally settling on an up-twisted coiffure.

Once I had been dressed and coiffed, my gown and shoes brushed, I swept down the stairs behind Aunt.

Father caught us as we were leaving. "You're not taking the Victoria?"

"We are."

"But I might have need of it this afternoon!"

Aunt hardly paused in her step. "You will just have to tell your patients to be patient."

"There are such things as emergencies."

"And anyone who expects you to attend them under such circumstances between the hours of four and six o'clock must be told to die some other day."

———

AT SHERRY'S, OUR cloaks were taken from us and we were ushered into a fantasy world of extravagance. Multiple tables had been laid out at the head of the room. One for tea, one for meats and savories, and one for ornate desserts.

My tea table at home had been interspersed with flowers. Lizzie's tables had columns of fruit extending near to the ceiling, dripping with cherries and gooseberries, fanning out at the top with frondy pineapples. And beside them were stationed pillars of flowers that could only have come from exotic countries. Candles were reflected in mirrors and from the hollows of countless cut crystal decanters and vases and pots.

It was a glimmering, shimmering show of elegance and refinement.

"Well." For once, Aunt's observation was followed by . . . nothing at all. In truth, I did not think there was anything for her to criticize. But she only needed a moment to gather her thoughts. "If they meant to serve dinner, then why did they specify tea? Only common people serve up supper at this hour."

———

The New York Journal—Society
November 17, 1891

Everybody, and that's everybody, congregated at Sherry's on Monday afternoon to honor Miss Elizabeth Barnes's debut. If the crowds are not mistaken, Miss Barnes is clearly the debutante of the hour ... if not the year.

LIZZIE'S DEBUT HAD been a social triumph. But that was not what she wanted to talk about on Thursday when we met behind the hedge.

"Did you see what Emma Vandermere was wearing? To church?"

Emma Vandermere? Had she been there at all? "Should I have noticed?"

"No. Not at all. Because she was wearing *last season's blue!*" Lizzie's eyes had grown wide at the pronouncement. "Can you imagine? To church! Where everyone would see."

"But doesn't blue become her?" She had the most startling pale blue eyes.

"Yes. Maybe. With those limpid eyes. But honestly! Last season's blue? To church? Didn't she know everyone would notice?"

Lizzie seemed to be offended, though I couldn't quite understand why. "Maybe she thought everyone would be concentrating on the sermon."

"The sermon?"

"It was quite good."

"I hadn't noticed."

I'd always had the feeling that most people didn't. I don't think they paid much attention to the hymns either. But on Sunday, the choir had sung one of my favorites. One of Mama's favorites. And it was then I had recalled something Mama said when I was younger. As she was having her hair done to go out to a ball.

I had heard her, throughout the day, humming a tune that even then I had recognized was from church. But it was only that evening, from five o'clock until six—the hour that was mine, alone with her—that she had begun singing the words.

Just as I am, tho' tossed about
With many a conflict, many a doubt,
Fightings and fears within, without,
O Lamb of God, I come, I come.

She had turned to me, after the maid finished with her hair, and hugged me with an unaccustomed fierceness. "Would it not be wonderful if God loved us just as we were, darling girl? Without affectation or pretension?" Her tone had been deliberate and vehement.

The maid and I had exchanged a look.

Mama smiled and grabbed a handful of earrings from her box of jewels. "Without bustles or corsets or falls of false hair?"

I nodded simply because it seemed that was what she wanted me to do.

She bent and kissed me on the forehead. Then she held a pair of earrings up to her ears. "Which do you think? Do you like these?" She let them dangle for a moment and then put them down on her dressing table and held another pair up to her lobes. "Or these?"

I chose the pair I always did. I chose the amethysts that swayed from a setting of diamonds and sapphires. They were the exact shade of the best candied violets.

"The amethysts, then." She looked into the mirror and screwed them onto her earlobes without hesitation. Then she spun around toward me. "How do I look?"

"Perfect." Mama always looked perfect.

She smiled and bent to kiss my cheek. "Then I suppose it's worth every pinch and poke and squeeze."

I threw my arms around her neck and pressed my face into her hair. It smelled of spicy lavender and sweet jasmine. "You're beautiful, Mama."

She hugged me hard, and then stood me away from herself so she could rise from her stool. "I fear it's simply artifice, darling girl."

"I like you just the way you are."

She then bent and gave me an additional kiss. "That's the nicest compliment anyone has ever thought to give me."

She had gone from the room after that, a vision in coral, ivory, and green, leaving in her wake the impression of tumbles of ruffles and lace. And the question of why no one liked her. Truly. Just the way she was.

———

"DO YOU THINK, Lizzie, it matters so much if we wear just the right colors or say just the right things?"

"What do you mean?"

"I mean, what if—why do we have to pretend to be people that we aren't? Why do we have to seem thinner than we are, and happier than we feel, and know the uses for dozens of kinds of forks when usually just one will do?"

She looked at me as if I had just asked her to translate my words into Latin. "Because we have to."

"But wouldn't you like me just the same? Even if I wore last season's blue?"

"Of course I would. But I might not invite you to dinner. Once I've married."

"You wouldn't?"

"I couldn't." She began to shrug, I could see, but then she yanked her shoulders down. "Not if I wanted to be fashionable and you weren't."

"So you would just cut me?" Lizzie would cut me? Me—her dearest friend? I would never have thought it of her!

"I wouldn't cut you. I would never cut you! But I might have to confine myself to visiting on your at-home day or meeting you at the art museum. Unless you became one of those marvelously eccentric people. Like Aunt Beulah down in Vicksburg. Mama says she has an enormous ear trumpet that she leaves strapped to her head *at all times.*"

"Is she deaf?"

Lizzie's eyes began to sparkle. "No. She's just convinced that everyone talks about her and she doesn't want to miss one word. You could be eccentric like that and no one would mind."

"Really."

"Don't pout. I'm only telling you what's true. It's what anyone would do. What any of us *should* do. And besides, you aren't like that at all."

But that was just it. I was.

Lizzie leaned forward to kiss me on the cheek. "Don't forget to meet me next week. And bring a fan!"

CHAPTER 9

$\mathcal{M}$Y FIRST AT-HOME arrived more quickly than I had wanted it to. I tried to summon some happy anticipation for sitting beside Aunt for several hours, conversing with people I didn't know about topics that didn't really matter, but the only emotion I felt was anxiety.

I didn't want to leave my room.

I wondered what would happen if I sat down in one of my pansy-covered chairs and refused to leave it. What would Aunt do? What could she do? I frowned as the maid wound my hair into a bun. It wasn't what Aunt would do ... it was what Father would think. I couldn't bear to disappoint him. My father worked tirelessly; I owed him this debut. And if I had to undertake it, then I would do everything within my power to make a success of it.

The house gown I was helped into was close-fitting and rather stifling. Made from a rose-colored wool, its high neck was encased in lace that ended in a point below my throat. The puffed sleeves fell straight and free to my forearms, where they had been caught up with more lace that descending to my wrists. The bodice clung to my corset cover and then eased over my hips and fell straight to the floor. I was encased. Completely. From head to toe. But still, my form was revealed in all its curvaceous glory.

I looked nothing like myself.

But I rather liked the image. The girl in the mirror before me looked as if she belonged in society circles. The girl in the mirror was the definition of elegance, grace, and charm. She would know how to dance; she would know how to converse. A room filled with strangers would never send her fleeing to her bedroom for refuge.

I only wished I felt the way she looked.

———

WE DESCENDED TO the parlor just before three o'clock and waited on the sofa a full half hour before Aunt moved a muscle.

Beneath the sleek lines of my gown, I was being eaten alive. My corset bit into my sides like an asp. The fine lace at my throat scratched at my skin and the delicate points of my slippers nipped at my toes.

"Why don't you play the piano. While we wait."

I rose from the sofa, relieved to be allowed to move.

"No. No. Better not to. We wouldn't want our first caller to think you had no other callers."

I took up my place beside her once more.

At four o'clock we heard the butler answer the door.

A moment later, he stepped into the parlor, carrying a silver tray well out in front of him. Stopping before us, he offered up the tray.

Aunt snatched the calling card from it and took it to hand.

"Mr. Ira Hooper." She frowned. "Ira Hooper. Ira Hooper. I think he must be related to those Hoopers that live in Boston. If I remember correctly, his mother was a sister to Charles Wilson of the Boston Wilsons who made their fortune in boot-blacking. Back at the time of the food riots. In the thirties."

She had lost me at "sister to someone of the Boston some-ones." I was still trying to trace that rather vague lineage in my head.

Aunt nodded. "Yes. Send him in." She turned to me as the butler left us. "At least when the other callers come, they'll discover someone else here before them."

The butler's disappearance coincided with the appearance of a rather cadaverously lanky young man. I thought I remem-bered him from my tea. If I had placed him properly, and I was almost certain that I did, he was the one who had stood in the corner near the piano and glared at me. Just as he was glaring now. If he didn't like me, then why had he come? Twice?

I tried a smile on, to see if it would cause him to speak.

It did not.

We stood as he approached.

He bowed.

We nodded.

Aunt smiled. "Mr. Hooper. So kind of you to visit us."

"I could think of nothing else since Miss Carter's tea."

"So nice of you to attend, wasn't it, Clara?" Aunt had clearly passed the impetus for the conversation on to me.

"Have you . . ." Where was it Aunt said his family had come from? Boston! "Have you been in the city long, Mr. Hooper?"

"Yes."

He had? "Are you well-acquainted, though, with Boston?"

"Not particularly, no."

"Would you like to be?"

"No. What I would like to be is in the company of my sister."

I felt my brow rise as I tried to make sense of that non sequitur. "Your sister. Is she debuting this year?"

"She ought to have been. Yes."

Ought to have been? But then that meant she wasn't. "Is she ill?"

Beside me, Aunt coughed. Apparently, I had ventured into dangerous conversational territory.

"She *was* ill."

"Then she's cured." And so, I hoped, was my faux pas.

"Minnie is dead."

"Oh. My. My goodness! I am so very sorry."

"And so am I. And so ought Dr. Carter to be."

"Dr. Carter?"

"Dr. Carter. Your father." After that extraordinary pronouncement, he simply continued to stare at me in that same bilious, unblinking way that he had been. Speaking with him was going to be like talking to one of Aunt's Pomeranians. And so that was exactly what I pretended to do. And in truth, Mr. Hooper's stare was so like that of Aunt's beasts that it was not difficult to undertake such an endeavor. I chattered on about nothing. For a full quarter of an hour. Until the bell chimed.

And it was then, finally, that Mr. Hooper decided to speak. "I do hope I'll have the pleasure of seeing you at the opera this season."

Did he? But it seemed quite obvious that he hated me.

"Or at one of the balls?"

Aunt rose.

I popped up beside her, thankful to be doing something, anything, besides talking to someone who had so very little to say.

Our rising required that he do the same.

I nodded at him, wishing nothing so much as to be rid of his ill temper. "I am sure that you will. Good day, Mr. Hooper."

Aunt enfolded my hand within her own as Mr. Hooper made his way from the parlor. When he was gone, she pulled me down to the sofa beside her. "What a contrary young man!

You managed admirably in spite of his ill manners. Just as I told you, it is always to your advantage to know how to carry on a conversation with a person who cannot or will not speak."

As I was contemplating the pleasures of an empty parlor with no one to speak to and nothing to do, the butler appeared, silver tray in hand.

"Mrs. Isaac Hobbs." Aunt nodded to the butler, placed the card back on the tray. And then she spoke to me as she pushed to her feet. "Mrs. Isaac Hobbs is the wife of Mr. Hobbs."

Evidently.

"And the mother of Mr. Jeremiah Hobbs, who will be following Mr. Hobbs into business."

Hobbs. Hobbs. It seemed like I should know that name. "What is their business?"

A woman appeared in the doorway and Aunt had only a brief moment to whisper an answer. "Mortuary services. The finest in the city."

I felt my brows peak and struggled to tug them back down into place. Mortuary services! Of course. *Hobbs Mortuary Services: Your death, our sacred trust.* But that was—that meant—I scarcely dared contemplate what that meant. And was exceedingly glad that I was destined for a different, more earthly-minded suitor.

"Mrs. Hobbs! How lovely of you to call."

"Such a splendid tea you gave for your niece. Miss Carter." The woman nodded toward me.

I returned the gesture.

She sat on a chair as we sat on the sofa. "Debutantes are so lively these days, Mrs. Stuart. Not like they were in our day. In our day one would cough as soon as smile. And languish as soon as dance. Don't you remember it?"

"I do. We were positively consumptive. All of us."

"That's true, that's true." She plucked a handkerchief from

her sleeve. "We were none of us long for this earth. And we knew it." A nod punctuated her reminiscences.

Aunt smiled. "We did."

"It's so important to contemplate one's eternal future." She dabbed at an eye.

"It is. I heard Mrs. James Cole passed last night."

"She did. A lovely soul. But . . ."

Aunt cocked her head. As did I.

"But. . . the coffin chosen for her was unaccountable."

"Really?"

"Yes. Mr. Cole chose . . . well... I shouldn't say . . . not really."

Aunt folded her hands into her lap. "I would hate to intrude upon Mr. Cole's private affairs."

"Of course. Think no more about it." Mrs. Hobbs turned toward me. "And who are you debuting with, my dear?"

Though the question was for me, Aunt answered it in my stead. "With the Barnes girl, several Vandermeres, and a Remstell. A Moffat and a Sturbridge as well as some other young girls."

Mrs. Hobbs smiled at me.

I smiled back.

She turned her attentions back to Aunt. "I really do wish I could say something about Mrs. Cole's coffin. But I shouldn't."

"Don't say anything you don't want to."

Mrs. Hobbs sat there on a chair across from us, looking doubtful. "No. No, I probably shouldn't." Her face brightened. "Have you heard about the Vanderbilts' new livery? For their servants?"

"I hadn't. Didn't they just order new? Several years ago?"

"They did. But they weren't noticeable enough."

"But isn't that the point of having servants? One shouldn't notice, should one?"

Mrs. Hobbs lifted a brow. "Well, whether they should be or shouldn't, they will be now. They've all been done up in red."

"Red!"

"Well. Burgundy. Burgundy *satin*." She turned to me once more. "Tell me, Miss Carter, how do you feel about your prospects?"

My prospects? I blinked. I felt intimidated by all of them. And plagued by Mr. De Vries in particular. But that was not what she wanted to hear, and it was certainly not what Aunt would want me to say. And so I tried, furiously, to think of something polite and charming instead. "I think, that is, I'm sure —" I smiled and started once more. "I can't believe that my debut has finally come." Which was nothing but the truth. I had been hoping I could put it off for another year. Or two.

In truth, I had been hoping to go to Vassar instead.

Mrs. Hobbs's own smile faltered. Then she nodded. "Yes. But better to do now those things that you may not be able to do later. Like poor Mrs. Cole. If only *she'd* had a choice."

If only I had a choice. If I had a choice, I would make Mrs. Hobbs divulge whatever secret it was that was trying to worm its way out of her.

She leaned toward me. "Are you healthy, dear?"

"Am I--?"

"Healthy." She overpronounced the word in both volume and syllables. "Oh dear. They say hearing is usually the first to go."

"Hearing?"

"No. Healthy. Are you healthy?"

"Yes."

"Oh. Because I've always thought young girls make the most lovely corpses. And you're so tall and thin. Not like that Mrs. Cole."

Aunt's smile had become rather thin. "I expect that Clara will be among us for some time to come. Some *long* time to come."

"Because we were thinking about a new advertisement. For Hobbs. Think of it, dear: What better way to leave this earth

81

than to know that your face would be on every milk truck in the city."

"Oh dear!" Aunt had half risen from the sofa and was looking toward the mantel. "I think our clock has stopped working again, Clara. I'm sure it's long past four o'clock."

Mrs. Hobbs looked over her shoulder at the mantel with a jerk. "Is it? Well then, I must be going." She gathered her voluminous skirts and pushed herself to standing. Then she removed a card from her reticule and handed it straight to me. "If you start to feel peaked, let me know. What a sensation it would be to have a debutante die during the season!"

I glanced down at the card. *Hobbs Mortuary Services: Your death, our sacred trust.*

Mrs. Hobbs moved from me toward my aunt. "I wish I could have told you about Mrs. Cole, but I just can't. So sorry."

"Think nothing of it. Thank you for visiting."

"Miss Carter's face just kept floating in my mind after the tea. Like a vision. And it came to me this morning that she would be the perfect corpse." She leaned close to Aunt. "Do you think it's prophetic?"

"Probably not. Good day."

Mrs. Hobbs smiled at me and then wandered out toward the front hall.

Aunt glared at her back until she disappeared around the corner. "She has no idea just how uncouth she is!"

"She wanted me for an advertisement. As a dead person!"

"Honestly, that woman has only ever had one thing on her mind. And no one has ever been able to discover what it is at any given time!"

I held a hand to my mouth and swallowed an importunate giggle.

"Just remember: It never pays to alienate a mortician. One never knows when one might have need of his services."

"Have I—did I meet Mr. Hobbs? The son?"

"Yes, of course you did. He came to your tea."

"He did?"

"Yes. But don't worry. He was much more interested in the tea table and talking to the older people than he was in talking to you. A nose for business, one might say."

I felt my own nose curl in distaste and I felt, for some odd reason, as if I should wash my hands. And my face. And my arms.

"Don't let her worry you. She had consumption when she was younger and somehow came to be cured. She's thought ever since that it was some cruel hoax that left her among the living instead of the dead. And she believes everyone else ought to think the same. It's good for their business, you know."

"Yes, but will I ever have to talk to Mr. Hobbs? The younger?"

"I sincerely hope not!"

We remained seated on the sofa for nearly another hour and then the clock struck five. "Well," Aunt said. "I shall have to consult the papers. I had thought Tuesdays were a safe day for our at-home, but there must have been some other event this afternoon. I am sure we'll see an increase in callers next week. And you can wear that lovely gown again."

CHAPTER 10

ON THURSDAY AFTERNOON, Thanksgiving Day, I slipped downstairs while Aunt was dozing. I noticed the door to Father's study was open. He looked up at my knock. "Ah—the season's loveliest debutante! And to what do I owe the pleasure of your charming company?" There were times when my father could make me feel like the most beautiful girl in the world. And there were times when he seemed to forget my very existence.

I smiled. "I would like to ask the good Dr. Carter a question."

"A question? Questions are free. It's the answers I charge for." As he leaned back in his chair, the springs protested the motion.

"Did you ever have a Miss Hooper as a patient?"

His chair bobbed upright. "Hooper?"

"Miss Minnie Hooper."

"Why do you wish to know?"

"I met her brother. Mr. Ira Hooper."

"Ah. Her brother. I thought I saw him at the tea. Lurking in the corner?"

I nodded.

"I was hoping I wouldn't have need to protect you from him. He was quite distraught at his sister's death, and I'm afraid his grief has altered his mind."

"He came to my first at-home as well."

Father frowned. "I'd rather he not come anywhere near you. He's prone to wild accusations. Accused me once of quackery!" His lips pursed as if affronted by the very thought.

"What happened to her?"

He shrugged. "She had always been delicate. Fainting spells and hysteria. Dyspepsia." He coughed. "In any case, I was treating her with strychnine, but by last spring, it no longer seemed to help. So I increased the dose. She began to seize—it was quite terrible. She bent nearly double. But there was nothing I could do. Nothing anyone could do. I still don't understand. It was working before. A simple increase in dose shouldn't have done anything at all but cure the problem. I told them that. She should have responded. Perhaps . . ." His voice trailed away as his eyes fixed on something that I could not see. "That's never happened to me before. Such a terrible seizure."

"I'm sorry."

"So was I. But at least she died in her own bed."

"Mr. Hooper said she would have debuted this year."

"She probably would have. With you." He took up a sheaf of papers. "But don't give it another thought." He picked up a pen, and I interpreted the gesture as permission to leave.

Don't give it another thought.

I would try not to. But I was quite certain that it was all Mr. Hooper ever thought about.

———

AN HOUR LATER, I went out to meet Lizzie in the garden. Though I wasn't certain that she would come, since it was, after all, Thanksgiving, I brought a fan, as she had ordered me to.

"Don't just stand there!" The hiss came from the hedge. "Come here!"

I sidled toward the hedge and then, once I was hidden from view of the house, I pushed aside some branches to peer beyond them. "There you are."

"Did you bring a fan?"

I pushed through the hedge into the space by the gate. And then I pulled the fan from my sleeve and threw it open with a flourish.

Lizzie began to frown. "I didn't think you knew any of this."

"I don't. That's all I know."

"Good! I'm going to teach you. Mother had a woman come to the house last week. We spent endless hours on fans. First. . ." She leaned forward to inspect my hand. Then she tsked. "You must always hold it like this." She demonstrated the proper technique.

"Like this?"

"Yes. Exactly. This is going to be so much fun! We can talk to each other without speaking."

"How?"

"With our fans. If I twirl my fan like this"—she twirled it in her left hand as she was speaking—"it means that you're being watched."

"I'm being watched!"

"By a suitor. That's the first signal to learn. That way we can tell each other how many beaux we have."

"But isn't he supposed to be Mr. De Vries?"

"We can't have just one."

"Why not? We can only marry one."

Lizzie rolled her eyes and sighed. "Just pay attention. Pretend you're my beau."

"Right."

She set the fan in motion. "If I want to tell you that you've won my heart, I place the fan just here." The fan paused for a moment above her heart and then it started once more. "You try."

"If I want to tell you that you've won my heart, I place the fan just here." I stopped the fan; knocked myself against the chest, and started fanning myself once more.

Lizzie laughed. "You don't want to tell him that he's bloodied it. You just want him to know that he's won it. Gently. Just a delicate touch. Like a butterfly's wings."

I tried again.

"Well done. Now. If I want to say, 'I love you,' I do it like this." She raised the fan so that it hid her eyes. And then she withdrew it, raising her brow at me.

I did as she had done. "But why wouldn't you just tell him so?"

"You would. Later. But the point is that you could do it in the middle of a ball. On a crowded dance floor even. You could send a message that only he could interpret. Isn't that romantic?"

I supposed. I tried to imitate the gesture.

"A bit more gracefully would be nice, but yes. Just like that. And now, since you've told him that you love him, you can kiss him. And you invite the kiss like this." She folded the fan up partially and touched it to her lips.

I did the same.

"Perfect."

She drilled me for several minutes, calling out "Heart! Love! Kiss!" in rapid succession. By the time she had tired of the game, my wrist ached and we were laughing from the sport of it.

"But really, Lizzie, will the men truly know all of this?"

"The ones we want will."

"How do you know?"

"Because I do. There wouldn't be tutors if it weren't important."

THE NEXT DAY, Aunt asked for me to meet her in her bedroom after lunch. When I appeared, she gestured for me to sit in the chair opposite her own.

"There is an ancient but useful language that I wish for you to learn." She snapped her wrist and a fan bloomed as if by magic. "The language of the fan. It might seem old-fashioned, but it's worth learning. And sometimes, it can prove to be useful. Not, of course, in flirtation, for well-bred girls never flirt, but useful in communication." She leaned forward and offered me the fan, taking up another one from her lap.

I opened it with a flick.

Aunt raised a brow. "Listen well. This is a tedious business and I do not wish to repeat myself."

I nodded, feeling for once quite worthy of the task.

"If one wishes to tell a suitor such as the De Vries heir that he has won one's heart, the fan is placed just here above one's heart."

I debated about whether to display my knowledge, but in the end, efficiency won over prudence. If I could finish this lesson quickly enough, Byron awaited. And so I mimicked Aunt's gesture with perfect ease, just the way Lizzie had taught me.

"If one wishes to declare one's love, it is done like this." She raised the fan so that it hid her eyes.

I did as she had done.

"These gestures are not to be used lightly and must not be undertaken at all without the greatest of discretion. It would not do for you to flash about your sentiments indiscriminately. Understood?"

"Yes."

"Now, it might, under certain circumstances, be desirable to invite a kiss. One does it like this." With a deft turn of her wrist, the fan retreated partially into itself and she touched it to her lips.

I did the same. Or tried to. I'd had trouble with that one the day before as well.

She sighed. "A man will not want to kiss a girl who handles her fan like a patrolman's baton. Like this." She repeated the gesture, only at a lesser speed.

This time I could see exactly how she turned her wrist. And soon I was able to do it without pause, without thought.

"Perfect. Now repeat for me the gestures. Heart."

I tapped my chest above the heart in just the way Lizzie had said to.

"No." She sighed once more. "The whole goal is to avoid any conspicuous motion." She put her own fan into motion, gently using it to stir a breeze in front of her face. Her head became mobile, her eyes lively. And an illusion took hold. The years seemed to drop from her face and her eyes took on a certain sparkle. She turned first this way and that. Nodded as if to some unseen suitor across the room. "The goal is to be graceful. And elegant. And completely inconspicuous. Do you see?"

"Yes." Indeed I did. If a fan in Lizzie's hand was a toy, a fan in Aunt's hand was a tool. I had watched a young girl at play. Now I was watching a master at work.

"And did you see that?"

"What?"

She rolled her eyes and then went into that strange trance once more. She fluttered and bowed and simpered and then . . . there! The fan had touched a place above her heart and lingered for just an instant. Then she nodded at me.

I tried to do the same. I fanned and nodded and smiled.

"No. No, no, no. The fan must become an extension of the arm. It can only be done properly when one is unaware of it's being there. Do not mistake me—you have natural talent with your lean, slender arms. There is a certain grace already evident in your gestures. But you must grow into yourself. Do this:

Carry a fan about for the next week. Wherever you go. Eat with it. Read with it . . . for I know you will."

As she paused, I blushed.

"Sleep with it. And in that time, if I am not mistaken, it shall append itself to your body."

At least she hadn't told me to stop reading. Lizzie's mother had commanded that very thing of her daughter. Said it ruined the eyes.

"Well. This proved to be a less difficult lesson than I had feared. Perhaps there is some hope for you after all. When did you learn all of this?"

I felt the blood drain from my face.

"I know you, my dear. This ought to have been a much more difficult lesson than it was."

How did I learn? I couldn't tell her I'd learned it all from Lizzie. I'd never be allowed out of Aunt's sight again. And then I was struck by inspiration. "Miss Miller knew more than just popular songs and Italian." It wasn't really a lie. She had known Latin and mathematics as well.

"Did she? Well." She sniffed as she pulled a handkerchief from her cuff. "Perhaps I underestimated the extent of her education. And your own."

CHAPTER 11

$\mathcal{A}$ S I LEFT the dining room after lunch on Tuesday, Aunt looked up from her newspaper. "Don't forget. We're at home today."

I might have slouched up the stairs if I hadn't been corseted. I hoped this one would be more exciting than the first one.

It wasn't.

"Well." My aunt eyed the clock on the mantel. "It's five o'clock."

It was indeed.

"And not one visitor."

Not a one.

Aunt had begun to frown.

"Perhaps they misread our cards. Perhaps they thought we are at-home on Thursdays."

"Impossible. No one misreads a calling card. I know how this game is played. And I can play it too." She pushed herself from her chair and sailed from the parlor majestically, the skirts of her black silk gown trailing behind her.

It was with relief that I mounted the stairs. After being shed of my house gown, I spent the time until dinner between the pages of Byron, revisiting my favorites among his poems.

———

THE NEXT DAY at noon, Aunt informed me that we would be at-home that afternoon as well.

"But didn't our cards say Tuesday?"

"They did."

"Then why . . . ?" There must be a rule involved. Some rule I didn't know. Another rule I could never hope to understand.

"Because this is how it is done: a card for a card, a call for a call. For years I have left cards all over the city, storing up connections against your debut. I knew from the moment Brother married your mother that she would never be able to cultivate the proper relationships. Not the way it ought to be done. You've only to look to the Barneses! Your mother made her closest friend of the woman. Why Reginald Barnes went to Mississippi for a bride when there were plenty to choose from right here is beyond my comprehension. And most of those in good society cut her years ago."

"But then why was Lizzie's tea attended by so many people?"

"I said *good* society."

It was plain that the Barneses weren't included among them. At least not by Aunt.

"They fit in well enough with the Vanderbilts and their ilk. But they have nothing to do with us. In any case, others from all parts of the city have left cards for me. It is time to elevate these relationships from cards to calls."

"But—"

"We will only call on our social equals. At first. And then we will start calling on Brother's patients. And you will see: They cannot fail to receive us. Not on days when they are at-home.

They cannot risk the possibility of offending us. Now leave me in peace so that I can plan our course."

That day, Aunt deigned to accept all of the callers who came instead of merely taking their cards. If they had thought they could simply get away with leaving their card on a tray, they were sorely mistaken! We were soon joined by a group of women who were of Aunt's generation. Many of them wore a widow's cap. Others dressed in skirts with hoops so unfashionably wide they looked like apparitions from our nation's Civil War. They all seemed vaguely surprised to have been invited into the house. And Aunt always said the same thing as she greeted them.

"It has been such a long time since I have talked with you that I couldn't let you escape without a chat." And chat we all did. About the weather and the season and who it was that had recently passed.

The next day we ventured out to make calls. The women we called on all seemed rather surprised at our visit, brows raised or furrowed as they greeted us, but the welcome they offered seemed genuine.

Aunt would give her card to the butler, who would disappear with it into a parlor. And then we would wait for an invitation to enter. As the afternoon progressed, sometimes our wait stretched on for several minutes. It was only when we visited the home of a particularly deaf old dowager that I realized what the delay was about.

"Who?" The shout came floating toward us through the open door.

"Mrs. Lewis Stuart and Miss Clara Carter." The words were tinged with the butler's foreign accent.

"I don't know any Carters."

"Of the Dr. Willard Carters."

"Dr. Carter you say?"

"Yes, madam."

"Then I expect I shall have to see them. Send them in."

The butler returned, his manner cool. We went into the parlor and sat for the appointed minutes. And we talked. About the weather mostly.

The family names of those we called on were familiar— Howard, Knowles, and Clayton—though their connection to our family was not. Indeed, as Aunt explained on our ride home, most of them were related to Mr. Lewis Stuart, her late husband. By blood or by marriage.

"Are you listening, Clara?"

"Hmm? Oh. Yes." I had been—just barely—while looking out upon the city we were passing through.

"That went very well indeed."

"But none of them seemed to want to see us. At least none that we visited later on."

"Of course they didn't. But they did, didn't they? And now, if I'm not mistaken, they shall all feel obliged to visit us. And then we shall visit them, and don't you see, my dear—I have just gained you entrée into the highest circles in the city!"

But at what cost? I couldn't help but question. Clearly none of those women really wanted to know us. So why then had they felt compelled to receive us?

It was a puzzle that had no solution. And by Sunday, I was bored to death of conversation with no real meaning and etiquette that seemed to serve no purpose. It was with relief that I anticipated church.

As we walked down the aisle, I braved a look at the De Vries pew. They were there, all of them. And as we came abreast of their aisle, I looked once more.

The fashionable, dashing one leaned back slightly and, if I was not mistaken, he winked at me!

My face flamed as I sat down, praying that no one else had seen him. Flirting in a drawing room was one thing. Flirting at church? Was that even proper?

After service, as we filed out of the pew, the De Vrieses filed out of theirs. They fell into step beside us. Mr. De Vries beside Father, Mrs. De Vries beside Aunt. And then it was my turn. I was to be matched with one of the brothers.

The winking one.

I blushed again—I could not help it. To hide my face from his view, I turned my head away from him, took up my skirts with my right hand, and began to turn around the edge of the pew and into the aisle.

But the folds of my skirt got caught on the corner of the pew. When I tried to turn, I was jerked backward. The jolt sent my Bible flying from my left hand.

It landed in the middle of the aisle, right in front of the winking brother's shoe.

As I stumbled, a firm hand gripped me at the elbow. The scent of sandalwood enveloped me and a low voice spoke into my ear. "Are you all right?"

My face must have gone scarlet. I could feel it. And it could only have contrasted horribly with the green of my gown. In lieu of speaking, which I feared I would garble, I simply nodded.

I took an unsteady step forward, away from the hand that still cupped my elbow.

The other brother, the disheveled one, handed me my Bible.

I barely dared to look at him, merely nodded my thanks. Then I turned from them both, raised my chin as if nothing had happened, and continued down the aisle for all of Grace Church to see. At least I wouldn't have to speak of it to Lizzie. Her family had exited the church well ahead of ours. As I settled myself into the carriage, I waited for the rebuke that would surely come.

But Aunt only smiled. "Well done, Clara! Such a clever way to catch the heir's attention."

The heir? *That* one, the winking one, was the heir?

Lizzie had been right.

———

THE FOLLOWING DAY, among the mail was an invitation. Aunt handed it over to me.

Mrs. John Moffatt
   Requests the pleasure of your Company
   on Tuesday Evening, December 15, at Ten o'clock.
   1062 Fifth Avenue.
   Dancing.

"You've been invited to a ball, Clara! Well done. Not to the De Vrieses', perhaps, but at least you've been invited to the Moffatts'. It seems you have made an impression."

"To a ball? But there was no mention of a ball."

"It mentioned dancing. And being invited to dance at a private house is a private ball. It's the last word in vulgarity to invite someone to a 'ball' or an 'evening party.' No hostess of worth would ever think of such a thing. But to mention dancing? A ball is assumed."

"I can't dance."

"If it's at the Moffatts', then it's virtually assured that the De Vries heir will be there. It will be your chance to make a lasting impression."

She clearly hadn't heard me. I repeated my objection. "I can't dance."

"It will be cold, of course, and possibly snowy. But I think that you should wear your debutante's gown. It will be expected."

"But, Aunt, I can't dance." I spoke the words louder this time.

"What do you mean you can't dance?"

"I can't. I don't know how."

She sat up a bit straighter as her brows knit themselves together. "But surely you've had lessons."

"I haven't."

"You haven't?"

"No. I can't dance."

A lighter shade of pale swept her features. "You never, not once in your seventeen years, attended dancing school?"

I shook my head.

"Never?"

"No."

"You can't dance! What did Miss Miller teach you?"

"She taught me to sing."

"Yes. Good. But you should have been taught to sing *and* dance." Her cheeks flushed a furious shade of red. "You've been educated by halves! Why didn't you say something? Before now?"

I began to shrug but thought better of it.

"Didn't you know you ought to have had lessons?"

I could not lie. Not under the scorching heat of Aunt's glare. "I guess ... I mean, Lizzie was always telling me about her dance lessons—"

"And why didn't you realize you ought to be taking them as well? Why didn't you say something?"

Say something? And have to take lessons myself! "I just thought it was providential."

"Then you can thank Providence that you'll have to learn in one week what you should have been learning over the past two years. I should have left those Stuarts long ago!"

Aunt discussed my plight with Father over dinner and it was agreed that Mr. Drake himself, of Drake's Dance Academy, would be hired to tutor me at home because, as Aunt argued, "We can't send her to him and admit that she knows nothing at all. Not at her age."

At my reception I had only had to greet people and bid them good-bye. But at the ball I would be expected to converse. And flirt. And dance. This private ball could be my ruin.

———

TWO DAYS LATER, Aunt wrung her hands as she sat in the parlor watching me dance with Mr. Drake. "I don't know how you shall accomplish any of it."

I had just attempted a waltz with the instructor. It had not gone well.

"You learned the lancers and the schottische and the polka with perfect ease. What is wrong with you? The waltz is the easiest dance among them!"

The lancers had set figures. It was danced with several couples, in a square. The movements consisted of clasping and unclasping hands, stepping into the center and then stepping out, forming a chain to pass about the circle, and other simple patterns.

The polka had just several movements: the slide, change, leap, and hop. Depending upon the particular polka, they were performed in different arrangements. All I had to do was memorize the order. After having studied Latin and Italian and mathematics, memorizing a set of patterns posed no difficulty. And the schottische contained all the polka movements, though they were combined in different ways and set to different music. If I could commit the order of the sets to memory, and I believed I had, I could perform them as well as anyone.

But the waltz was different. The waltz had no predetermined pattern. Certainly, it was made up of very simple steps, but there was no predicting when the dance master would turn or reverse the course of the dance. "I just—I can't—he always goes right when I think he should go left." And he always seemed to vary the length of his step. It was impossible to foresee what he might do.

"Then stop thinking! It is not for you to anticipate; it is for the man to act."

"If the young miss would just allow me to lead, madam . . . and if she would dance up through her toes, then perhaps—"

"Clara! When one dances, one is to be as light on one's feet as a feather. You are not stuck to the floor with great blucher boots. You are, at any second, expecting to soar into the air on angel's wings. If your feet touch the earth, it is only for an instant." She waved a bejeweled hand at me to get me to come near.

At my approach, she reached out her hand and pulled on my own in an effort to rise. "I shall show you what I mean. A waltz, Mr. Drake."

The dance master took Aunt's hand in his own. Aunt extended her other hand to his shoulder, and his free hand went to the back of her waist.

Aunt turned her head slightly to the left as they waited for the music. Once the assistant began playing the piano and they circled about the room, a miracle occurred: Aunt's age fell away and she became that graceful angel of which she had spoken. And then the dance came to an end, and I helped Aunt back into her chair. "There. Now do what I have done."

I approached the dance master with some trepidation, but I took up his hand and tried once more. At least I meant to try. But I stomped on his foot at the first opportunity.

Poor man. He looked as if he could not decide whether to slap me or leave the room.

"Clara' If you cannot pretend with your eyes open, then pretend with them closed."

Closed? But how could I dance if I could not see where I was going?

"Now' Close them now'."

I closed them. After a moment I felt the dance master take up my hand in his. The music began and I panicked. How could

I dance if I could not see? But I did not dare to open my eyes. I didn't want to be reprimanded. Not more than I already had been. Neither did I want to step on the dance master's toes.

A pressure at my back caused me to turn to the right. Another slight movement at our hands caused me to turn to the left. A faint squeeze of my hand suggested that I lift my arm. And so I did. Around the room we went. And by the end of it I was smiling.

And so was Aunt.

At least I think she was.

"Again. Only this time, roll from your heels up to your toes."

CHAPTER 12

Y HEART CLATTERED within my chest like a trinket rolling around inside a box. This was it. Tonight, at the opening of the opera, I would officially start my season. No matter what happened, no matter whether I would be a great success or a great failure, I could not undo this night; I could not step back from this moment. I would either end the season engaged to be married or . . . the alternative did not bear thinking about.

I *must* end the season engaged.

And the engagement must be to the De Vries heir.

The sooner done, the sooner accomplished. I had to succeed. There was no other option. My family depended upon it.

———

OUR CARRIAGE BECAME entangled in a line of carriages waiting to deposit their occupants in front of the opera. At last, we were allowed to exit at the portico on Broadway. Father helped Aunt down and then he offered his hand to me. I took it and followed them into the Met.

From the first, I was overwhelmed by the crowds of people milling about in spaces not calibrated to their number. It seemed as though there ought to be some large foyer or some grand entrance. Some sign to indicate that here, through this way, lay the opera hall.

But there was nothing. Just an abundance of burgundy-colored walls accented with mirrors and gilded fixtures.

I followed Father and Aunt up a flight of stairs. There, on the second floor, was a crowd even more elaborately coiffed and costumed than the crowds below.

Father excused himself. Aunt frowned at his rapidly disappearing back, but then she nodded toward another flight of stairs.

Before I could respond I became transfixed by a group of women coming toward us. They wore tiaras, all of them, the bright stones glittering and gleaming like stars through their clouds of hair. Necklaces by the dozens were looped about their necks, and so many bracelets had been fastened about their wrists that they reached nearly to the elbows. One of them was kicking at a large stone. It dangled from a pearl necklace that had been looped about her waist.

The other women around her were laughing at her antics. Their voices were so loud and boisterous that I worried Aunt might be tempted to reproach them.

But she only clutched at my arm and pulled me out of the woman's path. And good thing! She was so busy kicking at the stone that she did not appear to notice where she was going.

"Mad. All of them! All that money and no good sense. It's truly, terribly annoying!"

We pressed ourselves to the wall as the woman stumbled by. The thing she was kicking appeared to be an enormous ruby. But though she was laughing and though she appeared to be enormously amused, the look she shot at me as she passed was one of ennui.

Across the foyer from us stood another woman. A grave and formidable woman, dressed in so many jewels that she sparkled like a ... well... a diamond. A large, human-shaped diamond. She, too, was watching the ruby-kicking woman.

Aunt saw me staring at the second woman. And then she pulled me from the wall and we continued on our way toward the stair. "That was Mrs. Jacob Astor. The Astors own New York City. Even more, they own society. And you can bet she doesn't approve of such antics! Not from a Vanderbilt."

————

ONCE WE HAD settled ourselves in a box on the third tier, I saw Lizzie and her family sitting in a box across from us. As I watched, she picked up a pair of opera glasses and trained them upon me.

I picked up my own and trained them upon her.

She was dressed in white, just as I was, and she wore a collar of pearls about her neck. Her hair had been caught up into a puff of white ostrich feathers. Sitting there in the box, her dress glowing in the dim light, her fair hair shimmering, she looked like nothing so much as a contented kitten. She lifted a hand and waved. And then she dropped her glasses and crossed her eyes at me.

I burst into laughter before I could check myself.

"Whatever are you laughing about? No good can come from braying like a donkey. The opera is no laughing matter! The sound you hear about you is the sound of money. Fortunes are gained on the suggestion of a look. And destinies are forfeited on the failure of a gown to please. You will never again experience anything so fraught with danger as the opening of the opera season."

"Unless I marry the De Vries heir."

"What's that?"

"Unless I marry him. Then I will experience it every season."

Aunt looked at me as if she suspected some untoward levity. But I was not teasing. Were I to marry Mr. De Vries, then I could see my life unfolding vividly before me, one social season, one gown after another, for as long as I lived.

Lizzie would have exulted at such a thought; I was rendered morose.

"Look there: We are surrounded by Schermerhorns and Goelets and Astors."

I was looking. The boxes beneath us, across the auditorium, glinted with the jewels of their occupants. The curving length of the box tiers made the room look as if it were encompassed by a diamond horseshoe.

"Get up—show yourself."

"But I just now took my seat."

"And so did Lizzie Barnes over there across from us, but look at her now!"

The whole of the opera was looking at Lizzie. She had pulled the blooms from her bouquet and was tossing them down into the masses below.

"Do something!"

"Like what? All I have are my glasses. And I'm not about to throw those." They had been Mama's glasses. Slim and elegant, they were sheathed with mother-of-pearl. I firmly pushed myself back into my seat just in case Aunt decided to insist.

She harrumphed around for a few minutes and then Father joined us, smelling of cigars and liquor. He was almost too handsome, too suave to be someone's father. To be my father. His steel gray hair swept away from his forehead, falling longer than was fashionable, to his collar. His skin had a pleasant ruddiness that his trimmed beard only served to accentuate. I wasn't quite sure why he hadn't married again, after Mama died. I had assumed that, like me, he was heartbroken. But watching him watch the women in the other boxes, I began to wonder.

Especially when I saw those same women looking right back at him.

––––––

BENEATH THE BUZZ of the crowds could be heard the sounds of the orchestra scratching and screeching. Plucking and whining. A great primeval beast come to life, slowly. Sleepily.

A moment later the lights began to dim and the noise of the crowd fell to a whispered hush. As the curtains rose on the opening scene of *Romeo and Juliet*, I soon forgot all those around me. I left my own world for Juliet's.

As I listened to Miss Emma Eames sing "Je Veux Vivre," *I want to live . . . in the dream*, I could not keep from sighing. She was at a party and had just seen Romeo, *her* Romeo, and it was love at first sight. As she sang about it, her voice wound through the opera house like an enchantment. I was entranced. A female version of Byron, her words were a hymn to the raptures of love. Faster and faster, up and down the scale she sang until, finally, she had exhausted the expression of her newfound love.

A girl, just like me, who was about to enter into the romance of a lifetime.

I want to live in the dream.

Oh, so did I! With a dashing, elegant man by my side.

––––––

AT THE INTERMISSION, Aunt tapped me on the arm with her opera glasses. "Get up. We're going out."

"I don't need anything." I wanted to stay in the theater, within the shadows of the box, and relive the songs in private.

"But we are here for you to be noticed. I haven't seen the De Vrieses, so their box must be below ours. If we hurry, we can make it down to their level before they reach the assembly room."

We might have hurried had we been the only ones with that idea, but all the female occupants of the boxes on our level flooded the stairs at the same time. And all had the intention of descending. Aunt grabbed me by the hand, poked at the woman in front of her, and pulled me through the small gap that was made as the woman turned to glare at us. "We'll never reach him at this rate."

At this rate I had no confidence at all that we would be able to find our way back to the box before the opera ended. Slowly, ever so excruciatingly slowly, we descended the stair. "Do you see Mr. De Vries? Do you see Mr. De Vries?" Aunt's queries began to sound like a chant.

The only glimpses I'd ever had of him had been at church, but I was certain that I would know him. His dashing manner, his elegant clothes, and his wink had been engraved upon my memory. To oblige Aunt, when we had gained the second floor, I stood on my toes in order to see past the feathers and tiaras of all the women around me. Just . . . there? In the corner . . . ? Wasn't that his head? With all that dark hair swept back toward his crown? "Yes. I see him."

"Where?"

"Over . . . just. . ." Attentive to her lessons about not pointing, I tried to indicate the direction with a tilt of my head.

"Where?"

"Over ..." I took my reticule and swung it in the direction of the corner, but it hit a woman in the elbow.

"Just point!"

"There."

Aunt managed to shove through the crowds until we had

almost reached the corner. Then she pulled me close and leaned toward my ear. "Whatever happens, do not drop me."

"What—?"

At that instant, Aunt fell clean away into a dead faint. It took all the strength I had not to drop with her to the floor. Especially since, with my corset cinched so tightly, I could hardly bend, let alone breathe.

A gasp rippled out from around us, and a space soon opened in front of us.

"Aunt?"

There was no response.

"Aunt?"

Her cheeks suddenly seemed to lose the rest of their color.

"Aunt!"

All at once, there came two voices at my side. One from each elbow.

"May I help you?" A man's voice. It sounded rather familiar, but before I could turn to him, Lizzie's voice demanded my attention.

"Clara! What's happened? Oh, Clara!"

"Lizzie, find Father!"

Tears trembled at the corners of her eyes. "But what—how did— Oh, Clara!"

"May I help you?" I turned toward the other voice, discovering it belonged to Mr. De Vries. The winking, dashing one. The heir.

Disaster! That he should find me in an awkward predicament. Again.

"Is she ... is she . . . dead?" At Lizzie's conjecture, the crowd around us fell silent and then a woman shrieked. And another and another until mass pandemonium ensued.

"Lizzie!" Oh, how I wished she would be quiet. It was difficult to think over her moans and sighs.

"Clara?" Tears glistened on Lizzie's cheeks, and her normal color had turned ashen. Her hand reached out to clutch at my elbow.

At the same time, a warm, firm hand gripped my other elbow. "Is there nothing I can do?"

I turned to him and said the only thing I could think of. "Please, will you stay with Lizzie and my aunt while I go find my father?"

Mr. De Vries stepped beside and behind me, taking up Aunt as I loosened my grip.

As I turned to go, though, I thought I heard her speak.

He must have heard her too. He had begun to ease Aunt toward the floor, but then he started and dropped her.

Her head hit the tiled floor with a thud. Her eyelids fluttered open for a moment, her eyes rolled back into her head and then her eyelids fell shut.

"Did he . . . did he . . . did he kill her?" Lizzie's words were tremulous.

"No, Lizzie!" At least I hoped not. But if he did, then perhaps he would marry me to make amends and save me from my nightmarish existence.

At that moment, Father pushed through the crowd, handed his cigar to Mr. De Vries, and then knelt beside Aunt. He lifted first one of her eyelids and then the other. Slipped a hand inside his coat and pulled forth a vial. Waved it under Aunt's nose.

She snorted.

Sputtered.

Opened her eyes.

Her gaze traveled the ring of people standing around her and then they came to rest upon me.

Father looked up from her to the crowds. "Just a concussion. She needs air. And may I remind you that intermission is nearly over."

The women began to rush toward the stairs and the hall soon became deserted.

Father placed his hands beneath Aunt's arms and hauled her to her feet.

Mr. DeVries handed Father back his cigar.

Father clamped it between his teeth. "I thank you."

Mr. De Vries bowed. And then he turned toward Lizzie and offered his arm. I felt a keen stab of disappointment. I would have liked to have said something to him. Something amusing or clever. I would have liked to have given him some other impression than that of a clumsy young girl in constant need of rescuing.

Aunt grabbed my arm as I turned to follow them. "What were you thinking? To leave Lizzie alone with the De Vries heir?"

"You fainted."

"I hadn't fainted. Didn't you hear me: *Whatever happens, do not drop me.*"

"I didn't. He did."

"He whom you were happy enough to leave alone with your rival!" She muttered all the way through the foyer and back up into our box. "And now my hair ornament is falling out!"

I put up a hand and tried to push the ribbons back into place.

"Stop poking!"

I did. After one last jab.

It stayed.

———

THE REST OF the opera was so terrible, so tragic, that by the time it ended, tears were streaking down my face, wetting my throat, and causing my nose to drip. As I held a handkerchief to my nose, my eyes wandered to Lizzie's box. And I couldn't believe what I saw!

I raised my glasses to my eyes and took another look.

Yes. It was true. Lizzie had fallen asleep! With her hands curled up over the railing and her cheek against an arm, she wasn't just resting. She was slumbering. True, the hour was late. Much later than I was used to seeing. But how could she have fallen asleep during an opera?

CHAPTER 13

*I*F I HAD expected some reprieve from society as a reward for my appearance at the opera, I didn't receive it. The next night was the night of my first ball. The day began early. At least it seemed that way. But when Aunt thrust open my curtains, I discovered the sun to be quite high in the sky. "Get up."

I groaned.

She stalked to my bed and proceeded to yank my pillows from behind me. "However can you sleep this way?"

"It's the only way I *can* sleep. The corset—"

"Enough sleeping. There is much to be done in preparation for the ball!"

The maid helped me into a breakfast jacket and then I went downstairs. As I ate, Aunt informed me of all the work to be done— the first item of which was a visit from the dance master.

I hurried back upstairs and was aided into a morning dress. The maid quickly twisted up my hair and buttoned my shoes, but still I descended to find the dance master awaiting my appearance. My head was too sleepy and my eyes too bleary for me to care very much where he danced me. Which pleased Aunt enormously.

"Well done, Clara. Very well done. I knew you could conquer it."

I put a hand to my mouth to hide a yawn.

Afterward, the maid drew a bath and perfumed it with the scent of violets.

Then, paradise: She released me from the confines of my corset. To breathe deeply again! To glimpse flesh where I was only used to corset cover! I sunk into the water to my chin. And I might have succumbed to the temptation of sleep, but the maid did not let me linger. Once dried, she squeezed me back into my corset and then dressed me in a combing sacque. Then she placed a chair before the radiator and bid me sit as she combed out my hair.

Aunt came in as she was doing so. "You're to stay there to hurry along the drying."

"All morning?"

"As long as it takes."

I persuaded the maid to bring me Byron before she left and I passed several hours there in front of the radiator in complete and total bliss. There were perhaps some small benefits to being a debutante!

Just before lunch, the maid came to help me back into my morning dress. She followed me upstairs immediately afterward to help me change into a house dress. Later that afternoon, once I had been tested by Aunt on etiquette, the maid returned to arrange my hair. By the time she was done, all my hairs were stretched so tightly across my skull that I feared they might pull themselves out by the roots at any moment to avoid further torture.

As I was being dressed, Aunt came in and asked the maid to cinch my corset tighter.

Though expected, the pull of those laces still threatened to undo me.

As I steadied myself and adjusted to the compression, the maid put out my slippers. They were beautiful. Made of satin and decorated with a bouquet of ribbons and silk flowers, they were made for dancing. And they were much too slippery. I stepped right out of them.

"Let me see those."

The maid handed them to Aunt.

"Let me see your foot."

I drew up my skirts on one side and stuck out my stocking-clad foot so she could see it.

She took my foot in one cool hand and then she turned and barked at the maid. "Fetch me the violet water."

The maid hurried to do as she requested.

Aunt took it from her and sprinkled it on the bottoms of my feet. "Try them now."

I pushed my feet into the slippers. The moistened stocking seemed to cling to the satin.

"You won't step out of them now."

"No, but what if—"

"It will have to do. Come. It's time to leave."

———

WHEN WE REACHED the Moffatt residence, it was already quite crowded.

I saw Lizzie over across the room and raised a hand to wave at her.

"Put your arm down! Do you want to seem taller than you already are?"

"But Lizzie—"

"You have no friend here this night but the De Vries heir. All of your attentions are to be focused on him. Do you understand?"

"Yes."

"Do you see him?"

"Yes." He was in the middle of the room standing with several other men. Though they seemed to be speaking to each other, none actually looked at the others. They were all concentrating on the pageantry of dresses that promenaded about them.

"Then you must pretend not to see him. Where is he?"

I had some trouble trying to explain where he was standing without actually looking at him, or toward him, or in any way indicating any sort of interest in him.

There was something about the set of his chin and the exactitude with which his dark hair had been pushed away from his forehead. He looked quite debonair. And more than a little intimidating. Though he had seemed the perfect gentleman at church, I could not help but remember he belonged to the family that had impugned the Carter name.

I tugged on Aunt's forearm. "Does it have to be the De Vries heir? Couldn't I marry someone else?"

"Of course. Why not? Why not condemn yourself to a life such as mine? Always at the fringes of society, never quite good enough to be included. Let there be no more talk about it. And let me see your dance card."

I held out my wrist to which it was attached.

She withdrew a pencil from her reticule and proceeded to claim several of my dances. A quadrille and a waltz.

"But—"

She let it drop.

As we stood there, several of Aunt's acquaintances passed by, men in tow, to beg an introduction. It was not long before all of my dances were filled. And none of them by Mr. De Vries.

"Hand me your card again."

This time, I loosed it from my wrist. After I handed it to her, Aunt pulled a rubber from her reticule and erased the two dances that she had filled in earlier. "There." She said it with quiet satisfaction as she secured it to my wrist once more.

And then another of her acquaintances stopped in front of us.

"Mrs. Stuart, I would like to introduce to you Mr. Culpepper. He is the son of Mr. Charles Culpepper."

Aunt tipped her head in greeting as the gentleman bowed. "This is my niece, Miss Carter. Unfortunately, her dance card has already been filled for the evening."

The young man's face registered neither disappointment nor relief. He simply bowed once more and they moved off together.

After they had taken their leave, Aunt grabbed me by the forearm. "Follow me. And do not stop for any reason."

I stayed as close to her as I could without treading upon her skirts. And when she stopped, I realized we were standing before the De Vries heir. And his mother.

"Mrs. De Vries? I would like to introduce you to my niece, Miss Clara Carter. Dr. Carter's daughter."

"Oh. I had not thought she would debut until next year." "Why should her father keep such beauty to himself?"

I chanced a glance toward the heir and found him to be looking at me. My cheeks flushed, and I wished that I could fan them.

While Aunt and Mrs. DeVries continued to speak, Mr. DeVries maneuvered himself to stand near me. "Do you have any dances still available?"

I could not bring myself to look up into his eyes. Not when those available dances had been maintained through trickery. But I nodded.

"May I have one?"

I nodded again, offered him the hand to which the dance card was attached. And this time I dared to look up.

I caught a glimpse of profoundly blue eyes before he bowed, straightened, and left me with a parting word: "I will come to claim you later." I watched him walk away, posture perfectly straight, suit pulled pleasingly taut across his shoulders, his hair combed back precisely from his forehead. He looked exactly the way an heir to a fabulous fortune ought to look.

Strains of "Je Veux Vivre" lilted through my head. *I want to live ... in the dream.*

Perhaps, incredibly, I already was.

As Aunt finished her conversation, I pulled up my dance card to see which one he had taken.

It was a waltz.

———

ONCE THE DANCING began, I handed my card to Aunt.

"Remember. Just close your eyes for the waltzes."

My first partner was a Mr. Hamilton. He was shorter than I, though he had a mustache that more than made up for his deficiencies in other areas. When he took up my hand, it only came to his ear. But I did what Aunt had said and I closed my eyes. And by the time the dance was over and I opened them, I was surprised to find myself bound by the confines of the ballroom. I had been imagining myself in Juliet's world, dancing through the gentle breezes of a Veronese night.

The next dance was a lancers, and I must say that I danced it admirably.

The dance after that one was a quadrille. And the one after that a schottische and soon the first intermission was upon us.

The first dance after the intermission was a waltz. I closed my eyes for it, just as before. The dance was nearly finished when my slipper came off. One moment it was on my foot and the next moment it was gone. I opened my eyes to discover where I had left it, but I nearly stumbled and so I closed them up tight again.

As soon as the dance ended, I cast wildly about the room to see if I could find it. With all of the voluminous skirts and the mad crush of people, I feared it was lost to me forever. But just then, I saw a man throw up his hands and fall from view, disappearing into a sea of skirts.

Oh no! Perhaps . . . was it my slipper that had caused it?

After a moment, he reappeared. He bowed to those around him, but then leaned away from that circle to look around the room. Could it be that he had found . . . ?

But no. He had extricated himself from the group and I could see him quite plainly. There was no slipper in his hand.

But . . . but wait! He was patting his chest pocket as if there were something of importance in there. Something which stuck out quite a bit. And then, his gaze came to rest upon me.

He raised a brow.

I bit my lip and then nodded.

He made his way through the crowd, stopping to speak to people on several occasions, and I despaired that he would make it to me before the next dance began. But finally, he did. And it was then, as he passed from the shadows into the light, that I knew him for who he was. The thick brows, the unruly hair. The eyes that sparked with curiosity. He was the young man in the De Vries pew. The *other* young man. The younger son. "I believe I have something that belongs to you."

"I do hope so."

"I was watching you before ... well." He held out the slipper. "I'm surprised that you can dance with your eyes shut."

I stifled a laugh, remembering only just in time that it was uncouth and that my mouth was too large and that I should hide it. "Then you have never seen me dance the waltz with my eyes open."

A smile lifted the corner of his mouth and then spread across his face. "No. I can't say that I ever have." He bent as if he were adjusting the crease on his trouser and somehow managed to fit my slipper back on my foot at the same time. "Do I want to?"

"Do you want to what?"

"See you dance? With your eyes open."

"No. No, you don't. I'm much too clumsy. I would rather know where I am going than follow some stranger around."

He straightened. "I can't say that I much blame you. It sounds perfectly sensible to me." He bowed. "It has been a pleasure to see to your lost slipper. But, as my mother so often says, 'The half is more than the whole.'"

I smiled beneath the hand I had placed in front of my mouth.

"Though I can't think what she means by it or why she even says it."

I laughed outright then. I couldn't help myself.

Aunt came just as he had taken leave. "Wasn't that a De Vries?"

"He helped me with my slipper. I had stepped from it while dancing. He found it and returned it to me."

"Surely he did not help you put it on again?"

I nibbled on my lower lip. What was the correct answer? Was I to admit that I had needed his help? Or was I to lie?

"Did he?"

"No. Of course not."

For the rest of the evening, as I danced, I looked around the room, wishing I could find the younger De Vries again. I wanted to properly thank him. But I never saw him.

The final set of dances began with a waltz, and the heir came to claim me just as he said he would. With a hand to my back, he swept me away from Aunt before she could counsel me. He was tall. Taller than I was. And he had the most peculiar eyes. A blue that was searing in its intensity.

Before I could forget to, before I could ruin the waltz, I closed my eyes and gave myself to the music. Though I anticipated a turn, or at the very least a reverse of direction, it never came. And by the end of the dance I found myself quite fatigued from dancing at the same pace, through the whole dance, in one direction. My head was spinning. But I had gotten through it, my first dance with Mr. De Vries, and I had not humiliated myself.

When he returned me to Aunt, I was loath to let go of his arm for fear that I would fall to the floor.

He seemed not to notice. "Have you no other dances left for me?"

"I ..." I took the card Aunt held out, wishing that I had one available.

He took it from me. "But this is perfect! How clever of you to keep one free. I'll take it." He bowed. "I will come for you then." Aunt beamed a smile at him as he left me in her care. "Well?"

"He said I had one dance left?"

"And so you did. I made certain of it. Well done."

I looked at the card. As I read the dance, I felt the blood drain from my face. Already feeling quite dizzy, it only added to my vertigo. "But it's called a waltz quadrille. I don't know how to do it."

Aunt looked at me, alarm evident in her eyes. "Let me see that." She pulled the card from my grasp and took out her lorgnette to read it. "Waltz quadrille? What is it?"

I had no idea.

"We must find out. And quickly!" She looked about the ballroom with an air of desperation about her. Then she sighed. "The only thing to do is ask Lizzie Barnes—and hope that your years of friendship will preclude her from speaking about it to anyone."

Lizzie? She was going to let me see Lizzie?

"We shall go this minute and ask her."

Dispensing with Aunt's advice about never going anywhere directly, we walked straight over to where Lizzie stood talking to her mother.

"Mrs. Barnes." I dropped a slight curtsy.

Aunt nodded, then gestured slightly toward Lizzie.

The murmur of the crowds seemed to swell as I moved to my friend's side. Threading an arm through her own, I whispered in her ear. "I'm to dance the waltz quadrille with the De Vries heir and I don't know what it is."

Her eyes widened.

"Can you tell me how to do it?"

"Of course. But. . ."

"Quickly!" The buzz of the crowds now seemed somehow to come from my own ears, and the colors of the women's gowns around us had become too vivid by half. I discovered myself to be squinting against their glare.

Lizzie patted my hand but addressed herself to Aunt. "I do so wish I could spend more time with Clara. The only time I ever see her is at a ball or the opera. It seems a shame to go through an entire season together without ever actually having the chance to talk. It would be so lovely to be assured of having a few moments to speak. Now and then."

I held my breath as I waited for Aunt's reply.

It was long in coming, but finally she nodded.

Lizzie grinned. And then she took me by the arm and pulled me close.

I couldn't hear the crowds anymore, but I couldn't hear Lizzie either. I knew she was speaking, her lips were moving, but I couldn't hear the words. "What?"

"Clara? Are you feeling well?" Finally! Though her speech had the sluggish quality of words spoken from a great distance, at least I could now hear her.

"I don't understand."

"It's the patterns of a quadrille, to the steps of a waltz. Do you understand now?"

"No!" The quadrille was a certain, predetermined set of movements. So how could I dance them to a waltz? I didn't understand. And I was going to have to do it with Mr. De Vries!

As if I had summoned him from some other realm, he appeared, asking for my hand.

In the urgency of the moment, with a lightness in my head and the extra constriction of my corset, I couldn't seem to get a proper breath. I held out a hand toward him, and as I took a second step, the world dissolved into a hundred black and white pieces, and I knew no more.

CHAPTER 14

$\mathcal{A}$UNT SPENT THE next morning in bed, while I spent mine with my books, in a chair placed by the fire, until she called for me just before lunch. Her bedroom was still dark, the curtains a barricade against the light and the chill of day. I had an urge to cup my fingers to my mouth and blow warmth onto them. It was no wonder she was still bundled abed.

She held the paper out to me. "Read it for me. The society page about last night. I have not the stomach to read it for myself."

———

"The New York Journal—Society
"December 15, 1891

"The first event of the season was attended well and spectacularly by all, the city's finest sons seeking to win the hearts of the city's loveliest daughters. What unions will be forged, what marriages will have been struck by this time next year? Who can say where

Cupid will aim his bow? One thing is for certain: Miss Elizabeth Barnes, who fell asleep during the opera's second act, would not hurt the prospects of any man.

"The John Moffatts gave an admirable start to this season of private balls. Miss Clara Carter certainly captivated the ball-room. And she captivated Mr. Franklin De Vries as well, dancing about the floor with her eyes closed as if she were listening to some celestial music. What heavenly melodies do you hear, Miss Carter? And how might the rest of us fallen mortals join you? Yet once Miss Carter fainted, Miss Barnes reigned supreme over the remainder of the evening."

"And?"

I glanced up at her from over the top of the paper. "That's all there is."

"There is nothing more about you?"

"There is nothing."

"So Lizzie is lauded for falling asleep and you get mentioned for fainting." Her voice had become louder, the tone more shrill.

I shrugged. They had mentioned my dancing as well.

"Don't shrug. It's vulgar! You must pretend yourself to be much too delicate for such common gestures. Here." She handed me another newspaper. "Read this column. The one for gossip."

The paper was called *The Tattler*, and it came out whenever there were tales to be told. It seemed to be composed of inside knowledge and discreet jokes. Very seldom did the columnists identify people by name if the news was compromising. Normally the words meant nothing to me. It was the sort of news one had to have witnessed to understand.

I read through the first of the column quickly; it had nothing to do with me, of course, but I paused at the items that I thought might catch Aunt's interest.

"And while one of our fair debutantes was sleeping, another had surrendered herself to the passions of the opera. Whatever one might think of the girl's good father, it seems his daughter is made of finer stuff. Would that all debutantes might listen with such abandon.

"Which fine son kept up his end of the social stratum by dancing with the season's most eligible debutantes? And some who are not quite so eligible? Be careful, young lad, there are thorns among our flowers, some lovely blossoms who issue from tainted stock. Choose wisely—choose well."

Was that? . . . had that first part been about me? I had surrendered myself to tears at the opera, but I had thought no one was watching. Who was The Tattler, that he had known how much it had moved me?

"Let me see that." Aunt held a glass up to her eyes as she read it. ".. listen with such abandon.' It reeks of vulgarity. Only a common person would be overcome by such emotion."

"Was he ... he wasn't speaking of me, was he?"

"Of course he was speaking of you. You were one of the only people present who actually *listened* to the opera. Most of the rest of us were more intent on who was there and what they were wearing. Good gracious, my dear, one would think you had never attended an opera before!"

I hadn't.

"You must not let yourself be moved. Not to the point where persons such as this one would notice. Far better to adopt Lizzie's casual attitude, if I must say so. And I hope it's the only time I shall have to." She handed the paper back to me. "Is there more?"

"No."

Aunt sniffed. "It left Lizzie in the best light."

"Not by name."

"Yes, but anyone who was there will know of whom he speaks. No matter what high esteem you seem to regard her with, Lizzie Barnes is your chief rival for the heir. Can you see that now?"

I could see that the abrupt end to my evening had left something to be desired. It was little wonder that it had been noted in the newspaper. "Lizzie is my friend."

"A friend who seems to want the very same thing that you do. Did you know that it was she who danced your waltz quadrille with the heir?"

Better her than me.

"I'll have the dance master come tomorrow to remedy that lamentable flaw in your education. If only you hadn't fainted. That's what everyone will remember first about last night."

"If only my corset hadn't been laced so tightly. I couldn't breathe! I don't know how I even managed to dance."

"The corset has nothing to do with it. You're too much like your mother. Given over to female hysteria and a nervous disposition. I'll ask Brother to prescribe you something for it."

I needed nothing so much as a loosening of my corset strings. As I was leaving, she said one thing more. "Until you fainted, you were doing just fine."

———

AT A MUSIC concert that evening, I was able to greet Lizzie before the program began. We talked for a moment under Aunt's begrudging and watchful eye. Lizzie's cheeks were still pleasingly pinked from the frigid breeze that had blown all of us into the concert hall, her blond curls charmingly displaced. When she took my gloved hand within her own, I felt the chill of her fingers through both of our gloves. But her first words inquired after my own welfare. "Are you well?"

"I'm fine." Still a little chilled perhaps, but I expected that the impending crush of humanity in the hall would soon remedy that complaint.

"I was so worried! You didn't hurt yourself, when you fainted, did you?"

I flushed in remembrance. "Only my pride."

"Debutantes faint all the time." She gave my hand a squeeze.

"But not all of them are mentioned in the *Journal*."

"You were mentioned in the *Journal*?"

"And so were you."

"Really?" She leaned closer. "What did they say?"

"They said you reigned over the evening."

She smiled, flashing a glimpse of her even, white teeth. "Did they?"

"Yes."

She wrapped my hand in both of hers. "Oh, Clara. I'm so sorry."

"Aunt said you danced with him."

"I did. Are you terribly upset? Someone had to."

"I'm glad! At least I know he didn't linger and witness my further humiliation." Such a true friend Lizzie was.

"No. We danced. Although . . ." Her gaze crept toward mine.

"What?"

"His brother . . ."

"Yes?"

"He was there. Stayed there with you. While you were—after you had fainted."

He had? Somehow that was even worse.

"But by that time, someone had found a doctor."

Humiliation heaped upon humiliation. I was to be responsible for lifting the Carter family name to the highest echelon of society? When I could not even save myself from disgrace? I had been foolish to even think that I had a chance of succeeding at my debut. "I don't think I want to do this. Any of this!" After just three events—a mere three days into our debut—the crush of people, the bloom of colorful gowns was threatening to suffocate me. I felt a sweat break out upon my brow and I blinked, hard. Clutched at Lizzie's hand.

"But you danced beautifully. Every single dance!"

"I didn't."

"You did! I wish I were as tall and graceful as you. And when you closed your eyes, it was as if you were living in some dream or something."

I want to live in the dream. The one in which I looked exactly as I should. And danced exactly as I ought. The one in which I knew, always, what to say, and always, what to do. I wished I could be the person Aunt and Father needed me to be. Though why they should be throwing me at a family they seemed to despise, I could not say. "Aren't you glad I said what I did?"

"What did you say?" What was she talking about?

"When your aunt asked me about the waltz quadrille."

"Oh. Oh! Yes. And she agreed to it, to us talking. Even though she's been insisting that you were the first among my rivals."

She lifted her chin and patted at the curls dangling at her neck. "I am." Then she grinned. "But I'm also the first among your friends."

"Thank you. I would never have dared to ask."

"I'll see you at the Posts'. And you'd better not faint! The next time someone collapses, it's going to be me."

"It wasn't at all amusing."

"But there were ever so many people concerned about you. You were quite the center of attention!"

———

AT BREAKFAST THE next morning, Aunt wasted no time in directing Father's attention to my shortcomings. "Clara has no champion in the pages of the society columns."

Father put down the newspaper and laid it next to his plate. "Is that so?" He looked over at me as if I were some peculiar species of person. A type of creature that he had never before encountered. "Her mother used to headline all of those columns."

"What do you intend to do about it?"

"What *can* I do about it? She will simply have to become more noticeable." He winked at me.

Aunt's lips stretched thin and she turned her attentions to her egg, whacking off the top of the shell with a sharp blow and plunging her spoon into its golden liquid center. "I should think that the problem could be corrected with some attention to a newspaperman."

"A newspaperman?"

"One of those who writes such columns. They come, often enough, to these balls. Cannot one be convinced to write in greater detail about our Clara? With a kinder tone, perhaps?"

"Perhaps." Father patted his lips with a napkin and then tossed it onto the table. "Perhaps he can."

———

THE NEXT DAY, the dance master put me through my paces. Indeed, the waltz quadrille was just as Lizzie had explained it, though it only made sense once I had danced one. Aunt made me dance four, just to make sure I had committed the steps to memory. Then she had me dance both a polka and a schottische to be certain I had not forgotten them.

After the dance master and his assistant had gone, I took to the stairs to return to my room.

But Aunt stopped me. "You are wanted by your father."

It was not often that I received such news. I reversed my course and went immediately to his study.

As I entered, my father pushed away from his desk. "Ah. There you are." He stood there as if he was not quite sure whether to advance toward me or to retreat from me.

It was then I realized we were not alone. A man stood by the window, looking out onto the back garden. I had done the same just that morning, watching the snow sift down upon the ground. But whereas I had been happy to be gazing at such icy beauty from inside the house, the set of his shoulders made me think he wanted nothing so much as to be gone from here.

While I had been looking at the stranger, my father had reclaimed the seat behind his desk. "This is Mr. Douglas."

The man turned. He was younger than I had expected. Pronounced of chin, with an air of disdain that the curiosity in his brown eyes belied. He bent at the waist in a fluid, elegant bow. "Miss Carter."

"Mr. Douglas is going to accompany you at all your functions."

"Accompany me?"

The man leveled his eyes at me. "I am a columnist for the *New York Journal*."

"He writes the social column." Father spoke the words with what seemed like an especial satisfaction.

"*And* a political one as well." The man was rather pointed in his tone.

Father shrugged. And then he rose once more and approached Mr. Douglas. "You do understand your obligations?"

The man turned his gaze from me to my father. "Yes."

"There is nothing further to discuss?"

"No."

Father nodded. And then he smiled, his shoulders relaxing. "I appreciate your willingness to be of assistance in this matter."

Mr. Douglas nodded. And then, with a slight bow toward me, he was gone.

Aunt slid into the doorway as his steps echoed down the hall. "Well?"

Father smiled at me as he answered his sister. "He'll do it. Our Clara will soon be the season's most celebrated debutante."

CHAPTER 15

*I*T SNOWED AGAIN the day of the Posts' Ball. I wished that it had made the carriage drive as sparkly and festive as they always seemed to be in novels, but snow that fell into the city was always corrupted by the atmosphere through which it passed. By the smoke from tens of thousands of chimneys, by the great spark-lit belches of the elevated trains, and by the grime and filth that it finally came to rest upon. By the time we reached the Posts', it had degenerated into ice-glazed puddles or turned into an ash-colored slush. I had altogether forgotten about Mr. Douglas and our shared appreciation of snowflakes when I saw him in the front hall.

I didn't know what to do. Should I acknowledge him? Or would that have been inappropriate? He was like an employee, as good as an employee, although he didn't look like one. He wore the same black tailcoat, black vest, and white bow tie that the other men did.

Aunt frowned. And then, as if making a great concession, nodded. Once.

Mr. Douglas inclined his head toward me. And then he came over. "May I have the pleasure of a dance?"

Aunt opened her mouth, but he pointedly ignored her and continued to speak to me. "If I must write about you, I should think it would be better to do it authentically."

I offered him my wrist.

"I'll take a polka. That way you can work your charms on someone else during the waltzes."

I didn't know whether he was criticizing me or complimenting me. And I had no chance to ask him, for once he signed the card, he disappeared into the crowd. But what the masses swallowed up, they also gave back. In the form of Lizzie.

She smiled at Aunt.

Aunt scowled.

Lizzie hooked her arm through my own and spoke to me from the private recesses of her fan. "I adore the Posts' decorations."

Only Dickens's Scrooge would not have. In every corner of their ballroom stood a Christmas tree, strung with tinsel and bedecked with candles. And underneath each tree had been stacked presents wrapped in colored papers and secured with lengths of lace or ribbon. There were dozens of them, and they were all of identical shape and size. It was not difficult to imagine that they would be given out as favors before the night was over.

Lizzie brought my attentions back to her with a whisper. "Who is that divine-looking man that you were talking to?"

"A Mr. Douglas."

"Not *the* Mr. Douglas?"

I took a swipe at her nose with my fan. "I have no idea which Mr. Douglas. He came to visit Father last week." I very nearly told her that the man was a columnist for the *Journal*, but I could not overcome the thought that I shouldn't. That there was something not quite fair about hiring a newspaperman to report on all of one's social doings. And so I said nothing.

"There's a Mr. Douglas who writes for *The New York Journal*. Do you think that's him?"

I should have guessed that Lizzie knew more of such things, more of such people, than did I. Wasn't Mrs. Barnes the last word in social flair? "Is there? I hadn't known." Least not before I had been told. By Father.

"He looks as if he belongs."

I glanced about until I saw him, and indeed, he did have an air of belonging. That air of studied indifference that seemed to plague the most fashionable of the city. The mien that Aunt had often suggested I acquire.

"And besides," Lizzie whispered, "it cannot hurt to have a handsome man follow you about!"

"He's not following—"

"He *is* following. At least with his eyes. But it's perfect. Haven't you seen how Mr. De Vries glares at him?"

"Does he?"

"Doesn't he! I wish I had a Mr. Douglas of my own. You must flirt with him, Clara, and use him to your advantage."

I *was* using him to my advantage in ways that Lizzie must never know.

As we stood together, a young man approached Mrs. Barnes. I saw Lizzie's mother try to catch her eye. I touched my friend's hand with my fan. "A suitor awaits."

She glanced beyond me toward her mother. Glanced back at me with a wry twist to her lips. "I'd rather stay right here with you." She wrinkled her nose at me. And then she smiled. "How do I look?" She asked the question through her teeth.

"Lovely."

"If lovely is as lovely does, I'd rather act like a toad."

I was sorely tempted to laugh aloud, but checked myself just in time. And good thing. For when I had turned back to Aunt, she requested my dance card. For the unfortunate Mr. Hooper. He of the malignant eyes, who was so fond of staring at me.

"I gave him a dance. A quadrille. He might have made a scene otherwise."

Perhaps with a quadrille he would be so concerned about keeping the sets that he wouldn't stare at me.

My dance card was soon filled. And Mr. De Vries had claimed a dance upon it. So had Mr. De Vries, the younger son. They had approached me together, and the elder had introduced his brother to Aunt. It was the first time I had seen the younger brother since he had found my slipper. He took a lancers. The heir took a waltz.

No waltz quadrilles to worry over.

I sighed in sheer relief.

———

THE DANCE WITH the younger De Vries came first.

He escorted me out onto the dance floor, accepted my gloved hand in his. "Are you in command of both your slippers this evening, Miss Carter?"

A flush crept across my cheeks. "I am."

"I'm sorry. I shouldn't have said anything. I'm always saying just the thing I shouldn't say."

Which was probably why he and his brother had been urged to cut their tour short. But he didn't look like a dissolute. Not that I had any great experience with them. He looked rather nice. His hair was a bit overlong when compared to the fashion, but it curled handsomely at his neck behind his ears. And where his brother seemed sophisticated and knowing, the younger Mr. De Vries seemed simply genuine and kind.

"Perhaps I should have signed up for a waltz, for that's all Franklin could talk about yesterday: 'dancing with that delicious girl who closed her eyes.' But I must confess that I rather like your eyes open. Much better to see them than to . . . not." As the music began, he bowed and I curtsied.

"Did you enjoy your tour, Mr. De Vries?"

We stepped to the center and greeted the couple across from us with another bow and a curtsy. Then we retreated.

"My what?"

"Your tour. Of the continent?"

I chained across the center of our square with the other girls and then took up my place beside Mr. De Vries once more.

"Yes. That is until . . . well, it was shorter than expected. I would have liked to have seen Italy."

Italy! Where Bryon had lived. And died. "I would like to see it too."

Our conversation was impeded by a series of sliding chassés, which took us in opposite directions.

"Would you?"

"Yes."

"Well, that's something. Something in common."

Such an odd way he had of expressing himself.

We joined hands in a two-hand turn. "It's so rare to be able to look at a person, at a girl, in the eye."

"My aunt says I'm as tall as a boy. Taller even."

We broke apart to bow and curtsy once more, this time to our corner.

"I wouldn't say that. Although, I am a boy. And you are as tall as me . . . only what I meant to say was that it's unexpected, considering that generally I'm looking down upon some pointy tiara or getting tickled beneath the nose by some wayward feather."

I smiled at his remarks as I chained once more in the center. "Oh, sure, you may laugh, but imagine me in the ballrooms of Vienna trying desperately not to sneeze because some baron's daughter has got a peacock's feather that will not stop waving itself beneath my nostrils."

Once again, we were obliged to chassé.

"Better a feather than a hatpin."

"Oh yes. Much better a feather. A hatpin is likely to poke a man in the eye. You have no idea how filled with traps these ballrooms are. I take my life into my hands every time I set foot in one."

"I wish everyone shared your sentiments. You have no idea how tiring it is to balance all of these jewels and feathers on my head."

We chained across the square and then chained back to our original position.

He gave my hair ornament an apprising look. "Doesn't seem that big an imposition."

Had I been complaining? I hadn't meant to complain. It wasn't polite. "It's not!"

He raised a brow.

"I'm not complaining. Because I wouldn't."

"I would." We looked at each for a long moment and then burst out laughing.

As the final bars of the dance were played, we bowed to the couples across from us and at our corners and then Mr. De Vries deposited me back at Aunt's side. Bowed. "Thank you ever so much, Miss Carter."

"Thank you, Mr. De Vries."

He stepped a bit closer. "Don't you think, since we spoke of feathers and hatpins, that you could call me Harry?"

I nodded. And as he left me at Aunt's side, I was smiling still.

———

THE NEXT DANCE was his brother's. He bowed toward my aunt and then he turned his attentions toward me. "Miss Carter."

"Mr. De Vries."

He escorted me out onto the dance floor.

We waited for the opening measures.

And waited.

And waited some more.

"I wanted to tell you, Miss Carter—"

The orchestra began. I closed my eyes and let the dance, and Mr. De Vries, carry me away.

When I opened my eyes after the last note faded away it was with no little sorrow. I had imagined myself in sunny Italy. And then in a ballroom in Vienna. I flushed as I realized just how far my wild imaginings had taken me from Mr. De Vries's arms. "Thank you, Mr. De Vries."

He smiled at me. A slow spread of a smile that started at one corner of his mouth and didn't quite make it to the other side. "It was my pleasure, Miss Carter, and *I* thank *you*. For a dance that was exceptional. No other girl has ever placed herself in my hands as you do. Never trusted me so completely. It was as if I could do to you whatever I wanted."

I looked up sharply at that comment, though I found nothing but regard in his eyes.

"You're like no one I've ever met," he said.

"Thank you, Mr. De Vries."

He linked his arm through my own and turned me toward Aunt. As he did, his chin grazed my ear. He looked into my eyes. "Call me Franklin."

For the second time that evening, a blush stole over my cheeks. "Thank you, Franklin."

CHAPTER 16

*A*FTER MY DANCE with Franklin, Lizzie found me.
"You look good with him, Clara. You're both so tall."

"No better than you do. With you being so fair and he being so dark."

Lizzie leaned closer. Peered up into my eyes. "What's wrong?"

I should have known I couldn't hide my thoughts from her.

"You look unwell."

"I can't sleep. I can't eat. I can't do anything in this corset. I hate it." And truly, *hate* wasn't a strong enough word. I despised it with the passion of a prisoner who can glimpse freedom from her cell. A freedom that was daily denied.

"Really? I rather kind of like it."

"You do?"

Her shoulder seemed to want to lift in a shrug, but it locked itself in place before it could do so. "I like the way it feels. So snug. And close. As if... I feel like it makes me stronger. As if, when I wear it, I'm ready for all of this. You probably think I'm silly."

"No." I wished I could say the same. Not even my feelings, it seemed, were conventional. If I could just see things the way Lizzie did, the way Aunt did, then maybe I would feel as if I belonged here.

"Didn't you see me twirling my fan over there?"

"What? Where?"

"Clara! You're hopeless. I was *twirling my fan.*"

Which meant . . . something. I knew it was supposed to mean something.

"Did you not see Mr. Porter?"

Mr. Porter? "Is he the one with the droopy mustache?"

"No. That's Mr. Hamilton. Mr. Porter is the one with the red nose. The tall one."

"Oh. No. I didn't see him. What did he do?"

She batted me on the arm with her fan. "It certainly seemed as if the only thing he saw was you!"

"I hadn't noticed."

"Oh, Clara. *The fan!* When I twirl it, it means that you're being watched."

"I'm sorry. I can never quite seem to remember—"

She sighed. "How are you going to flirt with all of your beaux when you don't even know that you have them?"

"I don't. I don't have any beaux."

"You do."

"I don't." How could I when I didn't remember even the simplest of things?

"You do. I'll show you. Come with me." Lizzie grabbed hold of my hand and led me toward the front of the ballroom. "Go on. Stand right there. In the middle, where there's that open space."

"In the middle? Of everyone?"

She shook her head. And then she seized my hand. Together we walked into the center of the room.

"Do you see? Over there?"

I realized Mr. Hamilton was indeed looking in our direction. "Do you mean Mr. Hamilton?"

"Yes! And beside him is a Lorillard. And over there is one of the van Rensselaers. And two away from him is a Gould."

As she turned me about the room supplying name after name, it seemed each one heard what was being said. For invariably, when Lizzie spoke a name, that man would look over. Straight at us.

"They're looking at *you*, Lizzie."

"No, they aren't. They're all looking at you." Her voice had gone quiet, and I had to lean close in order to hear.

"So, what do I do?"

"Do? You smile and you flirt, and in the end, you spurn them all for the hand of Mr. DeVries. That's what you do. At least that's what I intend to do!" She was smiling now. "And I thought that on that matter at least we were agreed. So go flirt, Clara. Amuse yourself while you still can."

"But why can't we just pursue Mr. De Vries?"

"And forego the flirting? And the dancing?"

"Yes. Exactly that. Forego all of it."

She shook her head. "Truly, Clara, you're too prosaic! There's no good in going directly after him. He'll run away. We must approach without seeming to approach. Do you see him there?"

I looked in the direction she had nodded and I did see. Mr. De Vries was by the punch bowl surrounded by girls. And he looked rather bored with it all.

For a while I pretended to be Lizzie. I flirted with my fan, casting all kinds of glances toward the men, trying to coax them to my side. And it worked! Of a sudden I had more suitors than I could manage.

Perhaps Lizzie had been right. Perhaps I could do this. Perhaps I would do this. But what if I did? And what if I succeeded? What if I won the heir?

———

THOUGH MR. DOUGLAS was a member of what Aunt so scathingly called the working class, there was no fault to be found in his dance steps. Every hop, every turn, every chassé was timed perfectly. And he corrected me a time or two. I could tell by a pull in this direction or a push in that.

The fact that he was a newspaperman was a great fascination to me. At first, I was rather nervous, knowing that he might report on the slightest of social infractions, but then I remembered that he had made an agreement with Father and curiosity soon displaced my unease.

"May I ask you a question, Mr. Douglas?"

"By all means, Miss Carter."

"Do you know Mr. Riis? Mr. Jacob Riis?"

His eyes narrowed as his gaze intersected mine. "Why do you wish to know?"

"I just ... I mean, is it true? All of those things that he wrote?"

"In his book?"

I nodded.

"Yes."

Yes? Then people really did sleep on roofs? And little children truly did wander the streets? "But then why doesn't anyone do anything?"

"Do anything? I'd think you would be the last person to advocate for *doing something*, Miss Carter."

"When people are being treated as animals? Someone must!"

"But those same indigent poor keep our city's finest in the manner to which they've become accustomed." His eyes seemed to send me a challenge.

I decided to meet it. "This is 1891, Mr. Douglas. Surely no one in the United States of America should have to be without food. Or shelter."

"I agree."

"You agree?"

"I agree. But the plight of the immigrant runs from the slums of the city into the very deep pockets of some of our finest citizens. If someone really wanted to help the city, they'd torch Tammany Hall and all the Democrats who nest there."

"Tammany Hall." I'd heard Miss Miller say those words before.

"That's right: Tammany Hall. They're the only organization that cares what happens to the immigrants. But that's only so they'll receive their votes. It's the only thing that Tammany Hall and those at the top of society agree upon: The immigrants need to stay exactly where they are. It's the only way no one gets hurt."

"No one except those poor, destitute souls."

"Exactly."

We danced the next few moments in silence. I couldn't have said whether or not he enjoyed the polka, but he did lean near as the dance drew to a close. "Why do you do it?"

"Do what?"

"You're an accomplished enough dancer. Is that why you close your eyes during the waltz? Because you don't have to work at it?"

I felt my face flush with color. "On the contrary. I am so poor a dancer that if I do not close my eyes, I risk dancing upon my partner's toes. It was never my intention to exalt myself. Only to mask my own inadequacies. Please forgive me for leading you to think otherwise."

For the first time that evening, he seemed to look at me with something close to interest. "Is that so?"

I nodded. And I very nearly nibbled at my lip. Is that what people thought of me?

"Then it was a pleasure, Miss Carter. You're very much better at dancing than you think."

———

I LEFT THE dance floor only to find that Mr. Douglas's eyes followed me wherever I went. I knew, of course, that he had to observe me in order to write his articles, but still, it was a bit disconcerting. And so, at the next intermission, when Aunt and I came to stand beside him, I spoke to him. But only, of course, after Aunt had begun conversing with someone else.

"Don't you ever dance? With anyone but me?"

"There's no point."

"No point?"

He leaned close as if imparting a secret. "There aren't that many among this crowd who are worth it. They're more interested in catching a man than in learning how to keep one."

"And what would that take?"

"Learning how to keep one?" His smile was colored by condescension. "Being more concerned about his character than his pocketbook. A fellow is more than his inheritance. At least some of us would like to think so. There ought to be a better way to do this; marriages ought to be contracted on something other than beauty and fortune."

"They are. They're contracted on the basis of. . ."

"Yes?"

"Well . . ."

"You, for instance. What do you have to offer?"

I felt my chin lift in response to his question. "I . . . well ... I know how to play . . ."

"Yes?"

"A rather difficult Hungarian dance." I'd worked nearly two months in order to master it.

"Very impressive."

"And I can sing. Several arias by Mozart."

"And I expect you know the difference between a lemon fork and a lettuce fork too."

He made it sound as if that were a very facile accomplishment. "What if I do?"

"What if you do? If you do, then bravo." He began to clap. "With all the injustice in this city, one more raven-haired debutante who knows her waltz from her polka is just what's needed."

"You don't have to be so sarcastic!"

"And you don't need to be so naive. Wake up. Read a book. Educate yourself."

He was becoming rather unpleasant. "If you're not enjoying this, then why don't you just stop? Stop dancing. Stop writing." And why didn't I stop too?

"Because I can't. God help me, I wish I could, but I can't." Desperation seemed to envelop his words. But then he smiled. "And besides, I want to see how all of this plays out."

"All of what?"

"All of your father's crooked schemes. I figure if I stay around long enough, I'll have something truly important to write about."

Crooked schemes? What was he talking about? "What do you mean? Explain yourself!"

He stared at me for the longest time, as if taking my measure. "Does Mulberry Street mean anything to you?"

Mulberry Street? I began to shake my head and then thought the better of it. Because, somehow, somewhere, I had heard of it.

"Stop asking questions and go play with your fan, little girl. There's a big evil world out there that you don't want to be a part of."

The New York Journal—Society
December 22, 1891

The Posts' ball was the site of something never before seen in this fair city. It was an event at which more than half the eligible bachelors in the city gave their hearts away. To the same girl. Of course, each year features a new debutante who sets the hearts of the city to beating double-time. But this year one debutante, Miss Clara Carter, is something quite extraordinary to behold.

The Tattler
December 22, 1891

. . . and this poor reporter finds himself wearied to tears of this generation of debutantes who profess to be nothing more than pawns in the hands of their mothers or fathers. If you asked any of them, they would tell you the same: They do what they do because they are told to do it. They line up every year and partake of the pageantry of the season because it is what they are expected to do. But can a girl who flirts with abandon truly be innocent of trawling for the fortunes of this city's wealthiest citizens? Does naiveté beget stupidity as well?

I retreated to my room the next afternoon and had the second man kindle a fire against the winter's chill. After he had positioned a chair next to the hearth, I picked up my embroidery and punched the needle through the cardboard. Drew the thread back and forth. In and out; up and down.

Punch. Pull.

Punch. Pull.

Punch. Pull.

The dull monotony of repetition did nothing to drive the

words of the newspapers from my mind. Did naiveté beget stupidity? And if it did, then what was I supposed to do about it?

The Tattler seemed to imply that a debutante had some sort of say in her future. That I, that all of us, could make some decision other than that which had already been made for us, on our behalf. By our fathers. By our mothers.

But in that, I knew that whoever wrote the column had erred. Miss Miller had helped me to see that our futures had been decided. Decided long ago. Though some of us had hoped otherwise, we had all known of this end since our beginnings. Since the day the doctor had uttered the words "No. It's a girl."

So this one thing at least we could do: We could aspire to great social heights, greater heights than our parents had reached. Greater heights than Aunt had reached.

Punch. Pull.

Punch. Pull.

And no, we had no choice.

The Tattler was wrong.

CHAPTER 17

I MET LIZZIE the next afternoon, on Christmas Eve, in the bushes as was our habit. She greeted me by waving two packages at me. "I have Christmas presents for you!"

"Presents?" In the plural? But I had only one for her.

"One for now. Mine." She gave me the gift that her right hand was holding. I prized open the gilded paper and found within it a pair of embroidered slippers.

"But they're perfect! With pansies!"

"Your favorite."

Yes, they were. The fact that she knew it brought tears to my eyes.

"And this one is from Miss Miller." She offered me the present that she held in her left hand. When I took it, she slid her hands into her muff.

"But—how—?"

"She had it sent to me and asked me to be her messenger."

I hid it within the folds of my cloak. And from those same folds I withdrew her gift.

Lizzie fairly snatched it from me and tore the paper open.

She squealed when she saw what it contained. "Friendship Love and Truth."

"I know you like mottos."

"I adore them!"

"Then, merry Christmas."

She reached out and wrapped her arms around me in an embrace. "Merry Christmas!" After letting go of my neck, she straightened the hat on her head. "I have to go. They're putting the pig on to roast soon. And the cheese straws should be out of the oven by now."

While we had always had a goose for Christmas, the Barneses always had roasted pig. A whole one, turned on a spit in their garden. "And what else will you be doing? Tonight?"

"We'll all eat an apple at midnight. Like always." Her smile wobbled for an instant. "Just a very little bite this year, you know . . ."

Oh, how I knew. I very much doubted whether I would eat another apple as long as I wore a corset, which appeared to be indefinitely long. As long, perhaps, as the rest of my life. Apples gave me the worst indigestion. "Will you have the bonfire?" Another Barnes eccentricity, it filled the air with woodsmoke if the wind happened to blow in the wrong direction.

"Of course!"

One of my secret wishes as a child had always been to spend Christmas Eve at the Barnes house instead of my own. As it was, I usually spent a few minutes on Christmas Eve night with my cheek pressed to a back-facing window trying to see over our garden and the neighbors' into theirs. Trying to catch a glimpse of the merry flames and dancing sparks that shot up from the inferno like firecrackers.

"And what will you be doing?"

I shrugged. "The same things as always." We would eat dinner. I would play the piano, Father would read. And then we would all go to bed. And sometime during the night, Father would be called out to attend to someone who had overindulged or over-imbibed. Just the same as almost every other night of the year.

———

THE NEXT MORNING, I awoke to an unfamiliar sound. The sound of silence. There was no activity on the street beneath my windows. No calling out of passersby. I heard the clatter of one carriage as I lay there, propped against my pillows, but not the noise of the dozens I usually did.

I drew on a breakfast jacket without the help of a maid and slipped down the stairs to the parlor. The Christmas tree had appeared in the night, magically, just as it always had. Trees of Christmases past had been done up in paper chains and popcorn strings, with ornaments made of folded paper and candles clipped to the branches. Trees of Christmases past had witnessed the singing of Christmas carols, the hiding of gifts. They had seen the kisses that Father had stolen from Mama when he caught her underneath the balls of mistletoe. This year's tree was much more stylish and much too elegant to suffer any foolish games. Draped with tinsel and hung with silvered glass ornaments, there was none of my childhood present upon it, but all of Aunt's fervent wishes for the future were displayed upon its branches.

Christmas used to be my favorite holiday. We had been whirled into a frenzy of activity every December, Mama and I. I had been allowed in the kitchen to watch the cook make her puddings and Christmas cakes and to put the finishing touches on those creations. And when I had not been in the kitchen, its scents had followed me everywhere. Cinnamon and ginger, orange peel and lemon. Of such things were my memories of Christmas perfumed.

This December, the house had smelled of roasts and turnips,

the way it usually did. In fact, no hint at the coming of Christmas had appeared at all until the tree this morning.

———

EVENTUALLY, FATHER APPEARED from his study and Aunt came downstairs. After a breakfast of boiled eggs and boiled ham, we exchanged gifts.

Father placed Mother's jewelry box in my hands.

I lifted the lid and gazed at the gems I knew so well. There were sets of garnets and rubies and emeralds nestled in its felt-lined boxes. And best of all, the amethysts.

"The season's most beautiful debutante shouldn't be without her jewels."

"Thank you." Tears had begun to prick my eyes. I blinked. Then I looked at him and tried to smile. "They're lovely."

"If I don't miss my guess, you'll be even more lauded than your mother was."

Than Mama? I very much doubted that. Before I could revel any more in that unexpected gift, Aunt presented me with hers. A tasseled fan that was set into mother-of-pearl sticks.

I gave Father a new paperweight for his study and Aunt an opera purse I had worked in beads.

Father took a look at his pocket watch, frowned, and then set it back into his pocket. Aunt busied herself with petting her dogs. And then, after a while, Father left.

Aunt excused herself.

And I went back upstairs, carrying the box and the fan.

———

LATER THAN MORNING, we reassembled for church. The silence of early morning had been overwhelmed by the clatter of carriages, seemingly summoned by the pealing of church bells all across the city.

As always, the whole of the church had been done up for the holiday, from the narthex to the sanctuary. Small fir trees decorated the platform and calla lilies and elephant ears had been placed on the altar. The pews were swagged with festoons of holly and laurel.

The DeVrieses went into church just ahead of us. Mrs. DeVries, resplendent in maroon, followed by the girl and a man I did not recognize. That man was followed by Franklin, who was followed by his brother. The men were so dark, the women so fair that they looked like a picture of a storybook family.

The minister outdid himself that morning with his sermon. And the choir outdid themselves with a Te Deum and a Sanctus and then with "Adeste Fideles" during the offertory. The best singing of the service, however, came not from the choir but from across the aisle. From the direction of the De Vries pew.

———

AFTER CHURCH WE returned to the house, and at three o'clock we sat down to a dinner of roast goose with chestnut stuffing, a salad course with celery and hot cheese balls, and a plum pudding with brandy butter for dessert.

Later that night, I opened the present I had most been looking forward to. The gift from Miss Miller. I unwrapped the package to discover a slim volume of verses. And though I would have liked to have devoured them with a crisp green apple in hand, I gave myself to their stanzas and forgot, for several blissful hours, that I was even wearing a corset.

The next morning, my first task was to write a letter to Miss Miller.

Dear Miss Miller,

Thank you so much for the lovely book of verses. How did you know that I have nearly memorized my entire volume of Byron? I found Emily Dickinson's poems to be delightful, if rather odd. I had not before heard mention of her.

If you do me the pleasure of corresponding in the future, please write to me in the care of

Care of whom? Though Aunt had agreed to let me speak with Lizzie at balls and other events we attended together, were she to discover our meetings in the hedge, I was not sure she would approve. Better, perhaps, not to rely on Lizzie as a messenger. But if not Lizzie, then whom?

Perhaps Harry? Though I did not know him well, and though it was probably completely inappropriate to beg such favors from a gentleman, I decided that I would ask him. I thought, I hoped, that he would agree. But in case I was mistaken, I would wait to send the letter until I could ask.

Mr. Harold De Vries; New York City.
   Your friend,
   Clara Carter

That evening, I attended a private ball at the Hamiltons'. And it was with some relief that I saw the De Vries brothers attending. Thankfully, Harry offered me a cup of punch during the first intermission. I wasted no opportunity in begging my favor from him.

"I hate to have to presume upon our recent friendship."

"I beg you, Miss Carter, to presume."

His generosity of spirit supplied me the courage to continue. "I would like to post a letter to a friend. And it's necessary that her reply, if there is to be one, not be posted to my house."

"To her? It is a *she*, then, to whom you write?"

"It is. My governess. At least she was, until I found out I was to debut."

He leaned toward me ever so slightly. "And you miss her." His voice was gentle. And understanding.

"Yes. Very much."

"So how, then, may I help you?"

"May I ask her to send any reply to your care?"

"And this would be whom?"

"Miss Julia Miller. Of Cortland."

"Miss Julia Miller, then. Of Cortland. If a message should ever come to me from her, I shall gladly deliver it to you."

I smiled my thanks.

He smiled in return.

An awkwardness hovered in the air between us.

This, then, was the danger of speaking intimately before such privileges had been earned. I never should have asked such a thing of him. *What must he think of me!*

Harry broke the silence. "I saw you at church on Sunday. Well, I mean, I see you at church every Sunday. But I thought the reverend's sermon especially thoughtful this past week."

"You did? I've often thought that I must be the only one who actually listens. Lizzie just spends the service noticing what people wear ... or fail to."

"But that isn't why you attend?" It was a question couched as an answer.

"I attend because—" Why did I attend? "Don't I have to? Don't we all have to?"

He shrugged. "We could refuse."

"And then everyone would notice we weren't there."

"Who cares whether they would notice. God would notice. And wouldn't that be immeasurably worse?"

"You really think He would? When He has so many more important things to think of?" If God cared for anyone, it was people like Mr. Jacob Riis. People who did important things. People who mattered.

"He made you, didn't He? Different than anyone else who has come before or anyone else who will come after?"

I supposed He had. But I wished He'd had the foresight to make me bigger in the chest and smaller at the waist. Then I wouldn't be trying so hard to correct His mistakes.

"I must insist that you matter to Him much more than you seem to realize." There was an earnestness to his words that reverberated inside me. If only he spoke the truth. I would like to believe that God cared for me. That He might love me no matter what anyone else thought. Because such an idea was so astonishing and because I could think of no reply, I deployed my fan, whisking it in front of my face until I decided upon a response. "If I go to church, it's because I must."

"But wouldn't you rather go because you want to?"

"Of course. And wouldn't you rather be standing in a cathedral in Italy than here? In this ballroom?"

He laughed and I smiled and we turned our eyes to the crowd. How nice it would be to live life with Harry's convictions. To be so certain that God thought of us. And so quick to dismiss the thoughts of others. But though admirable, his views were flawed. Harry didn't understand the way society worked. And how could he? He didn't have to worry about the style of his hats or the cut of his gowns. He didn't have to mold himself with a corset. And he didn't have to squeeze his hands into gloves two sizes too small. He was a man.

CHAPTER 18

*L*IZZIE WAS AT the opera on Monday evening. She fairly ran to greet me when she saw me. "How perfectly *perfect*! You're here! And now you can help me."

Me? Help her? If anyone needed help, it was me.

"We'll never succeed this season, Clara, if we don't take care of the other girls."

"Which girls?"

"The other debutantes. We have to get rid of them."

It took me a moment to reply, so surprised was I at her words. "You don't mean . . . what *do* you mean?"

"I mean we have to keep them away from Franklin."

Franklin? So he must have asked her to call him by his name too. And I had thought it a special honor, reserved just for me.

Lizzie had continued speaking. "Heaven knows *he* won't keep himself away from them!"

That was certain. He seemed to relish the attention he was receiving from this season's debutantes. And the previous year's. And the few left unmarried from the year before.

"There are entirely too many suitable girls in this city for our purposes."

"Then what did you have in mind?"

———

I FOUND MY way back to our box in a daze. The entire first two acts of the opera, *Aida*, went unnoticed by me. At intermission, it was with a sinking heart that I followed Aunt into the Assembly Room.

Gowns in brilliant reds and vivid blues assaulted my vision, and they were exacerbated by spots of pure, glowing white, by the season's other debutantes. One of them was Lizzie. And when I reached her, I meant to tell her that I couldn't do what she had asked.

Only she found me first. And under her confident stare, my fortitude wavered.

"I don't think I can do this, Lizzie. I really don't."

She took me by the arm and wound her own through mine. "Of course you can. All you have to do is open your mouth and say the words." Only Lizzie would have thought to have taken me literally.

"But they're not true. You're asking me to tell a lie."

She frowned as she looked up at me. "What *is* true is that if we don't find some way to rid ourselves of the competition, then someone else is going to marry Franklin out from under us."

"But then we wouldn't have to marry him. And he wouldn't have to choose between us."

"Better one of us than one of them."

I supposed that Lizzie was right. "Fine."

"Ready?"

I hesitated in doing so, but eventually gave her a nod.

"It's only going to work if we say it comes from your father.

Remember, you only have to tell the Vandermeres and Addy Remstell."

"And you're going to do your part?" I didn't like it, I really didn't. But Lizzie was right: We had to do something about the other debutantes.

"I'll tell all the others." She laid her other hand on my arm and gave me a squeeze. "You know that he'll eventually come to decide that we really are the two best debutantes in the city. We're just going to make it easier for him to come to that conclusion."

"But do truly have to do this?"

"Yes. Because it will keep everyone from wanting to marry him. Why would any girl want to if his fortune is destined for his brother?"

"But—"

"Shh! No more delay."

"But—"

"It's what Mama told me to say."

"You involved your mother in—!"

"My mother suggested the whole scheme." There was something very much like pride in Lizzie's words. "Don't worry. No one will be harmed in the end."

"I suppose ... I mean if your mother thinks—"

"She does." There was no deterring Lizzie. Not when she had her mind set on something.

———

AS I WALKED back through the Assembly Room, I let space grow between Aunt and myself. And when we passed by the Vandermere cousins, I slowed just a bit. "My father let slip something I thought you should know."

"Oh?" Emma, the older one, aimed her upturned nose in my direction.

"Yes. Mr. Franklin De Vries is ..." I truly didn't want to say it.

"What? He is what?"

"He is known to be sterile." The words came out in a rush.

Her eyebrows shot up toward the ceiling. "Really!"

I shrugged and continued on my course, pausing when I reached Addy Remstell to tell her the same thing.

"Are you sure?"

"My father seemed to think so." Lies! Lies, lies, lies.

As I left the room, it was with the knowledge that I had left a roiling, reeling trail of deceit behind me. I couldn't even concentrate on the next act of the opera, except to note how romantic it was when the hero forsook the arms of the king's daughter to find true love with an outsider.

When the opera was over, I spotted Lizzie in the foyer. She tipped her fan to her left.

Another signal? But what did it mean? Was someone watching me? I examined the crowds around me. But, no. There didn't seem to be anyone looking in my direction.

Except for Lizzie. She tipped her fan again. And then she tipped her head in the same direction. Twice.

Why couldn't she speak to me in equations? Or Italian? Then I would know exactly what it was she meant to say.

She jerked her head once more to the left.

Did she mean . . . ?

Finally, she threw her arm out and pointed. As I followed the gesture, the thrill of triumph and the shame of guilt warred within me. For the first time during the season, Franklin De Vries was standing quite alone . . . while his brother Harry was surrounded by debutantes.

———

THE NEXT WEEK, my nerves frayed and my conscience wracked by guilt from the lie, I barely slept at night. So when the scream came, I almost confined it to the realm of my imagination. But then it came again. From the parlor.

I ran down the stairs as quickly as my corset would allow me.

When I reached the front hall, servants were already appearing from the basement and the back stairs. As they saw me, they cleared a path, leaving open the entrance to the parlor.

I crept toward it, not quite certain that I wanted to know what was happening inside. As I entered, I saw Aunt, nearly reclining on the sofa, waving one hand in front of her face as she clutched a letter in the other. When she saw me, she said no word, but she held out the letter to me with a trembling hand.

"What is it?"

"Read." Her face, which had theretofore been pale, flushed red.

"It's an invitation."

She nodded.

"To a . . . Patriarch's Ball?"

"*The* Patriarch's Ball."

I handed it back to her.

"You're going to the Patriarch's Ball!"

"Yes." Yet another ball.

"That I should live to see this day. The Patriarch's Ball!" She sounded as if I had just been transformed from mortal to goddess. She pushed herself to sitting and turned, full body, to look at me. "There are only ever four hundred people on the invitation list. Just four hundred worthy to attend. And we were never among them. If you have secured a place among the four hundred, then you have succeeded. The De Vrieses must have convinced someone to add you to the list."

"How do you know that it was them?" And why would they do that?

"Who else could it have been?"

HAD I KNOWN the amount of work entailed in readying myself for the ball, I would have intercepted and destroyed the invitation before Aunt could read it. There were visits to be made to the dressmaker. Hair ornaments to be altered and new slippers to be ordered. And worst of all, there were more dancing lessons to be endured. Apparently, the patriarchs demanded nothing so much as novelty at their balls; there was a new cotillion to be learned in advance of the event.

My only consolation was that Lizzie was suffering such agonies as well. She had to be if she was attending the Patriarch's Ball. It was with the goal of commiserating that I mentioned my torturous dance lessons that Thursday when I met her. "I just can't seem to remember the order of the patterns."

"Which patterns?"

"For the ball."

"Which ball?"

"The Patriarch's Ball."

"You've been invited to the Patriarch's Ball?" Her look was akin to the one Aunt had given me.

"Weren't you?"

"No. I wasn't."

If I could have taken back my words, I surely would have.

But Lizzie had already brightened. "The Patriarch's Ball? You'll have to tell me everything about it. Can't you just not wait?"

I could. I could wait for a thousand years. Or more.

———

I SPENT THE days before the ball in a state of nearly constant fear. What if I tripped stepping out of our carriage? What if I didn't remember the sets for the cotillion? What if I couldn't think of anything to say during the dinner? What if I fainted at some point that night?

And worse, there was a whole opera to sit through before the ball even began!

As Tuesday's night turned into Wednesday's dawn, as the hours ticked into minutes and the clock finally tolled four, my anxiety knew no bounds. Except, of course, those of my corset. When my breathing came too quickly, when my heart beat too fast, I closed my eyes against the world and sought to bring my breathing back within the confines of my laces.

I was coiffed and gowned, shod and brushed. And then I was bundled into a cloak and whisked to the opera. And from there, to Delmonico's restaurant, where the ball was to be held.

Pink was the color of the evening and the rooms smelled of nothing so much as money. It was evident in the scent of the pink roses that had been draped from every chandelier and which decorated every wall. It showed itself in the fronds of palms and ferns masking the rooms' corners. And most of all it was exhibited in the glittering jewels that the girls displayed with each wave of their fans.

For an hour there were informal dances. I spied Harry and Franklin—the one kind and affable, the other so confident that he was intimidating—but I did not have the chance to dance with them. At half past eleven we discovered we were to be seated for dinner at a table with the De Vrieses.

Aunt gave me an arch look. And then she leaned close. "We are going to thank Mrs. De Vries for the invitation."

Right now? When we would all be seated together? When both Franklin and Harry would be able to hear what I was almost certain would be Aunt's overly effusive gratitude? I didn't want them to know that I didn't belong. "Is it not one of those favors that it's best just not to acknowledge?"

Aunt raised a brow. "Not acknowledge? Not acknowledge the person who has secured you an invitation to society's most elite group? Who has guaranteed you access to the fabled Four Hundred? Who has decided to make your path straight?"

I supposed not.

"An invitation such as this one cannot be bought. We have tried. It must be granted. And we must thank her for granting it."

I worried overmuch, for by the time we reached the table, weaving in and out of the clusters of people, Franklin and Harry were nowhere to be seen. And so it was with much relief that I joined Aunt in thanking Mrs. De Vries.

"It was my pleasure." She leaned forward and glanced around as if she were imparting a secret. "My son would not give me peace until I had her invited."

Aunt smiled.

"And truly, we consider it payment. For services rendered by Dr. Carter."

I felt Aunt's hand stiffen around my arm. "Really."

Mrs. De Vries's smile seemed to freeze for just an instant. "It was the very least that we could do."

———

LATER, AFTER DINNER, after I had successfully unbuttoned my gloves around my wrist to free my hands and then tucked the glove's fingers up inside, after I had successfully avoided feeding my nervous stomach by pushing duck and creamed onions about my plate and rearranging them into various piles, the formal dancing began. Knowing that Franklin himself had urged my invitation, I wasted no time in thanking him for securing it.

But he held up a hand to stay my words as he commanded two glasses of champagne. Then he walked us over to a quieter part of the room. He pulled a cigar from his coat pocket. "Do you mind?"

I shook my head.

He lit it. Took a draw. "Now what was it you were saying?"

"I wanted to thank you."

He replied with a lazy smile. "For what?"

"For having secured me an invitation."

He took the cigar from his mouth. Blew the smoke away behind me. "Thank Harry. He's the one who pleaded and prodded and cajoled to get Mother to wedge your name onto the list. In fact, you can thank him yourself. Here he comes."

I turned in the direction Franklin had pointed with his cigar and, indeed, Harry was coming toward us.

I greeted him with a smile. "I must thank you. For having me added to the list."

He smiled and bowed. "It was for the most selfish of reasons, I assure you." He straightened then and frowned at his brother. "You shouldn't smoke those here. Not around the ladies!"

"Ladies? Where?"

My cheeks flamed at the implication.

But Franklin winked at me and then blew a ring of smoke in Harry's direction. "I'm only quoting you, little brother. The very same words you used when you extracted me from the Moulin Rouge in Paris." He turned his attention to me. " 'Ladies? Where?' That's what he said. To the Comtesse de Valois's face."

"I didn't know she was a countess. She wasn't acting like one."

"Don't worry. She thought it quite amusing." He flicked his ashes to the gleaming marble floor. "Shame we couldn't have stayed in Paris ... to see how that might have developed."

"Into an international incident."

Franklin laughed. For a moment. "You have the most annoying attachment to propriety, Brother. I'll bet Clara doesn't, do you, Clara? You have more imagination than that."

Harry responded before I could even open my mouth. "That's some question! How do you expect her to respond?"

"I was paying her a compliment. I think there's more beneath that regal carriage and gentle gaze than one might guess. But you probably think I've insulted her."

"Someone has to protect her honor."

"She won't lose it with me. Unless she wants to. And then I would be very happy to oblige."

Harry just shook his head as Franklin sauntered off. "He thinks he's being sophisticated, but he doesn't realize how arrogant he sounds. He's really not quite so bad as he'd like to be. Although, well, I'm sorry."

I tried to smile. Franklin hadn't insulted me. Not really. Not exactly. But I wondered how it was that two brothers could be so entirely different in their natures.

———

THERE WERE TWO ballrooms in use that evening, manned by two separate orchestras. I danced an admirable cotillion, though I had a hard time hiding my yawns as the hours passed. At half past three, the last dance ended. Once home, Aunt's maid helped me from my gown and exchanged it for a nightgown. I was famished, not having eaten at dinner. I wrapped a breakfast jacket around myself and crept down the back stairs to the kitchen.

I would have liked to have devoured the remainder of a cake that was sitting on the sideboard, but instead I found a roll and ate it plain, with a cup of cream to help it down. Too late I remembered the indigestion that cream had lately seemed to inspire.

Feeling a bit green, I walked back through the kitchen and out into the front hall. It was then I heard the voices. Father's and Aunt's.

So late at night?

I inched toward his study's door.

Aunt was speaking. "That's what she said: 'We consider it payment. For services rendered by Dr. Carter.' "

"At least they understand the debt that must be paid."

"But they think that now it's been paid in full!" Clearly, she had been affronted.

"I don't read that into her words."

"You would if you had heard what she said in parting."

"Which was?" Father's patience seemed to be reaching an end.

"It was the very least that we could do."

"That sounds benign."

"Not the way she said it. She said it as if it were the most that they could do. The most they *would* do. And there are not even two months left in the season. You're going to have to do something."

I stifled a belch. The indigestion was going to be worse than I had feared. And so, I left them to their conversation.

If I had hoped for sleep that night, I was disappointed. As my stomach roiled under the influence of the cream, the questions in my head kept me company through the few dark hours that remained. What could the De Vrieses possibly owe my father? And why had their debt not yet been paid? According to Aunt, they owned half the city. Surely they could afford a mere doctor's bill.

CHAPTER 19

*I*N SPITE OF his personal rancor toward me, Mr. Douglas appeared to be keeping his agreement with my father. And though *The Tattler* told a different tale, according to Mr. Douglas and his society column, I was the season's most celebrated debutante. It wasn't true, of course. Not at first. But the more he wrote it, the more people began to believe it. People who should have known better!

Mr. Tiffany sent a spangled bracelet to me for consideration. Mr. Constable of Arnold, Constable & Co. sent an opera cloak as a gift. And one night, when I had been walking into the Astor residence for a private ball, a woman standing on the sidewalk squealed, "That's Miss Carter!"

A journalist from *Town Topics* magazine had been dispatched to interview me. A corsetiere had written to persuade me to offer an endorsement of her corsets. And an artist from *Ladies' Home Journal* was sent to draw my portrait for a piece on the debutante's life. Lately, I was remarked upon even when I was simply stepping out of my own front door. A wave of whispers followed me about like a shadow.

"Miss Carter!"

"That's her!"

"Who is she wearing?"

"Where is she going?"

I had become the main arbiter and chief mistress of every-thing that was fashionable. Lizzie thought it hilarious. "What do you think, Clara? Orchids or roses?"

"For what?" We had met behind the bushes where I had been telling her about the Patriarch's Ball.

"For decorating."

"Yes, but when? And for what?"

"At a dinner party. For table arrangements."

Table arrangements? Did it truly matter? "I don't know."

"You don't?" Lizzie was laughing at me. I could tell by the sparkle in her eyes. "Because they say you know everything."

"Who says?"

"*Society*."

That was Mr. Douglas's column. "No, they don't. He—*they* just report on where I've been." I hoped Lizzie wouldn't notice the blush I felt staining my cheeks. I still hadn't told her about Mr. Douglas.

"Well... maybe *they* don't. But everyone else does. Mother and I went into McCreery's yesterday for a new hat and do you know what the clerk did?"

"What?"

"She brought out this truly terrible, hideous hat. It was made of orange bombazine with plum-colored ribbons, with a great big mass of blue feathers perched right on top. She said, and I quote, 'I delivered a hat just like this one to Miss Clara Carter last Tuesday.' "

"She did. Or, rather, they did."

"They did!"

"Yes. But Aunt sent it right back. She said no debutante should ever be caught wearing orange or plum!"

Lizzie began to giggle. "If you look hard enough when you're about the city this week, I bet you'll see more than a dozen girls wearing hats just like it."

"No."

"Yes."

And Lizzie was right! I had started a trend for a hat I would have been loath to wear. And it seemed to have stuck.

———

MY WEEKS HAD fallen into a tedious if predictable routine.

Sunday: church

Monday: opera

Tuesday: at-home

Wednesday: opera and private dinner or ball

Thursday: musical performance or other event

Friday: private dinner or ball

Saturday: private dinner or ball

And then back to Sunday when it began anew. And in between each social event I worked every minute at embroidering pillowcases and monogramming napkins that Aunt assured me I would soon need.

At least we were receiving callers on Tuesday. Whatever war Aunt had commenced by visiting people in person and receiving callers out of turn, she had won. And now our Tuesdays were spent not waiting for visitors but in discriminating between whom I would see and whom I would not. At times, there were several people waiting in the front hall together. And there were even other days of the week when people called, though they risked our not being home.

One afternoon as I joined Aunt in the parlor, the butler entered with the silver tray. "The gentlemen are waiting to be received by Miss Carter."

Aunt took the tray from him and dumped the contents into

her lap. "Mr. Hooper." She dropped the card directly into the wastebasket. "If he thinks he can come in here and brood again, then he's sadly mistaken. He can go darken someone else's door."

I couldn't keep from shuddering.

Aunt picked up more cards. "Mr. Hobbs. Mr. Harold De Vries."

"Harry!"

"Pardon me?"

"I mean Mr. De Vries. The younger."

"Yes. Brother to the heir." Aunt waved the butler over. "We will see *him*. But not the others."

The butler bowed and disappeared. Harry walked through the doorway a moment later.

Aunt and I stood.

Harry bowed.

Aunt smiled and she and I sat.

"Well." Aunt's brows raised as if she expected Harry to say something.

He said nothing.

Aunt inclined her head toward him, in the slightest degree.

The conversation was to be my responsibility then. "It was a lovely opera last night."

Harry blinked as if my words had startled him. "Oh! Yes. Lovely. Quite."

"The orchestra was . . . lovely."

"Very. Lovely." Harry was standing, hands clasped, rocking back and forth on his toes.

"You may sit. If you'd like to."

"Oh. Of course. Thank you." He looked around for a moment and then moved uncertainly to a spare, plain chair, our one and only Revolutionary relic. And then he sat in it.

I hardly dared to look at Aunt. But then I hardly dared to

look at Harry for fear he might fall through the chair at any moment. He didn't. But he did lean back into it.

The chair wheezed.

I had to do—to say—something. "That's truly a relic of history in which you are sitting, Mr. De Vries."

He leaned forward.

I found myself able to breathe a bit easier.

"Is it?"

"Yes. It was the chair my father's father's father was sitting in when he decided to join in the War for Independence."

"Imagine that. My mother has such a thing in her parlor. Only it's a footstool. Went through the war as well. Got a bullet through its leg."

I smiled.

"We were never allowed to sit on it when we were little. For fear of breaking it."

"No. I don't suppose you were."

Harry smiled. Let his gaze wander around the room. But then it came back sharply to rest upon me. "Oh. Oh! Perhaps ... I shouldn't be sitting here, should I?" He jumped to his feet. "Maybe I should be going. Just came to say hello, really. Nice to see you." He bowed toward me. Turned toward Aunt. "Thank you. For receiving me. Have a ... be assured ... be well. Farewell."

We rose.

He turned around and walked right into a pedestal, which supported a vase.

The vase began to totter and I lunged past him to right it.

"Oh—I just—" He turned from the pedestal and attempted to move around it, but a marble-topped table blocked his way. "I didn't—" He reversed his step right into me. I took up his sleeve to keep from falling, and he reached out an arm to keep me upright. "I'm so sorry!"

"Harry."

"What?" His eyes sent mine a message of desperation. And misery.

"There is a pedestal to your right and a table to your left."

"Pedestal right and table left."

I nodded. Released his sleeve.

He dropped his arm.

"You must step straight back and then you may turn around."

"Right."

"No!" I clutched him by the lapels. "Straight back."

"Right. Directly back."

"Yes."

He stood there, looking at me for a long moment as I held my breath, waiting to see what disaster could possibly happen next.

"If you could just...?" His gaze was directed downward.

I followed it, and noted my hands were still gripping his coat. "Oh! Of course." I let him go.

He carefully stepped backward. Once. Twice. "I'll see you tonight? At the Vandermeres' ball?"

"Yes."

He turned around and walked right into the doorframe.

"Harry!"

He held up a hand to stay me, then walked out through the door and into the front hall.

"What an odd young man!" Aunt frowned and went over to inspect the chair. "I don't know what young people are taught these days. Perhaps we should find another place for this chair."

———

THAT EVENING I danced a polka with Mr. Hamilton and giggled with Lizzie over Mr. Porter's dogged pursuit of her. Then Harry found me for a lancers.

"About this afternoon—" he said.

"Are you all right?" I lifted a hand to feel along his cheek where he had struck it against the door. There seemed to be a faint purpling beneath the fine stubble of his whiskers. But he captured my hand within his own before I could commit such an indiscretion.

The music started and he pulled me forward toward the couple across from us.

"I'm fine. What I meant to say is that I can think of nothing to say when I'm supposed to. When I'm calling and we're sitting across from each other like two marionettes and the only things I'm to mention are the weather or the opera."

"I know."

"It feels like my collar's too small and my tie is too tight and then I can't breathe and before I know it I've made a fool of myself. Again."

I very nearly smiled. "It doesn't matter. Not to me."

We chasséd in opposite directions and then came back together. "It doesn't?"

"No. I understand. I feel exactly the same way myself."

"You do?"

"Yes!" It was so good to talk to someone who understood! "Imagine that week after week I sit in the parlor waiting for callers to come so that I can talk about nothing at all to people that I don't even know."

"What a miserable existence."

"And the worst of it is that I'm doing it this year, with Aunt, as a kind of training. So that once I've married I can do it for the rest of my life by myself."

He grimaced. "How perfectly horrid!"

"Yes. But I can do it. I've practiced. I practiced speaking to Aunt's dog for a whole hour once. About. . ."

His left brow peaked. "Absolutely nothing?"

"Absolutely nothing."

"And why is that a good thing?"

"Because—" What was it that Aunt had said? "Because the city is built on connections. The more connections one has, the more prominent one is."

"And these connections consist primarily of women who spend countless hours sitting in their parlors hosting other women, whom they know very little, to whom they say nothing of great interest?"

How dull it all seemed. How bleak my future suddenly looked.

We bowed and curtsied to one corner couple and then to the next.

"I'm sure you'll do very well at it."

"Thank you." I couldn't summon the enthusiasm necessary to accompany my words with a smile.

———

AFTER THAT DANCE came an intermission. And I didn't mind when Harry remained at my side. He offered me his arm. "Come! There's someone I want you to meet." As he walked us over to the side of the room, a woman stood. It was the one from the De Vries pew. When we reached her, Harry made the introduction. "Miss Clara Carter, this is my sister, Katherine. She usually lives abroad, in Germany, but she decided to grace us with her presence this season."

"I am so pleased to meet you." And incredibly, it looked as if she was. She was as fair as Harry was dark. An angel with eyes the color of a summer's sky.

There was a cough at Katherine's elbow.

Harry turned in that direction. "And this is her husband, Baron von Bergholz."

The man snapped from the waist into a bow, grayed hair

flopping over his forehead. And then he took up my hand and kissed it. "You must be pleased."

I must? But. . . why? He had spoken with a distinctive accent. Perhaps he didn't understand what he was saying. I looked from Katherine to Harry.

Harry gave his eyebrow the slightest lift, then took his sister by the hand. "I must tell you about Miss Carter, Katherine. She has the amazing ability to dance around a ballroom with her eyes closed!"

"But I—it's not—" I turned from Harry to his sister. "It's not the way he makes it sound."

Her eyes were fairly lit with laughter. "Then tell me. How is it?"

———

FOR THE FIRST time since my debut, I woke that next morning not with regrets, not with memories of some foolish thing I had said or some important thing I had forgotten to do, but with complete and utter contentment. It took me a moment to work out why, but once I had, I leaned back against my pillows with a smile on my face.

I had met Katherine.

I had made a friend.

Which is not to say that Lizzie was not a friend. She was a very good one! But Katherine had already gone through her debut. And what's more, she had survived. There was a person I could look to when despair threatened hope. When the only life I could envision was one filled with dull conversation and innumerable parties and dances in which everyone said the same thing over and over and over again.

And Katherine had put to rest my last fears of marrying into the De Vries family. They may have denigrated the Carter family honor, but surely they had not done it through any conscious effort. There was no evidence of malice or greed among them. If there had been, then how could Harry and Katherine have issued from such stock? If people such as Katherine inhabited the world to which I was destined, then that world might not be so barren, so mean a place as I had feared.

CHAPTER 20

*T*HE NEXT AFTERNOON, as we were deciding which private balls to attend the following week, I heard the ringing of the door. Soon the butler appeared, offering up the tray to Aunt.

Aunt plucked the card from it. Gasped. "Franklin De Vries!"

My hands flew up to my head to check my hair. And then down my front to smooth my gown. Why was he here? It wasn't our at-home day. And what was I going to talk to him about?

Aunt nodded at the butler. Fluffed her skirts a bit. "Clara?" She pointed to her cheeks, which I took to mean that I should pinch mine.

Franklin strode through the door, and Aunt and I rose.

He walked to the center of the room. Bowed. As he straightened, I caught a glimpse of my reflection in the fathomless blue of his eyes.

Beside me, Aunt favored him with a nod. And a smile. "How nice of you to call, Mr. De Vries."

Franklin smiled. "It is a pleasure, madam, to be able to observe the beauty of your niece in the calm light of day instead of in the maddening crush of humanity at the opera. Or a ball."

"It has been quite an exciting season, hasn't it, Clara?"

God help me, it was my turn now. "Yes, so exciting! Don't you think so, Mr. De Vries?"

He smiled again, his eyes fastened upon me. "Excitement in the supreme." He turned and surveyed the room. Stepped toward the Revolutionary chair and put a hand to its back. "Is this the chair Harry sat in?"

I didn't know what to say.

Aunt replied in my stead. "It is."

"Harry's a good enough fellow, but not so skilled in parlor manners. You can't imagine the excuses I made for him all across Europe! It was quite amusing. Couldn't seem to remember the simplest of rules."

So Harry didn't have the best of manners. Why did Franklin have to go on and on about it?

He creased his pants at his thighs and sat in a chair opposite our sofa. "It's terrible! And embarrassing in the extreme. He once broke a chalice that belonged to Charles the Great. Charles the Great! Can you imagine? Over a thousand years old!"

Words leaped from my mouth before I could stop them. "I once read that there are so many artifacts of Charles the Great that they would fill half the museums in the world."

"What's that?"

I smiled. And I tried to make it look pleasant. "A chalice? From the time of Charles the Great? A thousand years ago? Come, Mr. DeVries, who but a family grasping and desperate for honor would believe in the provenance of something like that?"

Aunt's eyes had narrowed to slits and she was glaring at me.

Franklin smiled. But it flashed for just a moment and was gone. "It was rather garish, come to think of it—"

Aunt broke in on him. "The museums you must have seen on your tour! Tell me, did you get to visit the Louvre?"

He told us about the Winged Victory of Samothrace and the Mona Lisa.

"They call it *La Joconde* in French." He said it as if I couldn't possibly have already known it.

"Yes, and *La Gioconda* in Italian."

Franklin continued talking until the clock intoned the hour. Then he pushed to his feet. Bowed once more. "A very great pleasure."

"Thank you for your call." Aunt kept her smile on her face until Franklin had left the room. And then she turned to me, eyes lit by indignation. "Really, Clara! Grasping? Desperate for honor? You insulted our guest by presuming knowledge you had no right to presume."

"But he was criticizing Harry. In his absence!"

"His brother, the younger Mr. DeVries, is a very unconventional young man. And besides, this one is the heir. Why should it matter if he maligns his brother in our parlor? Your duty was to steer the conversation. And be *polite*."

Polite? I had been much more polite than he had even tried to be.

———

IT WASN'T UNTIL after we heard the butler show Franklin to the door that Aunt took out the society columns of the newspapers. She passed them to me after she had finished with reading them.

———

The New York Journal—Society
January 15, 1892

Miss Carter dazzled at the Vandermeres' last night, her dress a perfect confection of lace and satin in shimmering gold. When asked if she was intent upon capturing the hearts of all of the men in our fair city, the lovely Miss Carter demurred. Are there any stars in the firmament which shine brighter? Are there any butterflies in Central Park which dance on lighter feet? Beware you angels in the heavens, there is one still more fair who dwells among us mortals.

The Tattler
January 15, 1892

... and at the Vandermeres' ball, other intrigues were afoot. Let the observer remain vigilant. If the lives of past debutantes of this fair city are any indication, what is expected or predicted does not always occur. And many a presumably faithful heart has been known to wander.

I had been at the Vandermeres' ball, of course, but I hadn't noticed any such intrigues. I made a note to ask Lizzie. If any flirting had taken place, if she hadn't been a part of it, she would know who had been.

A faithful heart—known to wander? Whose could it be?

I still hadn't solved the mystery by the time of the New Year's Ball. It was held at Madison Square Garden. And since the guest list was expanded to one thousand, Lizzie was to be there. As was Harry. And Franklin.

A BOY DRESSED in livery handed me out of the carriage that night. Thankfully, the arcade in front of the Garden had been enclosed so none of the assembled crowds were able to catch a glimpse of me. But even so, I heard a few whispered "Miss Carter!"s as I walked into the building.

As I did so, I was enveloped in a jungle. Winter's chill grip found no hold here. There were palms and other exotic plants lining the entrance. And branches of cypress had been woven overhead. The main ballroom had been decorated with masses of pink blossoms and light-colored greens, a perfect portrait of an early spring. And the lights had been draped in pink gauze so that their electric brilliance was dimmed.

The throngs were so great that it was difficult to move. I ran into Mr. Hooper as I tried to push into the interior of the building.

I turned from him as soon as I saw him open his mouth, praying that he would not ask to sign my dance card. He did not. But Harry signed for a lancers and a polka and Franklin for two waltzes.

During the first intermission, Harry escorted me up to where his sister was watching the dancing from a box. Along the way I saw Mr. Douglas, lurking in the shadows. I nodded his way and he nodded back before I was pulled into the box by Harry.

"You've brought Clara to me!" Katherine extended a hand and drew me down to sit in a chair beside her.

"She was my excuse to evade all those fluttering debutantes. I don't know what they want with me when Franklin is the heir."

I did. And the memory of my deceit still had the ability to prick my conscience.

We stayed there speaking of his travels and her life in Germany until the orchestra took up its place again. But as they launched into the lancers, Harry didn't move to take me out onto the dance floor. It was actually quite refreshing. I enjoyed being able to listen to the music without having to dance to it.

When the music to his polka began, still we stayed in conversation with Katherine. In fact, I sat right there talking with Harry until his dances were over. Both of them. And he only realized it as the second one came to an end.

"But I haven't even danced with you yet!"

"I know. You claimed two dances on my card and didn't even bother to show me to the dance floor!"

"Really, Harry. How could you?" His sister looked only mildly distressed.

"But I have to have at least one dance."

"You had two dances."

"And danced neither of them! Give me your card."

Katherine was laughing at him. "Don't do it, Clara. Someone has to teach him some manners."

"I can't, Harry. They're all taken."

I felt a tap on my shoulder and turned to find one of the Lorillards. "Forgive my haste in removing you from this box, Miss Carter. Our polka begins and you hid yourself so well up here that it was difficult to find you!"

"But—" Harry's protest was loud but ineffectual.

"I'm sorry." I left the box with Katherine's laughter tinkling in my ears.

———

AFTER THAT, FRANKLIN came to claim me for the first of his two dances. As it ended, he turned me into a whirl and then spun me into the arms of Harry.

"But—"

Franklin bowed. "I leave you to a better man than I." He disappeared into the crowd.

Harry let go my hands and took a step back from me. "You aren't disappointed?"

"No." In fact, I wasn't. I was relieved. It was fatiguing to keep up with Franklin's waltz and put on a smile and think up something to converse about just in case ... all the while dancing with my eyes closed. I needed a respite. And Harry was just the person to provide it.

"While you were dancing with Lorillard, I convinced Franklin that he needed a cigar."

A cigar? I ought to have been annoyed, but I couldn't be. Not when he had rescued me.

"Look at what a mania you've started."

"What mania?"

"The one for dancing with your eyes closed."

"I haven't."

"You have. Look. Just keep your eyes open for a moment as the dance begins."

I did it. And Harry was right. All around me, girls closed their eyes and raised their chins, leaned into the music as if it might carry them away from all of their trials. As we turned first this way and then that, the skirts of the gowns blurred together into one fabulous palette of color. It was magical. Glorious!

His hand wrapped around my waist. "It always reminds me of Holland in the spring."

"What does?"

"A ballroom. With all of the colorful gowns. It's like the tulip fields in Lisse."

"You've been to Holland?"

"I have." He paused to look at me. "And what's more: I want to go again."

This then was one advantage to wealth. "I've always wanted to travel. To Italy."

"That's one place I haven't yet been."

"Why not?"

"We were recalled. A year early. It has been ordained, you know, that Franklin must wed."

Oh, I knew.

"But if you've always wanted to travel, then why don't you?"

I very nearly shrugged before I remembered not to. "I can't."

"Why not?"

"Because it's just not done. How would I do it? What would I say?"

He grinned. "*Bon voyage*—I'm off to the Continent. That seemed to work for me."

"But you're a man."

"Yes. Yes, I am."

"You can do whatever you want. But I'm a girl—"

"Yes, indeed you are!"

I frowned. He was teasing me.

"Forgive me. As you were saying?"

"I cannot just go wherever I want whenever I please. I have to be escorted. And who would escort me abroad?"

"I would."

I laughed.

"I would!" His protest was tinged by his own laughter.

"You can't."

"And why not?"

"Because we aren't—" I was going to say married, but that would have been presumptuous. "Because you can't. It wouldn't be proper."

"Far be it from me to know polite from improper, but I believe you just danced your first waltz properly. With your eyes open."

I had? I had! I had done it! I had danced an entire waltz with my eyes wide open.

AS THE CARRIAGE sped through the night toward home, it seemed that shadows fled at our approach. I blinked, hard, several times, certain my eyes were simply overtired. But then, at the next block, the shadows seemed to take on actual shapes. Of children.

"What are they doing?"

Aunt lifted her head, glanced out the window. "Who?"

"Are they children?" Jacob Riis's children? Orphans who spent their nights on the streets?

She squinted for a moment into the darkness, then she fell back against her seat. "They're urchins. Fleeing before they get caught."

"Caught doing what?"

"Sleeping under the stoops. Or on top of the grates." She said it as if it were reasonable for people to do such things.

"If only they had someplace to go, someplace warm. And something to eat."

"Well, they've nowhere. And nothing. And we can't have people sleeping on the street wherever they please."

"But shouldn't—"

"Forget them."

I couldn't. They had resurrected the images in Riis's book.

———

WE STEPPED INTO the house as the clock tolled four. And as soon as we had done so, Aunt began to scold me. "There was altogether too much laughing and too much conversing tonight."

"With Franklin?" I hardly ever talked to Franklin, let alone laughed with him. We mostly just danced.

"With the younger son. He is a De Vries and such an alliance is not the worst of things. But you would not want the heir to get the wrong impression."

"And what impression would that be?" The night's activities must have made me bold.

"You would not want him to think you preferred his brother to himself."

Perhaps not, even though I did.

"Just be careful."

Of Harry? There was no one I could think of who was less dangerous. "Why does it have to be Franklin?"

"Listen to me. I was in your situation once, so don't think I don't understand. I do. Only it was Franklin's father who courted me."

Mr. De Vries had courted Aunt?

"Don't look so amazed. I was beautiful once, the belle of the city. Only I had no money. All I had was my fair skin and my glossy hair and my smile."

I could not bear to look at Aunt. Not when what I saw was so different from the image she had just painted. I could not reconcile it with what she was telling me.

"My mother told me it was enough. But it wasn't. She told me I was as good as any De Vries. But I wasn't. Oh, he danced with me and he kissed me in the moonlight, but after the season was over, it was Edith Wentworth he married, not me."

"Maybe it wasn't you, Aunt. Maybe it was him. Maybe Mrs. De Vries was his heart's choice." I had meant to try to release her from the burden of the past, but my words didn't come out as I meant them. And as soon as they had died in the air, the illusion of youth that had passed over Aunt's features dissolved too.

She sighed.

"But you did marry."

"Yes. I did. I married into one of the old families. One of the old, fabled, *poor* families. I married a second son—the son who had all the proper connections but none of the money to go with them. And when my parents died, Brother was left to my care. The little I had, I put on deposit for him at the De Vrieses' bank. But when the Panic of '73 hit, we discovered it to mean nothing. All the money vanished in an instant." She laughed, but it was bitter and filled with rancor.

"Oh, we had ancestors and artifacts and relics. But in this day, in this gilded age, family means nothing. Money means everything. Your father had meant to marry some, but what could be done? He had nothing left to offer. It was while he was taking solace in Newport that he happened upon your mother. She was the most beautiful girl he had ever seen. As beautiful a girl as New York City had ever seen. And he vowed then that one day he would own this town. That one day all the money that the De Vrieses had lost would come back to him. With interest. And make no mistake. With you, that promise will be kept."

"But what if—"

"Money means everything, and we mean for you to have as much of it as you can get. You must redeem us. And you will do it by marrying the heir."

I bowed my head to her words and started up the stairs.

Aunt called out from behind me. "Whether he knows it or not, Franklin will marry you. And it's in your best interest to let Lizzie know sooner rather than later. Do you not agree?"

"But how will I? I don't know if I can--! How can I make Franklin marry me?"

Her gaze seemed to soften. "You are enchanting, in spite of being so tall, despite your wide mouth and lack of bosoms. You really are quite striking. So, if you had nothing else at all, you have your looks."

"But you just said—"

"Looks have been known to entice even the most staid of men. But do not worry. Franklin is smart. He will know what choice to make."

"But what about me? Don't I have a choice?" Shouldn't I have a choice?

She reached out to pat my hand. "Of course, you do. You may choose orange blossoms or roses for your wedding."

"But what if I don't like him?"

"Don't you?"

"I don't know." I really, truly didn't.

"Well, let me tell you: Whether you do or whether you don't, money makes life much better. And it's easier to live with a rich man than a poor one."

"But what if I don't want money?"

"Don't want money!" She gave a short bark of a laugh. And when Aunt looked at me, it was with something close to pity. "Oh, my dear girl, you don't know what you want, and you're too young to know what you need."

"But shouldn't I at least be happy?"

"Pray for happiness and hope for the best. Happiness has never been sufficient grounds to marry. Or not."

"If marriage is so important, then why have you never remarried?"

Her smile seemed to freeze upon her face. And then it with-ered. "I have earned the right to wear my widow's cap. I paid for it with years of unhappiness and many tears. And I'll surrender it to no man!" She paused, and when she began again it was with a lower, more controlled voice. "You cannot understand it now, but the best legacy Mr. Stuart passed on to me was the use of his name. And the right to place the word *Widow* before it. When Mr. De Vries approaches, you must smile and be captivating. And maybe one day, you too will find yourself to be a widow. With all the vast means of the De Vries family at your disposal. And then you can turn your attentions toward happiness."

CHAPTER 21

$\mathcal{L}$IZZIE WELCOMED ME into the hedge that Thursday, eyes shining. "I'm to have a dinner party!"

"A dinner party?"

"Yes! And you're to be invited."

"Aunt will never let me come." And it was too bad, for I would have dearly loved to.

"Of course, she'll let you come."

"She won't. She wants me to have nothing to do with you."

"But you have to come. I've already forced Mama to send you an invitation."

"Forced her?"

"She says that you're my only rival. And it's even odds on which of us will end up with the heir."

Mrs. Barnes didn't like me? Didn't want me? She'd been Mama's closest friend!

"But I said that if she didn't, I'd cry myself sick and wouldn't attend any events for a week."

"You didn't!"

"I did."

"You would never have done it."

Her smile, when it came, was sly. "She seemed to think I might have."

"Lizzie. You're incorrigible!"

"I know. That's why you have to come."

If I could, I would. "When did you send the invitation?"

"This morning. By messenger."

Then Aunt might already have received it.

"Just tell your aunt I plan to trap Franklin into marrying me, that you overheard me say it. And I did. Just now."

"It's still a lie, Lizzie."

"It's a partial truth. For a noble cause. Please."

"She'll find me out."

"She won't. She's too blinded by her ambition. The thought of Franklin being alone with me will frustrate her to no end. Just watch if it doesn't!" Lizzie disappeared behind the wall with a flounce.

———

THAT AFTERNOON I was called to Aunt's room.

"I have received an invitation. For you. To *Lizzie Barnes's* for a dinner party. It would behoove you to discover who she has invited."

"A dinner party? I think maybe . . ."

"Yes?"

"I remember overhearing Lizzie say . . ." How exactly had she phrased it?

"Yes?"

"I overheard her saying that she planned to trap Franklin into marrying her."

"She did?"

"She did."

Aunt held her lorgnette up to her eyes and then studied the invitation. She turned it over and turned it back. She set it down on her lap, then picked it up once more. And at last, she reached over and began to scratch one of her dogs on the belly with it. "Then I have no choice but to send you. You'll be accompanied by your father." She tossed the invitation in my direction. "Cheap. Cheap pasteboard. And not even engraved. They are not a respectable family. Not now. Though perhaps they were before the war. Before he married that Southerner."

I ignored Aunt's slurs and picked up the invitation. It was lovely. Pink in color and typeset in an ornate filigree, it looked just like Lizzie.

"You may go, but you are not to arrive until half past eight."

"But the invitation reads eight o'clock."

"Then the dinner party will not be able to start until you have arrived, will it? Take up a piece of paper and a pen. We'll see how well Miss Miller taught you."

I did as Aunt requested.

"You will write, 'My dear Mrs. Barnes, Miss Carter and her father are delighted to attend. Thank you for your kind invitation. Sincerely . . .'" Aunt gestured for the paper and pen, then signed it.

"Now put it in an envelope, but do not mail it until Monday."

"But—"

"We do not know what invitations await you next week. Lizzie's dinner may be the least of them."

"Won't they wish to know if I'll be attending? So that they can plan—"

"Of course, they'll wish to know. But we do not always, any of us, get what we want, do we? It will do no harm to keep them guessing. And you must not seem so eager. I'm of half a mind not to let you go."

I did not respond, though Aunt sent a keen glance at me from behind her lorgnette. "That is all."

I walked through her door and shut it behind me as I heaved a sigh of relief.

THE NEXT WEEK'S mail held invitations to even more dinner parties and more balls. Aunt, sitting at her desk, attacked them with ferocity.

'Another for you." She removed the envelope from the bunch and then slit it open, pulling out a card. She smiled. "Delmonico's! A dinner party to be given by the Schemerhorns! I'll have to find out who's on the guest list."

"Delmonico's?"

"Where the Patriarch's Ball was held. But this is to be a dinner party. So only the very best of the best society will be attending. And dining on oysters."

"Oysters?" I couldn't help pulling a face.

Aunt looked up at me. "Oysters. If you go to Delmonico's for dinner, then you must eat oysters."

"I don't like oysters."

Her mouth seemed to tighten. "If you go to Delmonico's for dinner, then you must eat oysters."

"Oysters make me retch."

"Then we'll just have to practice eating them, won't we?"

Practice began that very day. Oysters for lunch, in a stew. And for dinner, on ice with lemon. "I think it's the way they smell. And the way they look." Stewed or on ice, they still made my stomach heave.

"You may *not* close your eyes while eating them."

I hadn't thought I would. But if I could just somehow avoid looking at them, then perhaps I would actually be able to eat one. Because I hadn't yet succeeded. They truly did make me retch. That's why Mama had never served them. "Why do they have to be so slippery?"

"They aren't. Not when they're stewed."

"Then they're chewy." And I had not been able to decide which was worse.

She watched me as I took one up and squeezed a bit of lemon juice onto it.

"Very good."

I speared one with an oyster fork and raised it to my lips. Determined to eat it, I opened my lips and—I dropped it to my plate.

"If you would just taste it, then you might like it!"

"I can't. And I won't."

"You can't not eat oysters at Delmonico's. It's just not done."

"Well, perhaps I can set another trend. I *am* Miss Carter, arbiter and mistress-in-chief of all that's fashionable. And oysters are not." I rose, putting my napkin on the table beside the plate, and left the room.

———

THE NEXT DAY was Lizzie's party. Aunt summoned her maid to dress my hair. "Not too ornately. It's only a dinner party given by the Barneses."

At least, due to her disapproval, I was given a coiffure that didn't poke or pull. I had expected to wear my new dinner gown —a gown that one of the dressmakers in town had sent me. Aunt, however, asked for the old one.

"But—"

She stared at me.

"The De Vries heir will be there."

She sighed. Pressed her lips together. "So he shall. No"—she waved the old gown away—"we want the new one."

It was a simple gown of yellow net with ruching about the bottom, but sprays of embroidered pansies had been scattered about the skirt and lined the edge of the collar. It was both elegant and charming and one of the prettiest dresses I'd ever seen.

I WOULD HAVE walked to Lizzie's house that evening, but Aunt insisted on the carriage. And so we sat within it, Father and I, for the twenty seconds it took to arrive.

Once there, we were greeted by a butler, had our cloaks taken by a footman, and then were shown further into the front hall, where Lizzie stood to greet her guests.

"Finally! I kept assuring Mama that you were coming. I don't think she believed me."

"I'm sorry. My aunt." Those two words were all it took to erase the rebuke from Lizzie's eyes and replace it with sympathy. She linked her arm through mine and together we walked toward the parlor.

I could see Harry and several other guests, as well as Lizzie's mother and father.

But . . . "Where's Franklin?"

"Over in the corner."

As I walked into the parlor, I could see that the rest of the guests were also bachelors. "So many men!"

"Franklin mustn't think he's the only contender for my affections."

"Of course not."

"And neither must he think it of you." She smiled brightly and twirled her fan.

I smiled at her and twirled mine in response. It was only then that I noticed that there were quite a few pairs of eyes trained upon us both.

She left me then and went to talk, not to Franklin, not to Harry, but to Mr. Porter and Mr. Lorillard, who were standing together in front of the fireplace. But Mrs. Barnes called us to dinner shortly thereafter. And I can't say that I was disappointed. The table was magnificently set with silver and decorated with orchids. There were spoons and forks and knives in abundance.

I was seated between Father and Harry.

As Harry took his seat, he glanced over at me. "Good evening, Miss Carter."

"Good evening, Mr. De Vries. Father? Do you know Mr. De Vries?"

Father glanced over my head at Harry. "We have not met."

"No." Harry was smiling genially.

"I have, however, attended your family in the past."

"Father is a physician."

Harry nodded.

"I believe it was your sister I saw most recently."

"It can't have been that recent. She's been living abroad for —"

"Eight years now, if I recall correctly."

If he recalled correctly? With Father's bright eye and precise speech, there seemed little need to doubt the veracity of his memory.

"Yes." Harry seemed more attentive now. "Yes, she has. Eight years now."

"I trust she is doing well."

"Quite." Harry spoke that one word with the finality of the end of a conversation.

"Good." And Father did the same.

Harry ate through the courses with practiced ease. Through a lobster bisque and salmon with cucumber. Through a roast of lamb served with mint jelly. It was obvious that he had no difficulty remembering which knife to use or which spoon to take up . . . until a dish of beef marrow was served with points of toast and a lemon salad.

He began to attack the bone with a regular knife and spoon.

Until I nudged him with an elbow. "The marrow shovel." It

was meant to reach down to the bottom of a bone and lift the marrow out.

He reached for the utensil. "That's right. I always forget!"

He wouldn't if Aunt had been his teacher.

"Why do you think it is that we can't just use a knife?"

I smothered a laugh as I remembered that I had asked Aunt that very same thing. "I don't know."

"Neither do I. This table is a pigeon trap. A dozen different forks and knives and spoons. Four different goblets, all of them just waiting to be knocked over or misapplied and mishandled. It's a wonder anyone is ever tempted to eat!"

"You're doing quite well."

"Franklin's much better at all of this than I am."

"But you're much better at conversing."

"And making you laugh? Am I better at that?"

I smiled. "Yes. I would say so."

"Good. Because that, at least, is something worthwhile."

CHAPTER 22

*A*FTER DINNER, Mrs. Barnes played the piano while Lizzie sang. She performed "Deh Vieni, Non Tardar" from *The Marriage of Figaro.*

Oh come, don't delay.

I hoped Franklin was listening. If he married Lizzie, then he wouldn't have to marry me. And I would be freed ... to marry someone else.

Then Lizzie sang her mother's favorite. "The Jewel Song" from Faust. And then "Funiculi, Funicula" and "Oh, Promise Me."

It was while she sang the third song that I began to feel a most peculiar sensation in the deepest regions of my stomach. A growing pressure that pushed, unlike my corset, from the inside to the out. I shifted in my seat, trying to relieve it.

Harry, sitting next to me, glanced over.

I smiled. Much more cheerfully, I hoped, than I felt. As I sat there, listening to note after note, song after song, the pressure within me built to a near intolerable level. At the end of the last song, I was the first to leave my chair and applaud. And there, standing on my feet, some of the pressure seemed to subside.

As Lizzie and her mother left the piano and headed toward the other end of the parlor, the guests followed them. Harry glanced over at me. "Would you like to play a duet?"

And risk sitting down again? "No! No. No, thank you."

His smile dimmed. "I understand."

Understood what? That . . . Oh no! He understood that I hadn't wished to sit beside him. "No, I might not wish to play a duet, but would you not rather like to . . ."What? What could I offer in its stead? "It's so difficult, while playing the piano, to be able to talk. Don't you think?"

He nodded.

"Then why not let's just talk. We could talk right here. Away from the rest, where we can see each other. And hear each other. Wouldn't you much rather? And I could show you ..." I knew the Barneses' parlor like I knew my own. But what would be of interest to Harry? An international traveler who had seen the latest of what Europe had to offer? "I could show you Lizzie's collection of skeleton leaves!"

"Her skeleton leaves? Then by all means, lead on."

I walked over and gestured to a shelf above the piano. Lizzie's handiwork was displayed under a glass dome. In fact, that particular work was a phantom bouquet made entirely of skeleton leaves arranged in a cut glass vase. "Lizzie's so very good at these." I couldn't do the work; it was too tedious. But Lizzie reveled in boiling leaves and then rubbing the flesh away to reveal the skeletal structures beneath.

"Is she?" His mouth quirked up on one side.

"She's a genius with leaves. And it exhibits such beauty in death." At least that was what Lizzie proclaimed. Though the pressure within me had subsided, I had begun to feel a bit light-headed. And a sweat had broken out behind my ears.

"Are you feeling well?"

"Yes. Fine. And you must see this example over here." I led him away from the piano to a small marble pedestal where another collection of leaves had been caged under a glass dome.

"Ah. Yes. A very fine example of handiwork."

"Yes."

We stood there, the two of us, looking at Lizzie's accomplishment.

Harry leaned close. "What is it for?"

"Why, it's . . . one just . . . I honestly don't know." What did one do with a skeleton leaf? "But her mother takes great pride in it."

"Mothers take great pride in all sorts of unreasonable things. Witness Franklin, for example. My mother's pride is based on the fact that he will, upon my father's death, take leadership of one of the largest banking empires in the country."

I glanced over at him. I was not quite sure what to say. Shouldn't mothers take pride in those sorts of things?

"Even though, if you ask him the difference between an acquittance and an acquisition, he could give you no decisive opinion."

"What is the difference?"

"I have no idea, but there must be one. Wouldn't you think?" He put the question to me in the same way Miss Miller might have.

"There must be."

"So we're agreed. There must be one. We don't know what it is, but don't you think Franklin ought to? If he's going to be in the business of dealing in them?"

"One would think."

"Of course one would."

We stood there for at least a minute, gazing at Lizzie's bouquets. And the absurdity of her handiwork and the extreme effort we were putting into appreciating it nearly drove me to convulsions of laughter. And so, to hide my mirth, I turned my back on the ghastly thing and asked him a question. "If your father's businesses go to Franklin, what is it that you want to do?"

He shrugged.

"Is there nothing that holds your interest?"

"There are some things."

"Such as?"

"Such as . . . art." He spoke the word as if it were a confession.

"Art?"

"Yes. I could spend all day looking at a painting." Enthusiasm had lit him from within. "A well-conceived one."

"Like a Rembrandt? Or a Rubens?"

"Yes. But there are some new painters. Gauguin. Bernard. Van Gogh. Not anymore, of course—unfortunate circumstances —but there's another like him. A fellow in Paris. Name of Signac. He paints in dots." His hands had begun to speak on his behalf. "Masses of them in all different colors. Quite structured and regimented. But really quite wonderful. I can't create art; I'm too literal. But I enjoy it. If I could do anything, I should like to deal in it."

"Acquire it?"

"Yes. But also support it. Nurture it. There's been some talk of sending me back to Europe. In the summer."

"Why?" The thought of the city without Harry made it feel much less friendly.

"To acquire dusty old antiques for the family's collections." He winked.

I blushed. "Would you like to?"

"There's almost nothing I would like better."

Almost nothing? It was on the tip of my tongue to ask him what it was that he *would* like better when I saw my father on the approach and thought it more prudent to turn my attentions toward Franklin instead.

"I hope they send you then."

"You do?" He looked as if my words had startled him.

"Isn't that what you want?"

Father had reached me and offered me his arm.

I smiled at Harry. "It was so good of you to spend your time in conversation with me." *So good of you?* I sounded like Aunt! Father turned me away from Harry. "Isn't the heir the other boy?"

"Yes."

"The one that Lizzie's been clinging to all evening?"

"She hasn't been clinging." And besides, it was her party. And if she held on to him, then I wouldn't have to talk to him. It would spare me thinking up something to say.

Father looked at me sharply. Grabbing my hand, he placed a finger to my wrist. "Are you feeling quite well?"

"Not exactly."

"A bit short of breath?"

"Yes."

"Light-headed?"

"Yes."

"Anxious?"

I nodded.

"The beginnings of female hysteria. Your mother was prone to it. Take a deep breath."

I breathed as deeply as my corset allowed.

"And another."

As I was breathing, he passed a vial beneath my nose. My eyes watered at the scent of it. I coughed.

"There. The color's begun to come back into your cheeks. You're pretty as a posy once more." He leaned close. "Introduce me to the De Vries boy. I haven't properly met him yet." Father stepped over toward the piano, where Franklin was playing a duet with Lizzie.

I had no choice but to follow.

We came up to them just as they were finishing a song.

Father clapped loudly. "Marvelous. I had not known you to be such an accomplished pianist, Miss Barnes. And at such a young age."

Lizzie looked a question at me.

I tried to shrug without shrugging. Certainly, Father should know how old she was. Hadn't he delivered her? Lizzie was nearly the exact same age as me.

Franklin had stood at the sound of Father's clapping. He put out his hand. "Franklin De Vries, sir."

"Dr. Carter. Aren't you the fellow who was so kind to help my sister at the opera opening? I assume you've been introduced to my daughter since then?"

As Franklin turned toward me, Lizzie slipped away from the piano bench, mouthing a *thank you* as she flitted away.

Father and Franklin talked at length about the different clubs in which they shared membership. I was beginning to feel quite left out when the topic turned to something I knew.

"The Riis book? You mean Mr. Jacob Riis?" I had blurted out the words before I realized I was saying them. I wished I had followed the conversation long enough to know how they had stumbled onto the topic. But since they had, why should I not be a part of it? I turned to Franklin. "Have you read it, Mr. De Vries?"

He frowned at me in such a way that I wished I hadn't said anything at all. "Isn't it about immigrants? Filled with lurid details and sensational stories?"

Father answered him. "It is indeed."

"And isn't Riis himself an immigrant?"

I spoke before Father could. "He is, but—"

"Then I can't believe any reasoning person would consider anything he has to say." Franklin spoke with finality.

Father was nodding in agreement, but I could not keep myself from speaking. "Then you haven't seen the photographs!"

"Photographs?" Father had raised his brow in a way that made me feel as if I were six years old again.

Franklin cast Father a look before he turned to me. "You may not know this, Miss Carter, but photographs can be staged. They can be prearranged, so to speak. In advance. And in that case, they're worse than a lie."

"But these weren't."

"And how can you be sure, dear girl, if you weren't there?" Father patted my hand as he spoke, but he clearly wanted me to be silent. He turned his back to me and fixed upon Franklin. "The book is clearly Tammany Hall and the Democrats at work. They're the only ones who seem to care about the immigrants."

"It pays them dividends come Election Day."

But they were wrong. "The book isn't about politics. It's about people!" Why could they not understand that? And why didn't they just read the book for themselves and then form an opinion?

"Forgive her, Mr. De Vries. Women shouldn't be allowed to discuss politics. They can never hope to understand them." He turned to me and winked. "My dear Clara, people *are* politics. Even if those poor souls down on the East Side are only fit for prison."

"But—"

Franklin smiled. "Don't worry yourself any more about them, Miss Carter. What was it our Lord once said? The poor will always be with us?"

Yes, perhaps. But hadn't He also said, *"Inasmuch as ye have done it unto one of the least of these my brethren, ye have done it unto me"*?

———

FATHER'S CURE FOR my light-headedness wasn't wholly successful. By the time the evening drew to an end, my anxiety had reached new levels. And I had a desperate wish to hide myself in some dark corner, sink to my heels, and rock back and forth against the growing pain and pressure in my stomach. Only I couldn't. And even if I could, my corset wouldn't have let me.

I clasped Lizzie's hand in farewell.

As I did so, she turned us away from her mother and told me to meet her in the hedge the next afternoon. I nodded before rejoining Father.

We had scarcely stepped through the door and shed our cloaks when Aunt began to question us. "What did they serve?"

I recited the menu by heart. "A lobster bisque and salmon with cucumber. Roast of lamb served with mint jelly. And a marrow with lemon salad." Why was it that food that had tasted so good now seemed to have staled in the remembering? "With kickshaws to start."

"*Kickshaws*! They are not kickshaws. They are *quelque chose*. French for . . . for . . ."

French for kickshaws I imagined, those small dainty morsels that were served before dinner. "And nearly every sort of dessert you can imagine." The novelty of all of the creams and custards and ices had dimmed in the ensuing hours. What I had eaten with relish had turned sour in the depths of my stomach.

Aunt sniffed. "You'll have a bellyache for sure."

I already did.

"And what did Lizzie wear?"

"Spotted tulle."

"She didn't! She must have looked like some overgrown child. What color was it?"

"Pink."

"Well. At least your gown was yellow. It must have shone by gaslight."

"The Barneses converted to electric lights. Two months ago."

"Electric! They do so little for the complexion. And change completely the colors of one's gown. Vulgarity in the extreme!"

I left Aunt clucking in the hall and went upstairs to my room.

————

TAKING TO MY bed did little to ease my discomfort. And sitting up eased no pain.

I took away all of my pillows only to discover that if I lay on one side, it sent a gurgle through my stomach. If I turned over, it sent the gurgle back to the other side. And if lying on my back pushed the weight of all I had eaten against my backbone, lying on my stomach was simply not an option.

I surrendered, finally, to a fitful sleep. Dreams of Lizzie's dinner intermingled with visions of roast lamb, puddles of cream, and my own mother. A red lobster began to chase me, and as I was trying to escape, I tripped on a rumple in the carpet. I stretched out my hands into the interminable fathoms of dreams and the skeleton bouquet I was carrying dropped away. It seemed to me then that we were in Mama's room. That I knew what would happen next.

She had been waiting for me, lying on her bed. And in her illness she was helpless to do anything but observe my approach.

I remember thinking that whatever I did, I must not touch her. must not harm her. And so, as I stumbled on the carpet, I made one last valiant effort to avoid her body. I threw my arms out, one hand missing her entirely, and the other coming to rest between her legs. I sighed in relief, knowing it had encountered only a pillow.

But as I was congratulating myself on saving her, she suddenly and terrifically paled. And then she fainted dead away.

And even in my dream, even though I knew that I was in fact dreaming, I knew what must happen next.

She sickened rapidly.

Her eyes were swallowed by massive bruises. The pastiness of her pale skin became tinged with yellow.

"I've killed you, Mama."

"No."

"But I hurt you when I fell on you."

"I hurt myself long ago. You had nothing to do with it."

"What will I do? Once you've gone?"

She had tried to smile. I could tell by the look in her eyes. And then she began to sing. "'Just as I am . . . '" but she didn't have the strength to continue on.

"I don't—I can't remember that one!" It had been ages since we had sung it at church. "Sing it to me so I'll remember it."

But, as she had so often done during those last days, she glided off into sleep instead.

———

I WOKE MYSELF with moaning. And I was not the only one I woke. Aunt had come to my bedside, holding a taper. A maid lurked in the doorway behind her.

"What is it?"

"I feel as if . . ." Oh, I hardly had words for it. I felt as if I were suffocating. But if I breathed too deeply, I feared I might stir the nausea once more. It felt as if there were some urgency deep inside that was driving me to stand, to walk. But what I wanted, more than anything, was to sleep. "I feel ill."

Aunt placed a hand to my head. "You're perspiring, but you have no fever." It was not her words that comforted me, but the fact of her presence. I could count the times she had touched me in kindness on one hand.

"I . . ." Whatever it was I had meant to say was forgotten by the throbbing of my head. And the churning of my stomach.

"Drink this."

"What is it?"

"Something that will cure what ails you."

I took it from her outstretched hand and drank it all.

She motioned a maid to my side.

I collapsed back against my pillows. But only for a moment, for in the next instant everything I had eaten at dinner the night before came barreling back up my throat in one great heave.

The maid offered up a silver bucket just in time.

Afterward, Aunt sat on the side of my bed and patted my hand. "There now. Don't you feel better?"

I couldn't respond. I was still trying to catch my breath.

Aunt gestured for me to roll to my side and then loosed the strings of my corset.

"Thank you."

She patted my hand again. The patting, the closeness, seemed to contribute to an awkwardness between us. I wished she would go back to her bedroom.

"Now then. You must be more careful in what you eat. The corset is limiting. Less meat, fewer sauces. No champagne. The corset cannot support it."

The corset? The corset supported it well enough. Too well, in fact. It was me who couldn't support it.

"I remember how it was with my own debut. Do not worry; we've all been through it. You will learn what to eat and what you shouldn't, and soon there will be no more mistakes."

CHAPTER 23

J MET LIZZIE the next day, out behind the hedge. It wasn't our usual Thursday, but she'd asked me at her party to meet this day instead. She appeared, wan and pale, like a wraith or a spirit. The cold had left an imprint of color upon her cheeks, but her eyes did not reflect the vigor. "Wasn't it amazing? The dinner party?"

"It was." We leaned against the bushes, burrowing our hands deeper into our muffs. I tried to remain as still as possible, to move as slowly as I could in order to keep my head from spinning like a top.

She put a hand to her head for a moment. Closed her eyes. "Oh, Clara, I was so sick last night." Her hand left her head to hover over her mouth. She closed her eyes once more.

"I was sick too."

"Mama said it was the food."

"That's what Aunt said."

She opened her eyes at last. "I'm never eating anything more than a leaf of lettuce again!" Her mood seemed to lighten. "Did you see Harry start to use his knife and spoon for the marrow shovel?" "He said he never remembers it's there."

"Truly? I wish we'd sat him near me. He's always so comfortable. So easy to talk to." She kicked at the knob of a root that was pushing up from the ground. Then she turned her face toward mine. "Thank you for rescuing me. At the piano."

"Rescuing you?"

"I'm never quite sure what to say to him."

"To Franklin?"

"Yes."

She could never think of what to say? "I would never have guessed."

"Why do you think I always propose playing duets or dancing or singing?"

"You always seem as if you're in high spirits with him."

"Do I?" Surprise colored her words.

I nodded.

"That's good." She was silent for a moment. "You don't think it will be like that for always, do you?"

"Like what?"

"I mean . . . after you're married to someone. Do you think it will be like that? Always having to think of something to do because there's nothing to say?"

Would it? "I don't know."

"It can't be, can it? Surely once you've married there are heaps of things to talk about." She said it as if she were trying to convince herself.

"There must be."

Lizzie laughed. "Otherwise, I'd run out of duets to play! And dances to dance. Surely once you've married it must be different. Otherwise, you'd have to travel. And keep giving parties. And moving houses. Or redecorating. There aren't enough things that can be done, are there? To escape from a man?"

I shook my head. There wouldn't be.

"Well . . ." She lifted her chin and glanced off toward the gate. "Franklin's not like that. He can't be."

"It's not like that with your mother and father. is it?"

Her mouth flattened as her eyes busied themselves with the foliage of the shrub. "I don't see them much. At least not together. They must talk . . . sometimes. When I'm not around."

"I'm sure they do. If it becomes too difficult with Franklin, just give me a sign with your fan. You know I'll come."

She smiled, leaned close, and kissed my cheek. "You're a darling. I know you will. And I'll always come for you too." She took a hand from her muff. Pushed back a branch to duck behind it. "I'm off now. We're to go to McCreery's. For another hat."

She disappeared and soon I heard the gate squeak open and then clang shut. She'd gone. But she'd left behind her troubles. Because I knew I couldn't always come for her. And I knew that she couldn't always come for me.

Not once we'd married.

And what would happen then?

———

AFTER MY EXTREME indigestion the night of Lizzie's party, a truce had reigned between Aunt and me concerning food. "If you don't think you can manage the oysters, then don't try," she declared the night of the Schemerhorns' party at Delmonico's.

"I can't. So I won't."

"Just remember: There is only a month left in the season. If it gets around that you don't eat oysters, I don't know if there will be time enough to fix the damage." Though she frowned, Aunt refrained from saying anything further.

As my foot hit the pavement at the restaurant, I heard a familiar whisper run through the crowd.

"Miss Carter!" "Here? Where?" "Who is she wearing?" "Where is she going?"

I raised my chin and determined not to think about them,

those unknown faceless masses that seemed to be waiting for me everywhere I went.

Once inside, once we had been delivered of our cloaks, we were shown into a private dining room. As we passed from the hall into the room, Aunt's hand clutched at me. "Ward McAllister." She said it with an undertone of great fear and great respect.

"Who?"

"Mrs. Jacob Astor's social secretary. For heaven's sake, please try to eat those oysters! If he decides not to like you, for any reason at all, you're finished! You might as well just drop out of the season."

As we took our seats at the table, I discovered that Mr. Hooper was among the guests. Thankfully, he was seated far down the table on my side. His malevolent stares would have to be directed at someone else. Mr. McAllister, however, was seated at my immediate left. And at my right, Aunt nearly swooned.

The first course was oysters. In ice. Not on, but *in*. Each of the guests was given a plate holding a small block of ice sitting atop a napkin and surrounded by parsley and lemon. I spied an oyster fork as part of my utensils, but no ice pick. Further inspection revealed that a cavity had been created in the ice and the oysters placed inside it.

Beside me, Mr. McAllister took up an oyster fork and fished one from his block of ice, deftly squeezed a bit of lemon juice onto it and then swallowed it whole. He turned to me as I was trying to decide what to do with my own oysters. Perhaps if I removed them, one by one, I could hide them between the sprigs of parsley. "I have been admiring your beauty from afar this season, Miss Carter."

"Your words are very kind."

"I speak the simple truth."

I leaned toward him. It was especially important that Aunt

not be able to hear what I was going to say. "Then you wouldn't fault a girl for being truthful in return?"

He stroked his mustache for a moment. "Absolutely not, though I must say that I find the thought of anyone here speaking the *simple* truth quite incredible."

Glancing around the table at the women wearing gowns that blazed with color and dripped jewels, I smiled. "The truth, Mr. McAllister, is quite simply that I could not eat an oyster if my life depended upon it."

"Does it?"

"Does what?"

"Does your life depend upon it?"

"Some might think so. Especially since I am sitting here, next to you, at Delmonico's, where the whole point, the whole goal even, is to be seen eating oysters."

He poked a fork into his ice, stabbed an oyster, and then lifted it to his lips.

I closed my eyes for one brief instant. When I opened them, the oyster had vanished.

"Yes. You're right. The whole goal at Delmonico's is to eat oysters. But there *are* finer things than oysters that may be eaten."

"Finer things?"

"Yes. That's what you intended to say, wasn't it?"

I nodded. What else could I do?

"And in that opinion, I am in total agreement." He leaned back and crooked a finger at one of the waiters.

The waiter reported instantly to Mr. McAllister's side.

The distinguished gentleman whispered into the waiter's ear, nodded once, and turned his attentions back to me. "Yes, my dear, I am in total agreement. And how marvelous to have found a kindred spirit in a city so lacking in true conviviality. Why eat oysters when one can dine on caviar?"

―――――

The New York Journal—Society
February 2, 1892

Our Miss Carter has done it again: She has started a new fad among the young, fashionable set. And was clever enough to do it under the benevolent, approving eye of Mr. Ward McAllister. Oysters at Delmonico's? How outmoded—caviar's the thing!

Just reading about it made me feel green again. At least Mr. McAllister was now an avowed admirer. That was worth something, in Aunt's opinion. I had seen Mr. Douglas lurking in the hallway just as the waiter was bringing the dish of caviar to the table. And if I was not mistaken, he had sent a wink in my direction.

Caviar!

I would as soon eat oysters.

―――――

The Tattler
February 2, 1892

. . . and who is trying to insinuate herself into a certain social secretary's good graces? Here's a word of advice to all who are tempted to follow that leech's lead: It takes one to know one.

Harry found me at a musical performance the next evening. Fie raised his eyebrows at me as Aunt and I took our seats. And then, during the intermission, he came to talk to me, Lizzie on his arm.

"I've heard you dine on caviar."

Lizzie giggled.

I felt myself color. I didn't know Harry read *Society*. "The truth is that I prefer not to eat oysters. I retch as soon as I smell one. Mr. McAllister misunderstood what I was telling him and took it to mean that I'd rather have something else."

"Caviar?"

"Yes."

Harry began to laugh. But it was no laughing matter! The more I thought about it, the queasier my stomach became. "Don't tell another soul."

"I won t."

Lizzie fixed her sparkling eyes on me. "We promise."

Harry laid his hand atop Lizzie's, which was resting on his arm. "We won't. I can't stand them myself. I only ever eat them because Mother used to tell me I had to. It's the worst part of Christmas: oyster stew. But it's tradition. Of course, Franklin loves them, so he always took a good share of mine."

I could just imagine the DeVrieses' table, filled with people and suffused with laughter. "And what else do you do? At Christmas?"

"Christmas? We sing. We sing till our lungs burst. Mother has always been a songbird. But Franklin and Katherine and I rebel now and then. Mother taught us to sing in thirds, but every now and then we pretend we're tone deaf and try to sing in seconds."

I cringed at the thought.

"It's truly terrible. But it's also very difficult. Have you ever tried to sing off-key?"

I shook my head.

"Try." He started humming a tune that I recognized in an instant: "With All Her Faults I Love Her Still." It was only thanks to Miss Miller that I knew it, or any other popular tune.

I joined in on the third measure, matching my alto to his baritone.

"And even though the worlds should scorn;
No love like hers, my heart can thrill,
Although she's made that heart forlorn!
Tho' other hearts have won her love,
I bear for her no dreams of ill.
Her face to me still dear shall be,
With all her faults I love, I love her still!"

I intended to sing counter to him, but somehow my will deserted me, and true to Harry's words we ended up in harmony, trying not to laugh as we sang.

"Stop it!" Lizzie was trying to be proper, but I could tell she was dying to laugh.

"See? It *is* difficult. And you didn't believe me, did you?"

I hadn't! "How long did you last? As a child?"

"As a child? We do it still! And it was Katherine who won this year. Of course, she always wins; she has an iron will."

"Let me try again."

Harry began to hum the notes of another song, and though I had better luck this time, I left off singing before the song was done and let him finish alone. Franklin walked up just then carrying a stem of champagne in each hand. He offered one to me.

"Oh! No. No, thank you. I don't think . . . not tonight." I had no wish to pass the nighttime hours writhing in my bed from pain.

He offered it to Lizzie instead.

She seemed to pale at its sight. "Er ... no, thank you . . . I'm just ... not quite ... not now. Thank you."

A wrinkle appeared on Franklin's forehead, but then he shrugged. "Harry?"

Harry took the glass from him and they toasted themselves.

———

AFTER THE CONCERT, Aunt and I walked beneath the arches of the Music Hall and onto a glaze of new-fallen snow. In this light it looked pure and brilliant, though I knew that by daylight it would have succumbed to the grime and dirt of the city just like everything else. As our carriage clattered through darkened streets, Aunt dispelled my notion that singing with Harry had been an innocent amusement.

"I heard a report that you were singing this evening. And doing it quite loudly. And poorly."

"It takes a great deal of effort to sing badly."

"And so why would you wish to do it?"

"Because . . ." Because it had made me laugh. And it was fun. "Because it was fun."

"Fun. There's nothing so inappropriate as fun when you're a debutante. This is serious, life-altering business that you are undertaking."

"Yes. And if there's to be no fun now, then when is there to be any?"

Aunt looked at me, appraisal in her eyes. "Fun? It might come upon you now and then, and startle you with its sudden appearance, but life is not about fun. And it's not about you. It's about who you marry. And then, it's about your in-laws. And your children. There will be no more talk of *fun*. Although I did see that Lizzie Barnes was in the company of the younger De Vries. Perhaps that signals your triumph."

"My triumph?"

"Perhaps she's lowered her expectations."

"You mean . . . ?"

"I mean perhaps she's no longer a rival."

Harry? And Lizzie?

CHAPTER 24

HE NEXT DAY, instead of our usual, studied preparations for an opera, Aunt had a different idea. "This afternoon we shall take to the streets. Put on your carriage costume."

"It must be thirty degrees outside!"

"Change."

She left me standing in the hall, her dogs watching me. One of them barked, startling me. Once in my room, the maid helped me out of my house gown and into my carriage costume, recoiffed my hair, and then aided me with my cloak.

The cloak had been done up in gray satin with marten fur around the edges of its swinging cape. Ruffles began at the neck and descended to my shoulders and down the back. It was beautiful, but it weighed at least fifteen pounds. I had to brace myself for it as the maid fit it about my shoulders.

"A hat, miss?"

"She'll have the gray felt." Aunt had come into the room and was contemplating my attire. She nodded as the maid set the hat upon my head. "Yes. That will do quite well."

It should. The hat was a perfect match for the cloak. A band of marten fur decorated its crown in a wavy pattern and tips of ostrich feathers sprang up from the back. The maid pulled the wide ribbon around from beneath the feathers and secured it in an enormous bow between my chin and my ear.

With the weight of the satin bearing down upon my shoulders and the slipperiness of fur threatening to tumble the hat from my head, I feared I would not be able to complete the drive in the manner in which Aunt expected. "I can't move."

"The goal is not to move; it is to be seen."

The hood on the carriage had been lowered and secured; we would have no relief from the wind. The coachman assisted Aunt into the Victoria and then me up beside her. Soon we were gliding away from the house, toward the city.

"We'll drive Ladies' Mile first," she ordered the coachman. And then come back for Central Park."

"Yes, madam."

We swept past places that I had only just discovered this year. The city was so big, so vast! After we had driven the length of Fifth Avenue housing the most fashionable stores, the coachman urged the horses into a turn.

But down the street came a careening cart, making a turn impossible and spurring our horses into a run.

Aunt stifled a scream.

The carriage, not being able to make the turn, continued on down the street. By coming to his feet and tugging on the reins, the coachman was able to turn the carriage to the east. But the horses' fear was not so easily diverted, and so as soon as they had recovered from the turn, they were off at a run again. Only the sight of a glass-sided hearse blocking the road ahead of us caused the horses to veer from their course.

I felt my hat slide off my head. It began to bounce at the nape of my neck.

We were headed south, and then, when traffic had blocked

an intersection, the horses twisted east once more, dragging our carriage, dangerously tilted, behind them.

"Turn around!" Aunt cried.

"Just as soon as I can, madam."

But we continued, block after block, until we found ourselves in the middle of a narrow street with no way forward and too little room to turn around.

The horses lurched to a halt.

After the wild pounding of hooves and banging of the carriage that we had endured, the silence seemed unnatural. And the scene before us unreal. The street was littered with a colorful collection of filth. A horse was stretched out before us, dead, its stomach bloated beyond comprehension. Across from it, on the other side of that narrow street, a man had been pushing a cart filled with rags past a wooden barrel leaking ashes. And just in front of him, where a hotel had left its door open to the street, the tinkling music of a piano could be heard.

And though I had never known this part of the city, I found I knew this place. I knew it from the pages of Mr. Riis's book. This was how the other half lived. They lived here in this place that stank of overripe food and overripe flesh.

The coachman hopped down from his perch and went to calm the horses. They were trembling with exhaustion, steam rising from their backs. In between their great gasping breaths, as the condensation of their breath thinned and dispersed, I saw people slowly gather. People with an unsavory look about them. Men in stained bowlers. Boys with greasy caps. And behind them, women with shawls pulled over their heads. And beyond them, on the sidewalks, close to the hotel, a group of women dressed far too nicely for the area and far too delicately for the weather.

Aunt must have been looking at the crowd too, for she clutched at my forearm with her hand.

"May I be of some assistance?"

I jumped at the words and Aunt grabbed at me.

But as the steam thinned and vanished, I recognized Mr. Douglas stepping from the crowds. "Mr. Douglas!"

"Help the coachman turn this carriage. Immediately!" Aunt had pushed to her feet and was trying to step past me.

"Perhaps we should stay seated, Aunt." More and more people were pressing around the carriage, staring at us. Little boys were hoisting friends to their shoulders so they could get a look over the sides.

Mr. Douglas was eyeing the crowds as he moved toward us. He put a hand out to one of the horses.

It snorted great clouds of breath at him.

"Yes, please remain seated." He cast an eye to the people around him. "Move on. The ladies need the carriage turned."

A collective mumbling rose up, but no one moved.

"Be off!" Mr. Douglas raised his cane.

I had never known before that I should be frightened in the city, but with the press of humanity that would not be moved and a dull flatness in the eyes that looked up at me, it crossed my thoughts that I might never find my way home again.

It must have been in Aunt's mind too, for she slipped her hand into mine.

I gave it a squeeze.

Then I heard the scuff of footsteps approaching and the crowd began to thin. Just a bit. To my complete and utter surprise, Harry pushed through. He came up to the carriage, hat in hand. "I saw what happened back on Fifth Avenue. I ordered my carriage to follow yours. May I offer you a ride?"

Aunt stood once more, but this time pulling on my hand, she moved as if there were no crowd and as if runaway carriages were a daily occurrence. "Thank you, Mr. De Vries. We would be delighted."

She reached down for Harry's hand, but there was no room for him to retreat to clear a space for her descent.

There was one tense moment when no one yielded, but then slowly a path was cleared. There were a few grunts and an assortment of coughs and sneezes, but no one reached out to accost us, and no one addressed us, and very soon Harry had led us away from our carriage and we were seated in his.

I pulled my hat from my neck and settled it once more atop my head.

As the horses pulled away, I glanced back. The coachman and Mr. Douglas were trying to coax the horses to step back, slowly reversing the carriage's path.

"We should do something nice for him."

"Who? Aunt asked."

"Mr. Douglas."

She sniffed. "We already are."

I might have pondered her enigmatic reply, but then Harry began to speak and further thoughts of the incident drifted away.

———

The New York Journal—Society
February 5, 1892

. . . and among the attendees at last night's opera, Lakmé, were Mr. Franklin DeVries, Mr. Harold DeVries, Miss Emma Vandermere, Miss Elizabeth Barnes, and the lovely Miss Clara Carter. .

. .

The Tattler
February 5, 1892

*Which of our city's lovely debutantes wandered far from Fifth
Avenue on a winter's afternoon when a runaway carriage pulled
her into The Bowery? Through some cajoling of The Bowery
element and the aid of a gentleman, all was put right. But that is
not the first time that a person of her name has ventured into the
bowels of our fair city.*

But—that was me. How had *The Tattler* known? Did news travel
so fast? And what was meant by that final line?

Even Lizzie read it. She asked me about it when we next met.

"Who do you think the debutante was?"

"It was me."

"You! But how did *The Tattler* know?"

I shook my head.

"So what was it like?"

I closed my eyes as I remembered that harrowing ride, then
opened them to try to forget the sights of The Bowery. But I had
only to go upstairs to my bedroom and open Mr. Riis's book to
renew them. "It was terrifying—with the carriage tipping this
way and that. I'm just thankful that it didn't overturn!"

"No. Not that. I meant The Bowery. What was it like?"

"It was . . ." How was it? Exactly? "It was nowhere I'd like to
find myself again. Ever."

"They say it's filled with . . . " She looked at me expectantly.

"People? Immigrants? There seemed to be an awful lot of
them."

She shook her head. "They say that there are *prostitutes*
there."

Prostitutes! Had there been prostitutes among those
wretched people? Lizzie had whispered and so I whispered
back. "I wouldn't know."

"You didn't see any?"

"I might have."

Lizzie's eyes grew round. "You did?"

I shrugged and tried to look nonchalant. "I actually don't know if I did or didn't. How do they look?"

"Not quite nice."

Then there very well might have been some. Most of the stares we received hadn't been nice. They had been threatening. Hostile. "At least Harry was there to rescue us."

"Harry rescued you?"

I nodded.

"He was the gentleman? Really?"

"Yes. He whisked us from our carriage into his own and back up Fifth Avenue."

"Just like that?"

"Very much like that." It hadn't taken more than a minute to make the shift.

"How romantic!"

"Harry? Romantic?"

"I've always thought so."

She had?

"Franklin wouldn't have been bothered to get his gloves dirty. So what did he say?"

"Harry?"

Lizzie nodded.

"He said ... let me see if I can remember it right. He said, 'May I offer you a ride?' "

Lizzie sighed. " 'May I offer you a ride.' "

"Lizzie! Don't be such a goose."

"I can't help it. The only thing Franklin ever talks to me about is hunting. Or horses. And then I'll look over to where you're talking with Harry, and I'll think to myself, It looks like she's laughing because he's actually said something truly funny. And then I'll wish I were you all over again."

She wished she were me? That couldn't be possible. Why

would the accomplished, adorable Lizzie Barnes wish she were me? And why did Franklin talk to her about horses? He'd never mentioned horses to me.

Lizzie began to giggle. "But I think I've finally discovered the secret: If I ask him about himself, then he's happy to talk on and on without any help from me! It's too bad Harry isn't the heir. I might have had to fight you for him."

"But he's not—"

She pressed a kiss to my cheek and left in a flutter of skirts.

"He's not mine."

I don't think she heard me.

CHAPTER 25

I WENT INTO the house through the kitchen after Lizzie left. Enveloped by the cozy heat, I snatched up a roll as they were pulled from the oven. As I cradled it in my hands, its warmth thawed my fingers.

Father was home. I heard him speaking as I passed his study. "He said they will give us the younger son."

I paused, passing the roll from hand to hand as I stood there.

"The younger?" Aunt's voice.

"That's what De Vries said."

De Vries? The younger? That meant . . . Harry? That meant Harry. Harry! They were going to give us—give me—Harry. A smile tugged at my lips, and joy filled my heart. Lizzie's words had been prescient. A heat crept up from my neck to my cheeks.

Harry.

They weren't going to make me marry Franklin after all!

I was just about to burst into Father's study and thank him when I remembered that the conversation was meant to be private.

"No. No! We don't want the younger. We want the elder! I hope you told him no."

"I did."

"And what did he say?"

"He said hadn't they done enough by securing the invitations to the Patriarch's Ball? Hadn't they done enough by seeming to welcome Clara's debut? He wondered why we had our sights set on Franklin when clearly Clara could have anyone she wanted."

"Anyone but their own eldest son?"

I backed away from the door because I didn't want to hear any more.

He'd said no? Father had said no.

It was then, as I slunk from the door and hid myself in the coat closet, as I examined my deepest thoughts and secret feelings, that I discovered I had been placed into a trap. And I knew a great longing for freedom.

———

I WAS NOT entirely myself the next day. It seemed to me disingenuous and false to dance and flirt when the outcome of my debut had already been decided. I truly was to marry Franklin. There was no question about it. Nothing I could do and nothing anyone could say would stop Father and Aunt from securing him for me.

Neither did I fear, anymore, being linked to one of the undesirable gentlemen. Such company could be nothing other than temporary. I was destined for grander things.

Did Mr. Hamilton wish to dance with me?

I let him.

Did Mr. Porter wish to talk with me?

Why should I try to dodge him?

Did Mr. Hooper wish to stare at me?

What did it matter? I had not the fortitude to avoid his gaze that I usually did. And so, I let him meet my eyes.

Only he seemed to view such access as encouragement.

As he started across the room, I began, too late, to reconsider my indifference. He barely bowed before he spoke. "Miss Carter? I will contain myself no longer. The invitation you sent by your glance . . . I must speak to you of my dear departed sister."

"Oh! Don't. . . please don't."

"I must. I must speak on Minnie's behalf."

"I'm sure you must not. Really, Mr. Hooper, is this truly the time or place to share such memories? I must confess that I never once met her."

"But your father did. She was so kind. So gay. She looked forward, with such anticipation, to her debut."

I could think of no reply.

"I have undertaken the study of medicine myself, in hopes of finding a true cure for the illness that plagued my sister." The light of undying loyalty and the pain of sorrow mingled in his eyes. The poor fellow. He wasn't mad; he simply missed his sister.

"That's very commendable, Mr. Hooper."

"But I will not remain silent: People like your father must be stopped!"

"My—my father?"

"Those who practice quackery under the guise of medicine."

Quackery? Father was right: Grief had altered his mind. But madness did not preclude tact. "I'll have you know that my father is the best doctor in this city!"

"I have only just begun my studies, but I can tell you without hesitation that no doctor worth his license would ever prescribe strychnine in the dose that he did."

"I know nothing of medicine, Mr. Hooper."

"And neither does your father."

"I will not stay here and listen to your insults." Though, as a matter of fact, I had to. Aunt had left me for the punch bowl.

Until someone passed by that I recognized, I had no other means of escape.

"How is it that you get to debut and my sister does not? How is that just?"

I shrunk from his accusation. If his sister had appeared at that instant, in the flesh or in spectral form, I would have gladly given her my own debut.

People were starting to turn in our direction and the look in their eyes was one of curiosity. I didn't want to give them something to gossip about. I threaded my arm through Mr. Hooper's as though he had made the valiant gesture of offering it to me himself. "I cannot tell you how sorry I am, Mr. Hooper, that your sister died."

"Sorry? Sorry—!"

I bent my head in toward his in an effort to make him reduce his volume. "But I cannot see how I can be of any help to you."

"Help to me? You disgust me! You and your father both. That he should squire you around New York City's finest ballrooms when he peddles such—such—!" His face was growing red and a vein was pulsing in his neck. "It's an injustice that I hope to find some way to right."

I pulled my arm from his. "I think, sir, that our acquaintance has come to an end."

He shook his head, then began to smile in a most malicious way. "Our acquaintance shall never come to an end. Not until you renounce the debut that Minnie ought to have had."

Renounce a debut? I might have credited the impossibility of his demand to grief, but he seemed, in that instant, quite sane. His eyes quite lucid. Would no one help me? I looked desperately around the room for Aunt, but for once she was nowhere to be found.

Mr. Hooper put his hand to my forearm.

I recoiled at his touch.

"Come now, Miss Carter. I would like—"

"There you are!"

It was with great relief and not a little loosening in my knees that I perceived those words to be Harry's. At just the right time. "Mr. De Vries!"

"I believe this next one is my dance."

"It is. You're quite right. Please excuse us, Mr. Hooper." I turned from him and then immediately attached myself to Harry's forearm.

He swung me away and walked me across the ballroom floor. "I didn't mean to interrupt if I shouldn't have. And I know that my dance is after the next intermission. But you seemed to need help."

I glanced at Harry, then gazed down at the floor. That Harry, of all people, should be the one to rescue me. Again. "I don't think he's in his right mind. He said I issued him an invitation. Through the glances I had given him."

"Glances! Only a fool relies on an invitation from a glance."

I smiled at his indignation. "And what would you rely upon?"

"A simple request. If I wanted a kiss, for instance, I would say, 'Miss Carter, may I have the pleasure of your kiss?' And you would say . . . ?"

If only he knew what I wanted to say. But no. I couldn't. "Miss Carter would respond firmly in the negative."

The sparkle went out of his eyes.

I couldn't let him think I cared nothing for him. "But *Clara* might be persuaded to say yes."

His lips crept up at one corner. "Really. Well. I must keep that in mind."

My cheeks flamed at the implication. Perhaps my relief at being saved had overcome my discretion. But Harry, thankfully, did not take advantage of my lapse in prudence. He returned me to my aunt.

And as he did so, Franklin came to claim me. He bowed to my aunt before casting a look from me to Harry and then back to me. "He hasn't embarrassed himself, has he? He's been known to step on quite a few feet in his time. Remember the count's daughter, Harry? In France?"

Harry smiled, but it contained no pleasure.

"She practically had to be carried from the dance floor. I shall never forget the stream of curses she cast after you. I learned some I had not known!" Franklin laughed as if he expected Harry and me to join him.

Harry excused himself.

Franklin took up my hand.

"That wasn't very nice."

"Old Harry's up to it. He's not so adept at the social graces. The best of intentions, but the worst of executions, you could say."

"You've made him feel bad."

"He'll get over it. In fact, he is right now. Look."

I looked in the direction Franklin had spun us, and indeed, Harry was leaning against a colonnade, speaking to Lizzie. As we watched, she smiled at him and placed a hand on his forearm.

He reached across and covered it with his own.

"Really, Franklin, for a gentleman you're quite rude!"

He twirled us away from Harry and Lizzie and then pushed me back a step and looked into my face. "That truly bothered you?"

"It did." And I wasn't sure what had bothered me most: Franklin's disparagement of his brother or the possibility that Harry and Lizzie were together. Why did Franklin always have to insinuate?

"Then I apologize. Forgiven?" He flashed a smile that had no more remorse in it than did a cat with a mouse caught up between its teeth.

Since it was a ball and since I would be eventually be marrying him, I simply smiled back. "Of course." But Lizzie's words continued to haunt me. *"It's too bad Harry isn't the heir. I might have had to fight you for him."*

My reward was a tightening of Franklin's fingers at my back, which pulled me closer to his chest. "You're quite fascinating, you know. I never know what you're going to do or what you're going to say."

The problem was, I didn't either.

"Every event is an adventure. Every dance is rife with possibilities." The possibilities of which he spoke sparked a gleam in his eyes.

My gaze faltered before that look.

He laughed, then danced me forward and back with a force that cast me against his chest again. And for a brief moment, he clasped me to himself. "Such intriguing possibilities."

———

AUNT TOOK ADVANTAGE of the ride home to chastise me about the evening's events.

"... and you must stop cavorting with the second son."

"With whom?"

"With Franklin's brother. You danced with him twice. Some might think you prefer him to the heir. And no good can come of it. At the next opportunity, you must cut him."

Cut him! "Franklin's own brother?"

"He knows he must give way to the heir, but it seems he needs a reminder."

"Please, don't make me—"

"You will do as I have asked."

Asked? She'd commanded!

As she looked at me, Aunt's expression seemed to soften. "Besides, it would be kinder. You must not dangle one man while you are angling for another."

"I'm not dangling anyone."

"Aren't you?"

Was I? "Of course not." Of course I wasn't.

"Good. Then it will make it that much easier for you to do as you must."

———

IT WAS WITH some trepidation that I caught sight of Harry as he was walking down Ladies' Mile two days later. We had been going from shop to shop, and I had begged to step outside for some air while Aunt settled our accounts.

He lifted his hat as he approached. "Miss Carter."

I dearly wanted to talk to him, but I knew I could not. Must not. And so I kept my eyes trained on the sidewalk before me.

"Miss Carter?"

I turned and walked away. Surely he would understand.

But he did not. "Clara?"

He had said it so loudly that I feared we would attract attention. And so I stopped.

When he caught up with me, I saw he'd taken off his hat. "What—why—?"

Standing rigid, eyes still trained on the sidewalk in front of me, I leaned slightly in his direction. And when I spoke, it was in whispered words. "I am trying to cut you."

"Cut me?"

I nodded once and prepared to move on.

"But... wait." He put a hand to my arm. "What does that mean?"

"I am trying to snub you."

"Oh. I see."

But it was quite clear that he didn't. "So you must not speak to me anymore."

"Why not?"

I raised my head and turned toward him. "Because I just

rebuffed you. I pretended to ignore you. Really, Harry, you ought to be quite humiliated! And I did it here on the sidewalk in front of everyone."

"Why would you do that?"

"Stop speaking to me!" There. Now maybe he would understand.

"If you insist. But . . . how long is this cutting to last? It sounds quite painful."

We were starting to gather no little attention. Aunt was right. Better to end it here and now. I couldn't have him anyway. "It lasts forever. You must remember that I've been unspeakably rude to you."

"Ah. Yes. Unspeakably rude. I'm beginning to understand. In any event, then—"

"You really must stop speaking." My voice was unaccountably beginning to rise quite beyond the range of our two sets of ears.

"You mean to say forever? We can't even—"

"Now. You must stop speaking *now*"

"You would not want to know if, say, a small insect had become entangled in your hair?"

I put a hand up to check. "Why? Has one?"

"No. But in that case, you *would* wish for me to speak."

"Of course I would wish for you to speak. Has one?"

"No."

"Really, Harry, tell me!"

"You ask me not to speak to you and then you order me to speak to you? I confess I can't keep up with all of this social nonsense." He was laughing at me. I could see his eyes twinkling.

I glared at him for one long moment and then I could not help myself. I burst into laughter too.

He joined me. And when finally we could speak again, he set

his hat atop his head and tipped the brim toward me. "Good day, Miss Carter."

I nodded. "Good day, Mr. De Vries."

————

AUNT CAME OUT of the store as Harry was bidding me good-bye. "I thought I told you to cut that boy!"

"I did."

"Then you must not have done it correctly."

I hid my smile as I turned from her and continued down the sidewalk. "He refused."

"He refused what?" Aunt hurried to catch up with me.

"He refused to be cut." I tried to say the words as if that was all there was to say.

"How could he? It was not his choice. It was yours!"

"How can I cut someone who refuses to be offended?"

"But did you do? What did you say?"

I stopped and turned to face her straight on. "I did everything. I didn't look at him. I failed to speak to him. I told him not to speak to me. But he did not understand and when the cut must be explained . . . ? It didn't work."

I nodded to the doorman of the next store as he pulled the door open for us, leaving Aunt stuttering her disapproval in my wake.

CHAPTER 26

*a*T A PRIVATE ball that evening, Harry and Katherine found me after dinner. He stepped close and began to speak. "I feel that I should apologize for my brother."

"For what?"

"You tell me. He must have done something."

I laughed before I could remember not to. "Did you do that often on the Continent? Apologize for him?"

"And pay people to be quiet every now and then too." Katherine put a hand to his arm. "Harry!"

"I did."

Katherine's husband walked over and offered her his arm. They moved off together, leaving us alone.

"When I read in the paper that the De Vries brothers had scandalized England, terrorized France, and appalled Germany, I assumed they must be talking about you."

"Me? Why?"

"Aren't younger brothers the irresponsible ones?"

"Only if they have a *responsible* older brother."

Why did they always have to insult each other? Is this what I had to look forward to? Defending one against the other for the rest of my life? "Franklin isn't irresponsible. He's . . . charming." He was. He just wasn't anything else.

"He can be. When he's not being ruthless and cunning."

"He doesn't seem as bad as that."

"Ah. But then you've never lived with him, have you?"

"You sound jealous."

"Jealous? No. I used to be. I used to wish that I'd been born first. But then I realized it's ineffectual to waste time thinking about who, and what, I wasn't."

Like me, I supposed, always wishing I were shorter. Or thinner. Or better.

"Besides, why should I want all the headaches of the bank and the burden of producing an heir? Why would I be jealous of that?"

"Because you'd probably be so much better at it." My cheeks colored as I realized I had actually spoken my thought.

"Then you're the only one to think so. And besides, that's not the life for me."

No. It wasn't. He'd be stifled, stultified, if he were condemned to a lifetime of ballrooms and opera houses.

Harry placed a hand to my arm. "Make no mistake. I was born for a purpose. And so were you."

A purpose. As if there were some grand task for me to accomplish or some great change for me to effect.

"Don't you believe that?" His eyes were so sober, so serious, as they probed mine.

"Born for a purpose? Some people are, perhaps. But what is there that I can do? Besides dance a waltz or play the piano? And even then . . ."

"Even then?"

"Even then I'm not good enough."

"Good enough for whom?"

I gestured toward the people that crowded the dance floor. "For them."

"But they don't matter."

I nearly laughed at him.

Harry grabbed my hands. "Don't you realize? You are exactly the person God intended you to be."

"Intended?" As if He would have spent time thinking about me. "God can't have thought of me."

"Then you were a mistake? Is that what you're saying?"

Was it?

"God doesn't make mistakes." As he looked at me, a smile began to soften his features. "I'm so thankful, Clara, that—"

I laid a hand on his arm to stop him.

He covered it with his own. Just like he'd done with Lizzie's. It was not the result I had hoped for. I had meant to stop him in his speech. His look had warned me: He was dangerously close to voicing a sentiment that I could never hope to return.

He looked up from our hands, a kind of regret coloring his eyes. "Is he worth it?"

"Who?"

"Franklin."

What was he asking? And what could I say? "It's not a question of worth." If it were, then Harry would have been the object of all my endeavors.

"Then it's a question of money?" There was something very much like disappointment lurking in his eyes.

"No."

"No?"

I shook my head. "It's a question of expectations. And I'm expected to do as my father and aunt request. I have no other choices. I'm a hothouse flower bred for one purpose only: to bloom beautifully enough that someone will pluck me and take me to their home for use in decoration."

"But couldn't you just—"

"What? Refuse them? What well-bred girl would do such a thing?" Why couldn't he understand? Why did he have to insist!

Why was it so difficult for him to comprehend the way it all worked?

"There must be another alternative."

"Of course. I could declare myself independent. Only how would I support myself? I don't know how to do anything. Nothing useful, in any case. I can sing and I can play the piano, but I'm no soloist. I can talk to someone for nearly an hour even if they never respond, but why would anyone wish to hire me for that? I might teach, but I've never had the chance to go to a teachers college. Who would hire me? What choice do I have, Harry?" Really, I had none. And if I hadn't known it before, I did now.

"You could marry someone else. You could marry for love." His hand tightened around my own.

"Yes. I could elope. And ruin my reputation forever. Whomever I wed myself to would never thank me for such a tainted dowry. And it would ruin him as well." How dare he speak to me of love!

"But what if there weren't any impediments?"

I looked him in the eyes. And as I did, my anger was eclipsed by great sadness.

"What if you could choose?"

"Ah! Mr. De Vries." It was my aunt.

Just as my chin began to tremble, Harry's gaze broke from mine. He dropped my hand as he turned toward her.

What if I could choose? Even if I could, what other choice could I make than the one that had been made for me? As I had just told Harry, there was literally nothing else that I could do.

———

AFTER I HAD danced with Franklin, and a Lorillard, and a Vandermere, I decided to spend my intermission with Aunt, by the piano in the parlor. My head was hurting, and I needed the relative silence that the room offered.

It was there that Harry found me. Again. And I can't say that my heart didn't skip a beat or two.

He gestured toward the piano. "Can you play by sight?"

"Yes." Of course I could play by sight. I'd spent hours and hours, days . . . weeks ... at the piano over the years, practicing anything my instructor placed in front of me.

"Would you play a duet with me, then?" He withdrew a composition from his coat. "It's a new one. From Italy."

I had made myself plain, earlier in the evening, hadn't I? He couldn't have failed to understand how things must be. And so, I gave him a long look before agreeing. But then I gathered my skirts with a hand and slid up the bench so he could take a seat beside me.

He did. And then he reached forward to settle the music on its holder above the keyboard.

A warmth rose from his clothes. A warmth scented with cedar and sandalwood. And with something else that tickled my nose with its pungence. Limes?

He placed his hands on the keyboard, as did I. Our shoulders were touching, the wool of his coat scratching against my bared skin.

"Ready?"

I nodded.

"One . . . two . . ."

I kept the time of his count by pulsing my fingers as he did the same. And on three, we began to play.

The composer had given me a lovely, lilting melody, and Harry a simple, if unimaginative, harmony. But then, inexplicably, the piece began to change. And very soon I was playing in his low octaves, and he was playing in my high octaves.

He leaned back a bit as I leaned forward.

Our fingers flirted, first nestling between one another and

then bounding away. The intricacy, the sheer ... intimacy ... of it all, left me rather flustered. But soon I began to anticipate those portions of the music. Those moments when Harry's breath would caress the curls dangling at the back of my neck and I would graze the backs of his hands, for just an instant, as I leapt over them to the next movement in the music.

But just as I was growing accustomed to our musical embrace, the melody and harmony wandered apart and I was returned to my own octaves, constrained by the music inscribed on the sheet. And then, in one last lilting phrase, the song ended, leaving us both breathless.

———

The New York Journal—Society
February 9, 1892

. . . the ball was well attended, and was especially graced by the presence of the charming Miss Clara Carter, who wore a striking gown by Madame Connolly. Composed of ciel blue ribbons and white taffeta, drifts of snowy white lace fell from its shoulders. It was cut décolleté, and flounces of lace decorated the bodice.

The Tattler
February 9, 1892

Which debutante appears most skilled in the art of flirting by duet? She was seen entwined upon the octaves while playing with one of our city's finest young Knickerbockers yesterday evening.

"Entwined upon the octaves!" I couldn't seem to keep my voice from rising.

Lizzie gave my arm a squeeze. "I knew you'd want to see it. That's why I sent you the message to meet me."

And Aunt had almost intercepted it.

Lizzie shifted the paper so that it caught the light filtering through the branches of the hedge. "Entwined. That's what it says." Worry clearly shone through the lines above Lizzie's eyes.

"Entwined!"

"I'm not misquoting. And you might want to keep your voice down. Just a little."

"I know you're not misquoting, but—we were not entwined! Our fingers might have gotten a bit mixed up . . . and I might have had to lean across him . . . and . . . he across me . . ."

"You were playing a duet. What did you expect?"

"That I would play a duet. Not that I would be portrayed as some . . . some . . . fallen woman!"

Lizzie began to laugh. "But duets are only ever played in flirtation."

"He said it was a new one. From Italy."

"Oh—from *Italy!*" Her laughter grew more pronounced. "Honestly, Clara. Didn't you know?" She quieted for a moment to look at me. And then, with a curious pity displayed in her eyes, she leaned forward and patted my hand. "You didn't know."

"But—but you and I play duets all the time. Or we used to."

"In practice."

"And you play them all the time with Franklin."

"How else can one expect to get five minutes alone with a suitor? Sitting side by side, breathing the same air? Duets were made for courting."

I closed my eyes with a groan. "And now Aunt will have one more thing to scold me for. I've been discovered courting the wrong man."

"Yes. Discovered *entwined* with him upon the octaves!" She couldn't seem to keep her giggles from bubbling forth.

"I suppose . . . there was an awful lot of . . . shifting . . . that occurred. And we did trade octaves more than once."

"Scandal!" Lizzie was laughing so hard that her face was beginning to turn red.

"But what if Franklin sees it? What if Franklin thinks—I mean— Harry's his own brother!"

That stopped up her laughter. "Franklin might see it, but he won't read it. Franklin doesn't read much of anything. Haven't you noticed?"

I hadn't. But as I thought upon it, I realized she was probably right. Franklin was such a restless, impetuous soul that I couldn't imagine him sitting in one place long enough to pick up a newspaper, let alone read it.

"Besides, the article didn't even name you."

That was little consolation. Anyone who had been there would realize that it was me. I let out another sigh. Vowed never again to sit next to Harry on a piano bench. Even if we both understood that it meant nothing.

The Tattler had to be stopped. He'd dogged my steps for the entire season and cast me in only the poorest of lights. At least I knew who he was. Hadn't Mr. Hooper signaled his intentions back at the beginning of the season? During my first at-home? Who else could it be but him? I could understand the depths of grief, but insulting me could do nothing to reverse his sister's death. Ruining my season would never result in any kind of triumph for her own.

She was dead!

Surely, he could be made to understand reason. I resolved to speak to him that very night.

———

"WHO?" A PALENESS seemed to wash over Aunt's cheeks.

"Mr. Hooper. The man who always stares at me." I had decided to enlist Aunt's aid so that my interview with Mr. Hooper could be accomplished quickly. And discreetly. But I hadn't yet seen him among the ball-goers.

"Oh, my dear! Please, don't speak of that. Of him."

"But he's been unbearably rude to me—you must agree—and I find that I require an explanation."

"You're not to mention him tonight. Or any other night. To do so would be to commit the *unspeakable*."

"But it is imperative that I speak to him tonight."

Aunt leaned close. "He's dead."

"Dead!" That was unexpected.

"By his own hand." The words were whispered viciously into my ear. "And it is not to be spoken of, will never be spoken of, in polite company."

A shameful relief overcame my initial revulsion. If he was dead, then The Tattler had nothing left to say. If he was dead, then I no longer had to confront him. I only wished I did not feel quite so triumphant.

Mr. Hooper had died.

May God bless his miserable, tormented soul.

CHAPTER 27

I WAS PACING in front of the window, trying to gather my thoughts. Lizzie's continued comments about the vaunted, ubiquitous Miss Clara Carter had left me in something of a state. If I stood on the tips of my toes, I could see beyond the lace curtains and out to the sidewalk. Just. There was a gathering of five or six girls out there. They were doing absolutely nothing but loitering as far as I could tell. "Have they nothing better to do?"

"Who?"

"All those girls out there. On the sidewalk."

Aunt looked up at me over the stack of invitations with a frown. "Let them look. Let them linger. It will only make your hand in marriage more valuable."

"I'm not a piece of merchandise. I'm a person."

"Who is destined for a great marriage. Why should they not look upon you with awe? You'll soon have the life of which every girl dreams. A veritable fairy tale."

I nearly laughed outright. A fairy tale? No. Those always included true love. And at that, I had not one chance. I turned away from the window. "No one told me it would be like this." Tripping home in the wee hours of morning, sleeping until nearly noon only to get up and repeat the performance again. And do it all in front of an ever-increasing crowd of admirers who were now all wearing hats of orange bombazine decorated with plum-colored ribbons.

"You've done far better than we had hoped."

"Yes. And now I can't go anywhere without Mr. Douglas. And I can wear nothing without it being dissected and analyzed in the newspapers." How could anyone think that I knew anything about any of this? How could they call me an expert on society? "Mama never told me . . . when she spoke of debuts it was always about the dances." About being whisked around a ballroom in the arms of a handsome man. She hadn't told me what hard work it was.

"Your mother never knew any of this. She never had a debut. She was a Newport girl."

As I had grown, I had come to realize that I didn't know much about my mother. I had only been ten when she'd died—much too young to wonder at the life she led before she had become the mother I had always known her to be.

"And not from a family that <u>went</u> to Newport. She was *from* Newport. She was a town girl."

"Oh."

"Yes: *Oh.* That's exactly what I said when Brother told me he had met her. There were Posts in Newport that year. And Livingstons. Sheldons. May Vandermere was there, with the bloom of youth and all her family's connections, just come from her debut."

"He was hoping for a match?"

"*I* was hoping for a match. In spite of our losses from the Panic. A Warren would even have done. Anyone besides a Newport girl."

"But. . . ?"

"He didn't listen. Wouldn't listen. Listened to nothing at all but your mother sing at church. She was a soloist, you know. in the choir."

I hadn't known.

"A summer of romance. Walks on the beach, dinners at the hotels. All fall and all winter there were quick visits to the coast out of season. He would not be dissuaded. And in the spring, they were married."

"Mama was beautiful."

"Oh, to be sure' And that was his argument. 'She'll be the most beautiful girl in the city, you'll see. We'll retake all I've lost, together.' And since there was nothing else to be done about it, I took her under my tutelage. I trained her up in the ways of society so that she wouldn't make a fool of Brother. I took her to the corsetiere's and the dressmaker's. To balls and the opera. Imagine: She had never seen one!"

"But she got sick."

"She was never quite well. Not after Brother brought her back from the sea."

She had missed her home. I knew it as surely as if Mama were speaking the words into my ear.

"She wasn't used to city ways. And how she chafed at her corsets! Just like a young girl." Aunt grimaced. "Just like you. But in time, she came to accept them. And then she used them for her benefit. In time and with guidance, she became the envy of every woman in the city: She achieved a sixteen-inch waist."

Sixteen inches! That was two less than my own.

"For a time, after we had groomed her for her new life, she brought Brother nothing but luck. She had a very simple way about her. Quite disarming. Charming."

"Did she never go back?" Because we never had. I had never once been to Newport.

"There was nothing to go back to. Her mother had passed away, and her father had her in his old age, after he had given up teaching at Cambridge. He died soon after she married."

"But she must have returned for the funeral."

"No. Brother couldn't leave his practice."

"He couldn't? But... not even in the summer? When everyone else goes to Newport?"

"Everyone else does not go to Newport. Not during the week. The men stay in the city. And that's where your father had to be."

Poor Mama. A child of the ocean, a child of the summer, without a wave in sight, with scarcely a breeze to be had in the city in summer. But she must have been happy. Hadn't she always been singing? At least until . . . she hadn't?

————

FRANKLIN CAME TO call later that afternoon. Inexplicably, Aunt rose and walked from the room, leaving me alone with him. But then a dog toddled into the parlor.

I glanced at the door through which Aunt had just disappeared. If the dogs were about, she must have kept herself near. I endeavored to ignore it, but the dog did not return the favor. It came straight over, stood in front of Franklin, and began to bark.

Franklin held out a hand toward it. "Nice dog."

The beast curled back its lips and grinned. And then, contrary to everything I knew to be true about it, the dog sat on its haunches, extended its neck, and whined as it pawed at Franklin's hand.

"Er . . ."

"They're my aunt's."

"*They*? There are more?"

"There are three."

As if responding to some unseen signal, the dog suddenly turned and sped toward the hall.

"Well."

I smiled at him. "Well." What was it that Lizzie said she'd spoken to him about? It was something he'd never mentioned to me and I'd kept it in my thoughts for a moment exactly like this one. A moment in which I could think of nothing to say. If only I could remember what it was!

"Would you like to go for a walk?" he asked.

I would have loved to, but I couldn't. Shouldn't. "I can't. It's my at-home day."

"Oh." He looked disappointed for just a moment, but then he smiled. "Perhaps I'll ask Lizzie then."

The clock tolled the hour.

I stood.

He stood. "It's been a pleasure."

"The pleasure was entirely mine. Thank you for coming."

And then he was out the door and off, apparently, to Lizzie's.

It wasn't a second later that Aunt appeared. "Well?"

"He asked me to go for a walk."

"And?"

The butler walked in and presented a tray filled with cards to Aunt. She riffled through them, replaced them on the tray, keeping back two. "We'll see these gentlemen." She turned her attention back to me. "Well?"

"I said that I couldn't. It's Tuesday." What other choice did I have?

"He asked you to go for a walk and you declined?" Her voice had risen with each word.

"Tuesdays are my at-home day."

"There's at-home and there's at home. I wouldn't expect you to be at-home on a day when the heir asked you to go out."

"But then visitors wouldn't find me at home." And wasn't that the point of having an at-home day?

"*Must* you be so literal? Is it too late to recall him?"

Probably. "He's on his way to Lizzie's."

"To Lizzie's? You sent him to the arms of your rival?"

I put a hand to my head, where the throbbing had grown more insistent. "There are too many rules. And I don't understand any of them!"

"Then let me make it clear: There is only one true rule, and that is to catch the De Vries heir at any cost. At the expense of any rule. Of every rule. Do you understand now?"

I HAD SOME time between my at-home hours and dinner, so I returned to my room and took my scrapbook from its box. I had been clipping the articles from *The New York Journal* and *The Tattler* along with some pieces from *Ladies' Home Journal*. I'd saved the menus from all of my balls and dinners too, so I set about pasting them into my book, beside the colorful scrap images that Mama and Lizzie had given me over the years.

As I pasted the articles, I reread them.

I paused when I came to *The Tattler* article commemorating our carriage's mad flight into The Bowery. Mr. Hooper must have kept a closer watch on my movements than I had realized. And he seemed to think my father had business in that part of the city. As I thought about the article and remembered a conversation with Father, I discovered a very great wish to know what business Mr. Hooper thought my father had in The Bowery.

I couldn't very well ask the coachman to take me back the way his horses had run. I didn't want to interrogate my father; and I couldn't drag Harry, the brother of the man I was to marry, into a place so disreputable. So I decided to ask the only other person I knew to associate with the incident.

———

"YOU WANT TO WHAT?" Mr. Douglas leaned close in order to hear me over the strains of the orchestra. His eyes had grown to the size of bread plates as I had explained my plan. But now they were staring at me through narrow slits.

"I want to go back to that part of the city where you helped my aunt and me that day when our carriage ran away with us."

"Why?"

"Because *The Tattler* implied that my father had some sort of dealings in that area."

"I know."

"You do?"

He blinked. Straightened. "Of course. I keep up with all of the society columns. Professional interest."

I wondered if he had known Mr. Hooper. "So will you take me?"

"To The Bowery? I'd as soon escort you to hell."

"Then I'll just have to go by myself. Thank you ever so much for your concern."

"Listen here." Mr. Douglas took me by the arm and pulled me further from the ballroom.

"Let go of me."

"No. Stop. Right now. And don't give another thought to going there. Ever."

"If you won't help me, then I'll go alone." My voice sounded much more confident than I was. Go alone? The one sacrosanct rule in my life, besides *Secure Franklin at All Costs*, was that I must never, ever go anywhere alone. I was never to be left unescorted.

"Don't you know about those people?"

"Of course I do! I've read the book."

"The book."

"Riis's book. I've read about those people. And I—" I pitied them.

With the same kind of pity I saw in Mr. Douglas's eyes when he looked at me. But just then it was colored with something quite near affection. "It makes a person start to think, doesn't it?"

I nodded.

"Listen." He said it much more gently this time. "There's nothing good to be found in The Bowery. And quite a bit of bad. The best thing you can do is just stay away."

"But—"

"There's lots of work to be done in The Bowery, but none of it can be accomplished by you."

"How can you say that?"

"What are you going do? March down there with your good intentions and sprinkle some money on them? They'd slit your throat before you were done. And no one would blame them." He threaded my arm through his and clasped his hand over mine with such a firm grip that when he turned to walk back toward the ballroom, I could do nothing but follow.

"Then why does my father go there?"

"Who says he does?"

"*The Tattler.*"

"Well, *The Tattler* doesn't know much of anything." He pressed his lips into a straight flat line.

"But why did he think my father—"

"There are some things you don't need to know."

"But—"

"And there are some things I'm not going to tell you. Just stay away from there."

"But why does he go there?"

"I don't know." But it was quite clear that in fact he did. "Ask *The Tattler.*"

"You're a newspaperman. You're supposed to know everything!"

"Tell that to my editor."

He wasn't willing to be persuaded. Maybe if I had been Lizzie, I could have batted my eyelashes and simpered. But I was only Clara. With a mouth that was too large and hands that were too big. And I was never going to find out anything. A tear slipped down my cheek.

"Don't—you can't—don't cry!"

"It's just that *The Tattler* . . . every time you wrote something nice about me, every time you flattered me in *Society*, he wrote something terrible. And not just rude, but venomous. He truly hated me." And now Mr. Douglas seemed to hate me too.

"I don't think so."

"I know so. And I'm just so tired." I lifted my hand to swipe at a tear. "And now you won't help me—"

"Because I don't want to hurt you. Please . . ." He fished a handkerchief from his pocket and offered it to me. "Please let this be the end of it."

"But—"

"No good can come from knowing anything at all about The Bowery."

"What is The Bowery, Mr. Douglas? Why is it so terrible?"

"It's a place where ..." He looked as if he wanted to be anywhere but here. "Where women who are not nice meet men who are not nice."

"For heaven's sake, just tell me the truth!"

"The truth? It's a place of prostitutes and extortionists. Where women die too young and men live too long. Now do you understand?"

Prostitutes? Then Lizzie had been right. And perhaps there had been some among the women I'd seen. But if it was a place of prostitutes and extortionists, then why did my father go there? If indeed he did. And more important, why had Mr. Douglas been there, in The Bowery, that day too?

———

MR. VANDERMERE CLAIMED me for a dance, and then Mr. Hamilton. Harry hadn't signed for a dance with me, though he danced a waltz with Lizzie. They looked good together. They complemented each other. She short and fair; he tall and dark. Perhaps Aunt was right, about the two of them.

As I walked with Aunt during intermission, I asked her to escort me to Katherine. She was standing by herself. One of the benefits of marriage. Once a girl was permanently attached to a man, she could go almost wherever she wanted by herself. I followed her gaze. She was looking at her husband. He was drinking in the corner, also by himself.

"Is the baron quite all right?"

She looked over at me. "He's fine. He doesn't like it here in the city. I had thought that I missed it, missed being here, so he came. For me. I owe him everything."

She must have seen my skepticism written on my brow.

"I do. I know it may not seem it, but he is a very kind man. Especially in Germany where I don't speak the language."

"You don't speak German?"

"My son does. But I never have. I'm trying. I have a tutor. But languages have always been so difficult for me." She spoke the words with no little regret.

"Then how do you speak to him? How did you come to know him?"

"I did a Tour."

"Of the Continent? It was there you met him?"

"Yes."

That one word seemed to preclude any other questions. It

would not have been polite to press for more information, not when she had shared so much already, and so I remained silent.

But she was not finished. "It was discovered that I had something the baron needed. And it's not a bad marriage. The bond only truly chafes when I come home. When I'm confronted with what it is that I have lost." It was then I realized she wasn't really looking at me. She was looking beyond me to the far side of the room as she spoke.

I turned to see what it was that had gained her attention.

It was Mr. Douglas.

CHAPTER 28

*L*IZZIE HAPPENED BY at that moment, with Franklin. He dropped her with us and then went in search of some refreshment. She greeted Katherine and then leaned close to speak of me. "I had a most delightful walk with Franklin."

"Yesterday?"

"Yes, it was. But how did you know?"

"He came to see me before he visited you. Tuesdays are my at-home day."

Lizzie wrinkled her nose in sympathy. "I hate having to be at home."

"Where did you walk?"

"With Franklin? Up to Central Park. With Mama. He bought me some chestnuts. And promised to take me skating on Friday!"

"Really?" I was glad he hadn't asked me. I didn't know how to skate.

"Yes! I shall hardly sleep in expectation of it. I've the most gorgeous skating costume. It's pink and trimmed out in fur.

With the most fetching little hat. And you know how I adore hats!"

"Do you know how to skate?"

"Of course. At least enough to get by, but not well enough that I won't have to hang on to his arm now and then." It looked as if. . . had she winked?

THE NEXT MORING, messenger came to the door. The butler delivered up his message to us. Aunt held the invitation out to the light as she read it.

"Mr. Harold De Vries solicits the honor of attending Miss Clara Carter to the skating pond in Central Park on Friday afternoon, February 12th, at three o'clock.

"The bearer will wait for your answer."

"That's tomorrow. How unspeakably rude to presume that you have not already made plans. Especially during the season! No. Absolutely not."

I looked up in surprise. She had said the words with such finality.

"But that's the day Lizzie's to go skating with Fr—the elder Mr. De Vries."

"Is she? And how would you know that?"

"I overheard her telling someone. Else. Someone else." Aunt glanced over at the butler. Glanced at me. Pressed her lips together in a firm and formidable line. "Very well. You may go. Write a reply."

I went to the desk and found a card. Took up a pen.

Miss Carter has much pleasure in accepting Mr. De Vries's kind invitation to the skating pond on Friday afternoon, February 12th, at three o'clock.

Aunt stood behind me as I wrote it, and as soon as I had sealed it inside an envelope, she passed it to the butler.

And it was only then that I dared to speak my one small reservation about the event. "I don't know how to skate."

"GLIDE. PUSH. GLIDE."

I was trying.

"Glide! Push! Glide!" It was easy for Aunt to say but not nearly so easy for me to accomplish.

I pushed just a little too enthusiastically. My other foot wobbled and then all of a sudden, I was sitting on my bottom, legs splayed in front of me.

The youngest maid giggled at my misfortune. I did not blame her one whit.

The footman extended a hand and held on to mine as I carefully clambered to my feet.

"Again."

"Wouldn't it be rather better to learn at the pond? With an instructor?"

"And admit to such a gap in your education?"

Apparently not. I sighed. Gathered my courage. And then pushed once more out onto the highly over-waxed parlor floor.

"Glide. Push. Glide."

I could glide well enough. It was the pushing I seemed to have a problem with. And it was difficult to keep my feet beneath me when the skates had rags wrapped around their blades. Though no more difficult, I supposed, than it would be once they were unbound. Once I was truly on ice.

"Push."

I tried, but my foot slid out from under me.

"Push!"

Once again, I collapsed onto the floor. And this time I made a vase wobble.

The footman put a hand out to steady it.

The door to Father's study flew open. "I cannot think with all the crashing and bumping going on—"

"Beware!" Aunt and I called out the word in unison.

But Father had already reached the parlor and his feet were sliding out beneath him. As he hit the floor, the vase wobbled from its display and joined him, shattering into shards as it hit the floor.

Oh!

I pushed forward and rescued its flowers from the debris.

It took two men to help Father to his feet. "What is the meaning of all of this?"

"Clara has been invited to a skating party."

"And?"

I blushed. "I don't know how to skate."

"So?"

"The footman is trying to teach me."

"Well, it doesn't look as if it is working!" Reaching up to rub at his head, he turned around and went back into his study, slamming the door behind him.

Aunt shook her head. "Really, Clara. You must concentrate. It's not that difficult."

"It's not that difficult."

———

I EYED HARRY with something that he must have read as suspicion.

"Truly. Just look at Lizzie!"

I had been. And I wished he'd keep his admiration for her to himself. My backside still smarted from all the times I'd fallen on it while practicing. And unbeknownst to Aunt, I had fastened a small pillow to my bottom, underneath my hoop skirt.

"Here. Give me your hand." Harry stretched out his to receive mine.

I wasn't quite sure that I should take it. Wasn't I to be the one to ask for aid? Or maybe ... was it that I, as the woman, should wait for aid to be offered? I could never remember. I ventured one of my skate-clad feet out onto the ice and my decision was made for me. I clutched at Harry's hand as my feet moved in two different directions. Two vastly different directions. I began to sway like a sapling, my free hand casting out to my side for something else to hang on to.

But then Harry's hand came around my waist with a gentle pressure, and as I leaned back into his strength, he pushed us forward. Into a glide.

And I could glide.

I did glide!

But then he pushed off again. "Stop trying so hard. Just let me push us." He let go my hand and took up the other. "See? It looks as if we're dancing."

What he ought to have said was that it looked as if I knew what I was doing. Circling the pond, with his peppermint-laden breath caressing my cheek, wasn't the worst thing I'd ever done.

We circled the outer circumference of the pond once. Twice. Three times.

By then, my ankles were becoming fatigued. I glanced up from the ice to the shoreline. Saw a woman sitting by Aunt wave in our direction.

"There's someone who—"

"Katherine! Let's go see her."

As we skated closer, I could see Katherine was accompanied. By someone much shorter than she.

"There's Fritz with her. You haven't met him, have you? He's their only child. Katherine spoils him terribly; the baron dotes on him too. He's the heir, you see. It was thought, until the baron met Katherine, that he could have no heir at all."

"How felicitous. He must have been so pleased."

We had reached Katherine and Aunt. Harry lent a firm hand to help me off the ice and up to the bench. As we approached, the boy looked up at me, brown eyes cool, appraising.

Harry bent toward my ear. "He doesn't speak much English."

"I do! I speak large!"

I smothered a laugh behind a hand as his mother tousled his blond hair.

Harry squatted before him. "You mean to say that you speak much?"

"Yes. Grand. Large."

Harry looked about to laugh, but chose not to indulge it. He spoke to the boy instead. "You must be growing tired of New York."

"I want home."

"I was thinking, next time I travel to the Continent, you can take me to the Tiergarten."

"Zoo. With . . . " he seemed to pause for a moment to think. "Animals!"

"Yes. The zoo."

"Bears?"

"And lions. How would you like that?"

"Grand."

"Yes, I think it would be grand. But this is even grander." Harry pulled the boy off the bench, hefted him onto his shoulders, and hopped back onto the ice. He skated in crazy circles, spinning round and round with Fritz.

"Harry—stop! Stop now!" Katherine had run to the edge of the ice to call out to them. "Harry. That's enough!"

Laughing, the two returned, red-cheeked and panting. Then Harry offered his hand to me again.

"No. I don't think—"

"Just once more."

"I can't—"

"Say yes. Please."

"Go ahead, Clara. Why don't you skate out toward Lizzie?"

Once Aunt had thrown her support to Harry, how could I say no?

Lizzie and Franklin were away on the other side of the pond, making graceful patterns in the ice.

"Shouldn't we skate straight over? Through the middle?"

"No." Harry pulled me over toward the shore. "The ice is beginning to soften. I told Franklin it was too late in the season for an outing like this, but he said he didn't care. He wanted to go skating. He had plans."

I'd noticed that before. Harry would profess one thing or state a well-thought objection to something, and Franklin would either disregard or overcome it. As he was doing now. He had taken Lizzie out into the very middle of the ice.

Harry slowed to a gentle stop and we paused a moment to watch them. There was something almost bewitching about the way they glided over the ice, Lizzie so confident and graceful. Franklin so sure and suave.

I knew a moment's regret that I could not trade places with Lizzie. That I could not be so elegant and self-assured.

But as I watched, Lizzie's foot seemed to catch on something. A look of horror came over her face and then she collapsed into a heap.

Harry left my side, racing out to the middle, toward his

brother. By the time they returned, Franklin carrying Lizzie, I had picked my way back around to the bench and Aunt had gestured for our carriage. But the Victoria only had two seats. Aunt arranged for me to take Lizzie's place in the DeVries carriage and then climbed into our own carriage next to Lizzie to take her straight to Father.

"You'll see Clara directly home?"

Franklin bowed in reply.

As soon as our carriage began to pull away, Katherine readied Fritz for the return. And Harry began to reprimand his brother. "I knew it was too late in the season for skating! I told you the ice was turning soft in the middle. Didn't you hear me?"

"No one can see a person if all they do is skate along the edge."

"Why can't—"

"Hush!" Katherine spoke to her brothers as if they were children. "Are you going to call for the carriage or am I going to do it?"

Harry called for the carriage while Franklin dug underneath the bench for a hamper and began to round up a group of rather exotic-looking people who were clustered beneath a tree.

As he was doing so, Harry returned and joined me as I sat to remove my skates. "Franklin had the hamper done up with toast and caviar. And hired a Russian to pour tea from a samovar. And another to come with a dancing bear." He inclined his head toward a cart, where, indeed, I could see a bear, ambling back and forth on a lead. And a matron bent over a smoldering fire.

Franklin could be heard shouting at them.

Harry only shook his head and helped the rest of us into the De Vries carriage.

Franklin joined us shortly after. "My Russian tea party is ruined."

"Let's just hope Lizzie's ankle isn't ruined." Harry looked a hard glance over at his brother. "From your stupidity."

"Let's sing, shall we?" Though Katherine was smiling, the look in her blue eyes could have frozen water. "Clara? Do you have a favorite?"

"I . . . well . . . " A little levity seemed to be what was called for. "How about 'Where Did You Get That Hat?' "

> "Now how I came to get this hat 'tis very strange
>   and funny;
> Grandfather died and left to me his property and
>   money.
> And when the will it was read out, they told me
>   straight and flat,
> If I would have his money, I must always wear
>   his hat!
> "Where did you get that hat? Where did you get
>   that tile?
> Isn't it a nobby one, and just the proper style?
> I should like to have one just the same as that!"
> Where'er I go they shout "Hel-lo! Where did you
>
>   get that hat?"

By the time the carriage stopped in front of my house, the three De Vrieses were harmonizing in song as if Lizzie's accident had never occurred.

———

I WAS ABLE, that evening, to see Lizzie since Father was going over to check on her.

She was lying in bed, pale as a specter. "I've spoilt everyone's good time. Did you know about the tea party?"

"The one with the Russians? And the dancing bear?"

"And the Cossack dancers. Yes." Lizzie said it in the chastised tones of a small child.

I hadn't known about the dancers. "But it's not as if you'd planned to spoil it. It's *you* Franklin should have thought about. Not himself. He shouldn't have taken you so far out on the ice."

"He'd only meant to amuse me."

"If he likes the idea so much, then he can do it again. At a later time, once you're well."

Her face brightened at my words. "I would have liked to have seen it."

"You know you must be his only concern."

"Do you think so?"

"I know so." At least, I hoped so. Because what would it say about his character if she weren't? I bent to press a kiss to her cheek.

"You're right. And you're going to the Hamiltons' ball tonight? I wish I could be there."

"But—you—" It was then that I fully comprehended the consequences of her injury. Lizzie wouldn't be attending the ball. Or any other ball. Not for a very long time.

"But what am I to do? Without you?"

"You're to go to all those balls and be fabulously beautiful. Breathtakingly lovely. And you're to capture the heart of the De Vries heir."

"No." I was shaking my head.

She reached over to place her hands on my cheeks. "Yes. If he can't propose to me, then he must propose to you."

"But it's only a sprain. That's what Father said. You'll be back on your feet in no time! And perhaps sooner if you put twice as many plasters on it and take twice as many tonics!"

Lizzie was shaking her head in such a mournful way.

"But you must be able to ... to ... go to dinner parties! And the opera?"

She took one of my hands between her own. "No."

"But I can't do this without you!"

She squeezed it. "You must. And after, you must endeavor to see me, just like always. And tell me everything that you've done." She pressed back into her pillow. The light had gone out of her eyes.

"I'm sorry, Lizzie. So very sorry."

"So am I."

I leaned forward and placed another kiss upon her brow before leaving.

———

I WALKED BACK home with Father. Once our cloaks had been taken, once I had changed for dinner, we met up again with Aunt in the dining room.

Aunt ate with great zeal that evening. "What incredible good fortune, that the Barnes girl would put herself out of contention!"

Good fortune? Poor Lizzie. I'd like to push Aunt down the stairs and give her a chance at "incredible good fortune"!

"Yes. I told them it would be at least two weeks before she will want to test the strength of her ankle. And at least several after that before she can dance."

Two weeks without her. At least. They stretched before me, bleak and desolate. I imagined one ball after another, one dinner after another, with no one to share them with and no one to provide a break from Franklin. I wished I'd sprained my own ankle instead. As I came out of my reverie, it was to find both Father and Aunt staring at me.

"Clara, this your chance. No more waiting. No more dithering about." Aunt had put down her fork to speak to me.

Father took a drink of wine and then addressed me as well. "You have two weeks to secure the heir. Perhaps a bit more if I can talk the Barneses into keeping Lizzie off her feet."

He would try to keep her in bed? For my benefit? But didn't

he understand? I couldn't do this, any of it, none of it without her!

"You must move quickly. And when the time is right—" Aunt looked toward Father.

He nodded.

"When the time is right, then we will act."

CHAPTER 29

$\mathcal{T}$HE NEXT DAY I snuck out of the house and over to Lizzie's just as soon as I could figure out how to do it. Though she had cheered when she'd first seen me, she'd taken to her pillow once more in a sulk.

"Illness becomes you. It's too bad Franklin can't see you like this."

Lizzie scowled.

"Truly. Especially since it's nearly Valentine's Day." She looked rather tragic with her golden curls askew about her head and her high color muted.

"I wish it became me to sleep all day. They won't let me leave my bed." The last she said loudly, for her mother's ears.

I leaned close. And then even closer. "You should really ask for an opinion from a different doctor."

Lizzie looked at me, confusion dimming her eyes. "But why? Your father treated me as soon as it happened."

"I know. But... just... please, Lizzie. Ask to see another doctor. Scream and yell. Have a conniption fit. Do whatever you have to, only don't—" *please, don't leave me alone!*—"don't surrender the season without a fight."

"Do you think? Do you really think I could come back? Before the season's over?"

I nodded. Rather vigorously.

She glanced over at her mother. "Then I'll do it."

———

BEFORE WE STEPPED outside the next night to join the waiting carriage, Aunt took one of my hands into hers and then presented me with a nosegay of red roses. "For Valentine's Day. And good luck."

Apparently, every other debutante's mother had been struck by the same idea. All of us stood around the room with red roses clasped between our hands. Until the dancing began. Then we thrust them into the hands of our chaperones.

Franklin had come equipped for the evening. He was walking around with a red rose in his lapel and a gilded bow and arrow between his hands. As he aimed it at various girls in the room, they shrieked and pretended to scamper for cover.

Eventually, he made his way to me, where I stood talking with Katherine and Harry.

Franklin closed an eye, crouched, and aimed his arrow at Harry.

Harry only frowned and pushed at him.

Franklin straightened. "Nah. Only succeeds when Cupid has promising material to work with. Can't shoot the thing anyway." He tossed it onto a table and took up a glass of champagne instead. He sipped from it as he looked about the dance floor. His face brightened. He touched my arm. "Wait here. For just a minute."

And where was I going to go? By myself? Without an escort?

True to his word, he returned a minute later. And then, with a bow and a flourish, he pulled a card from his coat.

A Valentine's Day card. Overly large, it glistened with

jewels and dripped with pearls. I could do nothing but hold it up in front of me, displaying it as a badge of honor or a prize of war.

He laughed as I exclaimed over it. Over the abundance of gems and the number of pearls. Then he took it from me and handed it to Katherine for safekeeping, offering to escort me outside. To take some air.

The two of us? Alone? Reputations had been ruined for lesser transgressions. I demurred, staying with Katherine instead.

"So he gave it to you." Katherine studied the card. "You know, he spent over one hundred dollars on them."

"Them?"

"Each one. He ordered one for Lizzie too."

I could tell by her tone that she considered the sum misspent. And so did I. "I can't accept it."

Her eyes softened in color as her glance turned from the card to me. "And why not? What does it really mean, except some foolish spendthrift has paid more for an ostentatious display of his affections than he ought to have?"

"But one hundred dollars!"

"Forgive me. I shouldn't have said anything."

The nights seemed so very long without Lizzie, managing Franklin on my own. Thank heaven I had remembered her advice. When all else failed, I asked him about himself. He seemed to have ready answers. That went on and on and on.

"The celebrated and feted Miss Carter." He twirled me through the steps of a waltz. "You look good with me. You lend me a touch of elegance. And grace."

Maybe he did read the papers after all.

I danced with Mr. Lorillard and Mr. Hamilton and Mr. Vandermere.

And Harry.

As he appeared to claim me for his dance, he withdrew a

small cluster of pansies from his coat. The petals were crushed and the stems bent, but they were charming in their humility.

"The French call them *pensées*. For thoughts."

"Then thank you for thinking of me. They're my favorites."

The tops of his cheeks colored unaccountably. "That gentian blue ... it matches your eyes nearly exactly."

It was my turn to blush.

Over the sounds of the crowds, the orchestra could plainly be heard, tuning their instruments. This dance was to be the highlight of the evening. The cotillion for which everyone had practiced. Harry offered me his hand.

I took it up, and between our palms we clasped the bouquet together.

After the dance, favors were offered up to the participants. A glittering heart carved from crystal for the girls. And a gleaming silver flask for the men.

There were only several dances left after that one. And at the end of the ball, in the rush to the cloakroom, I forgot to reclaim my card from Katherine. But she caught me in the crowd and gave it to me. And so I left that night, holding on to a hundred-dollar card, a heart made from crystal, and a fast-fading cluster of flowers.

When I reached the sanctity of my room, I put the card away in the drawer of my desk. I was exhausted. Franklin, Franklin, and more Franklin. Aunt was ecstatic, Father was pleased. I was miserable. And if I thought ahead to year after year of unalleviated, unrelieved exposure to Franklin? It made me want to run away.

I tossed the crystal heart into my chest of drawers and then I took that spent bouquet of pansies and pressed them between the leaves of my Byron.

FATHER WAS ABSORBED by his newspaper Monday morning at breakfast. We heard nothing from him until he emerged, red-faced, from behind the broadsheet. "He's decided to take on Tammany Hall!" Aunt started, dropping her piece of toast. "Who? What?"

"The fool reverend at Madison Square Presbyterian. Preached a whole sermon about corruption and politics. And then a reporter had to go and write it up. As if no one knew anything at all about how the city operates! You give a little to get. . . quite a lot."

"Please, Brother. Not at the table."

"Not at the table? It will end up in our own parlor before it's all done. He's out to ruin a perfectly good system."

I could not keep from speaking. Not after the conversations I'd had with Mr. Douglas about Tammany Hall. "But if the system is based on corruption how can that be bad? Isn't that what politicians protect us from?"

Father let the newspaper drop to the floor and then folded his hands on the table and leaned forward over them. When he spoke it was as if he thought he were speaking to a young child. "Here is the way that it works. Everything in the city is run through Tammany Hall. You need a factory built? Or a gas line extended? You can stand in line for a permit at City Hall or you can just go down to Tammany Hall, talk to a few people, and the job's done before your permit's even been approved. You must pay out a bit of money, of course. But in the end, isn't it worth it?"

"Worth it to pay for a permit that would be approved anyway?"

Father smiled. "Ah, but there's the trick. It might not get approved. Not if you don't find your way to Tammany Hall first."

"So you're required to pay? For business the city should conduct as a matter of course?"

"It's how politics has always been conducted."

It didn't sound quite right. I didn't know very much about politics, and it wasn't as if I would ever vote on anything, but still it seemed quite removed from the concept of democracy that Miss Miller had preached.

"And where do you think I got my workers for Dr. Carter's?"

"For the factory?"

"For exactly that. I went to Tammany Hall and told them how many workers I needed. The next day they showed up at the door. And a foreman to go along with them."

"But where did they come from?"

"Does it matter? They're immigrants."

Didn't it? If I ran a factory, I'd want to know who I was employing. Although, I'd seen Father's factory once. Miss Miller had pointed it out one day in passing. It didn't seem like a bottling plant, although I'm sure I didn't know what one ought to look like. It must have been much more sanitary on the inside than it was on the outside.

"I might have paid for the privilege, but I pay the workers less than I would have otherwise. Everyone wins."

Everyone except the poor immigrant.

———

"AREN'T YOU READY?" Aunt stopped in my room the following evening to collect me for the night's events. An opera followed by a private reception at the Astors'.

"Almost."

"What's wrong? The bloom has gone off your cheeks."

"Nothing."

Aunt approached me. Took my hand up in hers. The cool chill of it seemed to spread ice through my veins. "What is it? You can tell me."

I looked long and deep into her eyes and realized that,

perhaps, I could. "I don't know if I can put up with Franklin for the rest of my life. He's quite unbearable. And I just don't see how I could stand him." I hadn't meant to cry, but tears unbidden had begun to blur my vision.

"Oh, my dear! Marriage is nothing like the season. In marriage you'll have a whole host of obligations to distract you from him. Just think of them: You'll have your at-home days, your calls to pay, and your clubs. There will be rooms to redecorate and furniture to buy. Gowns to be fitted for and parties to plan. Newport in the summer and Europe in the autumn."

Europe. Maybe even Italy?

But Europe seemed too little a reward for being married to Franklin. It wasn't that he was a mean person. Or even a truly bad sort. He was just so . . . not someone like . . . Harry.

Aunt put a chill hand to my cheek. "You think too much. You worry too much. Marriage is not meant to be a paradise. It's an institution. One which you are destined to enter. Don't suffer such gloomy notions. Not when a season is in progress. This is the best part. Save the work, save your brooding, for later."

CHAPTER 30

ARRY SIGNED FOR two dances. His waltz came first. It was a welcome relief to dance with him. I didn't have to try to interpret or anticipate his steps. It just seemed as if he went the right direction at the right time and I happily followed along.

"You look a shade paler than normal."

"I worry about Lizzie."

"Lizzie's fine. She should be worrying about you."

"Why?"

"I should think *I* would be if you were intent on marrying a suitor out from under me."

I sighed. At least he seemed to accept the situation now. "I wish she were here."

"You won't be able to share him forever, you know."

There was no need to clarify the "him" of whom Harry spoke. "I know."

"What will you do when he has to make a choice?"

"I wish..."

"What? What do you wish?"

I smiled. "Nothing." I was going to wish that Franklin could be more like Harry, but that would have been foolish. "I'm a girl, Harry, I don't have many choices. I debuted this year. I have to marry. If I don't, then I would be like . . . like a hat that's seen one too many seasons."

"But what if you weren't a girl? What if . . . what if you were me?" He quickly reversed the dance and moved us in the opposite direction.

"If I'm you, then who are you?" I was having trouble keeping up. With both the change in the dance and the change in the conversation.

"I'm you."

"Well, then . . ."That was simple. "I'd marry me!"

"You'd marry . . . you'd marry me?"

"Of course. I'd call you my darling. My darling Clara." I smiled.

Harry twirled me. "And then I'd call you dear Harry. No. No. I'd call you *dearest* Harry."

"And we could talk all we wanted, forever even, and never worry about making calls or attending balls, or operas, or private dinners."

He guided me effortlessly on the dance floor. "And we could go to Europe. We could live there."

"Where?"

Harry raised a brow. "England?"

I frowned.

"Italy?"

I nodded.

"And I would ... I would love you forever, dearest Harry."

"And I you, my darling Clara."

We stared into each other's eyes for a long instant, and then I began to giggle and he began to chuckle and soon we were laughing together.

When the dance had finished and Harry escorted me back to Aunt, we were still laughing. Hard enough that I was finding it difficult to breathe. And not from the corset. The only thing that saved me was that I saw Franklin. He was standing against the wall, staring at us. And the look in his eyes stifled any mirth that I had felt.

———

AUNT AND I went to claim some cups of punch. As we drank it, the swirling, chattering crowds seemed to press in upon me and their bright gaiety proved more than I could bear.

I handed Aunt my cup. "I think I—"

"Clara?"

"I just need a bit . . ." Spurning convention, I walked from the ballroom toward the parlor in search of a bit of solitude, for a few brief moments, so that I could compose myself. Before me, I saw Harry duck into an alcove. Curious, I came up upon it softly so that I could know what it was that he was doing.

"You don't think so?" Franklin's voice was surprised. Astonished.

"No." Harry's voice was flat. Serious.

"Truly?"

"Truly. All in all, I have to say that I prefer Lizzie Barnes to Clara Carter."

Harry's words hit me like a blow to the stomach. I stood there for one long moment, and then I began to run.

I ran as fast as my satin-slippered feet would let me for as long as I found the space. I ended up, finally, in the kitchen— hiding my face as I pushed through the startled servants and let myself out the back door.

Harry preferred Lizzie to me? Really?

Truly. That was what he had said. *Truly, all in all.*

But. . . how could . . . how could Harry prefer her to me?

Across the lawn, by the garden wall, arose a scratchy feline yowl that I might have believed originated in the depths of my own soul.

It was joined by another. And back and forth, up and down the scale, those two cats hollered and spit until at last the chorus ended in a shriek and a hiss.

I let myself down on a bench and sat there, spent.

Harry preferred Lizzie.

What more was there to say?

If Harry preferred Lizzie to me, then . . . good. Fine! It made giving myself to Franklin that much easier. Why had I worried so much about Harry's feelings? Though it seemed he had quite a few of them, apparently none were directed toward me.

Good.

Fine!

I would go back into that ballroom, and I would dance with Franklin, and God willing, sometime this week or next he would propose to me. And I would say yes!

Yes, Franklin.

Yes, Franklin, of course I'll marry you.

Yes, Franklin, I'd be delighted to marry you.

Yes, Franklin, my heart's desire has always been to marry you.

But if it had always been my heart's desire, then why was I crying as if the moon had just fallen from the sky?

One of the cats slunk away along the wall and the other scrabbled its way up a tree.

I took off a glove, turned it inside out, and used it to dry my tears. It was much softer, much more comforting than my impractical lace handkerchief. I took a faltering breath. And another one. Then I put my glove to rights and pushed to my feet.

I checked the front of my skirt and brushed off the back. Made sure my bosoms were in place. And then I mounted the steps and went back into the house.

I took a pencil from my reticule and lined out Harry's name from my dance card.

On my way back to Aunt, I found Mr. Lorillard and tapped him on the shoulder. "I find I have been relieved of a dance partner for the first dance after intermission. Would you like to take his place?"

He bowed. "Of course."

I offered him up my card. "Just there. The lancers."

"Thank you."

As the music began, I made sure I was by Mr. Lorillard's side. He took my hand in his to begin the first steps.

But we were stopped by Harry.

"This is my dance."

"Miss Carter said—"

"I'm sorry, Harry. I thought you had gone."

"Gone? But I've been here all night."

"My mistake. So sorry." I pulled at Mr. Lorillard's hand, turned from Harry and did not look at him for the rest of the night.

When Franklin came to claim me for the last waltz, I made certain I closed my eyes and leaned into his chest just the way he liked. Only this night I leaned especially close.

And I felt his hand creep up around my side.

As the dance ended, he bent close to whisper in my ear. His breath tickled my ear. "You darling!"

———

THAT NIGHT, ABED, my thoughts would not rest. And my memory would not lie. It kept replaying, in perfect detail, the conversation I had overheard.

Had Harry just been pretending all this time? Pretending to hold an affection for me? But if so, why? So that he could remain in close contact with Lizzie? For where I was, she was never far behind. But surely he knew that her parents would never let her marry him. Just as surely as he knew my father would never let him marry me.

And honestly, what could he possibly see in Lizzie?

Hair that glistened like gold?

A laugh that rang out as clear as a bell?

And eyes that sparkled like sapphires?

Why would he not fall in love with Lizzie? Why would anyone not fall in love with Lizzie Barnes?

CHAPTER 31

THE FOLLOWING EVENING, there was a performance at the Music Hall. Katherine extricated me from the crowds during intermission. Concern washed her blue eyes with gray. "Has something gone wrong?"

"With what?"

"With you? And Harry?"

I kept my voice flat. "I have no idea."

"He's been so despondent. As if the heart's gone out of him."

Of course it had. "He misses Lizzie."

Katherine shook her head so vehemently, her hair ornament seemed in danger of flying off. "Harry is the best of my brothers, and I don't like to see him so forlorn. Please, has there been some argument between you two?"

"There's nothing between us."

"Nothing? Are you sure? Because I wish you would have him. Franklin will only play with you, like some shiny new toy, and then, once your novelty has worn off, he'll take up with someone else. He's not worth the money."

I couldn't keep my mouth from falling open.

"Shocked?"

I most certainly was.

"On the other hand, Harry is worth more than his weight in gold. Only he has none. Not compared to Franklin, though Papa will make certain he will never want for anything."

She made it sound as if I were a gold digger. But then, wasn't I? Hadn't my sights been trained upon only the best and the wealthiest of bachelors? And hadn't I been ordered to secure him? At all costs?

"You haven't been long in our circles. And perhaps it's best if you don't linger too long. Those who dance too close to the fire always get burnt." A great sadness weighted her words.

I tried on a smile to lift her spirits. "You seem to have survived without being scorched."

"What seems is not always what is."

"But you're married. To a baron."

"Yes."

We both looked over at him. As we watched, he took up a glass of champagne and then he tipped the glass to his mouth and drank it all in one great swallow.

"You're not happy." Perhaps I shouldn't have said the words.

"Happiness would have exacted far too high a price. And I am not unhappy."

As we watched, Mr. Douglas walked up to the baron and began to speak to him. The German had to crane his head to look up at him.

"I should not have come back."

I reached out to touch her arm. "I'm glad you did."

She turned her gaze upon me and when she smiled, it contained real warmth. "Thank you. That's the nicest compliment anyone has paid me this evening." She paused then and placed her gloved hand upon my own. "Remember, Clara: Not all choices are as terrible as we imagine them to be. When you must make a choice, choose with your heart."

"My wishes aren't my own."

"Perhaps they should be." She leaned over and kissed me on the cheek. And then, once Mr. Douglas had gone, she walked over to join her husband.

————

THE NEXT EVENING'S private ball brought a surprise: Lizzie's return to society.

How I had longed to talk to her scant days before—to tell her about the possibility of Harry, to see if she could think of any way for us to be together. But now – now that Harry had revealed his true sentiments, I didn't know what to do. Should I speak to her of them? But how could I, without revealing my own heart? And had she not once said that if it were Harry we were both after, that she would fight me for him? Perhaps she returned his sentiments. Perhaps she already even knew of them.

How stupid I had been. Of course she knew.

And of course she returned his affection.

How could she not?

Had Aunt not predicted their match weeks ago? And had he not been neglecting to sign my dance card even while he had been certain to sign Lizzie's? I felt so angry with her for taking something—which, in all fairness, had never been mine—that I found myself quite without words when she came up behind me and threaded her arm through my own. I turned and even as I recognized a terrible jealousy within my soul, I saw an agony at work behind her eyes.

"Lizzie?"

She looked up at me, eyes glazed, then leaned so hard upon my arm that I nearly staggered.

"What is it?"

A dew of perspiration lined her upper lip. "My ankle." She lifted her skirts with one hand. Just enough that I could see her foot had been wrapped in gauze, leaving her ankle about four inches too thick.

"Mama said I could no longer delay. She made me come tonight. And I have Franklin for a polka. You know how energetic he is. I don't think I can do it!"

Of course, she couldn't do it. And for the first time in memory, I despised Mrs. Barnes and her ambitions, for making Lizzie attend a ball when she clearly couldn't dance. "Let me see your dance card."

She flapped it toward me.

I found Franklin's name, took a rubber from my reticule and erased it. Wrote Harry's name instead.

And then I looked for that same dance on my card . . . Harry — perfect! I erased Harry's name and wrote Franklin's in its place.

"Here." I handed it back to her. "Dance the polka with Harry. And I'll dance it with Franklin."

The lines that had been etched into her brow eased a bit. "Oh, thank you."

When the polka came, Franklin and Harry appeared together. But when Franklin began to offer Lizzie his hand, I stepped in front of her. Pretended, in fact, to be her. And every other debutante at the ball.

I pouted. Tapped at him on the chest with my fan. "Have you forgotten? You promised the polka to me!"

For one moment, an uncharacteristic look of confusion rode his features. But then he shook it off. Smiled. "I always dance the polka with Lizzie. And I always dance the waltz with you—"

"Which is why I made you promise to save me one. Tonight." I pulled the card from my wrist and held it up for him to see.

"Polka. Mr. Franklin DeVries." He bowed. Offered me his arm. "My mistake."

As he escorted me onto the floor, I looked back and saw

Harry standing at Lizzie's side, gazing at me in bewilderment. But soon I saw him take up Lizzie's hand and follow after us.

I would not have known that her ankle was bound had I not seen it myself. She hopped and galloped around the dance floor with nary a stumble. In fact, I think I was the only one who saw her faint clean away.

A look of astonishment crossed Harry's face, for just a moment, and then he grasped her tightly and whisked her away to an alcove. He'd moved so quickly it looked as if they were still dancing.

I left Franklin's arms to join them.

"Can I help?"

"She's fainted!"

Franklin had trailed me. He looked at Lizzie and then shrugged. "We can't do anything about it now but finish our dance." He escorted me from the alcove and whirled me back to the dance.

I saw Lizzie return, leaning heavily on Harry's arm. He was looking down at her, adoringly. I saw him reach over to pat her hand.

There was no doubt. He truly did prefer Lizzie Barnes to me.

The dance ended as we galloped past the refreshment table. Franklin reached out and grabbed a flute. "Champagne?"

"Yes. Thank you." The bubbles scoured my throat as they went down and I knew I would soon regret them, but I couldn't seem to make myself care.

———

I DIDN'T UNDERSTAND what was happening to me.

Harry loved Lizzie. I couldn't marry him anyway. What did it even matter?

I ran up the stairs, intent upon the sanctuary of my room. But once I reached the door, I was loath to go in. I wanted something different, something more than the thoughts I had to offer to myself.

I walked farther down the hall and pushed open the door to Mama's old bedroom. It swung open on silent hinges.

It still smelled of jasmine and lavender. I slipped inside and closed the door firmly behind me. Stepped into the middle of the room and . . . stopped.

What had I come for?

What had I hoped to find?

There was nothing here of those last dark, dismal days. No odor of stale sweat. No hint of the cloyingly sweet stink of blood. No moaning, no sighs. And least of all, there was no wasted body, tucked away from view beneath the bed linens.

I walked to the bed and then sat down upon it. I lay my head on Mama's pillow and closed my eyes. A poem recalled itself to my memory, the words unfurling in Mother's soft, whispered voice. I whispered the words along with her.

> "There rose no day, there roll'd no hour
> Of pleasure unembitter'd;
> And not a trapping deck'd my power
> That gall'd not while it glitter'd."

She had repeated those lines over and over again like a refrain during her last hours. But hearing those words, over and over again, was not so terrible as seeing her clawing at her corset, insisting that she wanted to be freed. Father, finally, had dosed her with laudanum. It had made her stop, though her fingernails had collected tatters of the lace and ribbons she had tried to shred. After the dosing, she had ceased her frantic, fevered movements and had settled. Then she had folded her hands upon her chest and begun to sing.

> "I heard the voice of Jesus say,

'Come unto Me and rest;
Lay down, thou weary one, lay down
Thy head upon My breast.'
I came to Jesus as I was,
Weary and worn and sad,
I found in Him a resting place,
And He has made me glad. "

She sang that hymn until she sang no more. Until she could sing no more. She sang it with the last breath of her life.

"I came to Jesus as I was, weary and worn and sad."

What if I came to Him just as I was? What would He say? And what would Mama say to me if she were still living? Would she know what to do with a heart that had been shattered?

Mama, I need you.

I opened my eyes and pushed up from her bed. Walked about the room, eyes lingering on her perfume bottles, her brush and comb. I held up her mirror to my face.

It only reflected back my own image.

Opening her wardrobe, I breathed deeply of the lavender that still scented it. I pushed through her dresses. Pushed into them and draped their arms across my shoulders, wrapping myself in a phantom embrace. But then my shoe pushed into something hard, ushering reality into my fantasy. I stepped out of the wardrobe and knelt on the floor in front of it. I stretched out an arm to discover what my toe had hit.

A box.

I pulled it out and set it on the floor.

It was filled with an assortment of odd contraptions. Rubber rings and bowls and cups in varying sizes, each one attached to a steel bar or spring. Devices of a masklike shape with a hinge in the middle, fixed to a rod with a screw at the end.

I disentangled them from each other as I pulled them from the box and laid them before me on the floor. I had just reached in to retrieve the last of them when I heard the sound of the door shutting behind me.

I turned, prepared to defend my intrusion.

Father walked into the room and sat on Mother's bed. "I'll never forget the first time I heard her. It was in church and she was singing. And I knew right then that she could have the entire city at her feet if she wanted to." The features of his handsome face seemed touched with something. Sadness? Regret?

"Did she want to?"

"There were several years when she was the only person the papers ever mentioned. We were guests of the Lorillards and the Hamiltons. Even the De Vrieses. That's when I acquired all of them as clients. It was your mother's charm and grace that secured them for me."

"What did you like most about her?"

He turned his gaze from his memories to me, a smile upon his lips. "The way she used to look at me, when we first met, as if I were the only person in the world."

She used to look at me that way too. Right up until the day she died.

"She looked at me that way before we married. Before I brought her to the city." His eyes fixed on a spot somewhere beyond my shoulder. I wondered when it was that she had stopped looking at him that way. And why.

"She suffered from female hysteria. And a falling womb." He coughed. Cleared his throat. "Prolapsed, we call it. At the end, there was no pessary that could push it back up inside."

A falling womb?

Prolapsed?

I knew the words. I knew them all individually. But I didn't understand what they meant when they were all put together. A prolapsed falling womb. "What do you mean?"

"I could not keep it inside."

"Keep . . . ? I didn't understand. What was it that he couldn't keep inside?

"Of course, she worked with the corsetiere. I provided her with the best services that money could buy."

Corsetiere?

"The woman said she could provide a sort of structure for her, to keep it fixed inside."

It?

"But the tighter she laced, the worse the problem became. I should have known—I might have thought . . . but, she tried them all." He was staring at the pile of devices strewn about the floor.

I gathered them up and shoved them back into the box.

"They worked, each one, for a while. But none of them permanently. And then she developed the infection."

"Mama died of the fever." That's what I had always been told.

"Yes. A fever caused by a prolapsed womb which finally fell completely and then became infected."

"I don't understand what you mean when you say *prolapsed.*"

"She could not keep her womb fixed inside her."

"Her womb?" How could a womb not be . . . ? "But isn't a womb meant to be inside?"

"Yes."

"When you say that it wasn't inside . . . ?"

"It fell. Outside."

Her womb fell outside. "Outside of her--?" I couldn't make myself say the word. I tried again. "Her womb fell outside of her body?"

"Yes. She was in great pain."

"But couldn't you do something for her?"

"We tried. I tried." He gestured toward the box.

The box of devices. From small to large with rings, and cups, and bowls in varying sizes. Suddenly, I understood.

"I ordered every kind of support, every pessary. I tried

SIRI MITCHELL

everything I knew to do. But still, her liver atrophied. And then, when she developed the infection . . ."

Now I understood why she always winced when I sat on the edge of her bed. I understood why she nearly fainted the day I stumbled in my approach and threw an arm out to steady myself. And I understood now exactly what those devices had been used for. Bile rose in my throat.

"You asked the corsetiere to treat her?" I could no longer keep my tone modulated. Hysteria had spun my words into a shriek.

"It seemed best."

"She was clawing at her corset the day that she died! She wanted to be freed!"

"I did what I knew to do."

What he knew to do? He didn't know anything! "But don't you see? You're the one that killed her! You told her she had to do that to herself. In order to be beautiful to you! Can't you see?"

He stood there, staring at the devices, mouth working, but there were no words. He had nothing to say.

"Why couldn't you see? She was beautiful. She was perfect."

"She was. We made her into the most beautiful woman in the city."

"But she was already beautiful. You're the one that ruined her."

"I did no such—"

I pushed up from the floor to my knees, trying to gain my feet, but stood up on my skirts instead. My gait shortened, I stumbled. Throwing out my hands for balance, I plunged them straight into the box of pessaries.

I remember opening my mouth to scream. I remember feeling my fingers caught up in steel coils and rubber rings, and then the box began to swirl and the cups and bowls merged together as all of the color drained out of the world.

CHAPTER 32

I WAKENED SLOWLY, feeling as if my limbs had been weighted with something deliciously warm and downy. I felt as if I were floating, shrouded by a big, heavy blanket. It seemed too much trouble to move, too much trouble to even open my eyes, so I just lay as I was, uncertain where I was, but not truly caring to know.

"Give her another dose in three hours."

Wherever I was, I was not alone. That voice had been my father's.

I felt a hand touch my cheek. A warm hand. It slid to my temple. "And perhaps you should think about a larger corset."

"Larger?" That voice was Aunt's. "But her waist is gargantuan! No one would want her as she is. Not as she is now. And certainly not the De Vries heir. Not when there's Lizzie Barnes to consider. There's too much that depends upon this debut. And there are less than two weeks left in the season."

I heard Father sigh. The hand disappeared, and I regretted the loss of that warmth. "Then at least do not lace her any tighter. There is a point at which I can no longer be of any help.

The point at which her mother failed. If that happens, she's no good to anyone."

I heard Father's footsteps retreat. Heard a door open. Heard it close.

I had almost drifted into a place of perfect peace and contentment when I heard a sigh and came to realize that it came from beside me. I tried to turn my head, but could not do it. And so, not displeased, and certainly not anxious, I slipped back beneath the comfortable haze of oblivion.

———

WHEN I WOKE the next morning, my limbs were restless and my body longed for some useful activity. Aunt aided me to sitting. And then she helped me to stand. My head spun for a moment, but then slowly settled, like a swirl of autumn leaves.

Aunt gestured to the maid.

She came, hands ready to tighten my laces.

"It was the corset that killed Mama."

"Yes." Aunt looked me in the eyes. "But we didn't know it at first. Not until it was too late."

"The kind same corset that you've made me wear."

"The same corset that any girl of good breeding wears."

"It's killing me."

"It's molding you. In any case, we're not reducing you to the extreme that your mother reduced. And once you've obtained the heir, then we'll order new, larger ones."

Once I'd obtained the heir.

The maid pulled the laces tight. My breathing was severed, for just an instant. Then, slowly, my lungs adjusted and my breath returned.

Whenever I tried to turn my thoughts back to what happened in Mama's room, they slithered away from me like serpents. I couldn't reconcile the facts of Mama's death with my childhood's beliefs. I couldn't bring myself to comprehend the horrible, agonizing illness that she had endured. Or the fact that my father, a physician, a man who ought to have been her first defender, had failed her. And that he had chosen to sacrifice my own well-being in the same way.

> There rose no day, there roll'd no hour
> Of pleasure unembitter'd;
> And not a trapping deck'd my power
> That gall'd not while it glitter'd.

I understood the words now. And if I had any tears left, I would have wept from the knowledge. But a rage had welled up inside me against my father. If he had implicated himself in Mama's death, then what else had he done? Who else had he harmed?

And what had he been doing in The Bowery?

———

I KNOCKED ON the door to Father's study.

"Enter."

I turned the knob and pushed it open.

"My dear. Are you feeling better?"

I nodded and tried to smile.

He gestured toward a chair. "Have a seat."

I sat.

"What can I do for you?"

I wasn't quite sure. And now that I was in his study, sitting across the desk from him, I didn't know what to say. I couldn't just ask him outright. Could I?

He was drumming his fingers against the polished wood of his desk.

"There's a society column."

"Yes?"

"*The Tattler.*"

He nodded. Once. "I am familiar with it."

"There was a piece—not a piece, really, but there was a mention in it that you are familiar with The Bowery."

"The Bowery."

"I think it said 'the bowels of The Bowery.' " In fact, I knew that it had said "the bowels of The Bowery."

"And why does this concern you?"

"Because it seems that this column is usually right. And The Bowery is—"

"Unsavory."

I nodded.

He pursed his lips as he looked at me.

"Do you—I mean to say, you don't go there do you?" I needed him to tell me that *The Tattler* was wrong. But I regretted the words the instant they left my mouth. Looking at his studied good looks and respectable bookshelves filled with medical texts, I couldn't think why I imagined he would ever frequent such a place.

"What concern is it of yours, Clara? I am doing my best, everything I can think to do, to ensure that you gain a place in society. To ensure that you will never fall victim to the sudden poverty that I had to endure. Are you telling me that you're ungrateful for my efforts?"

"No! Of course not."

"Then why should you care about my methods?"

"Do you go to The Bowery to treat patients then?"

He laughed. But it wasn't at all in amusement. "I have plenty of patients uptown. They pay me quite nicely and rarely complain. My work is not difficult. I dose half my patients with laudanum and the other half with alcohol."

"Alcohol?"

"They're drunks, all of them. Or cocaine addicts."

"Cocaine?"

"What do you think is in my famous tonic?"

"Medicine."

He smiled at me as if I were simple. "Yes. Medicine for the nerves. Thirty percent of it alcohol. It would steady anyone's nerves. A nice bit of luck that I stumbled onto the recipe." He eyed the safe in the corner with something akin to pride in his eyes. "And it's locked away so that it can never be duplicated. Unless I choose to let it be."

"But—"

"They're not ill. At least not most of them. But if taking a sip of *Dr. Carter's* now and then allows them to put their minds at ease and face another day of drudgery, then why should I begrudge them?"

"Because it's immoral!"

"Yes. I suppose it is. Tragic. But they keep asking me for more. And more for them means more money for me."

He seemed quite imperturbable. "Is that what it's all about? Money?"

He laughed. "Of course it's about money. It's all about money — everything's about money! And don't look at me as if you're horrified by it. It's only thanks to me and my quick thinking that you've had the upbringing you've had. The Panic of '73 and those De Vrieses stripped me of our family's money. We owe everything we have to *Dr. Carter's* and the patients who drink it."

"It's all about money." At last, I was beginning to understand him.

"Yes. And if I hope to gain any, I must go where it is. The Bowery is one of those places."

The Bowery. A place of prostitutes and extortionists.

"Ah. I can see that I've shocked you. But any well-bred woman knows that it's best to just accept and ignore."

"Accept and ignore." My voice sounded as if it were coming from such a great distance.

"Accept that all men have their little peccadilloes and learn how to ignore them."

"All men?"

He shrugged. "Most men. There has to be somewhere to go to discuss Mr. Hamilton's affairs and Mr. Vandermere's perversions and Mrs. Remstell's unmentionable liaisons."

"I'm not meant to speak of things so disagreeable."

"Of course you aren't."

"It's what Aunt taught me."

He nodded approval. "Always listen to what she says."

"But if you—what I mean to say is—" I didn't know what I wanted to say. "I don't know how to speak of such things."

"And well you shouldn't. It's the way things are. Women agree not to mention the unmentionable, and men agree to pretend as if they never commit such transgressions. That's the way it works in polite society." His eyes narrowed as he looked at me. "I've disillusioned you. I've disillusioned me. But if this is life—then let's have the best of it." He smiled, but it was a smile devoid of animation. "That's what I'm working to secure for you. The best of it. If this is all there is, then at least you'll have it all."

CHAPTER 33

ITH THE TRUTH of Mother's death and the revelation of Father's life, society seemed a sham. A swirling, twirling, glittering façade. None of it of worth. None of it quite real. Except for Katherine. She, I believed, was real. And I had come to detect a deep sadness in her whenever she looked at Mr. Douglas. Which was quite often. But as far as I could tell, they never spoke. I decided to remedy the situation.

That night, once Lizzie relieved me of Franklin, I made my way to Katherine's side.

"There is someone you must meet. He has been a great help to me this season."

She turned to me and smiled. "Of course. I would be pleased to. It's always good to have a savior."

As soon as she saw who it was I was taking her to, she stopped walking and plucked at my sleeve. "I mustn't—"

It was too late; I had already alerted Mr. Douglas.

He had turned. Upon seeing my companion, he made a swift bow.

Katherine took a step forward, to my side. But it was not made with any quickness or grace.

"Mr. Douglas, I would like to introduce you to Baroness von Bergholz. Formerly of this city."

He inclined his head. "Baroness."

"Mr. Douglas." Her skin had gone translucent, her lips blue. "Miss Carter tells me you have been a great friend to her this season."

"Not a friend. Simply an observer. Everything I have written is the truth."

Her hand found mine as if it groped for some sure support.

"Madam? I can serve you?" The baron pushed into our conversation, eyes darting from Katherine to Mr. Douglas and back again.

"Oh, Gerhardt!" For the first time that I could remember, she said his name in relief and gratitude. She pulled her hand from mine and placed it into his. "I am not well."

He glanced over at Mr. Douglas with some alarm, his blue eyes clouding. And then he offered his arm to her, covering her hand with his own. They left without excusing themselves.

Mr. Douglas glanced down at me with cool appraisal and then he turned and stalked away, leaving me quite alone. Alone with the feeling that I had done something terribly wrong.

———

LATER THAT NIGHT, I chanced to overhear a conversation between Katherine and Mr. Douglas as I passed the library, on my way to the lavatory. I registered their presence in a glance as I passed the door. But it was the vehemence in their words that made me slow my pace. They were standing at the back of the room, by a window, the fire's light reflecting in its panes. He had stretched out a hand to her. She shrank from it. "Don't, Charlie."

"But—"

"Please. Stop." She took a step backward. "I can only remember that your *kindness* cost me everything."

His hand was still outstretched, as if he were trying to coax a wild animal close. "I didn't mean—"

"And neither did I. But the truth is, it happened."

He closed the distance between them and took up her hand. "If only you would let me see you."

"To what end?"

"Kate." His voice was a reproach. His hand had found her cheek. She flinched, then closed her eyes as she leaned into his hand. "I am Katherine, Baroness von Bergholz. That is who you have made me. Do not ask me to become anything else for you." The last words came cloaked in a sob as she turned from him.

I sped down the hall before they could see me.

I had done a very terrible thing indeed.

———

The New York Journal—Society
February 19, 1892

Among all the bright flowers that have graced this social season, we will mourn Miss Clara Carter the most. The Lenten season to come does not bear thinking about absent the charms of her grace and elegance. We can only say that we hope her future plans will include Newport for the summer season.

The Tattler
February 19, 1892

As the season nears its conclusion, we can only say good riddance to those debutantes who grasp at the proverbial golden ring, who flirt and dance through balls and pretend their enemies are bosom friends. Which debutante was sure she had her rival out of the way for the rest of the season? The same girl whose dreams of fortune were destroyed when said rival returned unexpectedly.

I felt the blood drain from my face as I read it. I'd thought The Tattler was done. I'd thought he was dead. But Mr. Hooper was already buried by the time Lizzie had recovered from her injury. He couldn't have been The Tattler. But if he wasn't, then who was?

After breakfast I returned to my room and found my scrapbook. I read each *Tattler* article and tried to recall who had been at each event with me. The first event at which my attendance had been noted was the opera. Everyone had been there. So everyone from Mrs. Astor down to Aunt herself was suspect. That didn't help at all.

I turned the page.

The Posts' ball.

The Tattler had voiced a dissatisfaction with debutantes in general.

I read those words again:

If you asked any of them, they would tell you the same: They do what they do because they are told to do it. They line up every year and partake of the pageantry of the season because it's what they're expected to do. But can a girl who flirts with abandon truly be innocent of trawling for the fortunes of this city's wealthiest citizens? Does naiveté beget stupidity as well?

Although the words applied to me, I could not quite convince myself that they were aimed at me in particular.

I went on to the next event. The Vandermeres' ball.

. . . and at the Vandermeres' ball, other intrigues were afoot. Let the observer remain vigilant. If the lives of past debutantes of this fair city are any indication, what is expected or predicted does not always occur. And many a presumably faithful heart has been known to wander.

Ah—she of faithless heart. Another piece that didn't apply to me. So perhaps I was simply prone to hysterics, discerning a spy behind every palm tree and spite in every *Tattler* article. But I reread it just to be certain.

No. Nothing.

I turned another page.

The dinner at Delmonico's.

Ah! Now that had been much more limited in scope. A private dinner party. Franklin and Henry. Lizzie. Mr. Porter. Mr. Hamilton. A dozen other older guests.

I turned the page.

The runaway carriage. The piece in which *The Tattler* had mentioned my father. And the participants were even fewer than those who had attended the Delmonico's dinner. There had been Mr. Douglas. And Harry.

Which of our city's lovely debutantes wandered far from Fifth Avenue on a winter's afternoon when a runaway carriage pulled her into The Bowery? Through some cajoling of The Bowery element and the aid of a gentleman, all was put right. But that is

*not the first time that a person of her name has ventured into the
bowels of our fair city.*

Slowly, as I went through the events, I discovered only one
name that kept appearing. One person with whom I had done
nearly everything this season.

Harry.

I went to sleep that night in utter desolation. Harry was the
only person *The Tattler* could possibly be. And it didn't make
sense. Why would the De Vries family strenuously and directly
oppose my match with Franklin when they could simply scuttle
it in The Tattler's column through insinuation and misrepresen-
tation? They could have simply let the paper do their work for
them. So what kind of game were they playing? Their words
and their actions seemed at odds. And why had Harry agreed to
such a task? I had thought, had hoped, that he liked me.

At least a little.

Had I misinterpreted everything? Wasn't Lizzie always
accusing me of doing just that? It was quite clear to me now that
he despised me.

CHAPTER 34

ℐT WAS WITH a heavy heart that I attended the Schemerhorns' ball the next evening. But thankfully, Harry was nowhere to be seen.

"He's at home in bed with a cold." Katherine had smiled from across the room when she saw me and at intermission had come over to kiss the air in front of my cheek.

"Who?" I had no idea of whom she spoke.

"Harry. He's quite miserable really. And even so, we nearly had to lock him in his room to get him to stay in bed."

"Oh." Not that it mattered. At least there would be no one this night who could tattle on me.

Mr. Hamilton danced two dances with me. And two with Lizzie. Mr. Lorillard flirted with us both during an intermission. And in between all of it, in between the wretched boredom of the dances and the tedium of observing such extravagant displays of wealth, I decided to imbibe in champagne.

Why not?

Who would it hurt?

And besides, what more could be said about me that *The Tattler* had not already said?

I drained my glass and gave it to a passing waiter. My lips itched abominably. I couldn't scratch them, of course, least not with my gloved fingers. But I could let my fan do the work. I tried to scratch them with my fan open, brushing it against my lips as I half turned toward the wall, but it didn't work. I only succeeded in putting a dent in the fan.

I smoothed it out. Turned back toward the crowds. Closed the fan a bit and tried again.

Ah, relief!

It felt so marvelous, so satisfying, that I even smiled at Mr. Porter as I did it. He of tall stature and red nose. I danced several more dances and then, at the next intermission, decided to take some air. I had just taken a step away from Aunt and plunged into the cool of the night when I was accosted.

"You darling creature!" It was Mr. Porter. And he placed his arms about me.

"Please—oh, don't. Please, stop."

"All my prayers were answered when I saw you flash your fan at me."

"My . . . my fan? At you?"

"Let me kiss you, my darling."

"No!"

He took up my hand and simpered. "Don't be coy."

"Really, Mr. Porter!" I tried to push him away with my other hand.

"Ah. Miss Carter, there you are!"

Mr. Porter stopped pressing his case at the sound of Mr. Douglas's voice.

I took the opportunity to remove myself from his embrace. "I must have been rather thoughtless in the deployment of my fan, Mr. Porter. I do apologize for any misunderstanding." I took my leave before he could say more.

Mr. Douglas was still standing in the doorway, silhouetted by the ballroom's light.

"Thank you." I whispered the words as I passed him by.

"May I claim a dance?"

"You may have as many as you like. As long as you can explain them away." I held my card up to him.

He glanced it over. "What happy fortuitousness. I see a dance has just opened up—I don't expect that Mr. Porter will be claiming his."

Later in the evening, at the appointed time, he escorted me to the dance floor.

"Thank you. Again."

"Mr. Porter is a dolt. You shouldn't have encouraged him."

"I didn't!" How could he even imagine that I would have?

"You must have given him some reason to hope."

"I gave him none. I merely scratched my lip with the tip of my fan. And then, perhaps, I smiled at him."

"No more than that?"

"None." I said it with conviction.

"Surely you must know the significance of such a display."

"But I was exhibiting no affection. I was only revealing a deep desire to scratch at an itch."

He raised a brow. "On lesser desires whole dynasties have been founded. And marriages arranged."

———

The Tattler
February 21, 1892

Which debutante escorted herself into the night air at the Schemerhorns' ball? And with which young scion did she have an amorous interlude? Careful, little dove, or you may find your reputation is soon irrevocably soiled!

What was *The Tattler* insinuating? That I would--! That I was some kind of base woman? Of all of the attacks, this was the most personal. And the most despicable. That Harry would think such a thing, let alone write it! If I never saw him again, it would be too soon. I was of half a mind to cut him the next time I saw him. And certainly, I would warn Lizzie about him.

I was pondering more humiliating, more vile things to do to him when I remembered that Harry had not been at the Schemerhorns' that night. But if *The Tattler* was not Harry, then who was it?

Aunt burst through my door at that moment. "Disaster has befallen us!" She sagged back against the doorframe, looking as if she might faint. "Brother has been felled. By apoplexy." Her eyes were wide in her pale face.

"Where is he?"

She tried to reply, tried to speak, but no sound passed her lips.

"Father?" I pushed past her into the hallway. "Father!"

I heard a cough come from behind me and turned to see Aunt's maid. She curtsied. "In his study, miss."

I found Father there, slumped in his chair. A trickle of drool slid from his lip and lost itself in his beard. I might have knelt beside him, but my corset would not allow it.

"Father?" By casting myself forward over my toes, I was able to lean low enough to take up his hand.

There was no response, no corresponding squeeze.

I tugged on it and he fell forward toward my legs.

Trapped by my corset, I could neither push him back into his chair nor could I keep him from sliding from it. I could do nothing but let him fall over himself to the floor.

"Help me. Somebody help me!" Holding on to his hand, trying to pull him to standing, I caught a glimpse of the maid, lurking in the hall. "Summon a physician. Quickly!"

But before she could do my bidding, Aunt appeared. "No."

No?

Pale, but in command now of her faculties, she entered the study and shut the door behind her. Taking Father's hand from me, she lowered him to the floor. "No. There will be no one summoned. If the other physicians in the city find out that he is ill, then they will steal his patients."

"But . . . what if one of his patients falls ill? What if he had appointments scheduled? Someone else will have to attend to their needs." Courtesy required it.

"Then we must simply say that he was taken from the city on an emergency."

"And those who need prescriptions filled?"

"He has a closet filled with *Dr. Carter's Tonic*. We'll fill them ourselves."

"But—"

"I said no!" Panic swam in her eyes. "He wouldn't want anyone to know of this. He might yet revive."

———

WE SPENT THE next day, Aunt and I, in Father's bedroom, at his side. And during that time, it became apparent that he could not move. Neither could he speak. He could do nothing at all, save drool. And eat a bit of bouillon, if the broth was carefully spooned into his mouth.

The next day, Aunt beckoned me from his room. When I joined her, she looked up the hall and then down it. When she finally spoke, her voice was low. "I must be frank."

I closed my eyes at her words. She was going to say what I had been desperately trying to deny. "He won't recover, will he?"

"It is not of that which I speak. My connection to the Stuart family was only able to crack open the doors of society to you. It was your father's vast knowledge that caused them to swing wide in welcome at your debut."

"I know Father is a respected physician—"

"It was not what he knew; it was *who* he knew." She folded her hands in front of her and looked down at them. "And what secrets they wished to keep."

Secrets? Why was she speaking to me of secrets? "What do you mean?"

She raised her head. Looked at me with impatience. "Did you never wonder how Brother kept such a fashionable house? On Fifth Avenue?"

"He made his fortune in tonic." Of course I'd known that.

"The tonic was the least of his assets. He was paid, and quite well, for keeping all of New York City's secrets."

"I don't understand what—"

"Are you so naive, Clara? It was that knowledge, those secrets, that have kept you in society!"

"But—"

She looked at me. A look that bored into my soul. "It was your father's knowledge that would have purchased you a marriage."

"Purchased?" If I said it with horror, it was because I felt exactly that.

"All marriages are purchased in one way or another. There's no shame in that."

"But there is shame! There is great shame when he would seek to use people's secrets for his own advantage." How could he have!

"And that is just the point. He can use nothing to his advantage. Not any longer."

"Why are you telling me this?"

"If you hope to make a brilliant match, if you hope to recover the family's honor—"

"Honor? You speak to me of honor? We have none!"

But Aunt continued on as if I had not interrupted her. "—then it must be arranged within the week. Before word gets out that your father will never be able to reveal any of his secrets. To anyone. Ever again."

I felt a curious freedom lift inside of me as the shackles of the family's honor fell away. There was no honor; there was nothing left to defend. Nothing to regain. I was free. "And if I don't?"

"If you don't? If you don't, then who do you think will marry you once word gets out? No one will have any time or any dances or any invitations for the daughter of a tonic salesman. If you don't marry now, then chances are you never will. Of course, that might not be all bad. I've heard there is always a position for a governess or companion for the right person who wishes a small income for their many troubles and a room that they can never truly call their own."

"Surely Father must have made some provision—"

"He did. And they were all leveraged away in calculation of your success."

My success? But I hadn't obtained any. Not yet. And who knew if I would? "I don't know if Franklin will—"

"He *must*. He must propose. And as soon as he does, we will announce it. You have no other prospects." "But. . . but what about Mr. Hamilton? Or Mr. Lorillard?"

"They haven't called in weeks. I sent them all away in favor of the De Vries heir. Because that's what we had planned. The De Vrieses gambled our money away during the Panic, and we were going to make them pay for it. We were going to regain our honor by your marriage. Now is the time. You must not fail." She gripped my hand between her own. "Mr. De Vries is your only hope."

"He's not my only hope. He's your only hope."

"Don't be a fool! You're nothing without a man, without marriage. You have no money. You have no prospects. None but him."

"But he doesn't—I don't—" I didn't like him. And any preference he had shown me I now knew to be only perfunctory. Because he had been made to. By my own father.

"Oh, my dear. I can see your vanity has suffered. But know this: Our work would have been difficult indeed had you been one of the chinless Vandermeres or a bulbous-nosed Sturbridge. Your looks have done you well—the heir seems to truly like you. But Brother's knowledge has guaranteed a proposal... or it would have. You should be delighted."

"I'm mortified! How can I ever look him in the face knowing that the whole season has been a charade?"

"Surely he knows you well enough by now to know that you knew nothing of it."

"But I know now!" And that made all the difference.

"If anything, it should make you more secure in your conquest."

"But it's no conquest—it's an ambush. If I have gained anything at all, it's been by treachery, not virtue." How could she expect me to carry out such plans?

"There is nothing else in these circles. Believe me: Marriages have been contracted for far worse reasons."

"But what sort of marriage can I expect to have? In these circumstances? What is there to base it on but secrets and extortion?"

"At least you have something to hold over his family's head. I had nothing. And look where it got me!"

"I can't do it." I couldn't.

Her last words were uncompromising. "You must."

Dearest Julia,

A marriage is being arranged for me by means so treacherous that I cannot write of them. To begin what is to be a sacred union in such a despicable way seems to me to be contrary to every good and decent thing that marriage represents. Father is

I paused in my writing, uncertain of what to say; unsure of how much I should admit. Which only showed me just how well I had learned my lessons. To be so devious with one I knew so well!

suffering a fit of apoplexy. He cannot work. He cannot move. He cannot speak. And so you see, I am his only savior. I must succeed at what I am to undertake. I have no other choice. I do not know why I write to you. Perhaps it is only to explain to myself why I must do what is to be done. Please do not feel a burden to respond to my private miseries.

I hope that this letter finds you well and happy and that if ever you chance to think of me, it is with fond memories of our time together.

With kind regards,
Clara Carter

As I wrote the letter, I had come to one conclusion: There was no other way. Not for me.

I might have fought for Harry once, but it was clear that he preferred Lizzie. And so why shouldn't he have her? In truth, he was too good for me. The only option left me was Franklin. And as Aunt had said, there was so little time. If I couldn't elicit a proposal in the next few days, then all was truly lost.

CHAPTER 35

$\mathscr{I}$ WAS ABLE to secure Franklin that evening during an intermission at the Music Hall. Several minutes later, I saw Lizzie approach us from the side. It was now that I would normally trade places with her. But with Father's condition and Aunt's admonition still ringing in my ears, I pretended that I did not see my friend. "Shall we walk to the other end of the hall, Franklin? It's so noisy here."

"If you'd like."

"I would." Swiftly, I pulled him around and away from Lizzie.

As we began walking, I saw her standing in the middle of the floor alone, hurt written in her eyes. Poor Lizzie. It was well and good to play at sharing beaux, but in the end, someone had to win Franklin's hand.

And in the end, that person had to be me.

———

The New York Journal—Society
February 23, 1892

Especially stunning was Miss Carter, in a costume of white brocaded satin decorated with hand-embroidered silver butterflies. As she promenaded with Mr. De Vries during the intermission, all hearts were heard to sigh.

The Tattler
February 23, 1892

It seems the battle for one of the city's most distinguished heirs has tipped decidedly in one of our young debutante's direction. Having given up any pretense of bonhomie or friendship, this young miss has firmly pushed all competition away. Well done, my dear. But one must wonder: Has the best woman won?

I crumpled up that page of the paper after I had read it and threw it into the fire.

Has the best woman won?

No. Because Lizzie was the best woman. But trust and loyalty and friendship would not last long in these circles. If I wanted something, didn't I have to reach out and grasp it? Franklin certainly hadn't signaled that he had come to any decision, and neither had Lizzie. The season had almost come to an end. Someone had to make a decision; someone had to do something.

That someone had to be me.

There was no one else who could influence my future. If there was to be any hope of anything at all, for any of us, it would have to be me who secured it.

Besides, Franklin wasn't complaining, was he? And hadn't I learned how to manage him while Lizzie had been laid up in bed? When he talked about himself, which was almost always, his words soon blended into a monotone buzz through which I could think or dream of anything I wished. And as long as someone was talking, what did it matter who it was? He was content to be talking, I was content not to be listening, and both of us were happy.

Or very nearly so.

Did I feel badly about it? About my betrayal?

Of course I did! I had made a promise to a friend.

But it had been a hasty promise, made by a naive young girl. How could anyone expect such a promise to be kept? How could Lizzie expect such a promise to be honored? If she had any sense at all, she would have made a play for Franklin long ago. In fact, hadn't she? Hadn't she been the one he'd invited to the skating pond? Hadn't she been the first to break our promise?

I picked up my box of needlework, found my project, and began thrusting the needle through it. The jab and pull of thread through canvas usually served to calm my nerves. And this time was no exception.

Franklin. Lizzie. Me.

A triangle thrown out of equilibrium.

But Lizzie didn't need Franklin as much as I did. He was my only prospect. Hadn't she dozens of suitors waiting in the wings? Hoping for even one word or a smile? And if I got Franklin, then Lizzie could have Harry. Isn't that what she wanted anyway?

Sometimes life wasn't fair. Sometimes you had to take what you could get. And if I had broken our promise, then hadn't I already been punished? Wouldn't I be spending the rest of my life married to Franklin?

I could think of no worse reward.

———

THURSDAY CAME QUICKLY. It was a cold, dreary day, the sky pregnant with snow. Flakes began to drift down about noon. And by three o'clock, all the world was white. I didn't relish going out into that blizzard just to talk to Lizzie. As I glanced out the window, it occurred to me that she probably wouldn't relish the thought either. And really, why would she brave such a cold trip through the garden just to talk to me?

She wouldn't. I was sure she wouldn't.

The clock chimed half past three and still I sat in my chair, doing needlework.

But at quarter of four, I wandered to the window and stood for a moment, looking out toward the hedge. I thought I saw a flash of blue along the wall. I blinked. When I looked again, it had gone.

———

WE WERE TO attend an opera that evening and then a dinner party afterward, which would be hosted by Mr. and Mrs. De Vries. I thought long and hard about marriage to Franklin that afternoon. If I didn't marry him, then what else would I do? Marry some other young man? Which other young man? Aunt had dispensed with all of my other prospects. And this late in the season, they would have set their sights on some other girl. Perhaps I could become a Miss Miller to some young charge. A girl of ten or twelve. I wouldn't mind doing such a thing. But who would I give as a reference? And what right had I to claim that I could teach anyone anything at all?

No, my only worth came from my position here, in the middle of society, and it would all be taken from me if I didn't act quickly enough. And further, Aunt was right. I had given Franklin every reason to suspect that I favored Harry. I only had a few days left to correct that impression. A few days left before Father's illness was bound to be discovered.

On the drive to the De Vrieses' I decided to ask Aunt for advice. "What's the surest way to get a man to ask you to marry him? I have waited long enough. I want to be engaged. To Franklin."

"I do not blame you. Well. There are certain things any man wants. He may not have them, of course. Not until after a wedding. But the thought of possessing them might just spur him on to proposing. Do you understand what I am saying?"

Did I? I wasn't quite sure. But Aunt seemed to be demanding an answer in the affirmative. "Yes. Yes, I do."

———

I WAS DETERMINED that night not to think about, not even to look at, Harry. If my thoughts veered from my mark for just one moment, the pain was too searing, the sense of loss too great. It must be this same ache that Katherine bore within her heart.

The party did not start until after the opera. And the Vandermeres were giving a tea in advance of the De Vries dinner. So it was not until half past eleven that I expected dinner to be served. My head was spinning, and not from the task I had placed before myself; I had not eaten since breakfast. And I did not plan on eating at dinner either. I did not want to chance another episode like the one at Lizzie's. Not on the night I was hoping to secure a proposal.

Franklin smiled when he saw me enter the DeVrieses' ball-room. He winked and then he inclined his head toward the back corner of the room.

I put a hand out to Aunt's arm. "Franklin wishes to speak."

"Then by all means, go! Where is he?"

"Over there, by the palms. In the corner."

"Then I will escort you to the refreshments table. And if you leave me quickly enough to join him, your absence will not be noted."

We did as Aunt suggested, and very soon I was holding Franklin's hand, being tugged down a dark, narrow servants' hallway. And then, down even narrower stairs into darkness. They ended before I was prepared. I stumbled into him and then right past him as I lost his hand.

"Franklin?"

"Just here."

He had turned toward me. I knew it when he grasped both of my hands in his. And still he pulled me forward.

"It's so dark. Where are you?"

He pulled me sharply to the left and then dropped both of my hands. I heard the sound of a match being struck and then a flame flared. In the haziness of that sudden light, the silhouette of his face began to spin in and out of focus.

"I always used to come here, to my valet's room, when I didn't want anyone to know what I was doing. Or what I had done."

The guttering flame of the taper illuminated a bed and simple chair. And then, in the next moment, Franklin's face. The flame had put a smolder to his cheeks and a blaze in his eyes.

My teeth found the inside of my lower lip.

"And I've done a great many things in my day, though none of them I've done with you. It's a shame, since I've decided I'd like to know you better." He sat on the bed and leaned back against the wall, smiling up at me, light reflecting from his teeth. "Say something."

"I confess I don't know what to say."

"Then do something." His eyes! As he looked at me it seemed he knew something about me that I did not.

"Do what?"

"You can come here for a start."

I walked toward him, dreading . . . I knew not what.

"Sit." He patted the bed beside his thigh.

The bed was so low to the ground that I knew I could not attempt it. Not in my corset. And definitely not with it so tightly laced. "I can't."

He sighed. "Surely you aren't stuck on your own morality like all those other girls."

"I did not say I wouldn't. I said I *couldn't*. Can't. Because of . . ." Because of my corset. I couldn't bend at the waist, and since it was so long, it was difficult to bend at my hips. I could do nothing but stand, and if a chair were placed high enough and shoved into my knees by a waiter, I could sit, with some trouble. Surely, he could understand without my having to say it. What decent girl spoke of corsets and other unmentionables in polite conversation?

He pushed to his feet, coming to stand quite close to me. "You can't. But you didn't say you wouldn't." His face was hidden in a shadow now. Somehow it was much nicer to listen to his voice than it was to look into his eyes.

"No. I didn't."

Before I knew what he was about, he had picked me up and swept me into his arms. My head began to spin once more, but then he sat down with me upon the mattress. And within the solid enclosure of his arms, my vision began to clear. I closed my eyes and leaned back against his shoulder in relief.

He nuzzled his nose into my cheek. The bite of the stubble of his whiskers on my neck was pleasantly scratchy.

He began nibbling at my ear.

I moved my head away from him so that my skin would stop going numb.

He used the opportunity to plant a kiss on my neck. His kisses had only ever been on my cheek. And rather chaste. This kiss was not.

"Franklin!"

"I could devour you."

"Franklin, please."

"I just want a taste of you." He pushed my sleeve farther down my shoulder and his mouth dipped lower, trailing kisses along my arm.

A shiver shot up my spine and a curl of fear whipped through my stomach. *"There are certain things any man wants . . .the thought of possessing them might just spur him on to proposing."*

"Clara or Lizzie? Lizzie or Clara? You can't expect me to decide between you without a small sample. Let me see you. Let me touch you." His grip on my waist relaxed, but then his hand found my glove and he began to roll it down my arm.

My skin prickled as my flesh, released from its sheath, met air. "Really, Franklin—"

He drew it down with one last swift roll and set my fingers free.

I pressed them against his cheek and tried to gently turn his head away.

But he captured them with his hand and interlaced my fingers with his own.

"Stop—I have to tell you something!" My own words surprised me.

"What is it? And, please, tell me it's something I'd want to hear. Something worth the interruption."

"I said something. I spread a rumor about you. Me and—" No. I wouldn't implicate Lizzie in my crime.

"And what rumor was that?"

"I told everyone—well, only several people, and they told everyone else, but it's my fault still because I knew they were going to. I planned on it."

Franklin was watching me, brows raised.

I took a deep breath and closed my eyes. While they were closed I felt Franklin kiss my neck again. They flew open. "I told them you were sterile."

He stopped kissing me. But he immediately started to laugh.

330

"Don't—why are you laughing?"

"You told them I was sterile? Why?"

"Because . . . because I wanted you for myself." Lies! Again!

"Really?" He said it as if this revelation were monumental. "You wanted me for yourself."

I nodded. But only because it made me dizzy to shake my head.

"Then you can have me." He leaned forward over the voluminous pleats and tucks of my gown and kissed me full on the lips.

I tried to push him away. "You aren't upset?"

He gave me one more kiss. "Upset? It depends on what you used for the cause." He caught my face up in his hands and planted a kiss on my nose. "I couldn't think why, all of a sudden, all the girls began avoiding me. But it was just you, telling a lie so that you could have me all to yourself. I hadn't thought you had it in you."

"Had what?"

"Such a clever capacity for deviousness. And deceit." He slid his hands down my bare arms and linked his hands with my own. "Someone, somewhere, is going to start to miss you soon. So what do you say . . . ?"

Somehow, I didn't think he was offering to escort me back upstairs. "*Franklin De Vries is your only hope. Now is the time. You must not fail.*" My aunt's voice, low and vehement, reverberated through my head. My nebulous thoughts had grown even more hazy with Franklin's kisses. Wouldn't it just be easiest to give him what he wanted? And wasn't that the only certain way to get what I needed?

CHAPTER 36

J RODE HOME in the carriage in silence, then slunk up the stairs. After the maid undressed me, I slid into bed, pulling the covers right up over my head. I closed my eyes, wishing I could blot the night's events from my memory. How would I be able to face Franklin tomorrow? And the next day? And the day after that? My skin still scorched where he had kissed me. My cheeks still burned where his whiskers had scratched me. And how long had we stayed, secluded, in that little room?

I wondered if Harry had noticed.

Who cared if Harry had noticed?

Still, if one could die of shame, then I would be dead, right now, at this moment, standing in front of St. Peter, gathering my soiled raiment around me.

Aunt would know. Of course she would know. Probably already knew. She would guess in that uncanny way she had. She would guess and she would give voice to her suspicions and then how would I deny it? How could I?

"There are certain things any man wants. He may not have them, of course. Not until after a wedding. But the thought of possessing

them might just spur him on to proposing. Do you understand what I am saying?"

Hadn't she made herself abundantly clear?

Then why had I bungled it?

Why couldn't I have just done the thing she had asked me to do?

In spite of what she had said, in spite of being quite clear about the strategy I was to employ, I had refused him. And not only had I not given him liberty, I had slapped him in the process—finally and completely—refusing his advances.

Hadn't I done what any decent girl would do?

But I was no decent girl. I was a girl with a charlatan for a father. A girl pretending that she had a right to a debut. A girl who was just trying to do as she was told to do. A girl with no options, save one. And even knowing that, I had refused him. I had kept my virtue and I had given up everything else. Girls didn't have choices; they had directives.

I should have done as Aunt had told me to do. As Father had wished me to do.

———

I SLEPT WELL past breakfast and dressed hastily for lunch, stopping in to check on Father on my way down the stairs. Aunt was waiting for me in the dining room. My bowl of bouillon had barely been placed before me when she spoke.

"Did he propose?"

"No."

She frowned. Dipped her spoon down into the soup, away from her. Brought it to her mouth and took a sip. "You need to hurry him along. I don't think I can keep our secret for much longer."

"I don't actually think he will be proposing."

The spoon slipped from her fingers and landed with a *plunk* in the bowl. The butler moved to take the bowl from her. She slapped at his hand. "I haven't yet finished!"

He bowed. "Forgive me, madam."

She picked up the spoon and placed it on the plate beneath the bowl, glaring at the butler while she did so. "I have not finished. Perhaps you need a pair of spectacles."

The butler's face colored.

She swung her gaze back to me. "Now then. You don't think Mr. De Vries will propose. Why not?"

I said nothing.

"Has he already asked for Lizzie's hand? I thought you had pushed her out of the way."

"I did. I had."

"Then what is it? If there is no one else then you must have given him some reason not to propose."

I began to chew on the inside of my lip.

"What did you do?"

"It wasn't what I did." It's what I didn't do.

"Then what was it?"

"He asked me to do something. I didn't want to do it."

"You didn't want—? You stupid, foolish girl!" The dogs at her feet began to bark. "I presume he asked you to sacrifice your virtue."

I didn't answer. Couldn't answer. Why would I want to admit to such a shameful thing? Why would I wish for her to know what he thought he might have had?

"What is virtue compared to fortune? Didn't you understand? I told you he *must propose*." Spittle flew from her lips. "How many chances do you think you'll get to marry the De Vries heir?"

"Franklin."

"Franklin?"

"His name is Franklin." He was a person, not a faceless fortune.

"I don't care if his name is Methuselah! What have you done? And more—can you undo it?"

"No!" I hoped all the horror and shame I felt showed in my eyes. Undo it? Why, that meant . . . !

Aunt worked up a smile. Reached out to rest a heavy hand upon my own. "No, no. I don't mean what you think it is that I mean. I just meant, might you be able to provide the opposite impression? Make him understand that at a different time or other place, perhaps . . . ?"

"Like . . . in Newport during the summer?"

"Exactly. In exchange for a proposal."

"Give him to understand that of course I would gladly give myself to him if we are soon to be married?"

"Would that be so difficult?"

It shouldn't be that difficult. What was wrong with me that I couldn't do as I was expected to? Especially now, since Father's fit, when my entire future rested upon my shoulders alone. This path, the path that Aunt had laid out, was the plainest. The simplest. The most expedient. Why couldn't I just do it? "I don't want to marry him. I want something more." I wanted someone like Harry. Not Harry himself, of course. He was set on Lizzie. But someone like him. There must be someone else like him. Somewhere. I wanted something more even if it happened to be much less in material terms.

"Something more?" Her face softened and her eyes hardened in the same instant. "I suppose you're waiting for true love."

I felt my chin lift. "And what if I am?"

"Let me tell you a secret: True love is an illusion spun for young girls to seduce them into marriage. It's nothing but a myth."

"It is not!"

"And I assume you derive your proof from all of those novels and poetry you're always reading."

I did. In part. "Perhaps. But even reason tells me there ought to be more."

"There ought be, yes. That, I concede. But there's not. True love gets girls to the altar, and after, it is reality that takes them by the hand and leads them away. So it's better not to look for it. Much more practical for everyone concerned. There's no disappointment that way. Marrying Mr. De Vries would save you from all kinds of disenchantment."

"And all manner of happiness." I shoved away my plate and rose to my feet.

"If that's what you're waiting for, you'll be waiting forever!"

"It's worth the wait."

Aunt rose to follow me. "Don't be a fool! Don't throw away everything for nothing. For some hopeless longing, for a fantasy."

"It's not a fantasy." It couldn't be a fantasy.

"And what if you never find it?" Her voice had followed me out into the front hall.

At least I will have looked.

———

OF COURSE, THERE were still dinners and operas and private balls to attend. But what little interest I once had in the season was gone. I felt cheapened. Exposed by my actions with Franklin.

Though Aunt still held out hope for some reconciliation, I did not. But still, I wished that I could take back that time in the valet's room. That he had even asked for what he had indicated that he had sensed in me some ambivalence. That he had asked indicated that he thought it might be a distinct possibility. And it was that which shamed me most of all.

Because it was true.

Had I not been afraid, I might have wavered. Might, actually, have bent to his demands. Had I any virtue, it was that of timidity. And what sort of virtue was that? It was surely no trait that I took pride in possessing.

But at least there was still Harry to talk to.

Since I had been told of Father's deceit, my feelings toward Harry had changed. My wounded heart had experienced a miraculous healing. Since, as it had turned out, I had never been worthy of his attentions, I found myself simply grateful for his friendship. His and Katherine's both. Their kind regard was nothing that I deserved.

Especially since Franklin had finally and exclusively turned his attentions toward Lizzie. He couldn't claim every dance on her card, of course, but those he did claim were danced with a certain telling intimacy. And during intermissions, it was she alone to whom he spoke, while Mrs. Barnes looked on with ill-concealed delight.

Harry brought me a cup of punch during one such intermission. I was grateful to turn my eyes from the spectacle of their happiness in order to focus on him. But I wondered, How did he feel? To be dropped so suddenly and completely by Lizzie? It was a poor way to treat a man so gracious and considerate. I smiled at him. "Thank you, Harry. You're too kind."

"Then perhaps I could ask you a personal question. Did something happen between you and Franklin?" He was trying to catch my glance.

I smiled. Refused to let him. "No."

"Are you sure? Because if—"

Beside us, one of the Remstell girls barked a laugh. A moment later, her companions joined in. I leaned toward Harry so that my voice could be heard. "Nothing happened. Can you believe it's almost the end of the season? It seems as if it just started."

"Clara?"

I surrendered. I had to look at him if I were to have a chance at convincing him. And he would never stop questioning me if I didn't. "I'm fine, Harry. Truly, I am." But why should he care so much? If anything, he should be alarmed at Franklin's new attachment to Lizzie. I drank up the last of the punch and then held out my cup toward him. "Would you be so kind?"

"Of course. If you're sure . . . ?"

"I've had plenty, thank you."

He frowned at my misinterpretation, but I relied upon the fact that he was too much a gentleman to press his question any further.

Aunt appeared the moment Harry had gone. "What are you doing? Go over there to the heir. Take him away from Lizzie'"

I shook my head.

"You must at least try. After all these weeks! After all our work."

There was really no point. And Harry was on the approach. I deployed my fan and wafted her concerns away, determined to stay my own course.

CHAPTER 37

J TRIED TO avoid Harry at church the next day. When I did happen to look in his direction it was only from habit. Only because I had forgotten myself, forgotten my situation. I tried to immerse myself in the sermon instead. And the hymns.

"Just as I am, tho' tossed about
With many a conflict, many a doubt,
Fightings and fears within, without,
O Lamb of God, I come, I come."

It was Mama's song! Tears threatened to leak from my eyes. I surreptitiously drew a handkerchief from my reticule and dabbed at my eyes as I glanced around the pews. Thank goodness no one was watching.

"Just as I am, poor, wretched, blind;
Sight, riches, healing of the mind,
Yea, all I need, in thee to find,
O Lamb of God, I come, I come."

What if, as Mama had said, God loved us just as we were? What if He loved *me*? Without affectation or pretension? Without corsets or hoop skirts? What if He didn't care whether I knew how to cut someone or if I had mastered the waltz? Just the thought of it, the notion of it, threatened to undo me. For a love such as that would be an unthinkable extravagance. And if I could believe God loved me in that way . . . why, it would change everything!

"Just as I am, thou wilt receive,
Wilt welcome, pardon, cleanse, relieve;
Because thy promise I believe,
O Lamb of God, I come, I come."

If I closed my eyes, I could imagine her standing beside me, singing in her clear, bell-toned voice. The voice of my child-hood. Not the one of her later years that came out breathless in raspy whispers. When I was a child, Mama had the best voice of all the members of the church. She had loved to sing. Her words had soared like an angel's over the swells of the organ. In fact, I now suspected, her entire theology had been taken from the hymnal. Any care, any concern that I had voiced, had found its answer within the verses of a hymn.

Had I trials and temptations?

What a Friend We Have in Jesus!

Was I unsure about the right thing to do?

He Leadeth Me: O Blessed Thought!

A song for every experience, a melody in answer to every question. Every question but this: Did God truly love me? Just as I was?

———

THE FIRST DAY of March. The final Patriarch's Ball. It was to the De Vrieses' generosity that I owed my invitation. But I could not muster any energy to anticipate it. For in the end, all the sounds and the fury of high society dances and parties and balls had signified nothing. I had reaped only the wind. And I would leave all of it behind me this night. But not before doing one last thing.

Among the web of extortion and deceit that Father had woven this season, there had been one deceit greater still. And I had to make it known that I knew. I had to assure myself of the identity of The Tattler. I wanted to know, without doubt, who had tried to derail my efforts. But more than that, I wanted to know why.

The problem was that I needed to use Harry to obtain that knowledge.

But Harry was the least of my worries. Just as, it seemed, I was the least of his. He cared about Lizzie far more than he cared about me. I had never deserved his time and attentions. And in truth, it would make my future easier to accept. After this night, there would be no connections left to the life to which I had aspired.

In my more honest moments, I recognized that I mourned what I thought I had discovered in Harry. Friend, confidant. My soul's true companion. But Aunt and Father would never have allowed me the freedom to pursue him. And clearly, his heart was bent in another's direction. He probably mourned for Lizzie the same way that I mourned for him. Harry was as unattainable, as distant as a star. If nothing else, my actions this night would prove it to me once for all.

They would also erase Aunt's hopes of securing a marriage for me. And then perhaps, once this night was over, I would be able to make one choice for myself. I didn't know yet what that choice would be, but surely there would be something left me to do. Left me to become. Just in case, I whispered a prayer. I prayed that if God truly cared for me, just as I was, that He would make a path for me. Because there would be no undoing what I was about to do.

———

I SCREWED MOTHER'S amethysts onto my earlobes and took one last look in the mirror. How far I had come. There was no hint left of the quiet, timid girl I once had been. But who was the woman that looked back at me in the mirror? And what would become of her after this night?

I wished her well. And then I went downstairs to join Aunt.

"You know how important this night is."

"I do." More important than she would ever know.

Aunt poked at the tulle on my bodice. Bent to rearrange a bow on my skirt. "There must be a proposal. And I cannot overstate how important it is that it happens this night."

"I know."

"You look so pale. Pinch your cheeks."

———

THE EVENING BEGAN at the opera, followed by the ball at Del-Monico's at midnight. Everything at Delmonico's seemed keyed to a fevered pitch. Laughter was calibrated to a higher timbre. The music played at a louder volume. People seemed more exuberant, more free.

My dance card filled quickly. Franklin's name was not among those of my partners, but Harry's was. He had reserved two dances for himself. The first was a lancers. In previous weeks I would have been happy to have danced it with him, oblivious to the steps and patterns, only concentrating on our conversation. But it seemed this night that there was nothing left to say.

He returned to my side after intermission for his second dance and led me away from Aunt onto the dance floor. Taking up my hand in one of his, he put his other to my back, but then, as I raised a hand to his arm, he stepped away. "Do you want—I mean—I don't feel much like dancing."

"Then what do you want to do?"

"Would you accompany me out into the hall?"

Just the opportunity I had been seeking! I searched the ballroom before answering. It was imperative that I locate Mr. Douglas. And Aunt. He must see us leaving. And she must not. Ah—there he was! Just several groups down from me, listening to another gentleman talk, though his eyes were on Katherine. And there Aunt was, looking about the ballroom with a watchful eye.

"Clara?"

"Of course. Perhaps . . . should we go this way?" I made a point of walking past Mr. Douglas. Saw him raise a brow. And well he should have. I was walking directly toward the exit, making no secret of my intention to leave the ballroom. And I was escorted by one who could be considered a suitor.

The orchestra started to play and the strains of a waltz followed us.

I turned to take up Harry's hand in my own, but he was lingering in the door. Hurry! I had only the time of a waltz to do what I had to do. I tried to smile, but then turned to speech when it failed to move him from the door. "Harry?"

"You are so beautiful."

I could not keep myself from blushing, but it didn't matter. The relative darkness of the hall hid my shame.

"Do you know Byron?"

I nodded.

"There is a poem he wrote that I think was meant for you." Finally, he left the door. He walked toward me in silence.

"Do you wish to share it?"

"Hmm? What?"

"The poem?"

"Oh—yes! Let me see if I can remember it. It starts . . ." He closed his eyes and lifted his head toward the ceiling as if it might help him to remember. Then he opened his eyes and looked straight at me. "It begins, 'She walks in beauty like the night—' "

Oh, Harry. " 'Of cloudless climes and starry skies' . . . it's my favorite."

"I've never really cared for it. For any of his poetry. He's much too maudlin."

"Oh."

"You look distraught. Have I said something? Of course I've said something. I always say something. The wrong thing. And you had just said that poem was your favorite. So." He bowed, clearly by way of an apology. "Why do you like him?"

"Byron? He was my mother's favorite poet."

"Well, then. I have no criticism to offer up against that. And I must say that his lines perfectly describe you. '. . . cloudless climes and starry skies and all that's best of dark and light meet in her aspect and her eyes.' " Harry's voice had grown soft. And serious. "It's almost as if he had known you. 'And on that cheek, and o'er that brow, so soft, so calm, yet eloquent . . . a mind at peace with all below, a heart whose love is innocent!' "

Oh no, he had not known me at all. And neither had Harry.

The waltz was half done. I had to accomplish what I had set out to do. And so, I smiled. Took his hand and pulled him farther away from the crowds. "Mother had a book of his, of poems, that he had signed."

"To her? Didn't he die ages ago?"

"It was to her father, really, but it's mine now. The only legacy she left me." I'd been given her jewels, of course, but it was only within the pages of the book that I could sense her soul.

"And you love it most because it was your mother's."

He had understood exactly. He always understood exactly.

"But do you truly like Byron? On his own? For himself?"

"Oh, yes!"

He was shaking his head as if he couldn't account for my opinion. "Why? I've never understood his allure."

"Because he writes of love. Of true love. A love worth waiting for."

"A love that you're waiting for?"

How had we come to speak of love? I had tried to tell myself that Harry did not matter. That he did not think of me with any sort of affection; he had told Franklin that himself! But then why was he looking at me that way? And why did his eyes hold such sweet promise?

"Clara?"

I put up a hand to hide my mouth from him. "Harry?"

He reached out and took my hand within his own. "Why do you always talk like that? With a hand in front of your mouth?"

"Because it's too large." And I could not remember to think of peas and prunes and prisms.

"Who told you that?"

"My aunt."

"And what else has she told you?"

"That I'm much too tall."

"Has she?"

"Yes." I said it in a whisper because Harry had come so very close and his lips were hovering just above mine.

"I'm afraid that . . . I might just . . . kiss you. If that's all right."

"Oh, Harry . ." What a strange sensation, to feel Harry's lips upon mine. So warm and gentle and giving. Especially when Franklin's had been so hard and urgent and demanding.

He broke away with a sigh. Placed a hand to either side of my neck and stared at me for a long moment. Just stood there looking deeply into my eyes. And then he slid his hands down to my shoulders and clasped me to himself. "It seems just fine to me." The words were whispered into my ear.

"What does?"

"Your mouth. And you. You're perfect just the way you are." He loosed me and kissed me once more.

The kiss, his kiss, was so full of assurance and absolute certainty that it made me wonder if I had been wrong about everything. Harry's kiss was not about questions, and not about persuasion—it was about answers and convictions. I forgot to notice whether Mr. Douglas had followed us. I had forgotten about The Tattler. And most of all, I had forgotten that Harry was supposed to be in love with Lizzie. I ran from the hall with the feel of his kiss still on my lips, passing Mr. Douglas on the way.

———

IT WAS THERE the next day in the papers for all to read.

I may have discovered the identity of The Tattler, but I had also guaranteed that no one in polite society would ever speak to me again. How could they when I had been discovered kissing someone at Delmonico's? Kissing a man who was the brother of the person everyone had assumed I would marry?

Aunt didn't come out of her room that day.

That evening I wandered into the kitchen when the cook wasn't looking and I took her sharpest knife and a firm green apple. Concealing them within the folds of my skirt, I went back upstairs.

Once I had gained the privacy of my room, I shed my gown, my corset cover, my petticoats, and hoops. Then I applied the knife to the bottom of my corset and, with a great deal of sawing and much effort, I freed myself from it. Let it drop in tatters to the floor at my feet. Pulled the chemise off as well.

For the first time in . . . *months* . . . when I looked down, it was at my own flesh. I fingered the dents where the boning had pressed into my skin. Ran my hands along the ridges of my ribs, the dip of my spine. Used a handkerchief to press against the nicks from the knife.

Assured that I was still there, that I was still myself, I took one deep, deliberate breath. And another. Then I pulled the pins from my hair and shook it out. Donning a dressing sacque, I found my Byron, took up the apple, and burrowed into my bed.

So we'll go no more a-roving
So late into the night,
Though the heart be still as loving,
And the moon be still as bright.
For the sword outwears its sheath,
And the soul wears out the breast,
And the heart must pause to breathe,
And Love itself have rest.

CHAPTER 38

*T*WO DAYS LATER, I waited for Lizzie in the hedge, praying that she would still come. Just as I had resigned myself to having lost her friendship forever, I heard the squeak and swing of the gate and then a rustling in front of me, behind the hedge.

"Hello, Lizzie."

"Hello." If only she wouldn't look at me with those wounded eyes! "Did you enjoy the Patriarch's Ball?"

The Patriarch's Ball. The one instance in which I had been given an advantage during the season. I shrugged.

She raised her chin then and looked me straight in the eyes. "You weren't here last week." A flush crept up her cheeks, and she glanced down toward her muffed hands.

"Did you come? I didn't think you would. It was so cold. And snowy."

"You know I'd always come for you."

I winced at the accusation, my gaze sliding away. Oh, Lizzie, what had happened to us? I stretched a hand out toward her and looked up. "Lizzie, I wish—"

But she had already gone.

———

FATHER DIED THE next day.

I sat with him as he breathed his last. Those long, terrible, halting, gasping breaths. There was so much I wanted to say to him. To this man I really hadn't known at all. "I wish you had been . . ." What? Different, better? If I wished him so, then why not wish the same for myself? I took up his hand and thought back upon the season.

I wished I had been different.

I wished I had been better.

I wished I could have been what he wanted. What he had needed. I had failed him just as much as he had failed me. *Just As I Am?* No. I had never been good enough for him just as I was. And neither had Mama. But perhaps . . . perhaps the failure was in being willing to be molded just as much as it was in the molding.

I squeezed his hand. "I wish you could have known me just as I was. I think you might have liked me that way." I kissed him on the forehead and smoothed back that thatch of distinguished gray hair.

My words must have been a sort of benediction. After that, I sat waiting for a breath that never came.

———

SHORTLY THEREAFTER, AS if summoned by the celestial realm, Mrs. Hobbs rang the bell. Gently. Softly. Once admitted to the parlor, she settled herself into a chair across from us, folded her hands upon her lap, and sighed. "When I heard there was a death at the Carter residence, I was so hoping that it might have been you, Miss Carter. Such a handsome corpse you would have made. That's what I told Mr. Hobbs as I walked out the door. 'I hope it's the young miss.' That's what I said."

I had a sudden urge to laugh outright. I put a handkerchief to my eyes and pretended to cry instead.

Beside me, Aunt shifted. "May we make the arrangements?"

"Yes. Yes, of course. Let's make the arrangements. But. . . could I just have a look at him?"

"A look?"

Mrs. Hobbs nodded. "Yes. Just a little peek."

Aunt rose and led her from the parlor up the stairs. They only remained a minute and then I heard them coming down. Mrs. Hobbs retook her seat and pulled a small book and pencil from her reticule.

Aunt remained standing.

"Now then. You'll want him in a suit of course."

"Yes. I'll have it sent."

"As for pallbearers?"

Aunt bristled. "What of them?"

"Who will they be?"

"I . . . don't know." Aunt's voice sounded perplexed. But I could understand why. I didn't know, not really, who he had considered his friends. And we couldn't call upon his patients for that task.

"You don't know?"

"I wouldn't know who to ask. Could you not handle that task?"

"Of course, of course. Mr. Hobbs has a dozen fine young men he can call upon. All quite handsome, yet suitably morose. Of course, you'll supply the gloves and the crape? For their arms?"

Aunt nodded.

"About the carriages?"

"We'll keep the funeral private."

Mrs. Hobbs looked up from her book. "Of course. But you'll still have friends coming."

Aunt shook her head.

"No friends?"

Aunt's mouth had gone tight. "No friends."

I very much doubted that we had any left anymore.

"Be that as it may, you'll need a carriage for the clergyman."

"Yes. I'll have it sent."

"And the name of the church? For the announcement?"

"We'll have it here. At home."

"At home." Mrs. Hobbs was writing somewhat viciously in her little book. "At home." She shook her head. Then she looked up from her book. "Might I inquire as to flowers?"

"Do as you think is best."

"Certainly." She had returned her attentions to the book. "If only it had been Miss Carter. There are such lovely displays to be made from white roses . . . *tsk, tsk.*"

I pushed to my feet and excused myself. Ran up the stairs to my room and clapped a pillow to my face. And there I laughed into it until I began to cry. I cried for a mother I had known for too short a time and for a father I had known not at all.

———

THAT AFTERNOON AUNT busied herself with ordering mourning for me. She needed none for herself. If she had gained anything from her marriage to a poor but respectable old Knickerbocker, it was the right to mourn his death. For as long as she wanted.

The dressmaker came the next day, by appointment, bringing all sorts of gloom with her. Samples of black crape and fringe. Lengths of gauze and Henrietta cloth. Caps and cuffs and collars. "What would you like made?" she asked Aunt.

"Nothing for myself. But for my niece, some simple gowns in crape."

"Yes, madam. With a full bodice? Or perhaps a habit-basque?"

"It doesn't matter."

"A jacket, perhaps? Or a cloak?"

Aunt did not respond.

The woman looked up from her book, a frown crimping her forehead. "Pardon me for asking, but . . . something for the funeral? For being out of doors?"

"It doesn't matter."

Aunt looked up toward me then, a sad truth clouding her eyes. It didn't matter because no one would be coming to the funeral nor anywhere near me afterward. One celebrated when a vehicle of oppression, when an extortionist, died; one did not mourn. Aunt sighed. "She'll need some petticoats and handkerchiefs. Hose and gloves. And some bonnets."

"Yes, madam."

"You can speak to the milliner on our behalf?"

The dressmaker nodded.

"And you're to put it on the account."

The dressmaker's eyes bounced awkwardly about the room. "Dr. Carter's? I'm afraid—"

"*My* account. Mrs. Lewis Stuart's." Aunt rose and began walking toward the hall.

"Oh. Well, in that case. Of course." The dressmaker rose to follow.

But there was one thing the dressmaker needed to know. I coughed. Politely. "My measurements . . . ?"

She turned, brow lifted in expectation.

"They've changed. I'm no longer lacing my corsets as tightly. I'll need to be re-measured. For a proper fit."

"SURELY PEOPLE WILL send letters of condolence." Aunt had been sitting in the parlor on the sofa where I had placed her, doing absolutely nothing at all since the dressmaker had left.

But my time had not been spent so uselessly. I lifted my eyes from my book. From Byron.

"They will have to send letters of condolence. It would be petty of them not to." Though Aunt was speaking, she wasn't looking at me. She seemed to be conversing with herself. "I'll order some cards. It's only proper. The only proper response to a letter of condolence. I'll have them done with a wide black edge. That's what I'll do."

I was curled up in a chair by the window. The old dress I was wearing allowed plenty of latitude for movement. Carriages passed by on their way into town. Carts rumbled up the other direction on their way out. It was so peaceful here, watching the world go by, knowing that nothing was required of me. And I felt nothing at all. It was strange to feel so little. I was an orphan now. A girl still, with an interrupted debut, and no one pledged to wait for me. I ought to feel alone, lost, abandoned. But I felt nothing at all.

Nothing but peace. And an odd sense of relief.

———

THE DRESSMAKER SENT a girl to take my measurements, and soon after the funeral the new mourning clothes were delivered. Severe, dull, stiff things with no brilliance and little elegance. They suited me perfectly. Stacks of cards were also delivered. They sat in the hall, on the hallstand, waiting to be distributed. But few condolence letters were received. Not nearly as many as Aunt had expected.

We had been cut.

And as sure as Aunt had once taught me, there was no doubt about it. The only thing to do was to turn around and pretend that being ignored was what we had intended all along. It wouldn't be difficult. There would be no more society for me. No visiting or receiving visits. No dancing or carriage rides or dinners. My life had been stopped by death and, according to custom, it would remain suspended for at least a year.

For six months I would be dressed in crape.

For six months thereafter trimmed in lawn.

And then I would be able to venture forth into the world once more. But what kind of world would that be for one orphaned and ruined and cut?

CHAPTER 39

HE NEXT DAY I ventured into Father's study. I sat in his chair and tried to see the world through his eyes. A world that owed him beauty and fame and fortune, things he had felt compelled to wrest from destiny through deceit and cunning. I could not find it within myself to feel sorry for him. Pity perhaps. I could find pity enough in my soul for him. For a man who gave up everything of worth for things of such temporal value.

I flipped through the pages of his calendar, noting the names written on the pages.

Schemerhorn. Vanderbilt. Pierpont. Gould.

All of them now freed from his grasp.

I eyed the safe in the corner, the repository of the secret formula for *Dr. Carter's*. I left the chair and bent in front of the safe. Tried the handle.

It was locked.

I spun the dial once. Twice. Three times. What could the combination be? I tried his birth date. The date of his wedding. My own birth date. Those were the numbers that should figure largely in any person's life. But my father had not been governed by passions of hearth and home. I paused for a long moment to think. And then I tried a different combination. September 18, 1873.

9-18-73.

The date on which the Panic of '73 began. The date upon which all of his money had disappeared.

It opened.

I reached into the dark void. Felt my fingers brush paper. I grabbed at it and pulled it out. Reached farther in and found some more. Pulling the papers onto my lap, I began to sort through them. The first paper my fingers had touched was the recipe for *Dr. Carter's*. It had been scrawled across the back of an envelope. *To four gallons of 60-proof rye add: One pound white sugar—50 grains cocaine—3 drams powdered belladonna root—2 drams sulphuric ether.*

Rye, cocaine, belladonna root, and ether. On these, my father's fortune had been built. I thought about the things he had said. How dismissive he had been of his patients. How contemptuous he had been of their need for his tonic. If one glass of champagne was enough to turn my head, surely a dose of 60-proof rye would be enough to render anyone a drunk. My father had never cured his patients; he had only drowned their symptoms in alcohol. Mr. Hooper had been right. My father had never been deserving of his title.

After opening a drawer of his desk and hiding the papers within it, I summoned a maid to light a fire for me. After she had gone, I took the recipe from the drawer and threw it atop the logs. It blazed green for one moment and then vanished in a frenzy of flames.

Sitting once more in his chair, I pulled the rest of the papers from the drawer and laid them on the desk before me. They were deeds. Six of them. The properties were all located along Mulberry Street.

Mulberry Street . . . Mulberry Street.

Hadn't Mr. Douglas once asked me about Mulberry Street? Even at that first mention, the place had signified something to me. But then, as now, I could not remember what, nor why.

Mulberry Street.

It came to me then in a torrent of revulsion. Mulberry Street was Mulberry Bend. 'The Bend' in Mr. Riis's book. The place most identified with the anguished suffering of the immigrants. And my father had owned six of its decaying, dilapidated tenements.

I very nearly threw them into the flames as well. But at the last moment, as I held them above the fire, I thought the better of it. Here was an opportunity for me to do something. Something to atone for the sins of my father. I put the deeds back into the safe to protect them until I could decide upon a course of action.

———

SURPRISINGLY, LIFE WAS not so solitary as I might have expected it to be. A week after Father had died, Mr. Douglas came to call. I greeted him in the front hall.

"I came for my money. Your father owed me payment. For writing the articles."

"Did he?"

"Yes. For twelve weeks of work."

He was only telling me what I knew to be true, so I led him into Father's study. Bid him sit while I looked for his cheque book.

I found it in one of his drawers. Placed it on the desktop in front of me. But before I opened it, I laid my hands atop it. "Why did you do it, Mr. Douglas?"

He flashed a dimpled smile. "Who would not? For that kind of money?"

"But why did you feel the need to tattle on me? In the *other* articles, for the *other* paper. What had I ever done to you?"

His smile disappeared and his eyes lost their warmth. "It was never about you. And I'm sorry that you ever thought it was. Or . . . perhaps you did not know? That your father was a seller of secrets?"

"And what kind of secret did he keep about you?"

"One that was not worth knowing. One that would have had me banished from polite society. And to my mind, it didn't seem right, his being able to blackmail your way into society. Someone had to do something." He looked at me, challenge firing those molten brown eyes.

And in that instant, I remembered something. I remembered where I had seen those eyes before.

But Mr. Douglas kept talking, unaware of what I had just discovered. "I was very ungallant several years ago. I thought I had found true love and I convinced my lady friend that we would marry. Only her father didn't see it that way. And by that time it was too late. She was sent abroad for my mistakes."

It made sense now. All of it. Especially the great sadness I had glimpsed in Katherine's eyes whenever she looked at Mr. Douglas. "She was sent abroad into a society that didn't look on illegitimate children as such a stain. To a man who found your mistake to be quite useful." What was it that Harry had said? *"Before the baron met Katherine, it was thought that he would have no heir at all."*

He snorted. "I would have married her. I would have taken care of her. Of them both! Only I wasn't given the chance." He looked up at me. "I loved her." He said it as if he wanted to convince me of his intentions.

"But she was married off to a baron instead."

He nodded.

"Have you seen him?"

"Who? The baron?"

"The boy."

He shook his head. "She won't let me. Says he's the baron's son now."

"Can you blame her?"

His jaw worked as he seemed to grapple with an answer. And then his face went still. "No."

"He looks just like you. He has your eyes. And your pride."

As he looked at me, his eyes cleared and a ghost of a smile flitted across his lips. "How did you find out? Did your father tell you?"

"No. You did. And she did. By the way you looked at each other." And of course, I had received no little help from eavesdropping.

"It was your father who pronounced her with child. And if word had gotten round to any in society, how could I have continued to be invited into their ballrooms and their dinner parties when I had disgraced one of their own?"

"I once asked you if you knew what my father was doing in The Bowery. You wouldn't tell me."

"No."

"Because you're a better, more honorable man than he was." I opened Father's cheque book and wrote him a cheque. Put it into an envelope and handed it to him. "I'm sorry, Mr. Douglas. For everything. Whether you choose to believe it or not, your secret is one I never wished to know and one I will never share. As well, I believe my father left something for you."

His eyes were wary. "What? And why would he leave me anything at all?"

I handed him the deeds to the tenement buildings.

Mr. Douglas fanned them out as if they were playing cards. And then he shook his head and tried to pass them back. "No. He didn't leave these to me. He left them to his heir. To you."

"I don't want them."

He laid them on the desktop. "You'll need them. The rents from them, in any case."

"I don't want them."

"Then how else are you to keep yourself in the manner to which you've become accustomed this season?"

"I don't plan to."

"Ah. I see. You're going to sacrifice yourself for the good of common man. No matter whether any of them will notice, whether any of them ever know or not."

"Whether anyone ever knows or not, Mr. Douglas, it's the right thing to do."

"And what will happen to you?"

I shrugged. It didn't matter anymore if it was vulgar to do so. I was no longer Miss Clara Carter, preeminent debutante and arbiter of all that was fashionable. I was simply and only myself. "I don't know what will happen to me, but I have no doubt that God does. And I shall have to rest in that belief." If Harry was right, if God had truly made me for some purpose, if Clara Carter without corsets and without pretensions is how He intended me to be, then He would find some way to look after me. He was obligated to if it was true; if I mattered to Him just as I was.

Mr. Douglas narrowed his eyes as he held my gaze. "How old are you?"

"Eighteen."

He frowned.

"In another six months."

"And that still leaves three years until you can hope to do anything at all with this sorry inheritance." He gathered the deeds together, struck them against the edge of the desktop to align them, and offered them back to me.

"You once told me there was nothing I could do for those people in The Bowery. But I can. I can give these to you. And then you can do something with them."

He was shaking his head. "They aren't mine to do anything with. They have his name on them. All of them."

"Surely you know people, Mr. Douglas. You can't tell me you've no clout at Tammany Hall. Not when you're a news-paperman."

He smiled then. Mischief at work in the corners of his lips. "I might. I just might." He folded the deeds and put them into the inside pocket of his coat. "And you, Miss Carter, might just do after all."

Color lit my cheeks at his compliment. "You were a very great help to me during the season. I thought of you as a friend during a time when I had very few. I will always be thankful for you."

For once, his eyes would not meet my own. "Yes . . . well . . ."

"Always, Mr. Douglas." I got up and left him then, knowing that he could find his own way out.

CHAPTER 40

*M*Y NEXT CALLER was as unexpected as the first.

My aunt had taken to her room since Father had died, since her work of ordering cards and tying crape on the front door had been completed. And so it was to me that the butler delivered the calling card.

Baroness von Bergholz. Katherine. Harry's sister.

I told the butler to show her in and stood when I saw her walk through the door. "I didn't expect to have the honor of your call." Not after all that I had done.

She quickly crossed the parlor carpets and embraced me. The cool scent of bergamot followed her. "I came to say good-bye."

At least she'd had the decency to come see me one last time. I fully expected that I would be cut by all my peers and their families.

She pushed herself back from me, keeping hold of me by the arms. "It's not as you think. The baron and I sail for the Continent in several days' time."

A flush lit my cheeks, but warmth suffused my limbs. And relief that I had at least one friend still. "Please, sit." I gestured toward the sofa.

"No. I shall only stay a moment. You are in mourning and your thoughts may be put to better use than idle conversation with me. I only wanted to say that you are fortunate. More fortunate than you know. I was worried about you and Franklin. You wouldn't have been happy with him."

"He has Lizzie."

She smiled. "Yes."

"But have you no fears for her?"

"No. Lizzie was made for all of this. She sees it as it is and has neither undue hopes nor unfounded expectations. She can make her own happiness. And somehow, I think she might just ensure Franklin's as well."

The warmth I had basked in vanished. I took a step back from her.

"It's not that you are any less a woman than Lizzie. It's that you are more of a woman than Franklin deserves."

"I see."

"No. I don't think you do. But perhaps . . . I hope you will. While there is still time." She moved in close, took my face between her gloved hands and kissed both of my cheeks. "You must begin to guide yourself. Do not be swayed by what might have been. It is my fondest hope that I might see you again. It would make drear Berlin seem quite gay."

Berlin.

How I wished I could see her again. But I might as well have wished to go to Italy.

———

MY VISIT WITH Katherine only made me long for my friendship with Lizzie. And so the next Thursday at half past three saw me heading for the hedge in the garden. No one went calling the first six months of mourning. If there was to be any contact between us, it had to be at Lizzie's initiation. And so I hoped against hope that Lizzie would remember.

And she was there waiting for me! "I didn't know if you would be here, but I decided to come anyway."

I moved to embrace her. "Thank you."

She put her arms around me. "I'm so sorry. For everything."

"No, Lizzie. It was me. I was the one who broke our promise. It's my fault. I just—I got scared. When Father had his fit. And then, with Aunt pushing me like she did, Franklin seemed like the only way. I'm sorry."

"You weren't the only one to be pushed. Mother would have had me cut you a dozen times these last weeks. At least!"

Mrs. Barnes? "No!"

"Oh yes! But I could never quite bring myself to do it. Because I knew you had put your trust in me. Every night before I went to sleep, I would look at that motto you made for me: *Friendship Love and Truth*. And to be truthful, I had placed no little trust in you too! I still don't know how I'll be able to manage Franklin all by myself." She clapped a hand to her mouth. "I didn't mean to—!"

"It's fine."

"Really, Clara, I didn't mean to imply—"

"It's fine, Lizzie. You deserve him. You should have him."

"But I don't really know that he'll choose me. What if--?"

"What if . . . you suddenly sprout wings and fly off to China?"

She smiled at the mention of our childhood game. "Or grow whiskers and start to meow like Old Puss."

I sighed and shook my head. "You're right. In such a case he wouldn't want you."

She turned the full force of her smile upon me and threw herself into my arms. "Is everything all right?"

It was now.

———

AUNT AND I sat in the parlor the next day. I expected no more visitors. None for at least the first six months of mourning. So I decided to ask her a question for which I had never been able to discover a true answer. "Someone once told me that Father was a frequenter of The Bowery."

Aunt stirred in her chair. Lifted dull eyes to mine. "He was."

"Did you know about him? About the tenements?"

"I did."

"But how could he own such things? How could he treat people as if they were little better than animals! He was a doctor. He was supposed to save lives. He was supposed to . . . he was supposed to save Mama's life."

"No one could have saved your mother's life. You can't blame him for that."

I could. And I did.

Aunt closed her eyes for such a long time that I thought she might have succumbed to a sleep of exhaustion. But then she opened them and began to speak. "How could he own the buildings? The better question might be 'How could he not?' "

"It's immoral—to keep people in--! Don't you know what they're like?"

She shook her head as though she had long ago forgiven such foolishness. "He was simply a man. Like all men. And he was trying to recover what had been lost to him. Many men make their fortunes off the poor. Or the immigrants. Or prostitutes."

"Not *all* men. Not all men are like that."

"Believe me or not. I've been trying to teach you how to survive in this world. As a woman. I've been trying to prepare you for what lies ahead. Whether we want them or not, one thing is certain: We need a man. We all need a man and I've been doing my best to teach you how to entice one and then secure him."

"Then you've only taught me how to catch the kind of man I don't want."

"There is no other kind of man." There was a sorrow, a great fatigue that underscored her words.

There was. There had to be. "What about the kind that marries for love? What about the kind I marry because I love him?"

"There is no love—I've already told you this! There is only an illusion. A poor approximation. And it is that which I am trying to teach you. To converse. To flirt. To dance."

"So that I can live my life trying to be someone that I'm not?"

"So that you can be the person others expect you to be."

"But isn't there anyone who would love me as I am?" A remembered conversation echoed through my head. *"God made you, didn't He? Different than anyone else who has come before or anyone else who will come after? I must insist that you matter to Him much more than you seem to realize."*

"As you are? Why, you can barely dance a waltz! How can you be of use to anybody as you are? Why--why are you smiling? I'm only trying to save you heartache."

"I'm smiling because I just realized that I don't need saving. I'm fine just the way I am."

"But don't you understand? *I don't want you to end up like me!*"

I didn't know what to say. We sat there, both of us, perched on a razor's edge of emotion. Perhaps she felt herself misunderstood. It was true that she had given freely of herself and her knowledge during the past year. I would never have made it through my debut without her advice. But if she thought herself misunderstood, I thought my own self misunderstood. And so, I decided to try again. With a softer voice and kinder, simpler words. "I don't want a compromise of broken dreams. I want love."

"Love? Love will only disappoint you. Love will only see you abandoned and humiliated, waiting up nights for a man who will return with the sun's rising, drunk, with the scent of some other woman on him. Love will destroy your dreams and corrode your heart."

"I'm sorry, Aunt. For your pain. But you do understand me, don't you? There must have been love for you. Or the expectation of it. Once."

"Oh, there was love. There was plenty of love right up until the day I miscarried our first child. After that, after Brother told us it would be dangerous to ever try again? Mr. Stuart took his love down to The Bowery. He's the one who told your father about the tenements. But it didn't matter, you see, because by then I understood. And then a few years later, he died." She was trying to speak louder than the tears that were streaming down her cheeks.

But she failed to remember one thing: I wasn't blind.

She pulled a handkerchief from her sleeve and swiped at her eyes. Then she sniffed a long, shuddering sniff and looked at me with stoic, red-rimmed eyes. "All is lost. What are we to do?"

"I see no reason why you shouldn't do exactly as you like. Have you no money left? Of Mr. Stuart's?"

"Not much; it's been spent. On gowns and gloves and lessons for you." To her credit, there was no blame in her eyes. No accusation in her words. She was simply stating a fact.

"Then we will sell the house and everything in it."

"And what will we do then?"

"I won't need any of the proceeds. I'll be taken care of." I had to be. I had no reason to believe it, but I had never been more certain of anything in my life. "Why don't you use the funds to take a little cottage by the sea and retire there?"

"By myself?"

"Why not?"

"But . . . who will take care of me?"

"I think you've managed to do an admirable job all of these years taking care of yourself, don't you?"

Something like her old indomitable spirit came back into her eyes. She lifted her chin. "Yes. Yes, I have, haven't I?"

I READ IN the papers the next week that Lizzie and Franklin had become engaged.

———

The New York Journal—Society
March 22, 1892

Barnes-De Vries

The engagement has been announced of Miss Elizabeth Wallace Barnes, the daughter of Mr. and Mrs. Reginald Barnes of this city, to Franklin Schuyler DeVries, also of this city.

Miss Barnes is the granddaughter of The Honorable John Eames and the great-granddaughter of Zechariah Carlisle. She debuted with aplomb just this season.

A graduate of Yale, Mr. De Vries is the son of Mr. and Mrs. Peter DeVries and is a member of the Knickerbocker Club, the Union Club, University Club, the Tuxedo Club, the Player's, the New York Riding Club, the Racquet and Tennis Club, the New York Yacht Club, the Jockey Club, the Turf and Field Club, and the Skating Club of New York. He recently returned from a several-year tour abroad.

The wedding will take place on September 15.

Truly, I was happy for Lizzie.

I was.

Except when I realized that she would always have something that I would not: proximity to Harry on a practically daily basis. As often as she wanted.

CHAPTER 41

*T*HE NEXT DAY there came a knock at the door. I might have let the butler answer, but I had released him from service. We could no longer afford to pay him. So, though I was clothed in morning dress, I answered the door myself.

It was Harry.

And he looked surprised to see me.

But no more surprised than I was to see him!

He put a hand into the front of his jacket and withdrew from it a letter. "For you. It came just the other day."

I took it from his hand and tore it open.

Dearest Clara,

There is another way. Although I have accepted a proposal from a Mr. Powell and am soon to be married, I have just become acquainted with the needs of a Miss Thompson. Being a woman advanced in years, but determined to see the Continent, she would be delighted with a companion such as you. And she is a woman of no little means. I feel certain that you would be more than pleased in this situation. Surely, if your father's illness is as grave as you say, he cannot be far from death. Forgive me if I have offended your sensibilities, but having been of your situation, I must tell you that it is far better to plan while you still have means at your disposal. Shall I speak to Miss Thompson of your interest?

> *With only the fondest of thoughts,*
> *Julia Miller*

I nearly sagged against the doorframe in relief This was it! This was what I had been waiting for: the path God had prepared for me. He knew, He saw. He cared.

"Good news?"

I folded the letter back into its envelope. "News from a friend. She is to be married."

"That's very good news indeed."

It was. Only, underneath my relief, I somehow felt completely abandoned. In a way that I had not even when Father had died.

"I just—I came because—I wanted to say—"

"I once told you, Harry, that I was unspeakably rude."

His mouth slid up on one side and his eyes began to twinkle. "I remember."

"But what I did to you, at the Patriarch's Ball . . ."

The twinkle in his eyes disappeared and his mouth settled into a line. "At the Patriarch's Ball . . . ?"

"Mr. Douglas, the newspaper reporter?"

"The one who followed you around all season?"

I nodded. "He wrote about me in the *Journal*, but he also wrote about me in *The Tattler*."

"I know he did."

"You do?"

"I read the papers. He was the only one who had been with you all season. Except for me, of course."

Except for him.

"He sold you out." Harry's accusation was more accurate than he knew.

"He did. But I knew he would. Especially that night."

Harry's eyes shrunk to slits. "You did?"

"Yes."

"So, that night, at the Patriarch's Ball . . . ?"

"Was to confirm what I had already suspected. About Mr. Douglas."

He nodded. Then he took a great breath and squared his shoulders. "It confirmed something that I had already suspected too."

I knew what he was going to say, for how could he have failed to feel what I had felt? Even if he had already given his heart to Lizzie. Of course, he would be disappointed in those hopes, but that didn't mean he should fix them upon me. Not now. Not when I had discovered my father's treacheries. And besides, I didn't want to be anybody's second choice; I wanted true love. On both sides of a marriage. So I stopped him before he could make a promise he shouldn't be allowed to keep. "Don't say it, Harry."

"Why not?"

Why not? "What good would it do? Especially now? Or don't you know about my father?"

"I know he had you for his daughter."

"He wasn't a good man."

"And what has that to do with you?"

Such kindness, such love, glowed in his eyes. And yet I could not accept them. They weren't meant for me. And even if they were, I didn't deserve them. "I'm trying to do what's right, Harry. Help me to do what's right." I turned my back on him and began to shut the door.

But he stopped it with his hand.

"Harry—I" I could not hold myself together if he did not leave. Why could he not understand that?

"I just wanted you to know. I'm going back. I'm going abroad."

I smiled then. Mostly from relief. If he removed himself from the city, then I would not have to think of him. "I'm glad."

"I just wanted--I wanted to let you know. I wish you could go." His eyes were asking all kinds of questions that I knew I did not have the right to answer. Not any longer.

"Good-bye, Harry."

WE COULDN'T GO anywhere, of course, until our period of deep mourning was over, but Aunt warmed quickly to the idea of retiring to the ocean. She even invited me to come live with her. I told her I would consider it. But I knew that she, like Father, had invested everything in the success of my debut. There may have been enough money for her to live comfortably, but to add me to her expenses would only have caused both of us to worry. And so I took out Julia's recent letter and began to write a response.

Dearest Julia,

Please do not think that you offended any of my sensibilities. Father is dead. I have none left. If you think there is still a chance of securing a position with Miss Thompson, I urge you to recommend me to her with all speed. Aunt is soon to take a house on her own. I find myself without

---

Without anything at all.

I sighed and reread what I had written. Then I took up my pen once more to continue.

---

any reason to stay in this city. As you know, I have always longed to travel abroad. Please assure Miss Thompson of my good sense and my reliability, and if you can find it within you, please remember me also to your kind self.

Clara

I may be reached here at home until September. I do not wish to presume upon the kindness of Mr. De Vries any longer.

———

"PSST! CLARA!"

I had been taking a turn about the garden, reveling in the peace the place provided. I could not go out in public, not while I was in deep mourning, but I had not expected the public to find me here, in my own garden. I was no longer the stunning Miss Clara Carter. I was the disgraced daughter of the charlatan Dr. Carter.

"Clara!"

I peered into the hedge, trying to discern from where the voice was coming.

A moment later, Lizzie's figure, clad in green velvet, pushed through the branches. Her hat had been knocked askew and stray leaves clung to her curls. But she was in high spirits. I could tell from the bloom on her cheeks. "He proposed!"

Although I had already read of the news in the paper, I pretended that I hadn't. "Congratulations."

"I accepted."

"Of course you did."

She stepped close and clasped my hand with her own,

glancing over at the house as she did so. "But not without some consideration." She glanced over at the house again. Then she turned me away from it and walked me a few steps toward the hedge through which she had come. "He made me a most ungentlemanly proposition!"

"Did he?"

"Yes! And I will never speak of it again, except to say that I would never have cheated on you, dear Clara, in that way. I just wanted you to know."

"Does it not worry you?"

"Why?" Her brows drew together for a moment, but then her forehead cleared. "Oh. Oh! No. Why would he marry what he could get just by the asking? And I seem to have acquired some sort of allure since then. Since refusing him." She giggled. "It's quite amusing." Then she sighed and squeezed my hand. "I'm sorry about your father. I feel as if. . . rather like ... I feel as if I won Franklin unfairly."

I dropped her hand and embraced her. Hard. "No, Lizzie. You won him honestly. And I'm happy for you."

"Are you? Truly?"

"I am. Truly."

"Then that makes me even more happy. But the wedding is only six months from now. And you'll still be in mourning."

"I will." Though we had always planned to be each other's bridesmaids, I was happy not to have to attend her. The simple fact was that I did not deserve to.

"I'll miss you."

"And I'll miss you."

She hugged me. Kissed my cheek. "I'll be thinking of you. On that day."

"I hope not."

She giggled. Hugged me again. And then she started off for the hedge. "I have to go plan my trousseau."

"Don't let anyone catch you."

"They would mob me! And they all ask after the legendary and reclusive Miss Carter. Did you know that's how *The Tattler* referred to you?"

"No."

"Yes!" She paused and held up a finger. "He said, and I quote, 'Society will be the less for having lost the singular beauty of the legendary and reclusive Miss Carter.' He actually referred to you by name that time! 'There is more than one soul, and more than one gentleman, the better for having known her. She has graced both our ballrooms and our hearts. Her style captivated us in a way not seen in this city for many years. Farewell, Miss Carter, and may fortune smile upon you.' Wasn't that nice?"

More than she knew.

And much more than I deserved.

CHAPTER 42

I COULDN'T SLEEP. I couldn't eat. I couldn't even read. I had left poor Byron who knew where, but I no longer had any interest in finding him. There was no time for true love—there were too many other things to be taken care of. We could not long afford to remain in the house. Without Father generating money, in ways both respectable and not, we had no income. And he had kept no savings.

We had let the servants go, one by one, until at last there was only the cook. It was I who filled the coal scuttles and cleared the table, made the beds and swept the carpets. It was I who did the laundry and took our clothes out back to dry.

By the beginning of August, not even Aunt could deny the obvious. No one had come to rescue us. When our six-month period of deep mourning ended, we would have to rescue ourselves. I had secured myself a position with Julia's spinster. A train ticket had been sent so that I could go to Boston to meet her in September. I would stay with her there until the time came, in spring, to leave for the Continent. And Aunt? Though she had taken to the idea of retiring to the sea, she had not yet made any plans to move there.

One day late in the month, as I joined her for breakfast, she broke her silence. "I have asked the man at the auction house to call. To ascertain the value of what has been left us."

I felt my brow rise.

"He's to come at half past ten."

I made sure that I was done with the fires, had dusted the parlor, and had made myself presentable by that time.

————

THE MAN WAS short and balding. He went through the house, pencil in hand, *tsking* and frowning. He only seemed to take an interest in several things. One was the card receiver. The other was the hallstand. "Very nice pieces."

Aunt took up a position right beside them. "They are not for sale."

"If they were, I could command quite a high price for them."

"They are not for sale." She turned from him, toward me. "If I were to show up at the shore without a hallstand, people might think me somehow reduced."

"But, Aunt, I hardly think a hallstand of this size would fit in a—"

"I will not have people thinking that I've become—that I've been—!"

When Aunt moved to show the man my father's library of books, I left them for more important work. There was mending to be done and a table to be laid for dinner.

————

THAT NIGHT, I served us boiled eggs and herrings. With toast. Then I took my seat opposite Aunt.

She looked up from her plate toward me. "The man will send his carters on Wednesday."

"What does he expect to get from the sale?" There were very few things that I needed, but a few new gowns were among them. I couldn't very well assume my new position dressed in the clothes of a young girl. The gowns from my debut no longer fit, and I wouldn't lift any aged woman's spirits dressed in unrelieved black.

Aunt sniffed. "He said he would advertise in the *Journal*. I'm sure his expectations are well below what the sale will bring. He didn't seem to know an ice-cream fork from a lemon fork."

"But did he tell you what he expects to receive?"

"No. He will send his final estimate with the carters. On Wednesday."

We finished the rest of our meal in silence, dining by the light of our few remaining candles. The food looked more appealing in the candlelight. It cast a much warmer glow than the gaslights. But it was not for nostalgia's sake that we had done it. I had asked for the gas lines to be turned off. We could no longer afford that luxury.

———

ON WEDNESDAY WE woke to a suffocating mist. The carters materialized out of it, as if they were ghouls bent on some morbid task. They handed Aunt a letter and then tromped up the stairs to their work.

Aunt opened the letter and gave a gasp. "But . . . but . . . he can't be right!"

"Let me see it." I took the letter from her hand and began to read the cramped but meticulously written estimate. Apparently, Aunt had only asked him to sell several things. The dining room set, Father and Mother's bedrooms, and Father's books. "We're going to have to give him more than just these."

"Then what will we have left?"

"We don't have to have anything left. We can no longer stay here. The less we have when we leave, the better."

"But—"

"Why didn't you put my bedroom on the list?" I would have no need of it where I was going. I turned the letter over and quickly began to annotate it with additions. I added Mama's jewels and my carpets. The china and all of the silverware. The Turkish carpets in the parlor and the chandeliers. "I'm adding the piano."

"You can't!"

"What are we going to do with it? There's no one to hear it played."

"There might be. Once we've come out of deep mourning."

I shook my head. "Once we've come out of mourning, I will journey to Boston and you will move to the sea."

"No. Please. I cannot have a parlor without a piano."

I clenched my jaw against thoughts that were too profane to share. Instead, I went upstairs to find the men. They were in Mama's room, disassembling her bed. "I have made some additions to your list. You may have to fetch another cart."

One of the men nodded toward a young boy. The lad left the room at a run and I soon heard him patter down the stairs. The others continued with their work, carrying the pieces of the bedroom set down the stairs. Taking paintings from the wall. Once removed, the frames left odd dark patches of wallpaper to mark their going. The ghosts of what once had been. And along the floorboards, balls of dust had been exposed where they had taken refuge under the chest of drawers and the wardrobe. I had not been as good a maid as I had thought.

The last man paused as he bent to pick up a painting. "Were it nice, miss? Living like this?"

Had it been? "Yes." Yes, it was.

He nodded. Hefted the painting. "Shame, miss. But there's nothing lasts forever."

———

IT WAS ONLY as the carters left for the auction house with most of our possessions that I thought to consider my book. I found Aunt in the parlor. "Where's my Byron?"

"Your what?" Aunt looked up from the chair she was sitting in. The only one left us. The floors had been bared of rugs. The silk curtains pulled down from the windows. She sat there in the bright light, motes of dust dancing in a lone sunbeam. The Pomeranians were lying at her feet.

"Mother's Byron. Where is it?"

"Her Byron?"

"Her book! The red one. With the morocco leather cover."

"I don't know." Aunt had not yet looked at me. She was gazing about the room in bewilderment.

"Where is it!"

The loudness of my voice must have broken through her thoughts. She flinched. Finally, she looked up at me. "The book? The Byron?"

"Yes."

"The one in Brother's library? It had been signed. By the author—"

"The *poet*." I spoke the words between my teeth.

"The auctioneer said such things have great value."

"You sold it?"

"There was so little in this house of worth."

"You sold it?" How could she have? She had no right!

Aunt blinked. "*I* haven't sold it. The auctioneer will sell it."

"You sold Mother's Byron?!"

"Your father left us hardly anything at all. If only we had managed to find the recipe for *Dr. Carter's* . . ."

"But that book wasn't Father's. It was Mother's! It was the only thing I had left from her."

A look of puzzlement crossed her face. "But what about the jewels?"

"I sold them. For you. For us. I didn't think you would begrudge me one small book."

"Then I'm—" She turned to look at me. "I'm sorry. A girl should always have something left of her mother's. I didn't know." There was something very much like regret in her eyes.

I stood there for a moment, thinking of all the things I wanted to say to her, but instead I went upstairs to survey what was left of my room. There was no use mourning Byron.

It was too late for true love.

CHAPTER 43

ONCE I TURNED the calendar's page to September, once we had changed from full mourning to half mourning, we took a train to Boston and then the boat train to Fall River. It was time for Aunt to find her cottage. The train continued on down to Newport, but Fall River was as far as she would go.

"Wouldn't you like something farther south? Along the Atlantic?" Somewhere like Newport?

"I *would* like something farther south. In Middletown. I just don't want to take a boat to get there. I've a great fear of boats that has only increased with age." From the train station in Fall River she hired a carriage to take us down to Middletown, over the stone bridge from Tiverton. We spent that night in an inn and the next morning with an agent. He had located a small but comfortable house for her with a view of the water.

"Yes." She began nodding as soon as she stepped inside. "I can see myself here."

I could too.

"Only, you were right." She had turned toward me. "We ought to have sold the hallstand. It won't fit in here."

After promising to secure the house for her, the agent returned us to the inn. Aunt had not planned to settle on a house so easily, so we had no plans for the rest of the day. And so I asked for something I had always longed for. "Could we go to Newport? We wouldn't have to stay for long."

———

WE HIRED ANOTHER coach to take us south, and soon we were on our way. The Newport we drove into was not the fabled Newport of my dreams. The haunt of the very rich and the scandalously famous. The town was composed of small houses and, out of season, seemed bereft of people. Wind battered the carriage as we rode through the streets.

"Would you like to see the ocean?"

I nodded. It was here my mother had lived. In one of these houses she had been raised. To be in her town and miss her ocean? I leaned toward the window, pressed my forehead against the pane. "I think I see it."

Aunt laughed. "No. You cannot see it from here. It hides behind the dunes." She thumped on the roof with her parasol and then shouted a command. "To the beach! Second Beach."

The carriage made a wide, sweeping turn, and then drove out from town.

"But—"

"Second Beach was her favorite. It's not far."

After a while, the carriage left off rumbling and rolled into an extended sort of glide. The horses' hooves stopped their clopping and seemed to have disappeared entirely. And then, the carriage stopped. Aunt inclined her head toward the door.

I hesitated. "Do you want to come?"

"Gracious, no! I'll stay here."

The coachman helped me out and my feet touched not

packed dirt, not cobblestone, nor asphalt. They touched sand. How curious!

I raised my skirt with one hand and walked away from the carriage toward the hills of sand before me. Each step I took seemed to lose itself. It was more work walking on sand than I had ever imagined. But finally, after a few false starts and a near tumble, I made it to the top of one of those hills. And there, before me, twinkling in the sun, was the ocean.

Miles and miles of it.

Some of it was shadowed under clouded skies, but other expanses of it sparkled like the most brilliant of sapphires.

With a hand on my hat, I ventured off the hills and down onto an expanse of flat sand. It tilted right down into the ocean. I walked along, parallel to the waves, not willing to wet my boots. But as I walked, I noticed a singular bird hopping along before me. Long of beak and slender of legs, it skipped to the point where waves lapped up on the sand. It was uncanny how it knew exactly how far to go. It never got its feet wet either.

Following that bird, I walked along rather farther than I meant to.

When I turned around, it was to find the wind in my face. I tightened my hold on my hat, but my arm soon tired. So I took it off and clamped it beneath my arm. The wind worked its fingers through my hair, loosening my coiffure and teasing tendrils that wrapped around my neck whenever I turned to look out at the ocean. It brought to my nose scents I didn't recognize. Salty, briny odors. Smells scoured and bare.

I followed my footsteps back to where I had come off the sand hills. Took one last look at the ocean and then returned to the carriage.

Aunt greeted me with a frown. "I thought you might have gotten swallowed by a whale."

I smiled.

"Well?"

I sighed as the carriage pulled away. "I don't know how she ever left it."

"She didn't. Not truly. In fact, she almost came back."

"She did?"

"It was shortly after they had married. Life in a town along the shore doesn't prepare anyone for the city."

I didn't imagine that it could.

"And Brother's hours were unpredictable at best. He could never be depended upon to be home, you see."

Of course he couldn't. He'd been a physician, after all.

"And then she learned that he had discovered The Bowery. That he had bought some of those old buildings. The ruckus she raised! The tears she cried! She questioned the state of his very soul."

"What happened?"

"I waited until he had gone, until she had quieted, and then I told her how it was. I explained to her what kind of life she could expect as the wife of a man with growing wealth."

"And she stayed?" How could she have? When she had known such things?

"She got restless now and then. She would fling open those windows in her bedroom once in a while and I could tell by the look on her face that she wasn't smelling the garbage or despairing of the soot."

"But she did stay."

"She did. And eventually there were no more scenes."

"Because she loved him." And she had decided to partake in all the pleasures that money could buy.

She shook her head. "Because she loved *you*. She had discovered that you were to be born."

So she had stayed. And she had given up the ocean for me.

"And he stayed? With Mama?"

"Yes. He never did take up with another woman. Because I showed her how to keep him. Did I tell you she achieved a sixteen-inch waist? Brother was right: She was the most beautiful woman in the city."

———

TWO DAYS AFTER our return to New York City, I rolled off my pallet and worked at removing the crape trimmings from my best gown. I sewed on a pair of lawn cuffs and a collar in their stead. Afterward, I took a piece of dry toast and some tea for breakfast. Then I took my hat from its box, plucked the black feathers from it, and set it on top of my head.

I was going out.

I was a bit late and so I hurried down the street, impervious to man or beast. I had nearly twenty blocks to go. At the end, I even ran a little. In a very ladylike way. But I made it. I reached the sidewalk in front of Sherry's restaurant. And I fit myself into the crowds that pressed around the place. It was Lizzie's wedding day, and I did not want to miss it. Not even if my only glimpse of her were from the edge of a crowd.

A shout went up as the sound of a carriage swung near.

It halted at the curb. The coachman hopped down from his seat and opened the door.

Lizzie emerged. Her hair had been spun up on top of her head and orange blossoms and diamonds had been woven through it. Her long-sleeved gown was made of white satin and trimmed with lace.

As she stepped from the carriage, she turned her head in my direction. Her eyes widened. And then, I'm almost certain of it, she winked.

I hid my smile behind my gloved hand.

And then they were out of the carriage and into the restaurant. They were gone.

The crowd began to dissipate, and I found myself standing

quite alone, pondering the turn of events that had made Lizzie Franklin's wife instead of me.

"They make a handsome couple."

I started at the words, and then I turned at the sound of a voice I knew so well. "They do."

"I always knew they would."

In spite of everything, everything I had said and everything I had done, Harry stood there looking at me as if I were the only person on that city sidewalk.

I searched his eyes, looking for sadness or jealousy or some other hint of emotion. I could find none. None but happiness. Contentment. "You aren't—you don't seem to be angry. You seem quite satisfied."

"I am. Everything worked out just as I planned!" He was smiling.

Just as he had planned? "But. . . ?"

"But what?"

"I thought you wanted Lizzie for your own."

Astonishment transformed his features. "Lizzie Barnes? Me?"

"Yes."

"She's rather adorable, but I confess that I have never quite understood her appeal."

"You never--? But I heard you, Harry!" How could he lie to me? To my very face!

"Heard me what?"

"I heard you say so."

"Heard me say what?"

I took a deep breath. Summoned the words that had pierced my heart. "I heard you tell Franklin that, all in all, you preferred Lizzie Barnes to me."

"You heard that?"

"Yes."

His face fell and he looked extremely disappointed. "You weren't meant to."

Of course, I hadn't been meant to. I pushed my shoulders back and took advantage of my full height. "None of us is meant to hear the things said of us by others."

He took up my hand and looked me straight in the eyes. "You weren't meant to hear it because it wasn't true."

"It wasn't?"

"No. You see, Franklin has always taken from me everything I ever wanted. And this time, I determined that he would not take you."

"You . . . what?" I was having trouble making sense of his words.

"What I mean is that, all in all, I much prefer *you* to Lizzie Barnes."

I found that I had nothing, absolutely nothing, to say.

"Clara? Are you all right?"

I nodded. It was the only thing I found myself able to do. Harry *much* preferred me to Lizzie? He preferred *me* to Lizzie?

"I found something a week ago that I thought you might like. I've been carrying it with me in the event that I should see you. May I give it to you?"

I nodded once more, for I still didn't seem to be able to speak.

He slipped a hand into the pocket of his coat. It came out bearing a slim book bound in what looked like morocco leather. He placed it into my hands. "It's been signed by the poet himself. Quite valuable, I'm told."

"Mother's Byron!" I couldn't believe it. I opened the cover and turned to the first leaf. Byron's signature sprawled across the page. I flipped further still through those beloved pages and I came upon Harry's pansies. They were still there, pressed between the leaves.

"My flowers?"

Warmth suffused my cheeks. I shut the book and clasped it to my chest. "How did you ever find it?"

"I bought it. At an auction."

"But how did you even know?"

He simply smiled in reply. And then he pulled out his handkerchief to dab at my tears.

It really wasn't fair that he should turn up on a sidewalk right beside me. And confess to me that everything I had known to be true about his sentiments was a lie. A lie spoken on my behalf. On *our* behalf. "I thought you were going abroad."

"Turn your head a bit. That way."

I obliged, sniffing.

He put a hand to my chin and dabbed at the other eye. "I was. Am. I will. Maybe in the spring."

"I am too. In the spring."

"Of course, you are."

But I wasn't going for pleasure. I was going for employment. "I'm to be a companion for a Miss Thompson. An elderly spinster."

"So perhaps we will see each other."

Perhaps. Though I didn't know how. And I couldn't think what else to say to make him understand my reduced circumstances. But most of all, I didn't know what to feel. My tears had dried up in the confusion, and so I pushed his hand away.

He pocketed the handkerchief. "The most delightful coincidences seem to occur in Europe among expatriates. I knew a fellow once who ran into a compatriot, quite by happy accident. She was traveling as an elderly spinster's companion. The spinster was the gentleman's favorite aunt, so it seemed destined somehow that they would meet. And three days later, they eloped."

"They . . . they did?"

"They did." He said it quite firmly.

"*Three* days later?" Somehow, I could not seem to catch my breath.

"Why? Does that seem excessively slow? I thought, I mean, it was necessary, of course, to establish their love clandestinely; to walk about the gardens in the moonlight and make eyes over coffee while sitting in one of those Viennese cafes."

"That sounds very romantic." Heart-stoppingly romantic. "But how did his family regard the match?"

"With great felicity. It seemed that he had given them cause to think he had an attachment to some unsuitably wild Italian girl."

"And did he?"

Harry shrugged. "No. And I don't honestly know how they had come by that idea. The good fellow had not yet even traveled to Italy."

"He hadn't."

"No." Harry's voice had dipped intimately low. "But he went there shortly after. On his honeymoon. With his bride."

I felt myself blushing. I couldn't help it. And I'm afraid the warmth swept straight up my cheeks and tingled at the roots of my hair. "But . . ."

He raised his brow.

"What about the young woman? She was obviously in reduced circumstances. What did she do to excuse herself from employment?"

He smiled. "Even elderly spinsters, *especially* elderly spinsters, seem to have a deep and abiding, if secret, affinity for true love. Particularly when it involves their favorite nephews."

"They do?"

"Yes." He said it with confidence. With finality. With great assurance. And then he leaned forward and kissed me, right there in broad daylight in front of Sherry's, for all the world to see.

The New York Journal—Society
April 14, 1893

It has been reported that Mr. Harold De Vries, of the Peter De Vrieses, and Miss Clara Carter, daughter of the recently deceased Dr. Willard Carter of this city, married in Vienna, Austria. They are honeymooning in Italy. Those who were in the city last year may remember Miss Carter for the elegance and grace she bestowed upon the season.

The Tattler
April 14, 1893

Which society gentleman and young debutante, having become reacquainted by the happy coincidence of being introduced overseas by the gentleman's spinster aunt, have eloped? This circumstance putting to rest rumors that this gentleman had formed an attachment with the daughter of an Italian count. The couple is reportedly honeymooning in Italy. They plan to visit the young man's sister, a baroness, in Germany before establishing themselves in Paris, where he has been tasked with managing his family's interests in art and antiques. It is speculated that he will soon be managing an art gallery in that city and spending the winters in Italy at an estate the couple recently purchased.

SO...DID YOU LIKE IT?

I'd love to know what you thought of Clara and Lizzie and Harry and Franklin. If you have a spare moment, can you leave me a review on Amazon? New reviews will help other readers to be able to find this book, too.

Want to keep up with my releases? Follow me on BookBub!

A NOTE TO THE READER

IN SPITE OF his self-righteous rhetoric and racist views, Jacob Riis's *How the Other Half Lives* electrified the citizens of New York City. At that time, 43 percent of the city's buildings were defined as tenements and fully two-thirds of the city's population lived in the squalor and destitution that Riis described in his book. On Valentine's Day, 1892, Dr. Charles H. Parkhurst took on Tammany Hall politics as a preacher at Madison Square Presbyterian Church. The power of New York's democratic political machine would reach into the 1960s, but the vile oppression and police corruption that was Tammany Hall would be quashed by a grand-jury investigation and the victory of reformists in the city's mayoral elections of 1894.

The late-Victorian period in America produced our society's first celebrity culture. Just as they are today, celebrities of the era were created through the media of their time: newspapers. It was between the pages of the daily newspapers that the first society columns could be found and where the luckiest of debutantes could achieve fame for the simple reason that columnists had made them famous. It was not unknown for the most celebrated among them to stay away from street-facing windows to avoid being seen by the mobs of onlookers clustered on the sidewalks below. Even the summer season at the beach in Newport became a publicity opportunity when journalists followed society there on vacation.

Victorian women were very much focused on appearances and achieving a certain "look." The words *peas, prunes,* and *prisms* were on every girl's lips in the 1800s in hopes that the pressures of speaking "p" would induce a fashionable bee-stung lip. They also religiously brushed their hair one hundred strokes before going to bed, as well as squeezed their hands into gloves too tight and their feet into shoes too small. But most of their allure was achieved through the use of molding. Through the corset.

Magazines like *Godey's Lady's Book* and *Harper's Bazar* were the *Vogue* and *InStyle* of the Victorian Age. And if, in the interests of fashion, illustrations were drawn to exaggerate the chest or minimize the waist to unrealistic proportions, what did it matter? They were only drawings, after all. But to many unsuspecting women, the advertisements became the ideal. And to achieve that sort of hourglass shape, tight-lacing of the corset was required.

The dangers of tight-lacing were many. But one of the most serious effects was anorexia. The narrowing of the waist placed tremendous pressure on the stomach, reducing its volume. The tight-lacer would notice an increase in instances of heartburn and indigestion and recognize that some foods led to an uncomfortable buildup of gas. Soon the tight-lacer would begin not only to eat less food less often, but also to choose only foods that were easy to digest. Foods like toast. Or tea.

The diagnosis of hysteria was widespread in women of the era. It was given for symptoms such as fainting, shortness of breath, insomnia, heaviness in the abdomen, and loss of appetite, all of which were produced by corsets. Many women of the time became addicted to tonics like *Dr. Carter's,* which mixed toxic ingredients such as chloroform, opium, belladonna, digitalis, and cocaine with a large amount of alcohol. In a time of enormous societal pressure, primitive medical knowledge, and the unquestioned expectation of conformity to unrealistic ideals, tonics provided a method of socially acceptable escape.

It has been rumored for over a century that some women had ribs removed to achieve the perfect sixteen-inch waist, but such claims have never been proven. It is much more likely that those drastic distortions were accomplished by tight-lacing, which would eventually relocate and reshape the floating ribs.

One unfortunate byproduct of tight-lacing was the displacement of internal organs. It is known that tight-lacing diminished the volume of the lungs and repositioned and reshaped the liver. It could also lead to the pinching of nerves and sciatica-like symptoms. The rigors of childbirth, combined with the external pressures of the corset, contributed to a large number of prolapsed uteruses. Happily, the solution was convenient and widely known. Pessaries were readily available by prescription or by mail order through the Sears, Roebuck & Co. catalog.

It's worth remembering that when, as a society, we deem something absolutely necessary to beauty or health or happiness, some people will do absolutely anything to obtain it.

READING GROUP DISCUSSION GUIDE

1. Have you ever wanted to 'fix' one of your physical attributes? Which one? Why?

2. Do you feel any sense of kinship with the women of the late-Victorian era? Did you recognize yourself in any of the characters?

3. How would you describe the Victorian mind-set?

4. Did you discover anything new about this time period? Did anything surprise or shock you?

5. The general Victorian attitude toward the poverty and racism can be summed up in Aunt's words: "Some races are simply inferior to our own. The Irish, for instance. And the Italians. If they're poor and they live in tenements, then it's their own fault. If God wanted the poor to prosper, then they would. If they're not, then they deserve what they get." How has our view of poverty and racism changed? How hasn't it?

6. The women in the late-Victorian era were put through a training regimen in order to prepare them to take on a role in society. What was that role? What is the role of young women today?

7. What sort of advice could Lizzie and Clara offer today's women?

8. Do you think we've retained any attitudes, beliefs, or mores of the Victorians?

9. Fashions through the ages have often been created on the assumption that people aren't shaped correctly. What apparent flaws does modern fashion try to correct? What is today's ideal standard of beauty?

10. Society will tell you who you are and how to be until you decide to answer those questions for yourself. What has society been telling you?

11. Reading Jacob Riis's *How the Other Half Lives* influenced Clara a great deal. Has there been a particular book that has opened your eyes in a similar way, challenging your point of view and your beliefs? How did it affect you, and why?

12. At one point, Clara and Harry have a conversation about God: " 'I must insist that you matter to [God] much more than you seem to realize.' There was an earnestness to [Harry's] words that reverberated inside me. If only he spoke the truth. I would like to believe that God cared for me. That He might love me no matter what anyone else thought. How nice it would be to live life with Harry's convictions. To be so certain that God thought of us. And so quick to dismiss the thoughts of others." Is it difficult for you to believe that God thinks of you? What kind of thoughts do you think He has?

ACKNOWLEDGMENTS

A BOOK IS never the work of just one person, and this book, as all my others, had much help from a contingent of people I feel fortunate to call my friends. My agent, Beth Jusino, helped to start me down the right path. My editors, Dave and Sarah Long, helped me find a better way to express my ideas. And a chance exchange with Wendy Lawton added an extra layer of authenticity to these words.

Once again, as always, I am indebted to my readers Maureen Lang, Linda Derrick, ReAnn Johnson, and Trudy Mitchell for taking the time to comment on my drafts. And I cannot help, once again, mentioning my husband, Tony Mitchell, for always loving me just the way I am and for never ceasing to tell me so.

Made in the USA
Las Vegas, NV
26 April 2024